IDENTITY

Ingrid Thoft

IDENTITY

G. P. PUTNAM'S SONS | NEW YORK

G. P. Putnam's Sons
Publishers Since 1838
Published by the Penguin Group
Penguin Group (USA) LLC
375 Hudson Street
New York, New York 10014

USA · Canada · UK · Ireland · Australia
New Zealand · India · South Africa · China

penguin.com
A Penguin Random House Company

Library of Congress Cataloging-in-Publication Data

Thoft, Ingrid.
Identity / Ingrid Thoft.
p.   cm.
ISBN 978-0-399-16213-8
1. Women private investigators—Fiction.   2. Paternity—Fiction.
3. Murder—Investigation—Fiction.   I. Title.
PS3620.H58I44   2014   2013050432
813'.6—dc23

Printed in the United States of America
1   3   5   7   9   10   8   6   4   2

BOOK DESIGN BY AMANDA DEWEY

For the usual suspects,

Doug Berrett
and
Judith Stone Thoft,

and a few new ones:
Erika Thoft-Brown,
Lisa Thoft,
and
Kirsten Thoft

IDENTITY

Blood trickled out of her nostril onto her upper lip. It tasted metallic when the tip of her tongue instinctively swiped at it.

"Really?" Fina asked.

"Oh my God. I can't believe I just did that." Haley stood rooted to the floor, her gloved hands limp at her sides.

Fina freed her hand from the sweaty glove and grabbed a towel to blot her nose. "At least we know you can get in touch with your inner anger."

"Aunt Fina, I'm so sorry." Haley wrestled off her gloves and followed Fina over to a bench at the edge of the gym. "Should I get some ice or something?"

Fina gingerly palpated her nose with her fingertips. "It isn't broken."

Haley leaned back against the exposed brick wall. "I'm so sorry." She looked genuinely distressed.

Fina swatted at her with the towel. "I'm fine. You think one errant punch is going to do me in?"

"I guess not."

"Hey, you've thrown your first punch and drawn blood. I'm proud of you, sweetie. You're a true Ludlow now."

Haley looked doubtful. "If you say so."

"How about a clean towel? That would help," Fina said.

Haley made a beeline for the desk near the front door of the small bare-bones gym. Fina didn't frequent the establishment, but it was in her neighborhood, and the signs for self-defense and kickboxing classes had piqued her curiosity. Her brothers had taught her to fight, and she didn't understand why it wasn't an equally valued skill set for girls and young women. Certainly it was more useful than sewing a button onto a shirt.

At the desk an older gentleman with cauliflower for ears handed Haley a fresh towel. Fina was dabbing at her nostril with it when her phone rang.

"Yes, Father?" she said when she answered.

"What are you doing?" Carl asked.

"Teaching your granddaughter essential life skills."

The line was silent for a moment. "I'm not sure I like the sound of that."

"Trust me, I'm doing you a favor."

"Well, wrap it up. I need you in the office."

"What's going on?"

The phone went dead.

Ahh. Another satisfying father-daughter interaction.

Fina Ludlow was the private investigator at the family law firm. Ignoring her boss—her father, Carl—wasn't an option. She walked Haley to the T, then grabbed a quick shower at home, where she pulled on some jeans and a fitted T-shirt and put her hair in a bun. When actively working a case, Fina opted for sensible shoes, but not knowing the nature of the summons, she grabbed a pair of black strappy sandals. It was the end of August, and the Boston weather couldn't make up its mind: Summer? Fall? Summer? Fall? It had settled somewhere in between; cool breezes alternating with humid, still air.

Carl was sitting behind his desk when Fina arrived, a remote control pointed at the TV. A fifty-five-inch version of her father stared back, urging them to call the 800 number at the bottom of the screen.

"You make a habit of watching your own commercials?" Fina asked.

"I approve everything before it airs."

As a teenager, Fina had been embarrassed by the television ads hawking Carl's talents as a personal injury attorney. It was bad enough that her friends saw them between episodes of *21 Jump Street* and *Cheers*, but a family trip to San Diego revealed the true extent of her father's reach: his ads ran nationwide. People she'd never met had formed a likely negative opinion of her family. When Fina and her brothers complained about the notoriety, Carl reminded them that there would be no fancy trips or designer jeans without the ads, which was true, but Fina couldn't help but notice that her classmates got the same spoils from parents performing arthroscopic surgery and building skyscrapers downtown. Over the years, though, Fina grew to understand that the family firm had its redeeming qualities. They were the top dogs who represented the underdogs. Sometimes, Ludlow and Associates was the only option for poor souls down on their luck.

Carl gestured at his doppelgänger onscreen. "That tie is bothering me."

Fina shrugged. "Looks fine to me."

"Not that I should be taking style advice from you," Carl commented, hitting pause, freezing himself. "You couldn't bother to dress up a little?"

"For what? You wouldn't tell me what's going on."

"We have a potential client. She'll be here any minute."

"Who is it?"

"Renata Sanchez."

"Renata." She contemplated the name for a moment. "Renata from the Ramirez case?"

"That's the one."

Renata Sanchez had been a peripheral witness in a lawsuit a few years earlier. Fina had done some basic background on her and a phone interview, though they'd never met in person. She was the director of the Urban Housing Collaborative, an organization dedicated to addressing the housing challenges of the poor. She was a heroine or a pain in the ass, depending on whom you asked, and she didn't shy away from controversy.

Fina walked over to the bar tucked into the corner of the office. She pulled out a cold diet soda.

"That stuff is crap, you know," Carl commented.

"You think?" Fina asked, eyeballing the bottles of booze on the bar. Carl took good care of himself—his broad shoulders and flat stomach belied his age—but he had a selective memory when it came to his own vices.

Carl ignored her and clicked his mouse. Fina popped open the can and sat down across from him. She took a sip.

"So, tell me about Renata." Fina put her soda on the desk and rocked onto the back legs of the chair. The furniture in Carl's office was high-end and contemporary. Glass and leather dominated and symbolized his approach to the law: Carl was interested in breaking new ground, not upholding the traditions passed down through generations. The space was dotted with sports memorabilia and black-and-white photographs of Boston's twenty-first-century landscape. An antique map of Boston Harbor would never adorn these walls.

"You break it, you buy it," Carl said, gesturing at the precarious tilt of his daughter's chair.

Fina rolled her eyes. "The case?"

"It's a doozy." He brushed the lapel of his jacket. "She wants to sue the cryobank that provided the sperm for her kid."

"Why? Is there something wrong with the kid?"

"No. She thinks she and her daughter have a right to know the sperm donor's identity, despite signing off on an anonymous donation seventeen years ago."

Fina gently squeezed her nose. "There's no way she can win."

"Maybe not."

"So why are we even meeting with her?"

"I want to see how it plays out."

"Sounds like a waste of time to me." Fina dropped the front chair legs back to the floor.

"Let me worry about that." Carl narrowed his gaze. "Is that blood?"

"What?" Fina reached up to her nose and dabbed at a lone drop that had materialized. "Damn. I thought I stopped it." She rummaged in her bag for a tissue and blotted her nostril.

"Very classy," Carl remarked.

"Ms. Sanchez is here," Carl's assistant, Shari, said, poking her head into the office before Fina could respond.

Carl nodded and straightened his tie. Shari returned with a woman who couldn't have topped five feet two, her short stature only reinforced by her bottom-heavy physique. She had short wavy hair that was rich dark brown and skin the color of light brown sugar. Her pantsuit was black and looked inexpensive, but any lack of sartorial prowess was compensated for by her posture. She stood erect and looked Carl in the eye when he got up and shook her hand.

"Carl," she said.

"Renata. This is my daughter, Fina." Fina stood and offered her hand. Renata's grip was beyond firm, but short of crushing. It was clear this woman meant business.

Carl gestured to the empty seat next to Fina. "Please have a seat. Did Shari offer you something to drink?"

"Yes. She's bringing me coffee."

They sat, and Carl leaned back in his chair. "Fina is the firm's private investigator. As I mentioned on the phone, I think she could play a role in your case."

Renata placed a beat-up leather tote bag at her feet and turned in her chair to face Fina. "I assume your father has given you the details?" She wore a thick gold ring on her right index finger. Her hands were small and doughy, almost like a child's.

Fina glanced at Carl. "Yes, but I'd like to hear it from you."

Renata pursed her lips in annoyance.

"I know it may seem like a waste of time," Fina said, "but there are things I'll hear in the telling that a third party just can't convey."

Renata placed her hands on the arms of the chair and crossed her legs. "Fine. I want to sue Heritage Cryobank."

"Okay." Fina took a sip of her drink. "And why do you want to do that?"

"To learn the identity of the sperm donor I used to conceive my eldest child."

"Why?" Fina asked after a moment.

Renata looked puzzled. "What do you mean, *why*?"

Shari tapped on the door and entered bearing a tray. She set a small French press coffeepot and the necessary accoutrements on the corner of Carl's desk. She depressed the lever and then poured a cup for Renata before taking her leave. You'd think Carl was Queen Elizabeth II the way she backed out of the room.

"Why do you want to determine the donor's identity?" Fina asked. "Presumably you went into the arrangement satisfied that he would remain anonymous."

Renata stirred a spoonful of sugar into the hot liquid and added a liberal splash of cream. Fina waited as patiently as a Ludlow could and took comfort knowing that however eager she was to get things moving, her father was even more so.

"Things have changed."

"What things? Unfortunately, changing your mind isn't going to cut it in court."

"I signed those papers seventeen years ago. There was no other way for me to start a family, and I was naïve. I didn't think the identity of Rosie's father mattered, but it does. It's a fundamental human right to know where you come from."

"Not everyone would agree," Carl said.

Renata took a tentative sip and placed the china cup back onto its saucer. "Did you know that they recently outlawed anonymous sperm donations in British Columbia? They ruled that keeping that information secret is unconstitutional."

"So, what now?" Fina asked. "They're opening all those files for the world to see, despite the promise of confidentiality?"

Renata sniffed. "No, but they've acknowledged it's wrong."

"That's Canada." Carl looked unimpressed. "This is the United States."

"And there are lots of kids who don't know their biological parents because of adoption or abandonment or being the product of an affair," Fina noted. "Not knowing a parent's identity doesn't doom them for life."

"You've done research on the matter?" Renata asked testily.

"Anecdotal research," Fina said, and took a long drink, struggling to swallow her annoyance. "I interact with a diverse population in my line of work."

"If you're not interested in the case," Renata said, rotating the coffee cup on the saucer, "I'm sure I can find someone who is."

"That's not what we're saying," Carl assured her, "but as Fina said, changing your mind isn't the basis for setting a new precedent."

Renata leaned forward in her chair. "Does a day go by that you two don't consider your blood connection?" Her stare volleyed between father and daughter.

Fina and Carl both squirmed.

"Our connection is hard to ignore," Fina said after an awkward pause.

"Exactly. Whatever the nature of your relationship, it's a vital part of your identities. I'm only asking that my daughter be given the same basic information. Times have changed. A piece of paper shouldn't stand in the way of progress."

Fina raised an eyebrow in her father's direction. Renata would have to be kept on a tight leash if they were going to take on her crusade.

"I've told Renata that the only legal precedent for breaking the contract is in the case of medical necessity," Carl said.

"Which doesn't exist in this case?" asked Fina.

"Correct," Carl said.

"But what if something were to happen to me?" Renata asked. "My daughter would be left with virtually no blood relatives. And what if she has a medical condition that we don't even know about? Medical testing has made leaps and bounds in the last two decades."

Fina touched her nose. "I don't know. It still sounds like a reach to me. Dad?"

"Renata, the chances of winning this case are practically non-existent."

"That's what they said about the low-income housing the Collaborative built in Dorchester. They said it couldn't be done, that we would drown in red tape. One hundred and fifty families moved in last year."

"Be that as it may, we're not talking about politics," Carl said. "We're talking about the law. You could fight a long, public battle and still end up with nothing to show for it."

She straightened up in her chair. "That's a chance I'm willing to take."

Carl drummed his fingers on his leather blotter. "We can approach it from two angles," he said after a moment of contemplation. "We can research the feasibility of filing a suit against the cryobank on the basis that maintaining the donor's anonymity is a violation of Rosie's human rights, and in the meantime, Fina can figure out the donor's identity, which might give us leverage."

Fina looked at Renata. "Why don't I just try to find out his identity? It could be done under the radar with the same result as a messy lawsuit."

Renata waved Fina's suggestion away with a flick of her wrist. "It wouldn't be the same result. As I've said, this isn't just about my daughter's father; it's a human rights issue. All cryokids have a right to know."

"How does your daughter feel about this?" Fina asked, draining her drink.

Renata licked her lips before speaking. "She understands that I think it's important."

Fina tilted her head. "Okay, but what does *she* think?"

Renata fiddled with the ring on her finger. "She's fine with it."

"Renata, anything you say is protected by privilege, but I can't be effective if I'm operating in the dark." Fina looked at Carl. He nodded ever so slightly. "What does your daughter really think?"

Renata met Fina's gaze. "She's reluctant, but Rosie's always been very independent."

Fina gaped at her. "We can't take this on if Rosie isn't on board."

"Why not?" Renata said. "She's seventeen. She's a minor."

"Because it's unethical, and frankly, it's creepy."

"Excuse me?" Renata peered at her. "How is my fighting for her rights creepy?"

"Because you're talking about digging around in *her* life, into *her* personal information. She may be a minor, but she's old enough to decide if she wants to pursue this."

Carl held up his hand to silence the women. "Fina and I will discuss this further, Renata. Did you bring the documents I requested?"

Fina opened her mouth to speak, but Carl shot her a warning look.

Renata reached into her tote bag and pulled out a dog-eared manila folder. "Here are copies of the relevant paperwork. I have more in deep storage."

Fina took the file and mustered up a sour smile. "Great. Thanks."

Carl walked Renata out of his office. When he returned a moment later, Fina was flipping through the file.

"You're kidding, right? Even Mom wouldn't do something this insane." Fina and her mother, Elaine, had a contentious relationship that was fraught with resentments and grievances. Fina seemed to perpetually disappoint her mother, which tapped into her inner adolescent. Annoying Elaine had developed into a hobby of sorts.

"You heard her." Carl settled back into his leather chair. "It's a human rights issue."

"That's bullshit. There's no way the cryobank is going to give up the name, and Rosie will be in the news regardless. The PR is going to be a nightmare."

"That's not our problem."

Fina closed the file. "I don't like this."

Carl studied something on his computer screen. "I don't pay you to like things. You find out who this guy is, and I'll worry about the lawsuit."

"I don't know, Dad."

His gaze fell on her. "What? You're not interested in the work I'm giving you? You're done with the firm, too, not just the family?"

Fina felt the blood creep up her neck. She'd broken ranks with Carl during her last case, and he wasn't going to let her forget it. "I'm not done with the family or the firm. Stop being so dramatic."

He glared at her. "Then get on with it."

Fina slipped the folder into her bag and stood. "Why are you taking this on? There's no money to be made."

Carl shrugged. "I have a hunch. I think sperm banks are the next big thing. Just you wait."

Of course.

Carl smelled blood in the water and just had to swim closer.

Ten minutes later, Fina sat in her car in the Prudential garage and mulled over her first move. She needed to talk with Rosie Sanchez at some point, but wasn't looking forward to that conversation. Fina glanced at the folder Renata had provided. She'd do a much better job digesting it lying on the couch at home, with a snack.

As she pulled out of the garage, her phone rang.

"I don't have anything to report yet, Dad. I'm leaving the parking garage."

"Your mother wants you at the club for dinner."

"You just gave me a case; I can't make dinner plans."

Fina jammed on the brakes to avoid hitting a car that was cutting her off. The driver gave her the finger. How did that work exactly? Someone cuts you off and flips *you* the bird?

"You can take an hour for dinner. I thought you wanted to do right by Haley. What's one dinner?"

There was no question that her fifteen-year-old niece needed all the help she could get. Fina's most recent case, the one that had brought the Ludlows to the brink, involved the murder of Haley's mom, Melanie.

"Fine. What time?"

"Six thirty."

Fina ended the call before Carl could.

Ludlow family gatherings had never been relaxing or carefree, but they'd taken on a new level of awkwardness given recent events. Fina was still struggling to digest the dirt she'd dug up about her brother Rand, Haley's father. If that weren't enough, the normal reactions people were supposed to have to death and depraved behavior seemed to be absent from the Ludlow emotional toolbox, at least on the parts of Carl and Elaine. Fina had hoped that her parents would rise to the occasion when faced with Melanie's death and its fallout, but she was starting to believe that they were emotionally bankrupt. They couldn't give what they didn't have, and the flashes of anger she felt were interspersed with moments of sadness. No family was perfect, but some seemed more broken than others.

Walter Stiles stroked his goatee and studied the brochure. It was high quality—thick paper, bright colors, and appealing photographs. Still, something about it bothered him. The idea that you could choose your donor based on a resemblance to a celebrity wasn't the problem; maybe the problem was that it had been Ellen's idea. Ellen was his second in command, well liked by the staff and increasingly a driving force behind new initiatives at Heritage Cryobank. Walter knew that she had strong marketing acumen and her ideas would benefit the bank, but her insistence on pushing her agenda irked him. Heritage had done just fine—better than fine—before Ellen came along. It would do just fine if she weren't there now.

In the thirty-six years that Walter had been at the bank, he had watched it grow from a small, unassuming operation to one of the most respected cryobanks in the country. Walter liked to think that he was largely responsible for that growth. True, it was the nature of the industry, but without him at the helm, he found it hard to believe that the bank would have a national reputation. Ellen was obsessed with data and algorithms and marketing surveys, but at the end of the day, Walter knew, it was about a woman holding her newborn child, beaming down at him or her. There was no better marketing than that.

Walter put down the brochure and leaned back in his commodious leather chair. He tidied the small stacks of paper on his desk before swiveling around to the window, where he studied his reflection. Perhaps he wasn't the most handsome man in the world, but Walter put time and effort into his appearance and felt he looked young for his sixty-three years. He'd recently upped his swimming schedule to four times a week. There was no doubt that his metabolism was slowing down, just one more tide he'd have to stem.

The management team was scheduled to meet tomorrow to discuss the new brochure, but Walter decided he had a conflict. He would call a meeting for this afternoon instead. Too bad Ellen would miss it; she had a prior engagement, away from the office.

Fina drove back home and took the folder up to her condo, which overlooked Boston Harbor and Logan Airport. Technically, it really wasn't *her* condo. Her grandmother, Nanny, had lived there until her death nine months ago. Fina had become a de facto squatter, and the arrangement satisfied her nomadic approach to life. Privacy and comfort were her only requirements—not that she didn't appreciate the view—and she achieved both of those at Nanny's without changing a thing. The blue velvet sofa, the glass-topped coffee table with wrought-iron legs, the wall of Ludlow family photos—they were all Nanny's touch. A visitor might conclude that the condo was the home of a sentimental octogenarian who wasn't big on housekeeping. Fina did spring for a better TV, but the rest of the decor remained the same—except that now it was buried under a layer of Fina's belongings.

Renata had given her a lot of paperwork, but not much information. After wading through the standard forms used by the cryobank, Fina found a two-page profile of the donor consisting of basic data about his education, interests, physical attributes, and the like. In terms of facts, it was slim pickings. Donor #575651 was born in Joliet, Illinois, in 1951, graduated from high school in 1969, and from UMass in 1972. Fina started with a search of all the high schools in Joliet and came up with four public high schools, two Catholic and two private. She'd have to cross-reference birth records, high school graduation records, and UMass class lists. It would be tedious, but presumably she would end up with a somewhat abbreviated list. The whole thing sounded like a snooze, but at least she would be paid good money for her efforts.

Fina decided to take a trip to Cambridge, where, seventeen years earlier, Rosie Sanchez had been just a dot on a petri dish. She probably wouldn't glean much from a visit, but in her experience, it always made sense to start at the source, and you couldn't get any closer than the cryobank.

After a few wrong turns and a one-sided argument with the GPS, Fina found Heritage. Located in a nondescript concrete low-rise office building practically in Harvard University's backyard, Heritage looked like an academic building or a lab, not ground zero for the conception of countless children. Fina sat in her car and took stock of the situation for a few minutes. There were a dozen cars in the parking lot, and she saw a handful of people come and go. These were mostly women, and nothing distinguished them from those you might see in the grocery store parking lot. The foot traffic on the sidewalk was dominated by young men and women, presumably students, who were most likely doing everything in their power to avoid pregnancy.

Fina pulled down the mirror in her visor and checked her appearance. She applied some lip gloss and ran a hand over her hair to smooth the frizzy strays. She couldn't complain about her looks and considered them one of the perks of being a Ludlow. A clear complexion, high cheekbones, and a wide smile served her well, not to mention her rapid-fire metabolism. Her appearance gave her an advantage, not only in her job but in life in general, and she tried to use her powers for good, not evil. Sometimes, though, it was hard to keep the two straight.

Inside the lobby, Fina shivered from the air-conditioning and approached the desk where a young woman sat. There was a small waiting area with couches and potted plants, the walls painted a soft yellow. Enya drizzled down from the speakers mounted in the ceiling. Beautiful babies with puffy quilted arms and thighs smiled out from enlarged photographs. There were no pictures of crying babies or babies covered in their own shit. None of them were ugly. So much for truth in advertising.

"Can I help you?" the receptionist asked.

Fina tried to appear hesitant, which isn't easy when assertive is your middle name.

"Well, I think so. A friend told me about you guys, and I just wanted to get some information."

"Of course." The woman stood and revealed her extremely pregnant belly as she reached into a cabinet and pulled out a glossy folder. Did they always have a pregnant woman manning the desk?

"We're the second-oldest cryobank in the nation. We offer the latest technology in reproductive science and state-of-the-art facilities. Our director, Walter Stiles, serves on the board of the National Reproductive Medicine Society." She opened the folder and began pointing out the different inserts. "Here's general information about our services: choosing a donor, sperm and egg banking, shipping and storage. You'll find lots of details, including staff bios and testimonials from our satisfied clients. We've helped thousands of families." She smiled widely.

"When are you due?" Fina asked.

"In a month," the woman said, and ran her hands over her belly. "I'm so ready. This little guy won't get off my bladder."

Gosh, that sounded like fun.

"Well, you look great," Fina said. "Very healthy and . . . glowy."

"You're so sweet. I'm a beached whale, but it's all worth it in the end."

Fina closed the folder and began to slip it into her bag.

"Would you like to sit down with one of our client liaisons? She can answer any questions you might have."

"Thanks, but I'm just getting information at this point." She leaned toward the mother-to-be. "I'm not quite ready to take that next step."

The receptionist squeezed her hand. "I totally understand. You take all the time that you need. We'll be here."

"Thank you."

Fina returned to her car and pulled the folder out. She glanced through the materials. If you were desperate for a baby, Heritage Cryobank certainly gave you hope. But the hope came with a hefty price tag. Fina thought people who wanted babies should have them—whether the potential parents were single, married, gay, or straight. Adoption and sperm donation were two different roads to the same destination, and she didn't think one was better than the other. But when people profited from the desperation of parents-to-be, things got dicey. Parenthood really wasn't for the faint of heart.

In the Whittaker Club parking lot, Fina shut off the car and leaned her head back against the headrest. She took a few deep, hopefully cleansing breaths and felt no better. Under the best of circumstances, Fina's relationship with her parents was fraught, but since the debacle with her brother, she'd been on parental probation with no clear end to her sentence.

"What are you doing?" Her brother Matthew stood outside her window. Matthew was two years older than Fina, and in her opinion, the best-looking of the Ludlow bunch. His wavy brown hair hadn't yet succumbed to any gray, and his right cheek boasted a dimple that women practically fell into. He wasn't in any hurry to settle down, and who could blame him? Being Matthew Ludlow was a pretty good gig.

"I'm trying to gather my strength. You know, center myself."

"Why bother? Your blood pressure soars at the mere sight of Mom."

"I know, but I can't change her, so I'm trying to change myself."

Matthew laughed. "Oh God, I love it. That's hilarious."

Fina glared at him. "Seriously, I leave every family gathering with a throbbing headache. They act like everything is hunky-dory."

Matthew leaned against the open window frame. "Would you prefer chaos and breast-beating?"

"No, but doesn't it bother you? It's like Melanie never existed and Rand is on sabbatical."

"Well, we can't talk about it all the time. That would be weird, too."

"There's no happy medium?"

"We're not good at this stuff, you know that." A caddy walked by, a large golf bag slung over each shoulder. He threw out a greeting, which Matthew and Fina returned. "Mom doesn't know about Rand and Haley, right?" Matthew asked.

"Right. Even if she knew, I don't think it would make much difference. Her unwillingness to accept reality drives me crazy."

"Come on." Matthew tapped the door. "I'm hungry. We'll figure it out."

"Okay, Suzy Sunshine, if you say so."

They walked up the path that skirted the landscaping and ended at a large swimming pool. Much of the Ludlows' childhoods had been spent at the Whittaker Club. They passed idyllic summers swimming in the pool, working on their tennis serves, and getting up to no good on the golf course. The next generation of Ludlows was being raised in a similar fashion, and the club continued to be the destination of choice for family celebrations and events. It also served as neutral territory where they could meet despite whatever battles were raging.

Chaise lounges littered the grass, and tables dotted the patio. The waitstaff, dressed in khakis and white polo shirts, hustled between the eating area and a swinging door leading into an enormous shingled clubhouse.

"They're over there." Matthew nodded toward the patio, and Fina followed him as he picked his way through fluffy towels carelessly dropped and small children careening with ice-cream cones in hand.

Carl was seated at the end of a long table, and Fina's brother Scotty anchored the other end. In between were Scotty's wife, Patty, their three sons, and Rand's daughter, Haley. Elaine, Fina's mother, sat to the right of Carl.

"I heard you had quite the morning," Scotty said, grinning. He and Matthew shared the same good looks and were softies at heart, but the energy that Matthew devoted to dating and sports, Scotty poured into his family. He was one of those people who were meant to be parents, who enjoyed watching their children develop and grow. Fina thought soccer games and band concerts were torture, but to Scotty, that was the good stuff.

"Hale and I had a great morning," Fina said. "Patty should come next time."

"I'll leave the boxing to you two," Patty commented. "As soon as you want to do a spa day, I'm in."

Scotty and Patty took Haley in when her immediate family imploded and provided a steadying force that had been sorely absent from Haley's life even when her parents were on the scene. Scotty and Patty were good parents, and being an older sister to her three younger cousins seemed to be having a positive effect on Haley.

"We're just about to order," Elaine said, and pushed menus in front of Fina and Matthew. "There's a salad special, Josefina."

Fina looked at her sister-in-law, who was struggling to suppress a smile. "I don't like salads, Mom, remember?"

Elaine sniffed. "They're good for you."

The waitress arrived and called them all by name, the usual deference from the country club staff. Fina ordered a bacon cheeseburger with fries, and her niece followed suit, much to Elaine's chagrin.

"What did you do the rest of the day, Hale?" Fina asked.

"Not much. Risa took me back-to-school shopping," she said.

Risa Paquette had been Melanie's best friend and known the Ludlows since childhood. She'd stepped up since Melanie's death and tried to fill the gaps that Patty and Fina couldn't. None of them would ever replace Haley's mom, but the women were doing everything they could to get Haley back on track.

"That's cool."

"Not really. It means I have to go back to school."

"True, but you'll be back with your friends."

"I can be with my friends during the summer, without homework and getting up early."

"Good point."

Fina inquired about the crappy reality TV that seemed to captivate her niece, while her nephews blew bubbles in their lemonades until Patty put the kibosh on that. Carl, Scotty, and Matthew discussed a case, which left Elaine unoccupied, a status that always put Fina on edge. Her mother usually cycled through a list of topics, most of them negative and invasive, including Fina's eating habits, Matthew's romantic prospects, and anything in life that wasn't up to snuff. Interacting with her was like letting a camel into your tent: All it took was one toe and then the whole thing stormed in, wrecking the place.

"Are the boys all set for school?" Fina asked Patty in an effort to avoid an inquisition. Patty detailed the exhaustive list of required school supplies as their food arrived and everyone dove in.

"*Romance Renovation* was awesome last night," Haley commented, whacking the ketchup bottle with her open palm.

"I'm behind," Fina said. "Don't tell me who got the wrecking ball."

"Is that the one with the renovation dates and the kitchen re-models?" Scotty asked.

"Yes," his niece remarked. "It's awesome. Even Aunt Patty is getting into it."

"One episode," she protested. "I watched one episode."

"But admit it: You're hooked." Haley smirked.

Fina shared a look with Scotty. Maybe some kind of normalcy really was within reach for Haley.

"Okay, maybe I'm a little hooked," Patty admitted.

Fina enjoyed every bite of her juicy burger and distributed most of her fries to her nephews. Elaine looked annoyed across the table, but who wouldn't be if they'd chosen a garden salad for dinner?

"I don't understand the appeal of those shows," her mother stated, throwing out the handiest gauntlet. "They just seem dumb to me."

"That's part of the appeal, Mom. They're escapism," Scotty said.

"It seems like a waste."

"Speaking of a waste, which did you think was more impressive on *The Next Superstar*?" Fina asked Haley. "The fire-eating or the hula-hooping with the chain saws?"

"Neither pays the bills," Carl commented.

"They're not looking for a job, Pap," Haley said.

Carl grunted and let the wave of conversation wash over him. He pulled out his phone. So much for being there for the family.

Once the plates were empty and cleared, Haley and the boys returned to the pool, and the grown-ups were left around the large table.

"Did you make some progress this afternoon?" Carl asked.

Fina glared at her father. "I started. I'll let you know when I have something to report, Dad."

Her mother was peering at her. Uh-oh. "You need to go see your brother, Fina."

Fina squirmed in her seat. "We'll see."

"What's there to see? He's your brother."

Fina was silent. It was true that Elaine didn't know the full extent of Rand's crimes, didn't know that he'd molested Haley, but a lack of information never stopped her from having an opinion. She couldn't trust that Fina had her reasons for her choices and that adult children should be left to navigate their own relationships with one another. Fina remained silent, as much as it pained her.

"Someday, your father and I will be gone, and you children will only have one another."

Fina opened her mouth to respond, but Patty beat her to it. "That's not going to be for a long time, Mom. No need to worry about that yet."

"That's exactly what I was going to say," Fina said, grimacing.

Back at Nanny's, Fina flipped on the Red Sox game and reclaimed her spot on the couch.

"Who is it?" she hollered when there was a knock on the door thirty minutes later.

"Milloy."

She swung open the door to Milloy Danielson, her best friend, massage therapist extraordinaire, sometime operative, and occasional friend with benefits. He held a plastic bag out to her.

"And you're bearing gifts? Come in, come in."

They passed the next hour watching the Red Sox and discussing Renata Sanchez in between innings while Fina nibbled on the Mallomars he'd brought.

"So what's your first move?" Milloy asked as he stretched his arms over his head, revealing a sculpted abdomen.

"Put myself up for adoption? Seriously, the whole thing is crazy."

"You could opt out of this one."

Fina gave him a withering look. "I'm running out of free passes, and I'm not worried about the family stuff. It's the work that concerns me."

"What? You think Carl might fire you?"

"He might."

"But you've had other clients in the past. You could go out on your own."

"Maybe, but he could make my professional life very unpleasant, and more importantly, I like working for the firm. The cases are interesting. On my own, I'll spend my time following chumps around with a camera hoping to catch them reshingling their roofs while on disability."

Milloy patted her knee. "Then I guess you need to take this case."

"I guess so. If I find the donor quickly, maybe Renata will stop pursuing the lawsuit idea."

"Where are you going to start?"

Fina thought for a moment. "The offspring. I need to talk to Rosie Sanchez and get a DNA swab."

Milloy grinned.

"What?" Fina asked.

"I'm just imagining you in a nurse's uniform."

"Yeah, 'cause I'm going to show up in thigh-high white stockings and a low-cut white top."

"A boy can dream."

2

The next morning, Fina ventured past Cambridge's leafy streets and sizable single-family homes to Somerville. It was formerly a working-class town, but artists, professionals, and members of academia ushered in gentrification in the 1990s, recasting the densely packed city as a place to be. As she navigated the narrow streets, the mid-rise brick buildings and triple-deckers seemingly crept toward Fina. She had grown accustomed to Nanny's extensive vista and appreciated a sight line that encompassed more than the neighbor's clothesline.

Yesterday she'd reviewed her old file on Renata and done a cursory background check on her in preparation for this visit. Renata and her daughters lived in a two-family house Renata had purchased more than twenty years before. The house wasn't anything special from the outside, but its proximity to Davis Square and Harvard Square made it a fruitful investment. She'd make a hefty profit if she ever sold, but in the meantime, the rental unit probably paid her mortgage.

Fina rang the bell twice before it was answered by a girl who looked to be a tween.

"Is your mom home?" Fina asked.

"Mom!" the girl yelled over her shoulder. "There's a lady here to see you." She stared at Fina.

"Are you Alexa?" Fina extended her hand. "I'm Fina."

The girl shook her hand firmly and leaned on the open door. She had light brown skin and curly hair to her shoulders. She was creeping from plump to fat, a trajectory that Fina hoped would be halted for Alexa's sake. Kids were cruel.

Renata came to the door. "Alexa, finish getting ready for camp." She gently nudged her daughter's shoulder. "You've caught us during our morning mad dash, Fina."

In Fina's experience, even the most organized households had morning mad dashes, especially if there were children present. It was just one of the reasons she relished her solitude. She could barely feed and clothe herself, let alone small, moody people.

"Sorry about that. I assumed you wanted to get the ball rolling. I'll be quick."

Fina followed her into the kitchen. It was a modest space overlooking a back porch and yard. The cabinets were white laminate circa 1985, and the appliances were also white. The granite and stainless steel de rigueur in today's kitchens were nowhere in evidence. Alexa sat at the small round kitchen table slurping up a bowl of cereal.

"Alexa, sit up," Renata said.

Fina pulled out the chair across from the girl and sat down.

"Would you like some coffee?" Renata held up a pot.

"Yes, thanks."

Fina would have preferred a diet soda, her caffeine delivery system of choice, but part of being a PI was making people feel comfortable. Generally, people felt most comfortable when you made the same choices they did.

"Cream and sugar?"

"Yes, please."

Renata poured the steaming liquid into a mug that read GIRL SCOUTS BUILD BRIDGES and handed it to Fina. A sugar bowl was already on the table, and Renata plunked down a small cardboard carton of cream. Fina doctored her drink and took a tentative sip.

"Alexa, could you please get your sister and your backpack?"

Alexa sat up straight. "Rosie!" she yelled.

"I said 'get her,' not 'scream her name,'" Renata said in exasperation.

Alexa pushed her chair back from the table and left the room.

"That used to drive my parents crazy," Fina said.

Renata nodded. "We did it, too, although when you live in a tiny space, you're usually already in the same room."

"Did you grow up in Somerville?" Fina asked. She knew Renata hadn't, but it was always interesting to ask questions to which you already knew the answer.

"Lawrence, with four younger siblings in a three-bedroom apartment."

"Sounds like a lot of together time."

"Yes, but it wasn't all bad. Sometimes I think kids today have too much of everything." She looked at Fina pointedly. You didn't need to know much about the Ludlows to know that they fell into the "too much of everything" category.

Fina shrugged. "I don't have kids, so I really can't say."

The smacking of flip-flops interrupted the conversation, and Rosie Sanchez entered the room. She was extremely pretty, with long curly brown hair. Her features were delicate and free of makeup. Cutoff shorts flattered her lean, smooth legs, and a stack of woven bracelets encircled one wrist.

"Rosie, this is Fina Ludlow, the investigator I told you about."

Rosie looked at Fina, then back at her mother. "Mom, I'm late for work."

"Don't worry. I'll call them and tell them you'll be late."

"What?" Rosie asked.

"It's not a problem," Renata said, and drank her coffee.

"You're going to call the animal shelter? Mom, I'm an adult. You can't call my work."

Renata gripped her coffee cup. "Rosie, this is important, and they'll understand."

Rosie threw open the refrigerator door and bent down to scan the contents. "You don't get it. It's not your place to call my work or manage my schedule."

"I was just trying to help." Renata looked hurt.

Fina's heart sank. She knew this dynamic well: the complete lack of boundaries that felt like a constant violation to the daughter, and the apparent lack of appreciation that felt like ungratefulness to the mother.

"You know what?" Fina said. "We can do this later." She took her coffee cup to the sink, then reached into her bag and handed her card to Rosie. "Why don't you call me, and we'll set up a time that works for you."

Rosie eyed her skeptically. "Fine."

"It won't take long. I just wanted to ask you some questions and do a quick swab."

Rosie's eyes narrowed. "What are you talking about?"

Fina looked at Renata, who avoided her gaze by studying the carton of cream. "You didn't tell her?"

Rosie slammed the fridge door closed. The cereal boxes on top swayed. "Mom, what's going on?"

"She knows all about the lawsuit," Renata reassured Fina. "We talked about this, Rosie."

"We didn't talk about any swab."

"Fina is trying to identify your donor while we proceed with the lawsuit. She needs a DNA swab to get started."

Rosie stared at her mother. "You have lost your fucking mind," she finally said.

"Rosie!" Renata stood up from the table and glared at her daughter. "Watch your mouth, young lady!"

"There's no way in hell I'm giving a DNA sample. I can't believe you would even ask. I'm not some science experiment, you know."

"It will help our case."

"*Your* case. This is *your* case, Mom. I don't want any part of it." She turned on her heel and flip-flopped out of the room.

Renata walked over to the sink. She took a deep breath and then looked at Fina. "She'll come around. We just have to give her time."

"This is a terrible idea." Fina looked at her. "Pursuing this could seriously damage your relationship with your daughter."

Renata turned her back to Fina and twisted the faucet on. The vigorous hand washing that followed would have met the surgical standards at Mass General. Renata flicked the excess water off her hands before rubbing them with a dish towel. She turned back toward Fina.

"Didn't you just tell me you don't have children?"

"That's right."

"Well, then, I appreciate your concern, but your parenting advice is not required."

"All righty then." Fina headed to the front door. "I'll be in touch."

Back on the sidewalk, Fina kicked an empty can with her toe and watched as it clattered across the street and into a storm drain. If Renata wasn't going to listen to reason, maybe Fina should stop wasting her breath.

"What can I do for law enforcement this fine day?" Fina asked Cristian when he joined her at a diner in the South End.

"Actually, I have a favor to ask, strictly off the books."

"Shoot."

Cristian Menendez was a detective with the Major Crimes unit of the Boston Police Department. He and Fina had met at a crime scene more than a decade earlier and had been friends and occasional adversaries ever since.

"I need you to run a background check on this guy." He pushed a slip of paper across the table and righted his coffee cup so the waitress could fill it. Fina looked at the name.

"Who's Brad Martin?"

Cristian nodded his thanks to the waitress, whose gaze lingered on him. His Spanish and Puerto Rican ancestry melded into a pleasing package of cinnamon-colored skin and wavy hair. Haley had once categorized him as a hottie, and Fina had to concur.

He had some coffee and cleared his throat. "Marissa's seeing him."

Fina grinned. "You want me to run a check on your ex-wife's new boyfriend? I thought you always took the high road."

"I couldn't care less who Marissa dates, but I want to know who's hanging around my son." Matteo was Cristian's three-year-old.

"That seems reasonable, but why not just look yourself?" She sipped ice water from a clear plastic cup.

"Using city resources to snoop on your ex is frowned upon."

"As it should be, but I'm happy to do it."

"I don't want to hire you officially, though."

"No problem. I'm too busy for any other official jobs right now, so it won't be in my records. Just the usual stuff?"

Cristian nodded. "I owe you."

"Hardly." Cristian had saved her butt more than once.

"What are you working on that's keeping you so busy 'officially'?" he asked.

"Just a total clusterfuck of an investigation related to one of Carl's cases. It has the potential to blow up in everyone's faces."

"Sounds like business as usual at Ludlow and Associates."

"Pretty much."

"How's Haley doing?"

Fina unconsciously touched her nose. "She's fine."

Cristian didn't say anything. He looked at Fina.

"I *think* she's fine," she conceded. "Okay, I really don't have a clue. I took her boxing yesterday, and she nailed me in the nose."

He leaned toward her and examined her face. "Since when do you know how to box?"

"Since practically the day I was born!"

"You know how to hit. That's different from boxing. If you want her to learn some skills, I'll take her." Cristian was one of those cops who could actually run after a suspect and pitch himself over a chain-link fence. His father had died young from a heart attack, and he was determined to avoid the same fate, so he took good care of himself.

"I wanted to give her an outlet for her anger, blow off some steam. Plus, everybody should know how to defend themselves."

The waitress stopped by and expertly topped off Cristian's coffee, the two steaming pots like appendages on the ends of her arms.

"She's probably got anger to spare," he noted.

"That's why I think she needs an outlet. I don't want her to snap one of these days and shoot up her school or plant a bomb in her underwear."

"Is she seeing someone?"

"I assume you mean a therapist and not a boyfriend. Yes, Patty takes her twice a week."

"Does Haley talk to you about it?"

"Which 'it'? Her mother dying? Her father being a pedophile? Her brief foray into the world of escorts?"

"Any of it."

"Cristian." Fina put down her water and looked at him. "I think we can agree I'm way out of my depth on this one. So I asked myself, 'What would Oprah do?' and the answer I came up with was 'Listen, but don't push.'"

He gave her a pitying smile. "At least you're trying. What about the rest of the family?"

"Scotty and Patty and Matthew are on board. Carl and Elaine are on another planet."

"And Rand?"

"What about him?"

"What's his status?"

"I'm ignoring his existence right now."

"That sounds like a very mature approach."

"I thought so."

Cristian finished his coffee and reached for his wallet. Fina waved him away.

"Fine, but when you get the info, I'll take you out to dinner," he said.

"On a date?" Fina asked teasingly. Cristian and Fina hooked up occasionally, but their relationship was largely undefined. For the time being, both of them seemed to like it that way.

Cristian stood and shrugged. "If you want to call it that."

She watched him walk away and noticed a table of twenty-something women checking him out.

Maybe she should call dibs on such a catch.

After eating some leftover Chinese food at home, Fina started digging into the details of Brad Martin's life. Arrests and convictions, job history, education, driving record, civil court files, and property ownership were the pillars of a basic background check. That information was part of the public record and relatively easy to access now that so much could be found online.

Next, she turned to the Sanchez case. Fina called a friend at UMass and tried to finagle a list of graduates from 1972. Apparently, the class list was a closely guarded state secret, but her contact promised to do his best.

Since free information wasn't a sure thing, Fina went online and signed up for a few paid sites that promised to connect her with her long-lost classmates. She searched Joliet, Illinois, for male high school graduates in 1969 and watched a long—albeit incomplete—list unfurl from her printer. Fina considered looking for online yearbook pictures, but it would be a waste of time until she had pictures of the cryokids for comparison.

Fina poked around the online single mothers' community, in which Renata Sanchez was very active. Twenty years ago, it wasn't easy to find a like-minded group of single women craving motherhood, but today, all you had to do was hop online to do everything short of the actual insemination. Information on cryobanks, advice for choosing a donor, referrals to open-minded doctors, support networks for dealing with the questions posed by donor offspring—it was all there. Fina thought research and careful consideration were good policies, but it was a wonder anyone had kids after surfing the Net. Sleepless nights, saggy cervixes, vaccinations, play-group politics. It was a jungle out there.

Renata was the president of a local group of SMCs, single mothers by choice, and it seemed to be an active community. Fina clicked through a monthly calendar filled with potluck dinners, apple-picking outings, and discussion groups for tweens before landing on the list of other board members. Renata had suggested she speak with those women, particularly the one whose children shared the same donor as Rosie, Marnie Frasier. It wasn't unheard of for half-siblings to live in the same area, particularly in the early days of sperm donation when most sperm was acquired locally. It was only in the past decade or so that prospective parents had culled swimmers from a nationwide marketplace courtesy of the growing cryobank industry and FedEx Overnight.

Marnie's home was in Arlington on a pretty street lined with oak trees and single-family colonial-style houses. Fina rang the doorbell of her yellow house and peeked through the glass panel on the front door. After a moment, a pair of legs trotted down the stairs from the second floor, and Fina was greeted by a cute young man. He was tall and muscular with a swimmer's body, and his hair was growing out from a Mohawk.

"Hey," he said, and surreptitiously gave Fina the once-over.

"Hey. Is Marnie Frasier home?" She handed the young man her PI license and watched him scan it.

"Ahh, sure. She's out back."

"I'm Fina Ludlow." Fina offered her hand.

He had a firm handshake. "Tyler. Come on in." He held open the screen door for her, and they walked through the house toward the back. His walk was loose and confident. Coupled with his sandy blond Mohawk, he looked like he should be paddling a surfboard in the Pacific.

"I've never met a PI before. What's it like?" he asked.

"It's great. Never boring. I don't have to work in an office. I carry a gun." Fina patted her bag.

Tyler turned to her and laughed. His teeth were bright white and straight, and when he smiled, dimples emerged on his cheeks. Fina knew from the background info that Tyler was nineteen. Good thing; it was creepy when you started admiring the physical attributes of the underage.

A door in the kitchen led outside to a landing and a short flight of stairs. The steps ended at a brick patio on which a table, chairs, and a grill sat. The small lawn looked freshly mown and featured beds of hydrangeas and dahlias and other colorful blooms that Fina couldn't identify. In one corner of the yard, a woman was kneeling on a pad, her hands encased in gardening gloves, attacking the soil with a small hoe.

"Mom, this is . . . a private investigator." Tyler smiled at Fina. "Sorry. I'm terrible with names."

"Fina Ludlow. I'd like to ask you a few questions, Ms. Frasier, if you don't mind."

Marnie sighed deeply and sat back on her heels. "Questions about what?"

Fina glanced at Tyler. "Renata Sanchez."

Marnie gave Tyler a look that seemed to indicate her displeasure with his gatekeeping and brushed a lock of ash brown hair away from her face with her wrist.

"Fine," she said. "Do you mind if I keep hoeing?"

"Be my guest." Fina sat down on the grass, and Tyler walked back into the house. Fina studied Marnie for a moment as she dug into the earth with her hands. She was an attractive woman, her shoulder-length hair intermittently streaked with gray and loosely held back by a black fabric headband. She was wearing jeans that were obviously reserved for gardening, as evidenced by grass and dirt stains, and a faded T-shirt celebrating an event at Lesley University.

"So what can I help you with?" Marnie looked at Fina.

"Renata has hired the law firm Ludlow and Associates to sue Heritage Cryobank. Did you know she was planning this?"

"Yes, because she tried to get me on board. Has been bugging me for months," Marnie said as she stabbed the hoe into a clump of dry dirt.

"You're not interested?"

"In suing the cryobank? No."

"Because?"

"Because I signed a legally binding contract ensuring that the donor's identity would remain anonymous. Because I don't want to put my children through the wringer."

"We've told her the chances of winning are slim to none, but that hasn't deterred her."

"I wouldn't expect it to. Renata has fought the powers that be on more than one occasion and won. She believes she can defy the odds." Marnie paused in her digging. "Why does she need a private investigator for the lawsuit?"

"She wants to sue the cryobank, but she also wants me to try to uncover the donor's identity through other means."

"Such as?"

"Standard investigative techniques. Records searches, that sort of thing."

Marnie shook her head. "She's really outdone herself this time."

"What do you mean?"

"Renata has a talent for setting things in motion with little thought for the consequences." Marnie plunged her hoe into the earth. "Say you discover his identity. Then what?"

"She didn't say."

Marnie grinned. "Exactly. She probably has some fantasy about one big happy family. That the man will embrace Rosie as his own."

"You don't think that's likely?"

"Who knows? But she shouldn't toy with Rosie's emotions, and I don't appreciate her involving my kids. If they want to find their dad, it should be their decision when they're ready."

"She seems to think they have a fundamental right to know. Like she's doing them a favor."

"Uh-huh."

"So this is typical Renata, stirring things up?"

"Yes, and don't get me wrong; I like her, and many people have benefited from her zeal, but she has boundary issues."

Fina nodded knowingly. "When did you learn that you two used the same donor?"

"About four years ago. I didn't seek out the information. My son has a bad habit of digging around online." Marnie frowned and flicked a worm away with her gloved hand. "We already knew Renata and her family through the SMC community, but when Tyler got involved with a sibling registry, the biological connection came to light."

"You didn't support his research?"

Marnie shrugged. "I just worry, that's all."

"Is it a pretty tight-knit group, the SMCs?"

"You can be as involved as you want to be. When the kids were babies, those women were lifesavers, and I've met some of my best friends through the group." She hesitated.

"But?"

"But for some people, being an SMC becomes a cause of sorts, which is fine as long as that's in the best interest of your kids." Marnie struggled, to no avail, to pull a thick, gnarled root from the ground.

"Let me," Fina said, and got to her feet. She tugged at the growth and finally loosed it from the earth, nearly falling backward in the process. "You don't think Renata has the best interest of her kids in mind?"

Marnie slowly stood up. Her knee popped loudly.

"Yikes," Fina said.

"I know. It doesn't hurt, but I imagine it's only a matter of time." Marnie took off her gloves and smacked them against her jeans to loosen the dirt. "I think Renata is a wonderful mother in many ways, and she loves her kids very much. But do I think involving your child in a lawsuit related to her sperm donor is a good idea? No. Not under any circumstances, but particularly not when the child has no interest."

"Rosie. Right. I met her earlier today. She was pissed at Renata about the lawsuit. She seemed like a fairly private person."

Marnie shrugged. "Maybe she gets that from her father. She certainly doesn't get it from her mother." Fina watched as Marnie put her gardening supplies into a basket and grasped the handle. "I get the sense that you don't think this is a great idea, either," Marnie said.

"I try not to let my feelings come into a case, but it's not the best idea I've ever heard," Fina admitted.

"But you're going to do it anyway?"

Fina ground her toe into the soil. "Let's just say I have my own family-related reasons for taking this on." Fina swatted a bug from her face. "You aren't at all curious about the donor's identity?"

Marnie looked toward the house. "I think it might be Pandora's box. The only thing that matters to me about the donor is that he made it possible for me to have two wonderful children."

Fina handed her card to Marnie. "Thanks for talking to me. I'd like to talk to your kids, too."

"I'd rather you didn't, but they're adults." She smiled ruefully. "Even if they weren't, I couldn't stop them."

"If either of them is amenable, I'd also like to get a DNA swab."

"I'm sure Jess, my daughter, won't have any interest. I don't know about Tyler."

"I won't ask this minute. You can try to talk him out of it if you want."

Marnie snorted. "You think I can sway his behavior? That's the curse of raising independent, self-sufficient children: They really do have minds of their own."

"I'll be in touch," Fina said, walking away. She opened the side gate and returned to her car.

3

It was a short drive to Heritage Cryobank, and most of the spaces in the parking lot were occupied. Fina consulted her notes about the bank before heading to the front door.

The same heavily pregnant receptionist was behind the desk, but this time, the waiting room chairs were filled with an assortment of clients, and a few toddlers played on the floor.

"You're back!" the receptionist chirped as Fina approached the desk.

"I am."

"Ready to talk with one of our client liaisons?"

"Actually, I was hoping I could speak with Ellen Alberti." Fina had done a little digging, and Ellen's name figured prominently in the coverage of the bank.

The receptionist frowned. "Our associate director? She doesn't generally meet with new clients."

"I know, it's just . . . a friend gave me her name, and I'd feel more comfortable speaking with her."

"I don't know . . ."

"You know what? It's okay. I'll just—I'll try some other time." Fina fiddled with her bag.

"Well, hold on there. It's just a little unusual."

"I don't want to put you in an awkward spot. Really. I'll figure something else out." Fina turned toward the door.

"Just wait one second," the receptionist said, picking up the phone. "Have a seat, and I'll see what I can do."

Fina took a seat in a stiff-backed chair covered in a nubby mauve-colored fabric. The magazine options on the side table were limited: *Fit Pregnancy, American Baby, Pregnancy and Newborn, Parents.* Fina picked one up and flipped through the pages. Poor expectant mothers: Even they weren't given a pass when it came to meeting a ridiculous physical ideal. The women gracing the pages were beautiful, with perfect bodies boasting taut round bellies, nary a stretch mark in sight.

Fina was halfway through an article about keeping her nipples moisturized when the receptionist waved at her and smiled brightly.

"Ellen can see you now. Go through the door on the right, and her office is all the way back. Just keep walking. You can't miss it."

Fina thanked her and pushed the door open.

She couldn't believe access to the offices and labs wasn't restricted; allowing visitors to wander through the place unattended was sloppy. As Fina moved down the hallway, most of the doors were closed, but had signs identifying their purposes. There were client-counseling offices, exam rooms, labs, and client lounges. Fina poked her head into some kind of small waiting room, which could have passed for a nondescript living room or a shrink's office. It looked inviting, yet impersonal. The art on the walls looked to have been chosen for its soothing color palette and inoffensive subject matter—boating parties, fields of flowers, and café scenes. There was nothing state-of-the-art about it, but Fina assumed that claim applied to the actual medical facilities. She passed a nurse in teddy-bear-patterned scrubs in the hallway and kept walking until she reached an open door with the placard ELLEN AL-BERTI, ASSOCIATE DIRECTOR affixed to the wall.

"Goddammit!"

Fina peeked around the door frame. Ellen Alberti leapt up from behind her desk and dropped a stack of files onto the floor. Fina could see a disposable coffee cup on its side and dark liquid spreading across the surface of the cluttered desk.

"Dammit." Ellen mopped at the coffee with a small napkin.

"Here. Let me help." Fina stepped into the room and pulled a package of baby wipes from her bag. Baby wipes were a panacea.

Ellen looked at her and took the proffered wipes. She mopped up the liquid and tossed the used wipes in the trash can.

"I knew that was going to happen," Ellen said. "Do you ever do that, where you tell yourself, 'Don't put your coffee there, you'll spill it,' but you do it anyway?" She pulled a small package of tissues from her desk drawer and blotted the wet files.

As Ellen, who looked to be in her early forties, finished the cleanup, Fina took in her surroundings. The office was small, but a large window brightened the room. The bookshelves were stuffed with books and thick journals, and piles of folders covered every inch of surface space. Fina hoped that the Heritage labs were tidier than Ellen's office.

"I know what you're doing," Ellen said, and grinned. "You're judging a book by its cover, but you shouldn't. I subscribe to the 'messy office, brilliant mind' school of thought."

Ellen had medium blond hair that grazed her shoulders and a smattering of freckles across the bridge of her nose. Her makeup was tastefully applied. She wore a navy blue pantsuit, its tailoring a touch conservative, but that was offset by her funky dangly earrings. Her teeth were straight and white, and there were small wrinkles at the corners of her eyes and mouth. It looked like she smiled a lot.

She gestured toward the chair in front of her desk, inviting Fina to sit down.

Fina held out her hand. "Fina Ludlow. I'm a private investigator. I have a few questions." She settled into the offered seat.

Ellen sat down and picked up her coffee cup, forgetting she'd just spilled its contents. "I thought you were a prospective mother." Frowning, she put the empty cup back down.

"Well, aren't we all?"

She raised an eyebrow. "A prospective insemination candidate."

Fina tipped her head side to side. "I'm still on the fence about that one."

Ellen glanced at her phone.

"Wait," Fina said. "Before you call security, here's my ID."

Ellen studied it. "It concerns me that you got back here under false pretenses."

"I'm sorry about that, but it should concern you. Your security is seriously wanting."

Ellen smiled ruefully. "I've been saying that for months," she muttered under her breath. She tapped a manicured nail on her blotter. "So, what can I do for you, Ms. Ludlow? I'm a busy woman."

"You'll want to hear what I have to say."

"What is it you want to say?"

"I'm working on a case for an attorney, Carl Ludlow. He's my father, actually."

"I know who your father is, and I know your brother Scotty."

"Oh."

"We worked together on a fund-raiser for the MetroWest Children's Foundation."

"Great. Well, one of your clients is exploring the option of suing to learn the identity of her donor."

It was a tiny motion, but Ellen's shoulders seemed to rise ever so slightly.

Then she smiled. "Like pregnancy and childbirth aren't stressful enough. Throw in assisted reproduction and life really gets turned upside down."

"Meaning?"

"Meaning that sometimes our clients go through stages of uncertainty or ambivalence about the process. It would be odd if they didn't, but that's what it usually is—a stage."

"So the possibility of a lawsuit doesn't concern you?"

Ellen leaned forward and clasped her hands together. "What concerns me is the possibility that one of our clients is unhappy. We want all of our moms and dads to be completely satisfied with the Heritage experience."

Fina shook her head slowly. "I don't think she's satisfied."

"If you could tell me who it is, I could speak with her directly."

Fina smiled. "I can't do that. I'm covered by the attorney-client privilege that my father has with the client. But it doesn't sound like you're particularly worried anyway. It's all good." Fina stood to leave.

"I assume your father realizes that whoever the client is, she signed a confidentiality agreement, which is legally binding," Ellen pointed out. "You're welcome to talk with our attorneys, but they'll tell you the same thing."

"Every client signs a standard confidentiality agreement?"

"Of course. Potential parents either choose a donor who wants to remain anonymous or a donor who is willing to be in contact once the child reaches eighteen. Most clients think anonymity is a reasonable trade-off for a baby."

"But people must change their minds over time."

Ellen shrugged. "It's been known to happen, but that's why there's a legal document—to protect everyone involved."

"What about the sibling registries?"

"What about them?"

"Doesn't it put the bank in a vulnerable position if siblings connect with one another and compare notes?"

"Our mission is creating families. I think it's fine if half-siblings want to connect with one another, and it really doesn't have anything to do with the cryobank."

"Except it's a bigger data pool, and maybe kids have a better shot at identifying their donors that way." Fina knew of some cases where the donor babies had done their own sleuthing and discovered not only their half-siblings but their donors as well.

"A resourceful child might be able to ferret out his donor's identity whether or not there are half-siblings."

"Digging up that information doesn't worry you? In terms of the reproductive industry?"

"Not in the least. Some people say we're doing God's work here. What could be wrong with that?"

"Some people? Not you?"

Ellen smiled. "Whatever you believe in, I'm sure the powers that be would approve of our work creating happy families, and we can't ban the Internet, right?"

"Maybe anonymous donation will soon be a thing of the past," Fina ventured.

"Maybe." Ellen reached into a drawer and pulled out a card, which she handed to Fina. "Our attorneys. Feel free to call them. It's why we pay them such exorbitant fees."

Fina put the card in her bag. "Thank you for your time."

"Don't mention it. If you ever decide to get off that fence and have a baby, let me know."

"Just as soon as you create one that self-diapers," Fina said, and left the office.

"You're supposed to take me shopping for jeans," Haley said when Fina answered her phone.

"Okay."

"Like, now—unless you're too busy, say, shooting someone." Fina had shot a man a couple of months before in the course of Melanie's murder investigation. It was a fact that Haley revisited too often for Fina's taste.

"I only shoot people if they're trying to kill me, remember? And I didn't kill him. And you shouldn't be thinking about that."

"Whatever. Can you pick me up?"

"Yes. I'll be there in twenty minutes."

Fina put a quick call in to Marnie Frasier and asked for cell numbers for Jess and Tyler. She left a message for Jess and made a plan to stop by Tyler's workplace later.

"How's your nose?" Haley asked after climbing into the car.

"It's fine. I told you not to worry about it. I'm a tough old broad."

"Uh-huh."

"The good news is that Cristian has offered to teach us some real boxing moves." Haley looked out the window. Fina glanced at her. "I thought that idea would appeal to you."

"I like him, but I don't know if I want to spend a lot of time with a cop. After everything, it just seems kind of weird."

Fina nodded. "I get that, but he'd be there as a friend, not as a cop."

Haley shrugged. "Maybe."

"Think about it. You could bring a couple of friends. That might lighten the mood."

The Good Jeans boutique in Newton was small but crammed with denim and huge photos of beautiful people and their sculpted bodies. Fina and Haley had barely stepped over the threshold before a tall, impossibly skinny salesgirl confronted them.

"I help you?" she asked, a strong Russian accent making her offer of service more like a threat.

"She needs jeans," Fina said to "Vera," and found a comfortable seat by a three-way mirror. Vera interrogated Haley about her size and style preferences and amassed a stack of options. She carried them into a dressing room and directed Haley to start changing. While Fina scrolled through her messages, Vera tidied shelves nearby that already looked perfectly ordered.

Even after Fina had typed a few e-mail responses, Haley still hadn't emerged. "Hale? What are you doing in there? Do you need help?"

"One sec," she called.

"She need help?" Vera asked, straightening her spine.

"No, she's fine," Fina said.

A moment later Haley emerged, encased in a tight pair of skinny jeans, which she studied in the three-way mirror.

"What do you think?" Haley asked.

"What happens when you have to go potty? Call the fire department for the Jaws of Life?"

Haley rolled her eyes. "You're hilarious. I like 'em." She turned this way and that. Her long shiny blond hair blanketed her shoulders.

"Those good fit," Vera commented.

Fina ignored her. "They do look good, but did it take all that time to get them on?"

Haley bit the inside of her cheek. "It took some effort."

"I don't want other areas in your life to suffer because it takes you an hour to get your jeans on every day. When will you get your homework done?"

"You really do crack yourself up. Hold on. There's more." She disappeared behind the curtain.

Fina tapped her fingers on the arm of the chair. "Are these for school?" she called to Haley.

"Yes."

Haley reappeared in a pair that barely qualified as low-rise. The zipper only required half a dozen teeth.

"Those are obscene," Fina commented. "They barely cover your business." Fina looked at Vera. "Really? There's nothing that's a little more family-friendly? Not to start a family—to be around one?"

"You don't want her look like old lady."

"No, but I don't want her to look . . . inappropriate."

Haley looked down at her feet.

"I don't want people to only notice her physical attributes," Fina clarified. "And we need to keep Aunt Patty happy," she said to her niece.

"Fine," Haley said. "I'll try some others."

Forty-five minutes and ten pairs later, they settled on one acceptable skinny pair and one boot-cut pair. Fina handed over her credit card and nearly swooned at the $450 total. "Jeans used to cost about fifty bucks a pair."

"And people used to ride in stagecoaches," Haley said, reaching for the bag. "Do we really want to go back to the good old days?"

A couple of doors down, they went into an ice-cream shop and ordered frappes. Haley was slurping on her black-and-white when Fina spoke.

"You know, if you ever want to talk about . . . stuff . . . I'm happy to listen."

Haley shrugged. "I know."

"I don't want you to feel that any topics are off-limits, and I don't want to pretend that things that happened didn't. I know that's Pap and Gammy's favorite approach." Fina stirred her coffee frappe with her straw. "Talking, not talking, whatever approach your therapist thinks is healthiest, that's the approach we should take."

"Oh my God. Just have your frappe, Aunt Fina." They sipped in silence. "Aren't you going to ask me about my dad?" Haley looked at her pointedly.

"I hadn't planned to, but we can talk about him if you want." Why, oh why, had she said nothing was off-limits?

"Everyone else wants to know when I'm going to see him."

Fina took a long draw of her frappe and was instantly rewarded with a cold headache. She squeezed her eyes shut until it passed. "That's up to you. I would understand if you didn't want to see him for a while."

"Did you watch last night's episode of *Relationship Rematch*?" Haley asked after a moment. Fina had never been a big fan of reality TV, but in the past few months, she'd found the horrendous programming provided a common point of interest with her niece. And it turned out that watching other people's misery was surprisingly healing.

Fina parked in a lot a few blocks from Harvard Square and ducked into a coffee shop. She sat in a small booth, sipping a diet soda and reviewing a recent newsletter from Renata's single mothers' organization. These women were active and organized, but that didn't really surprise Fina; you had to be to take on single motherhood. She could see the wisdom of a supportive, like-minded community, but Fina wasn't much of a joiner. None of the Ludlows were. Sure, they were members of the Whittaker Club and some professional organizations, but Ludlows were their own little cadre with secret codes and handshakes. Membership in the family generally precluded membership in other groups.

She left some money on the table and walked to Astral, one of the hot new restaurants in the Boston area. Tyler Frasier was enrolled in a culinary arts college downtown and was spending the summer as a prep cook at the restaurant. He'd agreed to meet Fina before the dinner crunch.

Fina tapped on the glass door, and a bartender motioned that they were closed. After a small game of charades, he admitted her to the space, which featured lots of bamboo and enormous hanging lanterns. The menu was a fusion of French, Vietnamese, and various cuisines from the Pacific Rim. The bartender directed her to a set of swinging doors that led to the kitchen.

The kitchen was spotless, with shiny stainless-steel prep areas and enormous multi-burner stoves. Fina walked around a corner and found about ten Hispanic men in chef's whites seated around a table. They were eating family-style from large platters. There were bowls of tortilla chips and dishes of what looked like salsa in front of them. When she asked for Tyler, one of the men directed her to a counter at the other end of the room.

"Tyler." He looked up when she said his name. He was wearing a chef's coat and those baggy black-and-white-checked pants that you never saw outside a professional kitchen. A blue bandanna was tied around his forehead, and his feet were encased in black Crocs.

"Hey, Ms. Ludlow," he said, pausing his chopping.

"Please, call me Fina."

"Sure." Tyler looked around and called out to the men in Spanish.

A conversation ensued with Tyler holding up his hands and knife. Fina stood there awkwardly, but after a moment, an older man with a bright smile carried a stool over to Tyler's prep area and put it down next to Fina.

"*Gracias,*" she said to the man. "I could have gotten that myself."

"They just like giving me a hard time," Tyler said. "I would have gotten it, but . . ." He held up his hands once more.

"Got it."

"So, you wanted to ask me some questions?" Tyler grabbed a carrot from a heaping stack and began to julienne it. His knife moved in a flurry, and he was on to the next carrot before Fina could answer.

"You sure this is a good idea, talking to me while you're doing that? I don't want you to cut yourself."

"No worries. I could do this with my eyes closed."

Fina watched him produce a mini blizzard of carrot matchsticks. "Okay. Did your mom tell you about Renata Sanchez's lawsuit?"

"Yes, but I already knew something was up. Rosie told me a few weeks ago."

"She told you her mom was going to sue?"

"She told me that Renata had some plan up her sleeve."

"That makes her sound kind of sneaky."

"No, just that when other people might quit, Renata finds another way." Tyler was accumulating a sizable mound of carrots. The orange color popped against the stainless steel and white of the kitchen.

"So you know that Rosie is opposed."

"Yeah. We've kind of agreed to disagree on that one."

Fina decided to change tacks. It was often a fruitful interviewing strategy. "How long have you known the Sanchez family?"

Tyler paused for a moment, his knife hovering over the cutting board. "I don't really remember not knowing them, but I didn't know Rosie was our half-sister until about four years ago."

"You found out when you were fifteen?"

"Yup. I went on one of those donor registry sites and got a match right away. It's cool that she's our sister. Weird, but cool."

"So how does your sister feel about Rosie?"

"Jess likes Rosie, but she doesn't think of her as our sister." A roar of laughter erupted from the other end of the room. Fina and Tyler both looked in that direction.

"I left a message for Jess."

"Don't hold your breath waiting for a callback. She wants no part of SMC drama."

Fina nodded. "How did your mom feel when you uncovered the connection with Rosie?"

"Oh, she was pissed at first—not about Rosie, but that I'd been digging around." Tyler grinned. "I'm not known for my carefully thought-out decisions."

"Most people your age aren't."

"I stress my mom out on a regular basis. Nothing bad came from that particular decision, though. Rosie's cool. I like having a second sister. Do you have any sisters?"

Fina paused for a moment. "I kind of had one, but not really."

Tyler looked perplexed.

"I had an older sister who died before I was born. She was a toddler when she died." Fina had grown up acutely aware that she, Josefina, was a poor substitute for her sister, Josephine. It didn't take a shrink to see that much of the Ludlow dysfunction could be attributed to this tragedy in their family history.

"Sorry. Didn't mean to bring up a sore subject."

Fina adjusted her butt on the stool. "But what about the lawsuit? Did Renata ask *you* how you felt about it?"

Tyler took his container of julienned carrots and opened a large refrigerator behind him. He slid it onto a shelf and pulled out another tray stacked with peeled carrots. He put it down on the table with a bang and reached for one.

"She didn't ask Rosie; you think she asked me and Jess?"

"Well, that's obnoxious."

Tyler laughed. "Yeah, it kind of is."

"Do you want to find out the identity of your donor?"

At the other end of the room, the men were pushing back their chairs and standing up from the table.

Tyler shrugged. "It could be cool."

"What if he isn't interested in being a dad?"

Tyler pushed down on the knife and a carrot crunched under its blade. "I'm sure it will work out. Rosie worries about stuff too much. Just like my mom."

"I know your mom doesn't want you to give me a DNA sample," Fina said. "We talked about it this morning."

"She told me, but I'm an adult. I can do what I want."

"Indeed you can." Fina studied him. "So does that mean you're willing?"

"What are you going to do with it?"

"There's a lab in the city I'll send it to that is connected to a DNA database. They'll let me know if there's any kind of a match. The odds aren't high that your dad will show up, but it's not unheard of for a relative to match. It would give us something to go on."

"But then will they destroy my sample? It's not like I'm planning on murdering anyone . . ." He smiled and the dimples emerged on his cheeks.

"They'll destroy the sample, but not the test results. You have to agree to be a part of their database, which they can run other samples against in the future."

He twisted his mouth into a small frown. "I don't really like the idea that my info is on file someplace."

"I totally get that. It couldn't be accessed by law enforcement, though, not without a subpoena, but another half-sibling may use the service someday and get a match with you. They'd have your name. If you aren't comfortable with that idea, then don't do it."

Tyler put down his knife and walked around the table to Fina. "Renata is like a runaway train: better to hop on than stand in her way. And I like Rosie; might be cool to have another sister or brother."

Fina reached into her bag and pulled out the test kit. She ripped open the package, Tyler opened his mouth, and Fina swiped the inside of his cheek. Nearby, one of the other cooks eyed them suspiciously.

"I'll tell them that you're my baby mama," Tyler said, grinning devilishly. "That should get tongues wagging."

"I'm old enough to be *your* mama, but thanks for the compliment." Fina put the swab into a plastic test tube that came with the kit and dropped it into her bag. "I'll let you know if I get a match."

Tyler gave her a loose salute, and Fina threaded her way back through the kitchen.

4

Walter took his time filling his mug from the cappuccino maker in the kitchen. He had splurged on the machine, but good coffee was a necessity in life as far as he was concerned. Most of the staff seemed to appreciate his generosity. He carried the froth-topped mug into his office, where Ellen Alberti was sitting in front of his desk, engrossed in a conversation on her cell phone. He put down his coffee and sank into his large leather swivel chair. He tapped his wristwatch and looked at Ellen.

"I've got to go," Ellen said, "but that sounds terrific. Let's get a meeting on the books." She listened and then laughed. When she tipped her head back, a small gold charm fell into the hollow of her neck. Ellen was very attractive.

"That was Kevin Landry," she said after hanging up. "He's running the NRM conference this year." As a board member, Walter always attended the National Reproductive Medicine conference. It was an opportunity for him to hobnob with the other movers and shakers in the specialty and stay informed about the latest medical advances.

"Hmm," Walter responded.

"He has an idea for a panel. I think it's a great opportunity." Walter sipped his coffee as he listened.

"I'd be happy to participate. Just check my schedule with Jenny."

"Actually, Walter, he's asked me to participate."

"Really?" Walter's tone implied his doubt.

"Really." Ellen smiled at him. He could never tell if she was being genuine with her bright smiles. Sometimes they struck him as mocking punctuation she added to the ends of her statements.

"So did Margery fill you in on the brochure?" he asked.

"She did."

"Good." Walter had led a meeting the day before to discuss Ellen's newest project.

"I was concerned about something, though," she said, and looked at him.

Walter knew what she was going to say: that she was upset he had held the meeting without her.

"I don't mean to be indelicate, but I was concerned when you convened the meeting yesterday. Since you're well aware of my schedule, I wondered if you got mixed up?" She tilted her head. "Perhaps had a lapse?"

Walter stared at her. "A lapse?"

"Yes." She winced. "You wouldn't have purposely excluded me from my own meeting, so I wondered if you were feeling all right."

"I'm just fine, Ellen, but I appreciate your concern. Since Margery filled you in, let's move on to other business."

"Of course." She adjusted in her seat. "A private investigator stopped by earlier today. She's representing a Heritage client who is threatening to sue to reveal the identity of her donor."

Walter sipped his cappuccino. "That's absurd. No court will even hear a case like that, let alone rule on it."

"I agree, but it could stir up some unwanted attention, and the climate is changing. I'm sure there are other parents who share her frustration with anonymous donation."

Walter puffed out his chest. "They all signed the papers. They knew what they were getting into. Seems ungrateful to me."

"I don't think we want to broadcast that sentiment."

"I wasn't suggesting that we should. What did this PI want from you?"

"Nothing. I think it was just a shot across our bow, but I thought you should know."

"Good luck to her. It will rack up legal fees on our end, but I suppose that can't be avoided."

Ellen shrugged. "The cost of doing business, but I don't think we've seen the last of her."

"No?"

"You know Carl Ludlow, right? It's his daughter. They're known for being bulldogs."

"Well, there's nothing for them here," Walter said brusquely.

"I know, Walter, I'm just saying that I think she'll be back."

"We have better things to do than fend off frivolous lawsuits and overzealous investigators." Walter drained his coffee. "Let's discuss the new FDA recommendations, shall we?"

Ellen nodded her assent and consulted the notepad on her lap.

He was quite sure that he was irritating Ellen, and that was just fine.

Fina stopped at an office building in the Longwood Medical Area and submitted Tyler's swab to a private lab that promised results within forty-eight hours. The general public assumed that DNA tests took an extraordinarily long time, but that wasn't true. The testing itself was expeditious, but expensive. Police departments and district attorneys didn't have the money to run the tests, which explained the delays and backlogs. That was one of the benefits of working in the private sector: Fina didn't have to work hard to stretch her dollar.

She continued on to a modest ranch house in Newton, a home that would be considered comfortably sized in other towns, but was downright small by Newton standards. A collection of thirteen villages, Newton was a much coveted suburb of the city that offered strong public schools, parks and lakes, and prime marathon viewing. Houses went for millions of dollars, but there were also starter homes in the range of half a million. The street Fina turned onto was a mix of retirees who'd bought their homes decades ago and young families bringing in six-figure salaries. The small front yard of 56 Wellspring Street was tidy, and a welcome plaque hung next to the front door. Fina knocked on the screen door frame before letting herself in.

"Hello?" she called out.

"In the kitchen," a voice responded.

Peg Gillis was standing at the sink, looking out the window into the backyard. Her hands were covered in suds. Fina stood next to her and followed Peg's gaze. The freshly cut lawn sloped down to dense woods and was bordered on either side with rhododendrons.

"What the hell is that thing?" Fina asked. A large bird was poking at the grass with its beak.

"It's a wild turkey."

"It's huge. Is it friendly?"

"I haven't invited it in, but I'm sure Frank is doing his research."

"Is that how he's keeping busy? Researching the local wildlife?"

Frank was a semiretired PI who had taught Fina everything she knew. Actually, everything she knew that was legal. He couldn't be held responsible for her less ethical activities.

Peg rinsed her hands and dried them on a dish towel. "Are you joining us for dinner?" Five forty-five was the dinner hour at the Gillises' house. This schedule made Fina feel like she'd stepped into a wormhole straight to Miami and its early bird specials, but she also appreciated the consistency. Grown-ups are really toddlers at heart; they feel safer with routines.

"I'll sit with you, but I'm not going to eat if that's okay."

"That's fine. Frank!" Peg called toward the other end of the small house. "Dinner!" She turned to Fina. "Could you set the table, hon?"

Fina gathered plates and utensils and set two places at the round table nestled in the corner of the kitchen. Frank walked in a few minutes later, and the three sat. Fina watched them dig in to a traditional boiled dinner, otherwise known as corned beef and cabbage.

"Bet you're sorry you turned this down," Frank said, stabbing a pale, mushy potato with his fork.

"No offense to Peg, but no. I'm not a fan." Fina took a sip of a diet soda she'd found in the refrigerator.

"How are things at Ludlow and Associates?" Frank asked between mouthfuls.

"Never the same without you." Fina shook her head. Frank had left the firm a few years before, and Fina sorely missed his presence. "I'm still in the doghouse."

"Sweetie, you've been in the doghouse since the moment I met you," he said kindly.

"My recent sins may even be worse than flunking out of law school."

"I don't see how you could have swept your brother's behavior under the carpet," Peg commented. "You wouldn't have been able to live with yourself."

Fina rotated her drink on the tabletop. "I know, but now Carl can't seem to live with me."

Peg patted her hand. "Hang in there."

"I'm trying."

"So what are you working on?" Frank asked.

"Uncovering the identity of a sperm donor. A single mother by choice used a sperm bank seventeen years ago and now she wants to find the daddy. I've just started, and it feels more like a soap opera than a mystery."

"An anonymous donation?" Peg asked.

"Supposed to be. The mother has gotten it into her head that her child has a right to know the identity of her father, regardless of the legalities."

"You don't agree?" Frank asked.

"The mom signed a contract when she bought the sperm. She knew what she was getting into. I understand that times change, but then the law should be changed moving forward, not retroactively."

"Sounds like it could get sticky." Frank put a forkful of cabbage into his mouth. It looked like bleached seaweed.

"Especially when you factor in the mom. Do you remember the Ramirez case?"

"Remind me," Frank said.

"It was the slip and fall in public housing a few years ago. One of the witnesses was the head of the Urban Housing Collaborative. That's the mom: Renata Sanchez."

"It rings a bell."

"She's in the news a lot," Peg commented, and cut a piece of corned beef. "She does a lot for the lower-income community."

"I know," Fina said, "and she has my respect and admiration for her work. It's the other stuff I'm not sure about."

"What does the child say?" Peg asked.

"That's the part I'm not thrilled about. Her daughter has no interest in the case. Renata is convinced it's in Rosie's best interest, but Rosie doesn't want to find out her father's identity, at least not like this."

"The daughter doesn't get a say?" Frank asked.

"Her mother isn't too concerned with her opinion."

"So why are you involved?"

"Carl wants to attack from two fronts. He wants me to investigate less orthodox channels while he tries to push the case law. I'm not opposed to figuring out the donor's identity. Tech-savvy kids are already doing that on their own. It's the public crusade part I don't like."

"Having kids used to be so much easier." Frank took a sip of coffee. He was one of the few people Fina knew who drank coffee as an actual mealtime accompaniment, not just a pick-me-up or dessert in disguise. "Either you could or you couldn't."

"It was simpler, but I'm not sure it was easier," said Peg. "It wasn't easy if you wanted them but couldn't have them."

"Agreed, but now it's so complicated." Frank smiled at his wife. "We had it easy. The old-fashioned way."

"Oh, you know, I don't need to hear this," Fina said, sipping her soda.

"We're not *your* parents," Peg said.

"But you're old enough to be my parents." She gave them both a stern look. "The same gross-out rules apply."

Frank chuckled. "What's your next move?"

"I just talked to another single mother. Her kids share the same donor."

"Does she want to be involved?" Peg asked.

"No, but one of her kids is interested."

"Sounds like a lot of reluctant witnesses to me," Frank commented, sitting back in his seat. "You've got your work cut out for you."

"I know it. Enough about me. What are you two crazy kids up to these days?" Frank updated Fina on the recent influx of wild turkeys due to a construction project down the street. Fina offered to shoot one to shorten their Thanksgiving to-do list, but there were no takers. Conversation shifted to Peg's work as a school nurse, a career that often rivaled Fina's in terms of blood and gore. Peg was equal parts serene, loving, and tough, which made her perfect for her job.

Fina helped do the dishes and then walked to the living room with Frank, where he settled into his easy chair for some TV and his nightly dish of vanilla ice cream.

"I'll pull out my notes on the Ramirez case. Maybe there's something in there that will be useful, some background info on Renata," Frank offered, digging into his dessert.

"Thanks. I appreciate it."

"Keep in touch," he said as a farewell and a directive. "And let me know if you need help." Frank knew he'd done a good job training Fina, but he also knew that she flirted with danger on a regular basis.

"Always," Fina replied, smiling.

.   .   .

The Sanchez case was at a standstill until Fina got the DNA results, so she spent the next morning in a deposition and the remainder of the day working a car accident case. She photographed the intersection in question and conferred with an accident reconstructionist who did the math required in such cases. Accident investigations weren't exciting, but there was something satisfying about collecting all the data and reaching a solid conclusion. Medical malpractice suits were notoriously gray, but physics don't lie. There are rules that govern how objects move and interact with one another that leave little room for interpretation.

Back home later, Fina gathered her notes, computer, phone, and a bag of miniature Reese's peanut butter cups and settled on the couch. Her UMass contact had procured a list of graduates from the class of 1972, and she had an incomplete list from the high schools in Joliet. She typed her company credit card number into a site that promised a list of all males born in Joliet, Illinois, in 1951. Fina would end up with lists, lots of lists, but if there were any overlaps, she might be able to identify the donor.

She opened her door the next morning to Stanley, the doorman, who handed over a couriered package from the lab that had processed Tyler Frasier's DNA sample. Fina ripped open the package and scanned the results.

Bingo.

There were two men in the lab database with Y chromosomes closely matching Tyler's. According to the document, there was a 60 percent chance that Tyler and the two men had a common male relative in their family tree. The most promising piece of information was the names of the two men. The older of the two was Arthur Riordan of Davenport,

Iowa. The second was Richard Reardon of Springfield, Illinois. Fina pulled up an online map and found that in the scheme of things, Davenport, Springfield, and Joliet—the donor's birthplace—were within spitting distance of one another. Fina knew from past investigations that it wasn't unusual for the spelling of surnames to morph over moves and generations.

Fina went to the kitchen to give her brain a moment to process the information and also to find something to satisfy the grumbling in her stomach. It was ten in the morning, which seemed like a perfect time for cold pizza. She grabbed a diet soda and bit into a piece of Hawaiian, the sweet pineapple and salty ham mingling in her mouth. Back at her computer, she put aside the results from the lab and pulled up the lists from her computer.

Fina examined the first list, male births in Joliet, Illinois, in 1951, and felt her muscles begin to tense. The second list of high school graduates in Joliet in 1969 led to a pronounced ache in her lower back. By the time she finished searching the UMass graduates for 1972, Fina was fighting a full-on muscle spasm.

She had a name that matched all the criteria.

Oh, fuck.

"We've got a major issue," Fina said, striding into Carl's office a couple of hours later.

"Jesus, you really have no manners," Carl said, and looked up from his computer. A half-filled plate sat next to his keyboard.

"That's your takeaway from that statement? My lack of manners?"

"What is it, Fina?" He sat back in his chair. He was wearing a light gray suit, perfectly tailored to his frame, with a faintly striped shirt and a tie of blues and grays. Carl's clothes made a statement—that he was wealthy and had good taste—but he didn't take many risks on the sartorial front. Fina didn't think he was confident enough to mix patterns and colors, and if Carl wasn't good at something, he didn't like doing it.

Fina shut the door. She sat down in the chair in front of her father's desk. "I've identified the donor that Renata Sanchez used resulting in her daughter Rosie."

"Why is that an issue?" Carl cut a piece from the fillet of whitefish on his plate and put it in his mouth. Ludlow and Associates shared a corporate kitchen with a few companies on neighboring floors. For most of the employees, it offered tasty upscale cafeteria food, but Carl and the other executives often enjoyed individually prepared meals. Today, her father seemed to be eating halibut or cod and a mixed green salad.

"It's Hank Reardon."

Fina watched his chewing slow and then stop, as if a motor had gradually lost its power. Carl swallowed a sip of mineral water.

"What?" he asked.

"You heard me. Hank Reardon."

Carl put down his fork and wiped his fingers on a napkin.

"Hank Reardon?"

"Hank Reardon."

Carl rubbed his eyes. "Fuck."

"My thoughts exactly."

Hank Reardon was one of the most high-profile businessmen on the Eastern Seaboard, perhaps even in the whole United States. He'd made his fortune in high-tech while young, and everything he touched seemed to turn to gold. The father of a grown son, his first marriage had lasted twenty-four years, and his second was in its infancy—the marriage, although the bride wasn't much beyond that. Hank and the new Mrs. Reardon had recently had a baby girl. The possibility that Hank Reardon was the father of multiple cryokids promised a scandal of epic proportions. He had status in the community and the wealth to match it.

"You're sure?"

"I'm sure enough. I can't be one hundred percent sure until we get his DNA, but I wanted to update you in the meantime."

"Hank Reardon's not going to give you his DNA," Carl said.

"He doesn't have to."

Carl moved some lettuce around with his fork. He contemplated a cherry tomato, but lost interest. "I don't want to hear about it if your plan is illegal."

"It's not. But I do want you to know that you're now a proud supporter of the Greater Boston Fund for Children."

"What?" Carl put down his fork. "What are you talking about, Josefina?"

"You've made a generous donation, and Milloy and I will be attending their annual gala on Saturday night. You paid enough so that we'll be seated close to the Reardons."

"Tell me you're not going to swab him between courses."

"Hardly. I'm just going to emancipate a fork or a glass from his place setting once dinner's over."

"Sounds iffy."

"Not legally. There's no expectation of privacy for your cutlery at a public gathering, is there?"

"No, of course not. It just sounds hard to pull off."

Fina shook her head. "It's totally doable. I've done it before."

"Hmm. The skills you have." Carl pushed his unfinished meal away. "Put a twenty-four-hour rush on the DNA and tell me as soon as you get the results."

"Will do." Fina stood. "Once we confirm this, I think we should send Renata on her way."

"You've made your feelings abundantly clear."

"And yet it doesn't seem to make any difference. I don't think Hank's identity will remain a secret under any circumstances, but this case is leaving a bad taste in my mouth."

"As soon as you confirm the DNA, you'll be done. And then you can move on to cases that are more closely aligned with your values," he said sarcastically.

"Right. Thanks, Dad."

Carl focused on his computer screen. "I don't make enough money to deal with all this crap."

"Says the man who makes millions and doesn't lose a wink of sleep," Fina said, and left before her father could respond.

5

Fina was beginning to feel like Jerry Springer, given her recent focus on paternity matters. After the Fund for Children's dinner, she'd gotten the results back from the lab: Hank Reardon was the baby daddy. Identifying the donor was no longer theoretical.

A summit was arranged for Monday morning, which explained the motley crew gathering in the twenty-eighth-floor boardroom of Beekerton, Lindsley, Hobbes, and Lefowitz. Fina and Carl were representing Renata Sanchez and Marnie Frasier, and a lawyer named Jules Lindsley would protect Hank Reardon's interests.

Like the one at Ludlow and Associates, this boardroom was used when clients needed to be convinced that their attorneys were as successful as they were, if not more so. The room was oversized, with a polished cherry table that could comfortably seat twenty. There were sweeping views of Boston Harbor from two sides of the space. Another wall was dominated by a cabinet hiding AV equipment, and the fourth had a built-in buffet over which hung an ugly yet undoubtedly expensive painting. The whir of the air-conditioning was the only sound, and its constancy made it seem like the room was hermetically sealed.

Fina, Renata, and Marnie sat at the table while Carl paced near the windows.

A woman in her fifties wheeled in a cart and unloaded coffee, tea, juice, bottled water, and a platter of sliced fresh fruit and various pastries. Renata rolled her eyes at the spread arrayed on the table.

"They'll be right with you," the woman murmured before leaving.

A few moments later, Fina heard laughter outside the door, and two men and a younger woman came into the room. The elder man shut the door behind them, and they made the not-insignificant trip down to the end of the table where Fina and the single mothers were sitting. Carl remained standing.

"Carl, you look well," Jules Lindsley said, shaking Carl's hand. Jules was one of the old lions of the Boston legal community. Respected and well liked, he always seemed to be on the right side of issues. He was extremely successful, and his wife and children were shining examples of good, clean fun. He was everything Carl Ludlow would never be.

"Jules. Good to see you. This is my daughter, Josefina. I think you've met before."

"Please call me Fina," she amended, and shook Jules's hand. "We met a while back."

Jules was handsome, with white hair and glasses. His suit was elegant, but not flashy. Fina imagined that he went home at the end of the day and changed into khakis, a button-down shirt, a sweater-vest, and boat shoes.

"And this is my client, Hank Reardon, and his wife, Danielle." Handshakes were exchanged, drinks were offered, and they took their seats at the table. Fina studied Hank while the men prattled on about boats. He looked younger than his sixty-one years, or maybe Fina was looking at him through the forgiving lens afforded to aging men; they grew more distinguished, but women just grew old. Hank had sandy blond hair, straight white teeth, and a broad smile. His suit was expensive and, on the fashion spectrum, somewhere between Carl's and Jules's. He looked fashionable, but age appropriate.

Although the Ludlows were rich—extremely rich—they were paupers compared to Hank Reardon. Hank had made his first million straight out of college, but when he founded a company that developed one of the first e-commerce platforms, his income soared into the stratosphere. Fina wondered how her father felt being the poorest man in the room.

"Thank you, everyone, for fitting this into your no doubt busy schedules," Jules began. "Carl and I thought it was prudent to sit down and iron some things out."

Renata exhaled loudly.

"Yes, Ms. Sanchez?" Jules asked.

"I don't think there's anything to iron out."

"Well, don't be hasty. I think we have some common interests."

Fina watched Danielle Reardon across the table, her arm looped through her husband's. She was thirty-five years old, blond, and shooting daggers at Renata. She was wearing skinny pants with a subtle animal print in a moss green color, paired with a snug V-neck jersey in a baroque pattern. The whole ensemble was topped by a cutaway leather jacket of olive green with gold hardware. Had it been from a mall store, the outfit would have been tacky, but the impeccable tailoring and luxe fabrics elevated the outfit to a work of art. By Fina's rough estimate, Danielle was wearing close to five thousand dollars' worth of designer duds, and wearing them perfectly. She was tall and thin, and the clothing skimmed over her body. The black pebbled leather handbag on the table in front of her boasted a logo plaque for Dolce & Gabbana. *Cha-ching.* The diamond on Danielle's engagement ring was the size of a gumball, and Fina noticed Marnie gaping at it. Unlike her husband, who seemed calm, Danielle looked nervous and fidgeted in her seat.

"Ms. Sanchez, everyone wants what's best for the children involved. Your daughter, the Frasier children, as well as Michael and Aubrey Reardon."

"Oh, do they count more than my child?"

Hank's lip curled slightly.

"Renata," Carl warned.

"No, I just want to know, does Rosie count less than the heirs to the throne?"

"You don't know anything about—" Danielle started to interject.

Jules held up a hand to stop her. "I know that everyone is very passionate about this issue, but we can't let our emotions get the best of us." He looked around the table. "Hank is prepared to make a very generous gift to all of his biological children." He opened a folder and passed out a small packet to each person. "Our hope is to keep this private matter private."

Fina watched and waited as Renata and Marnie scanned the paperwork.

"Five million dollars?" Renata asked. She glared at Hank. "In exchange for our silence?"

"*Your* children would receive five million each, Ms. Frasier," Jules noted.

Marnie straightened the agreement on the table. "I don't imagine that my children will suddenly develop an interest in publicity, but I'm not entirely comfortable with the idea of a gag order, especially in exchange for money."

"And I'm not comfortable with five million dollars," Carl added. "Hank, last time I checked you were worth over a billion."

"Don't believe everything you read, Carl," Hank said.

Fina eyed Danielle. She was chewing on the inside of her cheek, though in anger or anxiety, Fina couldn't tell.

"I won't agree to any gag order," Renata stated.

"What about the kids, Mr. Reardon?" Marnie asked. "Are you interested in having a relationship with them?"

Hank glanced at Danielle. "I can't imagine that would be a good idea."

"Why not?" Renata asked.

"I may be your children's biological father, but I didn't make the donation with any intention of raising them. I have my own children."

"These *are* your children!" Renata exclaimed.

"Renata." Carl glared at her.

Marnie nodded thoughtfully. "This is a lot to take in. I need to think about it."

"There's nothing to think about," Renata said, staring at Marnie.

"Renata, what is it exactly that you want?" Marnie asked.

"Good question," Danielle mumbled.

"I want Hank to join my lawsuit."

A host of audible reactions emerged around the table.

"Ms. Sanchez, I will strongly advise my client against that," Jules said.

"I'm not interested in suing Heritage Cryobank," said Hank, "and to be honest, this whole thing is starting to piss me off."

"Hank, I don't think—" his attorney started.

"Let me finish, Jules." Color was creeping up Hank's neck. "I made those donations when I was young and naïve, with the understanding that my identity would be secret. Not only has that agreement been violated, but I'm starting to feel as if I'm the victim of extortion. This isn't just about you, Ms. Sanchez."

"I never suggested it was."

"Well, you're acting like it is. I understand you are advocating on behalf of your child, but her rights don't negate my own."

"But you're an adult and a parent. I thought you might be able to put her needs before your own," Renata replied. "We have the opportunity to improve the lives of our children and every cryokid who yearns to know her father. Think of the lives we could change."

Hank's mouth was open, yet words were failing him. Fina and Carl exchanged a look, each urging the other to act.

"In terms of your identity being revealed, Mr. Reardon," Fina said, stepping into the fray, "nobody could have anticipated the role the Internet would play in regards to anonymity. This is a scenario that's going to happen across the country. You just have a higher profile than most donors."

"She's right," Carl said. "Every anonymous donor is at risk."

Hank looked at his watch and started to push back his chair. "My wife and I need to be somewhere." He pulled Danielle's chair out for her, then shook Carl's hand. "Ladies." Hank nodded in their direction. He rested his hand lightly on his wife's back, and she put her purse over her shoulder and shook out her hair. They were almost to the door when Marnie spoke. "Mr. Reardon?"

"Yes?"

"Thanks for my kids. They're amazing."

Hank looked uncomfortable. "You're welcome."

Jules escorted the Reardons out of the room.

"Renata, this has gone far enough," Marnie stated. "I'm not going to be a party to your crusade." She looked at Carl. "I don't think I'll require your representation, Mr. Ludlow. My interests are not the same as Renata's."

"One of my sons can represent you," Carl said, never happy to lose a client.

"So, this is okay with you?" Renata asked Marnie.

"What? That the donor doesn't want to be a father? You may have harbored that fantasy, but I never did. Because of your crusade, now my kids will have to come to grips with that. I'm not okay with any of this."

"You're still entitled to the money," Fina said.

"And I can get you more than five million a pop," Carl added.

Renata sniffed. "It's always about the money."

Marnie picked up her belongings and walked out.

Fina, Carl, and Renata were silent. Fina looked at the plate of pastries that remained untouched in the center of the table. A cinnamon roll would really hit the spot right about now.

"So." Renata straightened up in her seat.

"Renata," Carl said, pacing at the end of the table, "let's go back to my office and discuss this."

"I'd rather discuss it now."

Carl stopped and leaned his palms on the tabletop. "Fine. My job is to advise you. As I said during our first meeting, this lawsuit is a nonstarter. You need to walk away."

"You told me it was a long shot, but you were willing to pursue it. What's changed?"

"We have new information, including the identity of the donor, and my advice is based on that. You have an opportunity in front of you that is tremendous. Your daughter would never have to worry about money. College, veterinary school, med school—she could do all three with what Hank Reardon can provide."

"That's all well and good, but I told you from the beginning that this isn't just about Rosie's father. There are thousands of cryokids who are being denied the most basic information about their identities."

"Information that their mothers or parents agreed to not have access to," Fina pointed out.

"I know that, Fina. I'm saying that times have changed and we should make every effort to right those wrongs."

"What would be the ideal outcome from your perspective?" Fina and Carl didn't always agree, but they were good at reading each other's signals, and Fina could tell that Carl's patience was running out.

"The ideal outcome?"

"Yes, blue sky scenario. What would that be?"

Renata sat back in her seat. She looked at her hands for a moment. "Hank would publicly acknowledge that Rosie is his child, he would be a father to her, the identities of other anonymous donors would be revealed—"

"What about the rights of the donors?" Fina asked incredulously.

"You asked me for the blue sky scenario. That's what I'm giving you. Please don't interrupt."

Fina rubbed her temples. It was best to keep her hands busy when she felt like smacking someone, especially a client.

"And," Renata continued, "the cryobank would no longer offer anonymous donation."

Fina and Carl exchanged a glance. "But wouldn't getting rid of anonymous donation significantly lower the number of donors?" Fina asked. "Wouldn't that mean that fewer women, fewer families, could have babies?"

"Perhaps, but that's a small trade-off for ensuring that these children would know their fathers."

Fina squirmed in her seat. She was irritated by Renata's cavalier approach to changing the rules now that she had what she wanted. Maybe the policies should be changed, but not like this.

"Renata, I urge you to go home and think about this," Carl said. "You don't need to make any hasty decisions. And don't do anything rash," he warned her. "Don't discuss this with anyone."

Renata gathered her belongings and rose from her chair. "I thought you would understand why this is so important," she said to Carl, and hustled out of the room.

"Why would she think you would understand? Has she met you?" Fina asked.

"Very funny. I think we've got a problem on our hands."

"I think you're right. We've created a monster."

Carl stared into space. "And we aren't even making real money on this."

"I know. It's outrageous," Fina said.

Carl contemplated for a moment. "Maybe a big check will sway her. Sometimes, it isn't real until people see all the zeros."

"I hope you're right." Fina stood up. "But I doubt it."

"So far, it looks like Marissa is dating the most boring man on earth."

Fina and Cristian were sitting on a bench, watching his young son, Matteo, in a sandbox. Cristian had picked Matteo up from day care, and Fina agreed to give him the update in his neighborhood park in Cambridge. A soccer field with withered grass claimed most of the space, and two basketball courts bordered the play area where a group of teens and tweens were shooting hoops. Some of them had their shirts off, and Fina marveled at what could happen in just a couple of years. Flat, undefined torsos became muscled, and voices dropped a register.

"Are you checking out those guys?" Cristian asked.

"No, just trying to wrap my head around adolescence. You couldn't pay me to be that age again."

"This age isn't always so great, either," Cristian remarked.

"True, but there's something particularly cruel about having your body calling the shots. At least adult angst isn't completely evident to the rest of the world."

He stretched his legs out in front of him. "So give me some details about this guy."

"Well, as you know, his name is Brad Martin. Can't get any more vanilla than that. He's thirty-six years old, works for an insurance company, and owns a town house in Burlington."

"Does he have a record?" Cristian asked, poking a tiny straw through the foil top of a juice box. "Teo! Juice?"

Matteo abandoned his work moving all of the sand in the sandbox out of the sandbox and trundled over. He smiled at his father, his cheeks plump like a little chipmunk's.

"You are one good-looking kid, Matteo," Fina commented, and watched him wrap his lips around the tiny straw. He sucked up the juice, which dribbled on his chin.

"I hungry, Papa."

Cristian rooted around in a Thomas the Tank Engine backpack and pulled out a bag of Goldfish crackers. Matteo draped himself over Cristian's lap, his head toward the ground. He shoved a couple of crackers in his mouth and chewed.

Fina tilted her head and looked at him. "That can't be easy."

"Teo, sit up. You can't swallow hanging upside down."

The child pushed himself up and continued chewing. He crammed the fish in his mouth like a prisoner breaking a hunger strike.

A light breeze ruffled the leaves. After a minute, Matteo pushed the near-empty bag into his father's lap and returned to his work in the sandbox.

"Matteo, you're supposed to keep the sand in the sandbox, buddy," Cristian called out to him. "He's totally ignoring me."

"Don't worry. I don't think he's got the attention span to finish the job," Fina commented. "Any moment now a leaf will blow into his peripheral vision that will require his expertise."

"So, criminal record?" Cristian asked.

"Nope. He's got a lot of parking tickets, but so do lots of people."

"I hate the parking ticket thing," Cristian commented.

"I know you do," Fina said, patting his hand.

"Seriously. Read the signs, and if you screw up, pay the ticket. How hard is that?"

"Very, it would seem."

"Debt?"

"Nothing jumps out. I just covered the basics but didn't turn up anything."

"Maybe you should do some surveillance."

"Of what?" Fina looked at him. "Him microwaving his Swanson TV dinner before sitting down in front of *Dancing with the Stars*?"

"It's not as crazy as you make it sound."

"It's a little crazy, but I'll keep looking. I haven't exhausted all the options yet."

Matteo ran over to the bench and inserted himself between Cristian and Fina.

"Ina!" he exclaimed, and wiped his snotty nose on her bare arm.

"I love you, too, Matteo." She held her arm, smeared with snot, toward Cristian. "Really?"

"And you don't think you're cut out for motherhood?" He laughed and ran a baby wipe over her arm.

Fina averted her gaze and enjoyed the physical contact with Cristian. There was a coolness in the light breeze, alluding to fall's imminent arrival. After a moment, Fina's attention wandered across the street, where a man lingered by a car. He pressed a phone up to his ear. Fina studied him.

"See that guy over there?" She nodded in his direction.

Cristian glanced up. "Yeah. What about him?"

"I don't know. He just looks familiar. Does he look familiar to you?"

Cristian stuffed the snotty wipe into a baggie and stared at the man. Aware of the attention, the man started walking down the block at a brisk pace.

"Not to me. Is someone following you?"

"I'm not sure." Fina ran her fingers through Matteo's dark brown curly locks. "If he is, our paths will cross before too long."

"Ah. Something to look forward to."

"Indeed."

Fina almost fell off the couch that afternoon when her browser refreshed and a large photo of Hank Reardon was splashed across Boston .com. Captain of industry, pillar of society, husband, father, philanthropist. And now, Hank had a new item to add to his résumé: donor baby daddy.

Carl was unavailable, and Renata's phone went straight to voice mail. Fina spent the next couple of hours watching as all hell broke loose in cyberspace. When she learned that Carl had left the office for the day, she knew a house call was in order, as much as she disliked visiting the familial home.

Juliana Reardon looked at the photo on Boston.com and sighed. The new Mrs. Reardon always got top billing—even when the news was bad—and the old Mrs. Reardon was generally relegated to a small link at the bottom of the page.

Juliana was the old Mrs. Reardon.

She'd married Hank Reardon before he was a household name, before his net worth numbered in the billions. They'd been college sweethearts and then raised their son as Hank built his empire. There had been happy times—or at least satisfactory ones—but that had ended five years ago when they'd divorced. Juliana had outgrown her role as corporate wife and started to care about things other than flower arrangements and ski vacations. Her more active participation in the community was okay by Hank, until it started taking her away from him. By that time she was more interested in choosing the paint colors for the Reardon Breast Cancer Center for Reflection and Rejuvenation, and the writing was on the wall.

It hadn't taken long for Hank to replace her with Danielle, a beautiful woman almost young enough to be his daughter. Juliana hadn't expected him to stay single, and his choice of mate wasn't really that surprising, but it wounded her deeply nonetheless. Juliana knew she had more to offer than Danielle—more intelligence and experience—but that didn't seem to matter much nowadays. Danielle was young and pretty in a stereotypical California beach girl kind of way. No matter how many triathlons Juliana did, her butt would never be as perky as Danielle's, her face never as unlined.

She could have accepted that given her other assets: She was the mother of Hank's son and the face of Reardon philanthropy, but Danielle was chipping away at those advantages, too. She'd given birth to a daughter, Aubrey, and was becoming increasingly involved in charity work throughout the city. Some organizations were even starting to favor the new Mrs. Reardon over the old Mrs. Reardon, which was appalling. When Danielle was in diapers, Juliana had already raised millions of dollars for Boston's needy, and this was how they expressed their gratitude? By replacing her?

Well, now the shit was really hitting the fan, and for once, maybe being the old Mrs. Reardon wasn't so bad. True, Hank had donated the sperm when he and Juliana were on a "break" shortly after college, but the focus right now would be on him and, therefore, Danielle. And the cryokids coming out of the woodwork? They were Danielle's problem, at least for the time being.

Carl and Elaine lived in an enormous stone and shingle house in a wooded neighborhood in Chestnut Hill, ten minutes from Scotty's house. Her parents had an affection for new houses that were built to look old, an approach that never worked as far as Fina was concerned. Those houses always had a Disneyesque feel to them, and it wasn't as if there weren't plenty of authentically old houses. They lived in New England, for goodness' sake.

The façade of the house had odd proportions: windows that looked too big and a circular outcropping of glass that interrupted the sight line. Fina pulled up to the four-car garage and let herself into the mud-room. She crept in, hoping that she could make it to her father's office unscathed, but her plans were torpedoed as soon as she entered the kitchen.

Elaine was standing in front of the open refrigerator in a nightgown and robe. She wore slippers festooned with feathers.

"What are you doing here so late?" her mother asked.

"I need to talk to Dad."

Elaine pulled out a bowl covered in plastic wrap. She peeled back a corner and sniffed.

"Looks like banana pudding to me," Fina said, looking over her mother's shoulder.

"I know what it is."

"Then why are you smelling it?"

"I'm trying to decide if I want any."

"I'm sure there's some stuff for a salad in there," Fina offered. "Nothing like a salad to hit the spot."

Her mother frowned and put the bowl on the spotless counter. She reached into a drawer and extracted a spoon, which she dipped into the thick confection.

"Is Dad in his office?"

"He's downstairs, in the wine cellar."

Fina left her mother to her pudding and took the stairs down to the lower level of the house, which had a workout room, screening room, laundry area, and wine cellar. Fina went to the end of the hallway and knocked before opening the door.

Her father looked up. The room was the size of some studio apartments, with every inch of wall covered by racks of wine bottles. There was a granite island in the middle of the space, surrounded by bar stools. Carl was examining a couple of bottles.

"We need to talk," Fina said.

Carl studied the racks. It was only in the last ten years that Carl had developed an interest in wine. Fina couldn't tell if he was genuinely interested or if it was a rich man's pursuit that he needed to get in on. She found the topic to be a complete snooze fest.

Carl reached over and pulled out two more bottles, which he set down next to the others. "This can't be good."

"Renata went to the press."

Carl stared at her. "That woman! I told her not to talk to anyone."

Fina rested her butt on one of the stools. "I don't think Renata's a great listener."

"I want you at her place first thing tomorrow."

"Why?"

"To see where she's going with this campaign of hers."

"She's made it clear where she's going, don't you think?"

Carl uncorked a bottle and poured a small amount into a red wine glass. He proceeded to swirl the glass, then study and smell the liquid before taking a sip. He passed the glass to Fina. She sipped.

"Can you taste the black pepper in the finish?" he asked, taking it back.

"No more than I can taste the pickle."

Carl snorted, poured himself a full glass, and corked the bottle.

"Just go over there and take stock. I'll call Jules."

"She's really screwed her bargaining position."

"Maybe. Maybe not. There's nothing like the court of public opinion to inspire people to be generous."

"I'll be in touch." Fina pulled the wine cellar door closed behind her.

It was kind of sad, her parents indulging their appetites alone, on different floors. But maybe that was the key to their long union.

6

Whoever was outside Fina's door was annoyingly persistent. It was seven thirty in the morning, and she wasn't in the mood for a visitor.

"Really?" Fina asked when she opened the door to Milloy.

He handed her a cup from the café across the street. "It's hot chocolate."

Fina took off the plastic top and inhaled the rich aroma. "What's so important? Not that I don't love seeing you."

"I was in the neighborhood, and I thought I was a better wake-up call than Carl. He's going to be calling you any minute."

"Why?" Fina asked, and led him back to the bedroom. She climbed under the covers and invited Milloy to join her. He sat on top of the duvet and sipped his coffee.

"Hank Reardon is dead."

Fina started, and hot chocolate jumped out of the cup onto her hand. "Ouch." She licked her hand, which then burned her tongue. "Dammit. Okay. Start over."

"Hank Reardon was killed last night or early this morning. Too soon to know."

"Please tell me it was an accident."

Milloy grinned.

"I'm having trouble wrapping my head around this." She looked at him. "This isn't good."

"Do you think it's related to your investigation?"

"It seems awfully coincidental. Fuck. I'm not usually involved in a case until *after* the victim dies."

"Don't jump to any conclusions."

Fina's phone rang. She reached over and looked at the screen. "Yes, Dad," she answered.

"You heard?"

"I heard." Fina raised her hot chocolate in salute to Milloy.

"Come in so we can get ahead of this thing."

"Will do."

"I mean sooner rather than later."

"You always do, Dad." Fina ended the call and sipped her drink. "He's so bossy."

Milloy narrowed his eyes. "I can't imagine what that's like, spending time with someone who's bossy."

She frowned. "I'm not bossy. I'm decisive."

"Just keep telling yourself that."

Fina put her hot chocolate on the bedside table and threw back the duvet. "I better make some calls. Carl's always nicer if I bring him information."

Milloy followed her to the living room.

"Thanks for the heads-up, Milloy. I owe you."

"Always," he said, and left.

Fina turned on the TV. Hank's death dominated the coverage, and like most explosive news stories it was filled with lots of conjecture but few facts. He'd been found around three A.M. in the parking garage of his company, Universum Tech, by a security guard. There was no word yet on the cause of death, but it definitely was suspicious.

What had Renata Sanchez unleashed?

Walter turned onto the street and saw a clot of news vans in the parking lot. Like many successful people, Walter had mixed feelings about the press. He loved to be the recipient of positive attention, but he didn't like it when he couldn't control the narrative.

He steered his way through the crowd, careful not to run over any feet, and emerged from his car wearing a confident smile.

"Dr. Stiles, can you comment on Hank Reardon's death?"

"Does it have something to do with the cryobank?"

"When did his cryokids learn his identity?"

Presumably, they got results from this rapid-fire approach, but Walter just found it annoying.

"I know you have many questions, and we will have information for you in good time," he said into a few microphones. "However, Heritage is private property, and our clients' comfort and safety are our first priority. I'll have to ask you to move from the parking lot."

They called out a few more questions as he strode to the front door and walked into the clinic. The receptionist popped up, her face shell-shocked. There were half a dozen women sitting in the waiting area.

Walter leaned over the desk and spoke to the heavily pregnant woman.

"Please call the police and tell them that the media are trespassing."

"Yes, Dr. Stiles."

"Any other problems I should know about?"

She gestured toward the reporters. "They came in before, asking questions, but Ellen made them leave."

"Good. She should have finished the job and removed them from the parking lot. I don't want this stress to be a problem for you, Debby. It's not good for your pregnancy."

She smiled at him. "I feel okay."

"Well, put your feet up if you don't. Doctor's orders."

Walter walked back through the hallway and stood in the open door of Ellen's office.

"Good morning, Walter," she said. She was wearing a dress in a turquoise and navy print. Her blond hair was pulled back into a bun that sat low on her neck.

He stood stiffly before her. "I was hounded by the press in the parking lot."

Ellen frowned. "I asked them to leave."

"That may be, but they didn't. I've asked Debby to call the police."

"That sounds like a good idea."

Walter exhaled loudly. No matter what he said, Ellen always seemed to twist things to her advantage. He hadn't been asking her opinion but rather stating what she should have done already.

"I'd like the management team to meet today to discuss this situation," he said.

"Already done." Ellen tapped her pen on her blotter. "I've told everyone to meet in the conference room at ten."

Walter nodded. "Good."

He left and walked down the hall to his larger, more luxurious office. Walter had a corner office with windows on two walls and room for a large desk and a bookcase that displayed the honors he'd received throughout his career. One wall was covered with baby pictures, girls and boys of every shape and size who existed only because Heritage had made their conceptions possible. There were a number of these displays throughout the bank; Walter liked visitors to constantly be reminded of Heritage's higher purpose. Yes, the cryobank was a business, but the most important thing they made was families.

There was a small closet in Walter's office, and before taking off his coat, he went into it and unlocked the bottom drawer of a gray metal filing cabinet hidden inside. He pulled out stacks of files and deposited them in empty banker's boxes. Once two boxes were packed and safely tucked under his desk, Walter took off his coat and settled down in front of his computer.

There. One less thing to worry about.

. . .

"What took you so long?" Carl asked when Fina arrived.

Fina sat down on the couch. "What, are you kidding? You called me an hour ago."

"You only live ten minutes from here."

"Do you really want to hear the details of my morning routine? Well, first I had to pee."

Carl grimaced. "At least tell me you have more information than what they've got." He gestured toward a flat-screen TV that was playing the local news.

"I called one of my contacts in the coroner's office. Hank Reardon was found around three A.M. in the parking garage of his company, Universum Tech. Looks like death from blunt force trauma."

"Who found him?"

"Security guard."

"What else?"

"Nothing else. The body is barely cold." She rested her head against the back of the sofa and studied the ceiling. "Are we to assume this has something to do with us?"

"It seems like a safe assumption." He exhaled loudly. "It means I'm going to have cops crawling all over my ass."

"Probably. Have you spoken to Renata today?" Fina asked.

"I got a voice mail from her, firing us."

"Really? Well, that solves some of our problems."

"According to our contract, the relationship can only be terminated in writing."

"And you're going to hold her to it?"

Carl shrugged and was silent for a moment. "You think she has it in her to murder Hank Reardon?"

Fina moved her head back and forth. "Maybe."

"She's a small woman."

"Blunt force trauma is an equal-opportunity means; with the right weapon, anyone can do a lot of damage."

"You better go see her, figure out if she needs a criminal attorney."

Fina stood. "You still think cryobanks and sperm donation are the next big thing in lawsuits?"

"Damn right I do. Murder means passion, and passion means lawsuits."

"Spoken like a hopeless romantic," Fina said, walking out the door.

Fina pulled up to Renata's house just as Renata was shepherding Alexa out the front door. Alexa looked camp-bound, with an overstuffed backpack and a towel in her hands. Renata was juggling a briefcase, an insulated lunch bag, and a plastic bag holding a pair of heels.

"Not now, Fina. I don't have time," she said while unlocking the car door.

"Renata, we need to talk."

"And I don't have time right now. Call me later."

"Have you seen the news?" Fina glanced at Alexa, who seemed altogether too interested in the conversation.

"I really don't have time for a guessing game." Renata leaned down and started the car.

"Hank Reardon is dead."

Alexa's eyes grew wide.

Renata's mouth opened and then closed. "Well, I don't know what I can do about it," she finally said.

"The police are going to want to interview you, and the press are going to be even more demanding."

"Well, this isn't my fault!" Renata protested.

"The murder may not be, but the media circus is. What were you thinking, going to the press?"

Renata studied the ground and avoided Fina's gaze. "I just wanted to set things straight."

"That really worked. Where's Rosie, anyway?"

"She stayed with a friend last night."

"Rosie was wicked mad," Alexa offered helpfully.

Renata glared at her.

"Is that so?" Fina asked. "What was she mad about, Renata?"

"She wasn't just mad at me, if that's what you're suggesting. She was also angry with Hank and his attempt to pay her off."

"For Pete's sake, why did you tell her about that?"

"It's her life. She has a right to know."

Fina shook her head in wonderment. "Renata, come into the office so we can talk about getting ahead of this story, and don't talk to the cops without counsel."

Renata ducked into her car. Fina watched her drive away.

In her car, Fina was scrolling through her e-mails when her phone rang. Cristian's number lit up the display.

"What's up? Did Brad Martin do something dramatic, like buy a new vacuum cleaner?"

"I'm glad you amuse yourself. You need to come by the station."

Fina looked out the window; a petite woman was on the sidewalk being walked by a large black Lab. "Because?"

"Because Pitney wants to see you."

"I don't know who killed Hank Reardon."

"She wants to talk."

"Oh, blah, blah, blah. I haven't even done anything yet."

"That we know of."

"Fine. I'll stop by."

"She wants to see you now."

"Well, I'm a busy woman."

"So is she, and she has the law on her side and a lot of people riding her ass."

"Don't antagonize her? Is that what you're saying?"

"Nothing gets by you, Ludlow."

"I'm on my way."

"I'm here to see Lieutenant Pitney," Fina announced at Boston Police headquarters twenty minutes later.

The desk sergeant gave her a weary once-over and pointed to the uncomfortable wooden benches across from his bulletproof perch. After tapping her toe for ten minutes, Fina got up and waited her turn behind a uniformed cop and his odiferous charge.

"Can you let Lieutenant Pitney know I stopped by? I'll try to catch her later."

"What's your name?" The desk sergeant asked.

"Fina Ludlow."

"Ah. In that case, 'sit down and cool your jets.' That's what she said to tell you."

"Ugh. Fine."

Fina sat and waited. Ten more minutes passed, but she was done cooling her jets. She started toward the front door.

"Ludlow!"

"Dammit," Fina said under her breath. She looked up to see Pitney at the top of the stairs, beckoning to her.

She led Fina to a room reserved for victims and family members; it was painted a neutral color and had two comfortable couches and framed prints on the wall. There was a small round table surrounded by four chairs. Pitney took a seat and pointed at another for Fina.

"Not an interview room? I think you're starting to like me," Fina said.

"Don't get ahead of yourself."

Fina and Pitney had a love-hate relationship. They were often on opposite sides of the fence, but each recognized in the other a smart, competent woman. Their interactions were fraught with lies, bickering, and grudging respect. They had most recently been at odds during the investigation of Melanie's death, but Fina had provided Pitney with key information and hadn't covered for her brother in traditional Ludlow fashion. Fina hoped this had earned her some points with the lieutenant.

"So you called, and I came," Fina said.

"I'd like to get some things clear about the Hank Reardon case." Pitney rested her hand on a folder on the table; her coral-colored nails looked like small wounds against the manila. They were a sharp contrast to her royal blue pants and red-striped blouse. Her gun sat on her right hip. Pitney was short and round and always brought to mind an armed garden gnome.

Fina sat back in her chair. "I know nothing about his death."

"How is it that every time I turn around, you're up to your neck in one of my cases?"

"You're being a little dramatic. We were hired by Renata Sanchez to identify her donor and possibly sue the cryobank. I investigated, learned Hank's identity, and the concerned parties were in talks."

"But now one of the concerned parties is dead."

"A man worth billions who had his share of enemies. I certainly hope your investigation is going to look at all possible suspects, not just the ones associated with my family."

"What do you think?"

"Just checking."

There was a tap at the door, and Cristian popped his head in. "Lieutenant, we're ready for you."

Pitney got up from her seat. "Don't get in the way, and tell Cristian what you know."

"Some of it is covered by privilege," Fina reminded her.

"Share what you can according to the law. Otherwise, you're looking at obstruction."

Fina scoffed. "You deem my very existence obstructive."

"And I'm the one who's dramatic?"

"I can't help it; it runs in the family."

"Good-bye, Fina." Pitney left the room, and Cristian took her seat.

"What do you have for me?" he asked.

Fina sighed and gave him an overview of her investigation into Hank Reardon and his offspring. It didn't take long.

"Have you seen that guy again? The one in the park?" Cristian asked.

"Nope. Maybe I was just being paranoid."

Cristian looked at her. "You're many things, but paranoid isn't one of them."

"Well, thank you." Fina smiled.

Cristian grinned and shook his head. "Watch your back."

"Oh, stop with the sweet nothings."

Fina left the station satisfied that she'd done her civic duty for the day.

Back at Nanny's, Fina fielded a concerned phone call from the building manager. Apparently, members of the press had connected her to Hank's "coming out" as a donor and were eager to talk to her. They'd spent the day hanging around, annoying the other residents. It wasn't the first time that Fina had brought the media to the building, and there was talk of her violating homeowners' association rules.

"You're not serious," she told the manager.

"It's disruptive, Ms. Ludlow. This is a quiet building, and the residents value their privacy."

"Well, the press aren't interested in them," she noted.

He was silent.

"Fine. I'll take care of it." She hung up and retreated to the bedroom. After stripping off her clothes and climbing into bed naked, Fina lay on her back and looked at the ceiling.

Renata Sanchez really was the gift that kept on giving.

7

"We've got to do something about this," Fina said, walking into Carl's office.

"What's the matter?" Matthew asked. He and Scotty were sitting with Carl at the shiny walnut table.

"We're in the middle of something," Carl said, flicking a glance in her direction.

"Well, *you* may be able to get work done, but I can't when I'm being followed by reporters." Fina had been trailed by a few when she popped out to get a hot chocolate and chocolate croissant earlier that morning. Forget the building manager—it was hard to detect when you were so damn detectable.

"What do they want from you?" Scotty asked.

"They seem to think that I'm going to lead them to some secret land populated by Hank Reardon's cryokids and his murderer. I can't do any investigating with an entourage, and my building manager is getting tetchy."

"What do you want me to do about it?" Carl asked.

"I don't know. Can't you threaten to sue them?"

"On what grounds?" Carl asked.

"It'll die down, Fina," Matthew said. "Another story will push it off the front page. You just need to be patient." He and Scotty looked at each other and burst out laughing.

"That's hilarious." Fina glared at her brothers.

"Why don't you just solve the case?" Scotty said. "That might shut everyone up."

"Who's going to pay for that?" Carl asked, suddenly looking alert.

"Just put her on it for a limited number of hours," Scotty suggested. "We did kind of contribute to the situation."

"I'm not in the charity business," Carl said.

Carl's assistant poked her head around the door. "Mr. Ludlow, there's a gentleman here to see you. His name is Michael Reardon, and he insists on speaking with you."

Scotty and Matthew glanced between their father and sister.

"That's his son, right?" Matthew asked.

"Yes. From his first marriage." Fina felt the stirrings of a headache. She walked over to the bar and pulled out a diet soda.

"Set up an appointment, Shari," Carl instructed.

"I don't think he'll take no for an answer," Shari whispered.

"Dad, let's just get this over with." Fina sat down in an empty chair at the table and popped open the soda.

Carl sighed. "We'll finish this later, boys."

Scotty and Matthew gathered up their folders and laptops and were barely out the door before Michael Reardon strode in.

"I called you last night and this morning," Michael said.

Carl stood and offered his hand to Michael. He then gestured to the chair that Scotty had vacated. "And I was going to return your call. Sit down, Michael."

Even though he was twenty-eight, Michael Reardon dropped into the chair as directed. Fina recognized the behavior. In her experience, young men raised by powerful fathers were often blustery to the outside world, but cowed in the presence of their fathers or comparable father figures.

"This is Fina, my daughter. She's a private investigator."

"I know who she is." Michael looked at her. "She's the one who outed my father. This is her fault."

Fina rolled her eyes. "It's a little more complicated than that, but yes, I did uncover your father's identity."

Looking at him, Fina could see the family resemblance. More cute than handsome, Michael Reardon had sandy blond hair and a lean physique. He looked like a stretched-out version of his father, who had been shorter and a bit beefier.

"What can we do for you, Michael?" Carl asked. To the untrained eye, Carl might appear solicitous, but Fina knew his question was in service of his goal of dealing with Michael and moving him along.

"You need to fix this."

Fina looked at Carl and then Michael. "What exactly do you want us to fix?"

"You need to find out who killed my father."

"I think that's a job best left to the police," Carl said.

"Aren't the first forty-eight hours the most important?" Michael whined. "After forty-eight hours, doesn't the chance of finding the killer dramatically decrease?"

"That may be true for most murders," Fina said, silently cursing *Dateline*, "but your father's case is hardly typical. I'm sure every available resource is being brought to bear to find his killer."

"It's not enough."

Fina sipped her soda and watched him clench and unclench his fists. When he felt her gaze, he slipped his hands into his lap.

According to a profile in *Boston* magazine, Michael had recently experienced an awakening of his social conscience and was seriously contemplating leaving Universum Tech for a more civic-minded position. It seemed to be an effort at atonement for having grown up the child of a billionaire, but his current attitude suggested that old habits die hard. He still fostered the belief that if you weren't signing someone's paycheck, you really couldn't count on them to get the job done.

"So you want to hire Fina to find your father's killer?" Carl asked.

Michael barked out a laugh. "I don't think I should have to pay you. You're the reason my father's dead."

Carl stared at him. "Did your father ever work for free, Michael? Is that how he ran his business?"

Michael swallowed. "No."

"Well, neither do we. You can hire Fina, but she doesn't do volunteer work."

Fina glared at Carl. She didn't want to do *any* work for the Reardons. She wanted to distance herself from them, not get more entangled.

"Fine. You're hired."

Fina opened her mouth to speak, but Carl cut her off. "Why don't you two continue this in the conference room? I have work to do."

"Dad."

"Fina." He stared at her. She relented.

"Michael," she said, and stood up from the table. "Let's go upstairs."

The Ludlow and Associates boardroom was an impressive space. It was vast, like Jules Lindsley's boardroom, with floor-to-ceiling windows and a conference table that could seat two dozen. Fina rubbed her bare arms and punched up the thermostat a few degrees. She took a seat at the head of the table and swigged her soda. Michael sat down next to her in one of the large leather chairs.

"I am genuinely sorry about your dad," she said. "I'm not taking responsibility for his death, but I regret any role I may have played."

Michael nodded, but was silent.

"But I need you to understand," Fina continued, "that I have to tread lightly if I'm going to investigate this. Pissing off the cops isn't productive."

"Understood."

"And we need to get one thing straight: When I investigate, I'm all in. I won't tiptoe around your family even if it gets ugly."

"Ugly? Uglier than Hank Reardon, businessman extraordinaire, fathering multiple cryokids?"

"It can always get uglier, Michael, and your description makes him sound like a pro athlete with a kid in every city. He was a sperm donor. Some people might consider that a selfless act."

A sour look overtook his features. "My father was many things, Fina, a lot of them good, but selfless was not one of them." He wasn't as cute when he was being pissy.

"I'm just warning you that I have to investigate everyone: the cryokids, you, your mom, and your stepmother, too."

Michael looked defiant. "Are you suggesting that my family had something to do with this?"

"I'm suggesting that I don't know. Neither do you. But if the prospect of my digging annoys you, then this isn't going to work."

He examined his nails. They were neatly trimmed and buffed. "Fine, but none of us killed him."

"But there may be other dirt that gets unearthed."

"I don't care."

Fina studied him. "All right. Why don't you tell me what you know?"

Michael took a deep breath. "A security guard found my dad in the Universum Tech garage."

"Okay. And the cause of death?"

"Isn't this public knowledge?" he asked.

"Not yet, and I want to hear what you know."

"He was hit . . . with something." Michael gestured toward the back of his head.

"How did you find out he was dead?"

He flinched at Fina's question, but she didn't apologize for her wording. She wasn't insensitive, but she had to be sure that Michael really had the stomach for an investigation. And she hated all the euphemisms for death; when people "passed" it was either gas or a test. You die and you're dead. That was that.

"My mom."

"How's she holding up?" Juliana Reardon and Hank had been divorced for five years, but according to the society scuttlebutt, they had a remarkably friendly relationship as exes. That was largely a credit to

Juliana's reasonable requests in the divorce. She could have taken Hank to the cleaners, but her own spiritual awakening precluded a nasty fight. The settlement left her an extremely wealthy woman, but it didn't burden her with the karmic baggage of a lengthy court battle.

"She's okay. Shocked. We all are."

"What about his business partner?"

"Dimitri? What about him?"

"Do you like him? Did he and your dad get along?"

"He's good at what he does. He and Dad didn't always see eye to eye, but they complemented each other."

Fina thought for a moment. "Who do you think killed him?"

Michael shrugged. "I don't know, but things were fine until Renata Sanchez showed up. This is all her fault."

Fifteen minutes ago it was all Fina's fault, but she was happy to share the blame. In her experience, few things were ever just one person's fault. There was usually plenty of blame to go around.

"When did you find out your dad had been a sperm donor?"

Michael cringed. "When the rest of the city did."

He learned his father's dark secret the same day as all of cyberspace? Ouch.

"Is there anything else you think I should know?" Fina asked.

"Like what?"

"Any conversations with your dad that seemed out of character? Had his behavior changed recently? Any fights or disagreements?"

Michael thought for a moment. "Nope."

"Well, if you think of anything else," Fina said, handing him her card, "let me know. I'll be in touch."

He followed her to the door.

"You should let your family know that you've hired me," she said. "I'll need access to investigate."

"I'll let them know right away."

"How are they going to feel about my poking around?"

"They want to know who killed Dad, too. That's all that matters."

Fina watched him leave.

Huh.

That didn't really answer her question.

The young Mrs. Reardon was currently unavailable, according to the woman who answered the phone, so Fina decided to shift gears and nose around Hank's professional world. The skies opened up as she drove across the river to Cambridge; her windshield wipers could barely keep up. People darted from building to building in Kendall Square trying to escape the deluge. Fina always thought there was something missing in that neighborhood that gave it a cold, sterile feel. Regardless of all the activity and progress in the buildings above, she was always struck by the lack of energy on the street level, despite the presence of humans. Say what you will about the grit and dirt of other neighborhoods; at least they had a pulse.

Universum Tech headquarters was located in an oddly shaped midrise building with glass awnings sculpted into undulating waves. It looked like a feat of engineering, but an ugly feat nonetheless. Fina pulled into a visitors' space in the garage and took the elevator to the first floor, entering an atrium that spanned seven floors. Glass-and-steel balconies bordered the space, and the ceiling that loomed above was made from frosted glass. The rain splattered down, the effect more noisy than soothing.

To the right of the seating area, a poster-sized photo of Hank Reardon sat on an easel flanked by large white flower arrangements. In the photo he was wearing a white Universum Tech golf shirt, which set off his tan nicely. He looked healthy and prosperous.

Fina turned toward the two twenty-somethings who were manning the reception desk that stood between two large potted ficus plants.

"Can I help you?" The young man smiled at Fina. His broad forehead, narrow head, and hooked nose called to mind an eagle. His name tag said TONY.

"I'm here to see Dimitri Kask on behalf of Michael Reardon." She handed over her ID.

His face assumed a downcast expression. "Of course. Let me call his office."

Five minutes later, Tony was standing next to her in the elevator, punching the button for the seventh floor.

"I'm sorry about Mr. Reardon," Fina said. "It must be hard on the whole company."

"It's awful," Tony replied in a hushed tone. "I mean, just dying would have been terrible, but murdered?" He gave her a knowing look. "I assume that's why you're here."

Fina smiled, but stayed silent.

"I understand. You can't talk about it," he practically whispered.

"Do you know Danielle Reardon?" Fina asked, stepping off the elevator.

"Well, not personally, but we all kind of *know* her. She comes to company events."

"With the baby?"

Tony thought for a moment. "Nah. She's so little."

Tony led Fina away from the atrium through an open space populated with cubes that looked corporate, but clearly there were no stifling rules about their decor. The ones she could see were decorated with pictures and posters and stuffed with comfortable furniture. In the corner of the building, two large glass-fronted offices faced each other with two assistants stationed in between. One office stood empty. In the other, a man with closely shorn black hair and a five o'clock shadow sat on a black leather couch under a window. He was not conventionally handsome, but even at first glance, Fina could tell that his clothes were expensive and he took care with his appearance.

"Ms. Ludlow for Mr. Kask," Tony told the female assistant. She announced Fina to the man in the office and ushered her into the room.

"Dimitri Kask," he said, and offered his hand.

"Fina Ludlow," she said, matching his firm grip.

"Dana, could you please close the door?" he asked the young woman.

As she pulled it closed behind her, Dimitri walked over to the glass walls that fronted the rest of the office and pulled the blinds shut. "Sometimes the fishbowl can be a bit much."

"I thought it was good for collaboration and all that," Fina said, sitting in an Eames chair next to the couch.

"It is, except when you need to think." Dimitri took a seat on the couch and crossed one ankle over the other knee. "What can I do for you?"

"I appreciate your seeing me without an appointment. I know how busy you must be."

Dimitri Kask was a technical wunderkind who'd made and lost his first million by the age of twenty-five. Now forty-five, he had an international reputation, the go-to guy when anyone needed a pronouncement on the future of technology. He was extraordinarily bright and generally well liked.

"Obviously, I'm here about Hank," Fina said.

"Yes, Michael told me you might be stopping by. You just missed the police."

"Who's leading the team?"

He peered at her. "Lieutenant Pitney. They don't know you're on the case?"

"I'll be coordinating with Lieutenant Pitney and her team." She mentally crossed her fingers behind her back.

Dimitri nodded. He picked a piece of lint off his expensive-looking black pants. He was wearing Italian leather loafers and a dress shirt without a tie.

"Can you tell me how Hank had been acting recently? Anything out of the ordinary?" she asked.

Dimitri chuckled. "There was nothing ordinary about Hank. Did you know he was one of the first people to market software platforms for e-commerce? Everything that we buy online nowadays, Hank had a hand in making that possible."

"But he was more a business guy than a tech guy, right?"

"Correct. He understood enough about the technology to hire the right people, and his instincts were fantastic. He was able to identify the next big thing and jump on it."

"When did you two start working together?"

"It's been almost ten years."

"So is e-commerce still the company's focus?"

"We have a number of companies and projects under the Universum Tech umbrella."

Fina nodded. His answer was pleasantly vague. "Did you two get along?"

Dimitri grinned. "Are you asking if I killed him?"

"Did you?"

"Do murderers usually confess to you?" He reached for a bottle of water on the glass coffee table and took a swig.

"You'd be surprised what people tell me."

"No, I didn't kill Hank, nor did I want to. I considered him a friend, not just a business partner."

"Anyone you can think of who might have been upset with him?"

Dimitri scanned the room as he thought. Most of the surfaces were free of paper, but pieces of hardware littered the room. There were computer towers and laptops and what Fina assumed were motherboards and other components. Some had exposed innards from which wires were sprouting. Black-and-white abstract photographs hung on the walls, and on the credenza behind the desk, family photos offered the only pop of color in the space.

"I don't know. Our competitors, maybe? Hank was arrogant—most hugely successful businesspeople are—and he didn't mind stepping on toes. I can't imagine anyone would kill him over business, though."

"What about Danielle?"

"What about her?"

"Do you like her? Did she and Hank seem happy?"

"They seemed happy."

Fina tilted her head. "You didn't answer the first question."

"Danielle is perfectly nice. Personally, I've always felt more of a connection with Juliana, but my husband is quite fond of Danielle."

"Do you still see Juliana?"

"Occasionally at functions. I try to support her philanthropic work."

Fina looked around the office. "I understand that Michael Reardon works here."

Dimitri took another swig of water. "Yes."

"But maybe that's going to change?"

"I don't know anything about that. You'll have to ask Michael."

"Was Hank grooming him to take his place?"

"He's a little young to take his place, but I think that was his hope down the road."

"And do you think Michael could fill his father's shoes? If he wants to, that is."

Dimitri pondered the question. "He's smart and certainly ambitious."

"But?"

"But his ambition comes from a place of having things as opposed to wanting things he's never had."

"I'm guessing the latter was the case for you and Hank."

He nodded. "Hank grew up in a working-class family in Illinois, and my parents were immigrants from Estonia. We both felt compelled to do better. It's a different dynamic than being the son of a billionaire."

Fina thought about her own family. Carl and Elaine had built their fortune from nothing, and she and her brothers had been raised accustomed to a privileged lifestyle. The Ludlow children were all ambitious—it was in their blood—but none of them knew what it was like to fret over the electric bill. That kind of worry was uniquely motivating.

"Anything else that may have been causing problems for Hank?" she asked.

Dimitri shrugged. Fina watched him and waited. He watched her back. Dimitri Kask wasn't going to fall victim to her usual bag of tricks.

"And the whole sperm donor issue?" she asked.

"What about it?" He shifted—just a tiny bit—on the couch.

"How did you feel about the revelations?"

"It wasn't my business." His expression was flat.

"So you didn't have any feelings about it either way?" Fina smiled at him. "I find that hard to believe."

"I wasn't thrilled with the publicity," he conceded.

"It is a little tabloidish. Donor babies coming out of the woodwork."

"As I said, it didn't really concern me."

"You weren't worried they would want a piece of the pie?"

"Of Universum Tech? There's no legal basis for that."

"There's no legal basis for Renata Sanchez's lawsuit, but that isn't going to stop her."

"With the help of your family's law firm, if I'm not mistaken." Irritation flashed in Dimitri's eyes.

"You're not mistaken. I make no excuses for my father."

"But you do for yourself?"

Fina narrowed her eyes and gazed at him. "I don't have anything to apologize for. I didn't reveal Hank Reardon's identity as the donor to the media, and now I'm just trying to find his killer."

"So no guilt by association?"

"No, no guilt by association." She leaned forward in her seat. "What about you? How's that investigation into your child labor practices in China going? How old were they? The same ages as your kids?" Fina looked toward a picture on the credenza. It was an eight-by-ten photo of Dimitri, his husband, and their two young children.

"I think this interview is over," Dimitri said, sitting forward.

Fina raised her hand. "Look, I didn't come here to have a pissing contest or give you grief about your business practices, but turnabout is fair play."

Dimitri looked at her, and then his gaze drifted to the picture be-hind his desk. "We resolved the China factory issue."

They were silent for a moment.

Dimitri glanced at his watch. "I really wish I could provide more help, but I don't know anything about Hank's death, and I have another meeting."

Fina rose from her chair and followed him to the door. "If you think of anything, let me know." She handed him her card. "Would it be pos-sible for me to see Hank's office?"

Dimitri looked at the empty room on the other side of the space. "I'll have to speak with our attorneys." He slipped her card into his pocket.

"Sure. What about the murder scene?"

Dimitri's assistant looked up with a pained expression and dipped her head again quickly.

"Just check in with reception before you go snooping around." He walked back into his office and closed the door.

Fina found Tony behind the reception desk engaged in a spirited dis-cussion with his desk mate. The snatch of conversation that Fina caught included the mention of boxers, Popsicles, and carpet cleaner. Tony was so engrossed in his story, he failed to notice Fina until his colleague nodded in her direction.

"How can I help you?" Tony chirped.

"I just spoke with Dimitri, and he said I should check in with you in order to see the crime scene."

Tony winced. "That area is still closed off to cars, but I think you can walk around if you like."

"That would be perfect."

He touched a button on his headset and turned away from Fina. The circumstances did lend themselves to a certain amount of intrigue, but Tony would probably infuse any job with mystery. Fina could imagine him whispering into the microphone at Dunkin' Donuts—"A sausage and egg croissant, please"—while stealing glances at the customers. It wasn't the content but the delivery that made life exciting.

A moment later, a security guard in a blue blazer and pants appeared from behind double doors and walked over. Fina couldn't peg his age— probably in his late forties—but the rest of his appearance did little to make her feel secure. He was about five feet five and overweight; most of the extra weight was around his waist, and when he walked toward her, there was a roll to his gait.

"This is the investigator who needs to see the area," Tony confided to the guard.

"Joseph Skylar." The guard thrust a beefy hand at Fina. "I'll take it from here."

Joseph led Fina to the doors from which he'd emerged and swiped a key card over an electronic sensor. The door beeped, and he held it open for her. Fina's height advantage gave her a bird's-eye view of the top of his head, which she could have lived without. Joseph's hairline was sneaking over the top of his skull, and he seemed to be attempting to compensate by growing his hair down the back of his neck. It was not a good look.

"So you're with the BPD on this one?" he asked as they waited at a bank of service elevators.

"I'm working with them, yes."

"But you're not a cop."

"Private detective."

The elevator dinged, and they got on. Joseph pressed the button for the third floor.

"I considered going the private route," he said, rocking back and forth on his feet. "Decided I could do more good in a corporate setting."

"Sure, I understand." Fina snuck a glance at his torso. He had a small collection of key cards hooked onto his belt and a walkie-talkie, but he wasn't armed.

"Did you ever consider joining the force?" she asked.

Joseph's lip curled slightly. "What's the point? Here, I do the work and get great benefits."

Fina interpreted this to mean that he hadn't passed the entrance exam at the academy.

The elevator moved at a glacial pace.

"I assume Mr. Reardon's death was unusual," Fina said. "I mean, this isn't a violent place to work, right?"

Joseph took a deep breath and pulled up his belt, which couldn't decide if it wanted to be above or below the pudge. "We keep a lid on things. People know that Universum isn't the place to go looking for trouble."

They emerged on the third floor, and Fina followed her guide across the parking garage.

"So you're probably more focused on prevention and support," she said.

"That's right. Stop it before it starts and help those in need."

Dead car batteries, flat tires, fainting spells, stolen wallets. These were the kinds of incidents that probably occupied Joseph's time, and he was probably very good at dealing with relatively minor crises. You weren't going to be locked out of your car, not on his watch.

They reached the southeastern corner of the parking garage; an area encompassing half a dozen spaces was roped off with police tape.

"Were you the one who discovered Mr. Reardon's body?"

"No, ma'am. You'll have to talk to our security director about that."

Fina looked at the tape. "The police haven't cleared the scene?"

"They did, but Mr. Hogan told us to leave it this way."

Fina looked out of the concrete structure toward the building next door. It seemed to house more offices. "What was Mr. Reardon like?"

"Oh, he was great. A really nice guy. I feel bad for his family."

"Sure. His son, Michael, works here, doesn't he?"

Joseph traced a pattern on the pavement with his shoe. "That's right."

Fina studied the ground. "I heard he might be leaving Universum."

Joseph shook his head. "I don't really know." He glanced over his shoulder and then leaned toward Fina. "They didn't always get along."

Fina raised an eyebrow.

"Michael and his father," Joseph added.

Fina nodded. "Yeah, I'd heard that." She hadn't heard any such thing, but that was a minor detail. "Did you ever see them fight?"

"Actually, they had a doozy on Friday, a few days before all this." He held his hands up in a gesture that seemed to encompass the scene before them.

"I guess that's what parents and kids do sometimes, right?" Fina remarked. "Where'd you see them fighting?"

"Right here. In the garage."

"I wonder what it was about," Fina mused.

"I don't know. I wasn't close enough to hear, but they both looked angry."

Fina was silent in case Joseph had anything else to offer. After a moment, the implication of his revelation seemed to dawn on him. "I'm sure it was nothing serious, though. I don't mean that they got physical or anything."

"I understand. Just a typical father-son thing. My brothers are always arguing with my dad."

"Sure, sure. That must have been it."

Fina dipped under the tape and surveyed the scene. Joseph stood on the other side and followed her gaze.

"Thanks so much for bringing me up here," Fina said. "You don't need to stay."

"I don't mind."

She smiled. "I'd feel terrible if you neglected your other duties on my account."

"I guess it's okay for me to go. I should probably do a recon of the other floors. Make sure everything is in order."

"Sounds like a plan," Fina said, and turned her back to him. After a moment, she heard his footsteps echoing across the floor; her junior deputy had moved on.

Fina scanned the pavement. Her eyes stopped on a dark stain a few feet wide. She dropped down to a crouch and examined the spot, confirming on closer inspection that it was in fact blood, not motor oil. The stain was close to what would have been the driver's-side door of a car parked in the space. There was nothing else of note, which didn't surprise her. Fina didn't expect the crime scene to offer any clues at this point, but seeing where Hank had been killed only raised more questions. Had his killer been lying in wait? Was it spur of the moment? Did the killer bring the weapon or find it at the scene? How long did it take for Hank to die? This was always the way in an investigation; the scope expanded before it narrowed, but that didn't make it any less frustrating.

8

One look at Mickey Hogan and Fina knew that security at Universum wasn't a complete joke. She'd requested ten minutes with him after visiting the crime scene. He was sitting behind a desk in a small, windowless room with a laptop before him. A door behind him led to some kind of nerve center that was dark and filled with screens. Fina sat down in a chair across the desk and stretched to get a better look at the control room; Mickey Hogan closed the door with his foot.

"Does Lieutenant Pitney know you're here?" Mickey asked after examining her license.

"She doesn't know I'm here at this exact moment, but she knows I'm on the case." Liar, liar, pants on fire. "I assume you're ex-BPD?"

"Yup. Thirty years."

"Let me guess: You took your pension, put your feet up, and got bored."

Mickey grinned. Given the math, he must have been in his mid-fifties, but looked ten years younger. His hair was cut close to his skull, and he wore a blue suit and tie. He was broad through the shoulders, and when he leaned back in his chair, Fina saw the gun at his hip. "Something like that."

"Sounds like my friend Frank Gillis."

"I know Frank. Didn't he work for your father?"

"Yup, and he trained me."

"He's a good guy. Still working?"

"Kind of part-time. He likes to keep a hand in things, but doesn't want to work that hard anymore. Did you consider going private when you left the force?"

Mickey shrugged. "I thought about it, but corporate was a better fit; good pay, great benefits, normal hours, no stakeouts."

"But peeing in a cup is so much fun," Fina said.

"Nothing stopping me from doing that if I want to."

She laughed. "True."

Mickey adjusted in his seat. "But you're not here to trade war stories, right?"

"Right. Michael Reardon hired me to investigate Hank's death. I've spoken with Dimitri Kask, and I've looked at the scene. Your officer Joseph Skylar was my tour guide." Fina couldn't help but grin.

Mickey sipped coffee out of a Universum mug. "Don't knock Joseph. He serves a purpose."

"He's not exactly intimidating, though."

"He doesn't need to be. He likes to keep an eye on things and solve the small problems. I never get any complaints that Joseph hasn't been helpful and courteous."

"Fair enough. Is there anything you can tell me about Hank Reardon's death? Like who found him?"

"One of the night-shift guys."

"Was it unusual for Hank to be here in the middle of the night?"

"It wasn't his usual schedule, but these guys, they work all the time. Sometimes when they've been traveling, they land at Logan at odd hours and can't sleep, so they come into the office for a few hours to work and then go home and crash, or they come back to the office after a function."

"So you wouldn't be surprised to hear that Hank or Dimitri was here at, say, one A.M.?"

"Not really. These guys"—he gestured in the air—"their lives aren't normal by any stretch of the imagination."

"Because of their wealth?"

"Their money, their ambition, their influence, their responsibilities. You name it, everything is on a grand scale."

Fina nodded. "They're not like everyone else."

"No, they are not."

"So what do *you* think happened? Hank drove into the parking garage, got out of his car, and someone bashed in his skull?"

"Basically."

"But I saw a lot of cameras when I was on the third floor, and you need a pass card to get into the garage."

"Hank's was the only car that came into the garage during that time."

"So the murderer came in on foot?"

"Or came in hours earlier and hung around."

"There's no footage from the time of the murder?"

"There is, but there's nothing to see."

"But the perpetrator left somehow." She was quiet for a moment. "Did he take anything from the scene?"

"You're assuming it was a he?" Mickey asked.

"No, I'm not, actually. Just trying to keep it simple."

"He didn't take anything that we know of. Hank still had his wallet and phone. His briefcase was open and papers were strewn about, but no one knows if anything was missing, since we don't know what was in there in the first place."

There was a tap at the door, and Mickey looked up at a young man in a similar blue suit.

"Boss, Mr. J. wants to see you."

Mickey pushed back his chair. "That's Mr. Jessup, our CFO. We'll have to cut this short."

"Of course." Fina rose and put her bag over her shoulder. "I'm assuming that you have some pretty serious security here, given the nature of the business."

"That's one of the reasons I like the job. I don't get a lot of blowback about resources. When I tell them they need to hire more people or update the systems, they do."

"Then it's got to feel pretty shitty that Hank was killed here."

Mickey massaged one hand with the other. "It does, but I'm not convinced that his murder had anything to do with the company."

"You think it was personal?"

Mickey cocked an eyebrow. "You tell me. It seems like the suspect list is pretty extensive." He held the door for Fina. She gave him her card and bade adieu to Tony at the front desk.

Things were starting to get interesting.

Fina hit the speed dial for Cristian as she approached the Longfellow Bridge.

"Menendez."

"In the interest of full disclosure, I wanted to let you know that Michael Reardon has hired me."

"To do what?"

"Find out who killed his father."

The line was quiet for a moment. "You're kidding."

"Nope." A bike rider weaved in and out of the cars ahead of her. Fina liked the idea of sharing the road in theory, but in practice, she wished her car were outfitted like a trash truck that lifted and overturned dumpsters. With the push of one button, pesky cyclists would be cleared from her path, easy peasy.

"Isn't there a conflict of interest with Renata Sanchez?"

"I finished my work for her."

"Pitney warned you to stay out of it."

"She can't actually tell me what jobs to take. That would be, you know, against the law."

"And you expect me to tell her this?"

"No, I'm happy to tell her; I just wanted to tell you first."

"Good luck with that phone call."

"Thank you!"

Fina was relieved to get Pitney's voice mail; she had every right to take the case, but nobody liked being chewed out. She'd just finished a chatty message describing her excitement at the prospect of working together when she arrived at the Reardon homestead.

The Reardons lived on Commonwealth Avenue between Fairfield and Gloucester, in one of the most expensive properties in the city. Their ten-bedroom, eighteen-bath mansion left little doubt of Hank's net worth.

When someone was murdered, the victim's spouse was always the go-to suspect, but this was even truer when there was a lot of money involved. And when it came to Hank Reardon, "a lot" was a drastic understatement.

Fina squeezed her Impala into a parking space and climbed the wide steps to the front door. If Mrs. Reardon had been closer in age to her husband, Fina might have worn a more conservative outfit, but they were the same age; looking like her peer, in a casual dress and wedge sandals, could only be a good thing.

Fina used the knocker, which was the size of a dinner plate, and waited for the large wooden doors to swing open. She was given the once-over by a fifty-something woman in a maid's outfit.

"Hi. I'm here to see Danielle. Michael, her stepson, asked me to stop by."

"And you are . . ."

"Here to see Danielle," Fina repeated.

"I mean, do you have some ID?"

Fina pulled her PI license from her bag and handed it over. The maid studied it and then closed the front door, leaving Fina on the stoop.

After five minutes, Fina sat down on the top step and fiddled with her phone. Under normal circumstances, she might worry that her ID was lost forever, but in a fifteen-thousand-square-foot house, it took considerable time to get from one place to another. She was in the middle of sending Haley a text when, five minutes later, she heard the door open behind her.

"Mrs. Reardon will see you now."

"One sec." Fina held a finger over her head. "I just need to finish this text." Fina made the missive newsier than necessary while the maid sighed loudly.

"Sorry to keep you waiting," Fina said with a smile as she hopped up and dropped her phone into her bag. The maid scowled, and Fina followed her inside.

"Wow," Fina said as she stepped over the threshold. The foyer was enormous and dominated by a dark wooden staircase that loomed two stories and featured an elaborately carved banister. The doors and windows were outlined with equally detailed molding, and polished wooden floors peeked out from underneath a twenty-by-twenty Oriental rug. "They don't make them like they used to."

"No, they don't," the maid agreed. She straightened up, and the corners of her mouth curved into a slight smile. Her workplace was a showplace; no wonder she felt proud. "This way." She beckoned Fina down the hallway to the right, where they stopped in front of a large wooden door. Fina heard a whirring sound behind it. After a moment, the maid pulled open the door, and the modern elevator doors behind it yawned open.

"Mrs. Reardon is in her studio on the top floor."

They stepped into the mirrored car, and the maid pressed the button marked 5. They rode in silence and emerged into what felt like a completely different house. A small passageway led to a large open space flooded with sunlight, which reflected off the white walls and white-painted floorboards. Skylights loomed overhead, and from the other windows Fina could see green and the Prudential Building. The rest of the urban detritus was hidden from view, leaving only an edited, visually appealing slice of Boston.

"Mrs. Reardon?" the maid called out across the canvases and easels that littered the space. "I've brought a visitor." She started across the room; Fina followed. They picked their way through drop cloths and canvases to a seating area by a window. There was an overstuffed sofa and a scratched coffee table. A couple of large wooden tables were covered in photos, clay, and other sculpting equipment. According to Fina's digging, Danielle had been a fine arts major in college and had met her husband while working at one of the tony galleries on Newbury Street. The rumor was that she was actually a talented artist.

The maid looked around. "Well, she was here." She walked back toward the elevator and picked up a wall-mounted phone.

"She's in the nursery," she said after a moment.

They took the elevator to the third floor and padded down a long hallway with high ceilings and intricate picture moldings. The maid knocked on the frame of an open door.

"Mrs. Reardon? The visitor." She made Fina sound like an alien.

Everything about the room, including the occupant, was camera-ready. Danielle Reardon was wearing a pair of dark-wash skinny jeans and a fitted white T-shirt, showing no signs of extra postpartum pounds. Her long blond hair was pulled back in a smooth, shiny ponytail. Her tan offset a star-shaped diamond pendant that dipped close to her firm cleavage, and on her ring finger she sported the walnut-sized engagement diamond and chunky diamond band that Marnie had gaped at during the meeting with Jules.

The room was bigger than most studio apartments and shared the same high ceilings and elaborate moldings as the rest of the house. Two floor-to-ceiling windows were covered by sheers and framed by heavy drapes and valances. Everything was decorated in shades of pink, including a sleigh crib with a canopy that dominated the room. There were also a changing table, armoire, couch, and rocking chair, but no photos, books, or pictures that Fina could see. It seemed ridiculously over the top. Didn't babies just need a drawer to sleep in and a diaper to poop in?

They listened as the maid shuffled out, and Fina walked over to Danielle. "Fina Ludlow. We met at Jules Lindsley's office." She offered her hand but was rebuffed by Danielle, who held up paint-stained hands.

"I would, but I don't want to get this on you." Her palms were spotted with green paint. "Just making some changes," she said, gesturing to a wall mural depicting the Public Garden and the Swan Boats. It was incredibly detailed, and the rich browns and greens popped out from the pink background. Fina took a step and examined it more closely. She pointed at a trail of ducklings behind a larger duck.

"Jack, Kack, Lack, Mack, Nack, Ouack, Pack, and Quack?" Fina asked.

Danielle rolled her eyes. "Obviously you grew up around here. You people are obsessed with that book."

"You didn't read it growing up? It's a classic." Fina's nephews still loved to hear *Make Way for Ducklings*, and a pilgrimage to the Public Garden and the Swan Boats was a rite of passage for Boston-area kids.

"Not that I remember, but I'm from Southern California; we were playing on the beach, not sitting inside, reading books," she said with a smidgen of bitchiness.

"You painted this?" Fina asked.

"Yup," Danielle responded wearily. "Not my usual work, and it's not like Aubrey appreciates it." Aubrey was Danielle and Hank's daughter, not exactly an art critic at three months old.

"It's amazing."

Danielle wiped her hand on a rag. "So Michael sent you, right?"

"That's right." Fina nodded. "He wants me to investigate your husband's death."

Danielle walked over to the velvet-covered couch and sat down. "Have a seat."

Fina sat at the other end of the sofa. "Congrats on your baby," Fina said.

"Thank you." Danielle smiled briefly. "She's taking a nap right now." The young Mrs. Reardon was making the standard hostess noises, but conveying little warmth.

"I'm sorry about your husband's death," Fina said.

"Thank you." She studied her hands. "I still can't quite believe it."

"That's a common reaction. It will take a while to sink in."

Danielle twisted the gigantic diamond on her finger. "I don't under-stand why Michael hired you. Your family's firm was going after Hank."

"Well, initially, we didn't know it was Hank we were 'going after.'" Fina made air quotes. "We were just looking for the donor."

A sour look crept onto Danielle's face. "Isn't there some kind of con-flict of interest?"

"No. We're not working for Renata Sanchez anymore, and Michael seems okay with it." The current relationship with Renata was unclear, but Fina couldn't worry about that right now.

"And Michael doesn't trust the cops," Danielle noted.

"Apparently not."

"No offense to you, but the cops are going to be all over this. We're talking about Hank, not some homeless guy." Her voice cracked, and she sniffled. Fina pulled a pack of tissues from her bag and offered it to her.

"Can you tell me who would want to hurt your husband?" Fina asked.

"You mean other than those women and their children?" Danielle dabbed at her nose.

"The cryokids? I'm not sure your husband is worth more to them dead than alive."

"Maybe not, but I wouldn't put anything past Renata Sanchez and her daughter."

"Anyone else you can think of who had it in for Hank?"

Danielle looked around the room. "Hank made his share of enemies in business. He was developing some land on the waterfront; maybe someone was upset about that."

"Dimitri Kask didn't mention that when I spoke with him."

"He wasn't part of the deal."

"By choice?"

"I have no idea. I didn't meddle in my husband's business."

"Of course not." Fina looked at the changing table, where a tiny dress covered in ruffles was laid out. Next to it sat a pair of pink tights that looked appropriate for a Lilliputian ballerina. "So you guys were okay?"

"Who? Me and Hank?"

Fina nodded.

"I don't see how that's your business."

"The cops haven't asked you that?"

"Of course they have, and that's bad enough. Now I'm paying for you to ask me these questions?"

"Actually, Michael is paying me."

"Same thing."

Fina shook her head slowly. "Not really. Maybe you should take this up with Michael. I have to ask questions in order to investigate Hank's death."

Danielle leaned her head against the back of the couch and closed her eyes. "I'm so tired, but when I try to sleep, all I can think about is Hank."

"Have you tried taking something?"

"Nah. I don't like feeling out of it."

There was a light tap on the door, and an older woman wearing a drab-colored dress stood in the threshold.

"Mrs. Reardon, the woman is here."

Danielle looked annoyed. "The woman?"

"You know, to discuss the breathing technique." She examined her shoes. "We've already rescheduled two times."

Color started to creep up Danielle's neck. "I'll be down in a few minutes," Danielle replied impatiently.

The older woman left, and Fina looked at Danielle. "Are you sure you're okay? Is that a yoga thing?"

Danielle pressed her lips into a thin line. "Yes. It's silly, but it helps with stress."

"Of course. Sorry."

"I need to go, so if you could see yourself out . . ."

"Right. I imagine I'll have more questions for you." Fina stood and reached into her bag. She pulled out her card and handed it to Danielle, who slipped it into the pocket of her jeans. Fina started toward the door. "Let me know if I can help in any way."

Danielle shook her head slowly. "We're beyond help," she said, almost to herself.

Fina walked down the hallway to the elevator, which arrived after a minute's wait.

Her job always reminded her that you couldn't buy happiness.

"How about some dim sum?" Stacy D'Ambruzzi asked Fina when she slid into a booth at the Golden Pagoda restaurant in Chinatown. She pointed with her chopsticks. "Help yourself."

"I don't know." Fina eyed the bamboo dishes littering the table. "It all seems like gelatinous sacs of goo to me."

"Fina! Shame on you. Here. Try some of these." Stacy used her chopsticks and placed two dumplings on Fina's plate. "You're not allergic to shrimp, are you?"

"No." Fina picked one up with her chopsticks and dipped it in a shallow dish of soy sauce.

"Well?" Stacy asked, popping a pot sticker into her mouth.

Fina chewed. "It's pretty good."

"So, what do you need?"

Stacy was a senior tech in the medical examiner's office and a good source of information. The Ludlows had provided her brother with legal representation in the past, and Fina had established a friendly quid pro quo with Stacy.

"What can you tell me about Hank Reardon's autopsy?"

A short woman wheeled a cart up to their table and took the tops off of the bamboo dishes to give Stacy a peek. Stacy pointed at two, which were deposited on the table. The woman scrawled something on the bill and left it behind.

"There's not much to tell beyond what was released to the public. Death resulting from blunt force trauma. Pretty standard."

Stacy was in her midforties and had spent most of her career in the ME's office. Her physical appearance—hair shorn close to her skull, a plethora of tattoos, and a collection of small hoops and studs in her earlobes—belied her inner softie. Fina was convinced it was this very quality that made her so good at her job. She didn't look at patients as slabs of meat, but instead tried to honor their humanity by treating their earthly bodies with respect.

"Any idea what the weapon was?"

"Small and heavy, like a mallet or a hammer."

Fina grasped a pot sticker with her chopsticks and dipped it into the soy sauce. The center was flavorful pork. She'd always assumed good dim sum was an oxymoron, but maybe she was wrong. She'd have to report her breakthrough to Milloy. He was half Chinese and found her aversion to dim sum maddening.

"Was he in good health other than that?" she asked.

"Very. He obviously took care of himself and had regular physicals. I'm sure he had to for insurance."

High-flying CEOs were usually required to undergo annual physicals for insurance purposes. Insurance companies wanted to protect their investments, and preventive care was a big piece of that. Too bad they didn't feel that way about the rest of their customers.

"What about prints, fibers? Any of that good stuff?"

"You know I'm not really privy to that."

"I know. Thought I'd ask anyway."

"Phoenix claw?" Stacy held up a scraggly-looking item.

"What is that?"

"A chicken's foot."

"Aaaand you lost me."

"It's delicious." Stacy widened her bright blue eyes. "Just try one."

"Look at the nails on that thing. I'm not interested in eating any-thing with which I can pick my teeth after the meal."

"You're missing out," Stacy said, gnawing on the scrawny toes.

"It's all yours. How's your brother?" Fina reached into her bag and pulled out a twenty.

"Staying out of trouble, for now."

"If he gets into it again, call me. Anytime." She put the money on the table and rose to leave.

Stacy looked at the twenty. "That's too much."

"I'm sure I owe you more than that," Fina said. "And if you hear anything . . ." She reached over and gave Stacy a hug good-bye.

Fina returned to her car. She needed to think about the why of Hank's death, not just the how. Means alone didn't translate to murder, but motive and means combined usually had disastrous results.

9

Fina listened to her messages, ignoring the annoying check-in from Carl, and found that Risa had called just ten minutes before. Since Fina was heading to the MetroWest area anyway, she decided to swing by her house rather than call. Plus, Risa was an amazing cook, and there was usually a tasty treat on offer.

The Paquettes' house was a three-story gingerbread Victorian in Newton that boasted a deep front porch. The untrained eye might not detect that the large addition off the back of the house wasn't part of the original structure since it featured the same intricate design. The fancy shingles were painted in a scheme of deep Bordeaux, two hues of mossy green, and white, which looked striking and expensive.

Fina rang the bell, and the door was thrown open by Risa's twelve-year-old son.

"Hi, Jordan. Is your mom home?"

"She's in the kitchen. Mom, Fina's here!" He rushed up the stairs, and Fina walked toward the back of the house. One of the features of the addition had been the expansion of the kitchen to incorporate a large family room and eating area. A granite island and a six-burner stove were command central, and the walls echoed the mossy green found on the exterior of the house. The space was warmed up by earth-tone tiles and brightened by white clapboard cabinets.

Risa was in her midforties and trim, with a quick smile and hazel eyes. Her hair was ashy brown and worn in a style that called to mind Princess Diana's look in later years. It looked breezy and simple, but probably required a lot of upkeep.

Sitting at the breakfast bar with a glass of iced tea, she looked up from a magazine when Fina walked in.

"Hi." Risa was surprised to see her. "I didn't expect you to stop by. You could have called."

"I know, but I have things to do out here. I thought it would be better to catch up in person."

"Do you want some iced tea?" Risa asked, and slipped off her stool. "And no, I don't have diet soda, so don't bother asking."

"Tea would be lovely." She perched on a stool and watched Risa fill a glass with ice and pour the amber-colored liquid.

"How's Haley?" Risa asked.

"She's okay," Fina said, and took the glass.

"I took her shopping, and I thought I might offer to take her to the movies one of these days. Do you think she'd like that?"

"I think it would be great for her. Why don't you run it by Patty? She's the teenager whisperer these days."

"I will," Risa said, and sat back down. She sipped her tea.

Since Melanie had been her best friend, Risa felt a sense of responsibility toward Haley, but Haley had never been the warm, fuzzy type, even before Melanie's death. She wasn't the easiest child to mother.

"So, in your message you said you needed my advice about something," Fina said.

Risa rotated her glass on the granite countertop. Fina waited. Silence was one of the most powerful tools in her arsenal.

"Yes, but I'd like to keep it between the two of us."

"Of course."

"Which means I don't want the rest of your family to know."

Fina grinned. "I am aware of what 'between the two of us' means. I promise I won't discuss it with my family. I'm good at keeping secrets."

Risa studied her short, buffed nails and took a deep breath. "I don't know why I'm nervous. I mean, it's not a big deal, and it's just you."

"It is just me. Think of it this way—there's nothing you can tell me that I haven't already heard in one form or another. I'm essentially unshockable."

"Okay." Risa looked around as if ensuring the kids weren't within earshot. She took a deep breath. "Well, you probably don't know that I was adopted."

Fina had a swig of tea. "I did not know that." What was it with her and babies these days? She was fast becoming the Dr. Spock of private investigation.

"I told Melanie, but she promised not to say anything. It's not a big deal, just, it's private."

"I understand."

"Nowadays, people talk about everything, but that wasn't the case when I was growing up. There was a lot of secrecy and shame associated with adoption forty-some years ago."

"Sure."

"The only people who know are Marty and Melanie." Marty was Risa's husband, a sweet, reliable bore.

"Your kids don't know?"

"No, I didn't really see the point. They're so close with my mom and dad. Why complicate things?"

"So what's changed?"

Risa slipped off her seat once more and walked over to the stove. She pulled plastic wrap off a deep plate and held it up to Fina. "Would you like a piece of ginger-peach galette?"

"What took you so long to ask?" Clearly it was a stall tactic, but any stall tactic that involved Risa's cooking was welcome.

Risa pulled plates from an upper cabinet, doled out two pieces, and handed Fina a plate and fork. She sat back down.

"I got a letter from a woman claiming she's my birth mother's sister, my aunt."

Fina took a bite of the galette. The peaches were firm but deeply flavorful, and the crust was rich with butter.

"You've never heard from your birth parents or their families before?"

"No, and I've never had any interest in finding them. I know some adoptees are dying to know, but I never felt like anything was missing."

Fina pressed her fork down into a slice of peach. "So how do you feel about this?"

Risa studied the kitchen cabinets, a look of consternation on her face. "I don't know. Confused. Curious. Want to run in the other direction and ignore the whole thing." She smiled.

"I don't think those are unusual responses," Fina said. "I've worked adoption cases before, and they usually bring up a lot of . . . stuff."

Risa picked at her galette. Fina's plate was nearly empty.

"What do you need from me?" Fina asked.

"I need you to verify that she is who she says she is."

"Does she have any documentation?"

"She claims she does, but how hard would it be to doctor something like a birth certificate, especially one from forty-five years ago?"

"Not that hard. Do you want to have a relationship with this woman or just verify her identity?"

Risa put a small bite of galette into her mouth. She chewed thoughtfully. "I don't know, but I definitely don't want to get invested unless it's legitimate. You hear about people being cheated out of money, and I'm not naïve, but when someone claims that they're your blood relative . . ."

"It's complicated. I understand."

"So, obviously, I want to hire you. Officially."

"I'm happy to do the work, but you don't have to hire me."

"But I want this to be a real case, not just something you fit in on the side."

"I will treat it as a real case regardless, but why don't we do this: You give me the information this woman has sent you, and I'll make some preliminary inquiries. If it ends up being especially time-consuming, then we can discuss a retainer."

"Okay. If you're sure."

"I am, but I insist you pay me in food in the meantime." Fina smiled.

"Like you've ever gone hungry at my house."

"True. You do know the way to a girl's heart. This is delicious, by the way."

"Thanks. I'm trying to enjoy peaches while they last. Let me get the info for you."

Risa left the room, and Fina took the opportunity to run her finger across her plate and lick the sweet crumbs off. She liked to maintain some modicum of manners in front of others.

"This is it," Risa said, handing Fina a plain white envelope.

Risa's name and address were handwritten on the front in a heavily slanted cursive, and the postmark was from Portland, Maine. Fina turned the envelope over, but there was no return address.

"And here is a copy of my birth certificate. The adoption version."

"Great. This gives me a place to start." Fina looked at the document. It stated Risa's name, the names of her adoptive parents, and her birthdate of July 17, 1966, at 3:43 A.M. in Rockford, Maine.

Fina tucked the items into her bag and followed Risa to the front door. "What about your biological mother? Did this alleged aunt say anything about her?"

Risa shook her head. "Nope. She said she'll tell me more when we meet in person."

Fina nodded. "I'm on it, and I'll treat it with the utmost discretion."

"Thank you, Fina."

"I'm happy to help."

Fina was climbing into her car when she saw a man down the street, seemingly tying his shoe. He was taking a rather long time to do it, so she started walking in his direction. He popped up from the sidewalk and broke into a jog in the opposite direction—which would have been fine if he hadn't been wearing jeans and slip-on Merrells. She couldn't be sure it was the man from the park, but it made her antennae quiver.

"Oh, no. The angel of death." Frank chortled as Fina took a seat on the couch in the Gillis's living room. Frank was in his recliner, his nightly bowl of vanilla ice cream in his lap. He muted the Red Sox game and looked at her.

"Very funny. *I* didn't kill him." She stretched her legs out in front of her. "In a related issue, I just got a weird feeling."

"If it involves a man, I don't want to know."

"It does involve a man, but not in the way you think."

Frank gestured with his spoon for her to continue.

"I think some guy is following me. I was over at Risa's, and he was hanging around outside. Tying his shoe."

"Did you inquire about his business?"

"Started to, but he took off."

"What makes you so sure he's interested in you? Maybe he was just out for a walk and needed to tie his shoe."

"And ran away when I went toward him?"

"You do scare some people," Frank murmured, grinning. "So what's your next move?"

"Hmm." She tilted her head from side to side. "I think I'll proceed with caution. Is that the right answer?"

"Someone taught you well, my dear."

"The best. When's Peg getting back from her book group?"

"You mean 'Masochists Monthly'? Who knew there were so many books about female genital mutilation and wasting diseases?"

Fina laughed.

"I expect her home in about a half hour."

"I'll stick around, if that's okay."

"There's diet soda in the fridge and ice cream in the freezer. Help yourself."

Fina got a drink and watched the rest of the game with Frank. She glanced at him occasionally. Her father and Frank were close in age, but sadly, the similarities ended there.

Fina was at Milloy's licking guacamole off her fingers. It was late, and they were sprawled on his couch, snacking and watching a reality dating show that made celibacy look appealing.

Her phone rang. "Yes, Renata?" She really wasn't in the mood.

"I don't suppose Rosie has been in touch with you," Renata said.

"With me? No." Fina reached for a napkin and cleaned off her hands. "What's going on?"

"It's nothing."

"Renata, wait!" Fina struggled up from the couch and walked into the kitchen. "Is everything okay?"

"No, everything isn't okay," Renata snapped at her. "I can't find Rosie."

"I know you don't want to hear this, but calm down."

"You're right. I don't."

"Start from the beginning. When did you last see her?" Milloy wandered into the kitchen and raised his eyebrows in question. Fina shrugged and watched him open a Corona. He held the bottle up to her, but she shook her head. Something was telling her she was suddenly on duty.

"As you know, she was annoyed with me on Monday night so she went to stay with her friend Laura. She didn't come home last night either; I assumed she was still pissed, but when I called Laura earlier today, she said Rosie had left her house on Monday night, and she hasn't seen her since."

"So she didn't stay with Laura on Monday night?"

"No, and she didn't stay with her last night." Fina could hear panic rising in Renata's voice.

"I assume you've tried calling her."

"Of course. She's not answering."

"Did you contact the shelter?"

"I just spoke to one of her coworkers. She says that Rosie didn't go to work Tuesday or today. She called in sick both days."

Fina dug a speck of avocado from under her nail. "So she blew off work. Sounds like she's playing hooky."

"Where? I've been calling her all day, and her phone just goes to voice mail. None of her friends have heard from her."

"Does she have a boyfriend?"

"She hangs out with a guy from the animal shelter. That's how she describes it, at least, but he says he hasn't heard from her."

"Renata, she's seventeen years old and has a lot to deal with right now. She's probably lying low with a friend, blowing off steam somewhere."

"Maybe, but it looks bad."

Fina looked at her reflection in the kitchen window. She looked good. Not a day over thirty. "What do you mean?"

"I mean it looks suspicious."

"What are you getting at, Renata? Are you worried that Rosie killed Hank Reardon?"

"Of course not, but I'm worried the police will think that."

"Have you spoken to the cops about this?"

"No, I didn't want to draw attention to her absence."

Fina walked back into the living room and perched on the arm of the couch. "What would you like me to do exactly?"

"Find her."

Fina thought for a moment.

"I know I fired you, but you're rehired," Renata said.

"I'm not worried about that. We can figure that out later." Carl wouldn't like such a loosey-goosey work arrangement, but when it came to a missing kid, Fina could be flexible. "E-mail me a list of her friends, including the boyfriend, and include any addresses you have, not just cell and e-mail info."

"Fine. I'll do it now."

"And we need to tell the cops. Aside from the benefit of their resources, not reporting a missing person looks extremely suspicious."

"But they'll read all sorts of things into it."

"Of course they will; that's what they do!"

"But she's my child, and I have to protect her."

Fina held the phone away from her ear and took a deep breath. Renata's maternal instincts were wildly inconsistent. "I have to tell them.
Just get me that list."

Fina ended the call and sat back down on the couch. Milloy muted
the TV, and she reached over and grabbed a handful of tortilla chips.

"Who's missing now?"

"Rosie, Renata's teenage daughter."

"She one of the cryokids?"

"Yup. I think Renata's more worried about the timing than her disappearance." Fina popped some chips in her mouth. "She thinks it
looks suspicious with Hank's death."

"You don't?"

"Yeah, but she's a teenager. You can't read too much into their behavior. I think they should all be sent to an adolescent leper colony
until their brains are fully developed."

"That seems like an excellent strategy." Milloy sipped his beer. "Do
you need some help?"

"Nah, not yet." Fina dipped her finger in the bowl of guacamole and
ate it.

"That's what chips are for, you know."

"Milloy, we have biblical knowledge of each other. Are you seriously
suggesting this is too intimate?"

"Not too intimate. Too gross."

She gave him a kiss on the cheek and grabbed her phone and bag.
"Bye."

Out on the street, she dialed Cristian's number, and he graciously
agreed to a drop-by.

. . .

Cristian was sitting on the front stoop of his building when Fina pulled up fifteen minutes later.

"Ah, okay. I guess you want to go for a drive," she said as he climbed into the car.

"Just a quick errand," he said.

"Okay. Where am I going?"

"Medford."

Fina pulled into traffic. "Why?" She knew that Cristian's ex, Marissa, lived there.

"Just drive. So what's up?"

"Renata Sanchez called me because she can't find her daughter Rosie. She's one of Hank's cryokids."

"I know who she is. I've been sorting through that gnarled family tree all day."

"Anywho . . . Rosie is MIA."

"Why are *you* telling me this and not Renata?"

"She's worried that Rosie's disappearing act looks suspicious given the timing."

"It does. Has she done this before? Taken off?"

"Not to my knowledge, but she's seriously pissed at her mom right now." They stopped at a light, and a car full of teenagers pulled up next to them. Music was blaring, and they were laughing.

"Do you think she might be in danger?" Cristian asked.

"I'm not too worried."

"Well, you know the drill. File a report."

"I will, but I wanted to let you know off the record. Don't you guys want to interview her?"

"Yes, but we've had our hands full with the immediate family. Take a right up here."

Cristian directed her to a neighborhood of small single-family houses. "It's the white one, so drive by and find a spot."

Fina followed his directions.

"Can you turn around so we can see the house?" Cristian asked.

"Yeah, yeah, Detective Bossy. What are we doing here?"

"Just checking things out."

They sat in silence and studied the house. It was a Cape Cod with dormers in the sloping roof and a small yard in front. A light was on in the bay window of what Fina assumed was the living room. One of the upstairs windows was illuminated.

"So her boyfriend's here," Fina noted. "So what?"

"How do you know he's here?" Cristian asked.

"That's his car." Fina pointed at a Toyota Camry parked in front of the house. "You asked me to run a background check. I'm a detective, too, you know."

He ignored her.

"Cristian, this is borderline creepy."

"I'm trying to figure out if he's staying over."

"How long have they been dating?" Fina looked at his handsome profile.

"Two months."

"Of course he's staying over. What do you think this is? Nineteen-fifty?"

"No, but not everyone is as horny as you are."

"Is that a complaint? And I'm not horny. I'm results-oriented."

"Well, Marissa isn't like you."

Fina leaned her head back against the headrest. "Just because she's the mother of your child doesn't make her a saint. She's a grown woman. Let her have sex, already."

"It's part of our custody agreement. She's not supposed to have people stay the night."

"I thought you were over her."

"I am."

"Then why do you care who she sleeps with?"

"I don't, but we're talking about my kid."

Fina looked at him. She knew that Cristian was motivated by his love for Matteo, but she also wondered if a tiny part of him was jealous of the new boyfriend.

"You need a hobby. Nothing good can come from this pursuit."

Cristian watched the house. "Fine."

Fina started the car and wound her way back through the residential streets. "Want to get a drink?"

"I can't. I've gotta get some sleep and head back in to the station. There's a lot of heat on us with the Reardon case."

They rode in silence.

Ten minutes later, Fina pulled up to Cristian's building. "Look, if you want me to run surveillance on the guy and document if he's staying over, I'm happy to. No charge," she offered.

Cristian climbed out and slammed the door. He leaned in through the open window. "I'll think about it."

"If you hear from Rosie Sanchez, would you let me know?" Fina asked.

"If you'll do the same."

"Deal."

Fina watched him unlock the front door of his building and disappear down a hallway.

Worrying about everyone else's children was wearing her out, and it was too late to contact Rosie's friends now. Instead, Fina went back to Nanny's and took a long hot shower.

As she lay in bed, she couldn't help but think about Hank. She couldn't ignore the sense of responsibility that was nagging at her. Maybe his death was unrelated to his sperm donation, but there was no denying that Fina was more than a casual observer. Usually, she assuaged any bad feelings she had about a case by reminding herself that she didn't cause issues, she just uncovered them. But there was no denying that she had helped alter the course of a stream, and Hank's murder had turned into a deluge.

10

Juliana Reardon, the old Mrs. Reardon, lived in a house on the ocean twelve miles north of the city. Fina had enjoyed the occasional meal in Swampscott, and another case had brought her there, so she was somewhat familiar with the setting. Its spot on the Atlantic offered prime real estate for those who could afford it, and as she wound through the streets, Fina saw variations on her parents' ginormous house, although these had more to recommend them architecturally. Like an actual style.

From the outside, Juliana's house looked generous but unassuming. It was a single story with a two-car garage and attractive landscaping. Fina took a moment to breathe in the ocean air before ringing the bell.

The door swung open, and an attractive woman of indeterminate age faced Fina. She knew from the files that Juliana Reardon was fifty-seven years old, but she never would have guessed from her appearance. She had short-cropped hair that was blond with a few hints of silver. Her skin was tan but taut, and her impressive muscles were on display in bike shorts and a fitted tank top that showed a stripe of stomach.

"Juliana Reardon?" Fina said.

She started to close the door. "I have no comment."

"No, wait." Fina stuck her foot over the threshold. "Michael hired me. I'm Fina Ludlow, the private investigator."

Juliana peered around her to see if she was alone.

"He's hired me to investigate Hank's death." Fina pulled her foot back.

Juliana nodded. "Of course. Come in."

Fina stepped over the threshold and was met by a stunning view of a sandy beach and the ocean behind it. She sometimes forgot that Massachusetts had sandy beaches, having been raised on a steady diet of pools and the occasional trip to a pebble-coated public beach. Floor-to-ceiling windows dominated the living room, which was furnished in a shabby-chic style. Two deep couches surrounded a fireplace, and the room led onto an open kitchen with quartz countertops, glossy white cabinets, and a professional-grade wok embedded in the cooktop.

"I hope you don't mind," Juliana said. "I was just fixing a late breakfast. I don't eat until after my training ride."

"I should apologize for not calling ahead," Fina said, not really sorry at all. Although common courtesy dictated that she should schedule appointments to see people, Fina was a big fan of the drop-by. First, people were flustered by a surprise visit and didn't have time to get their ducks in a row, and second, they could usually squeeze you in if you magically appeared on their doorstep.

"Have you eaten? There's plenty for both of us."

Fina looked at the ingredients gathered on the counter. Most of it looked dark green and leafy.

"Sure. That would be great."

How bad could it be? She'd endured worse in the name of detecting, like admiring a creepy ceramic clown collection for half an hour.

Juliana nodded toward a chair at the breakfast bar, and Fina took a seat. She watched as her hostess loaded the roughage into a shiny chrome contraption that looked part blender, part Mars rover.

"So what is all that stuff?" Fina asked.

"Spinach, kale, chard, flaxseed, beets, apples, and my secret protein powder."

The machine whirred to life, and Fina watched the ingredients rush by in a tornado of roots, seeds, and powder. Juliana poured the concoction into two tall glasses, and Fina followed her outside to the deck, where they sat at a table underneath a wide umbrella.

"To your health," Juliana said, and tapped her glass against Fina's. She took a long drink and smacked her lips in satisfaction. "Delicious." Juliana smiled at her. "Don't be scared. It won't hurt you."

"That obvious?" Fina said, and took a drink from the glass. It tasted like she imagined the clippings from a lawn mower might.

"It's a bit of an acquired taste," Juliana admitted, "but it's so good for you."

"I bet. It tastes very . . . earthy."

Juliana laughed. "Don't feel you have to finish it."

"No, no. I'm curious. You're obviously doing something right. You look fantastic."

Juliana grinned slyly. "For my age. Isn't that what you mean?"

"No, you look fantastic for any age. You're in better shape than most twenty-year-olds."

Juliana took another swig and leaned back in her chair. "So, you want to talk about Hank."

"Yes."

"I'll be honest; I don't understand why Michael has hired you. I'm sure the police are highly motivated, given Hank's status in the community."

"I told him the same thing, but he was insistent on having a third party investigate."

"I think that's his father's influence—throwing money at the problem when in doubt." Juliana looked at the ocean.

"I'm sorry. This must be difficult for you," Fina said.

"I'm very sad about Hank's death, but more for Michael than me."

She looked at Fina. "And I'm sorry for the world's sake; Hank was brilliant. Who knows what he might have done with the rest of his life?"

"How long have you two been divorced?"

"We've been divorced five years, and we were married for twenty-four. I assume you've met Danielle."

"I have."

A small smile crept onto Juliana's face.

"Do you have an opinion about the second Mrs. Reardon?" Fina asked.

"Well, I was certainly annoyed that Hank was acting out a cliché, and it put Michael in a weird position, having such a young stepmother."

"He seems okay with it."

"I think he's gotten used to it, and there is a twisted cachet having an attractive stepmother practically your own age."

"And the money? Is Danielle taking what's yours?"

Juliana's eyes widened. "You don't beat around the bush, do you?"

"It didn't strike me as necessary." Fina took a swig of the shake.

"You're right. It's not. Obviously, I did okay in the divorce, not that I asked for much, relatively speaking."

Fina raised an eyebrow.

"Oh, I could have bought the whole block, Fina—may I call you Fina?"

Fina nodded.

"I could have bought the whole block, if I'd taken what Hank had to give, but my days in the world of grotesque wealth are long gone." Juliana drained her drink. "That's part of the reason we split up."

"Too much money? That's a first."

"Once you've got ten million in the bank, how much more do you really need? Hank thought you could never have too much, but all you have to do is go to other countries—or even certain neighborhoods in the city—to realize there is such a thing as too much."

"You're not exactly slumming," Fina said, pointing toward the wide sandy beach.

"Hardly. My point is that there's a wide spectrum, and I didn't want to live at the very end. I have a pampered life, but I give a lot to charity, and I'm involved in causes in a way we never were as a couple."

"So you're not just writing checks."

"Nope. I'm trying to join the human race, as opposed to watching it from a luxury box."

"You're still active in causes associated with the Reardon name even though you're divorced?"

Juliana looked affronted. "It's my name, too. She doesn't get to take that from me."

"I wasn't suggesting that, but just like friends get split during a divorce, I assume the causes do as well. Unless you had the most amicable split in the history of mankind and work alongside your ex and his wife."

"You're right," Juliana conceded. "We did split the charities, or rather, I've kept the ones that are most important to me."

"Which are?" Fina continued drinking her protein shake, noticing that the residue of it clung to the side of the glass. She could only imagine what it was doing to her organs.

"I'm most involved with an orphanage in India and the Reardon Breast Cancer Center for Reflection and Rejuvenation."

"I'm familiar with the center. It's in Cambridge, right?"

"Yes. It's a wonderful organization, and we serve an extremely diverse population. We're focused on the spiritual component of surviving cancer."

"Which means what?"

"Alternative therapies and mental practices that support traditional medicine. We don't recommend patients forgo their chemotherapy or anything like that, but things like good nutrition, meditation, stress reduction, they can all play a part in recovery."

"It sounds interesting."

"It is. You should visit the center sometime. I think you would find it eye-opening."

"Is Michael worried about his inheritance? In terms of Danielle, I mean."

Juliana seemed surprised by the change in subject, but recovered quickly. "I think he's appropriately concerned. He likes Danielle, but on paper, she certainly fits the profile of a gold digger, and now with Aubrey and these other children emerging . . ."

"What do you think about that?"

"I think it's just like Hank to create a big mess from what was probably a brief period of impulsivity. And I feel bad for my son," Juliana added. "He didn't sign up for this."

Fina steeled herself to finish her shake. Blech. "Any idea who might have killed him?"

Juliana was silent for a moment and gazed down at the beach. A couple of kids were trying to launch a kite, but the wind wasn't cooperating. Kite-flying was one of those activities that Fina never really understood; say you finally got it airborne, then what?

"Hank wasn't overly concerned with people's feelings, and he played in the big leagues, but killing him is a whole other thing." She looked at Fina. "I couldn't hazard a guess."

Juliana carried the empty glasses into the kitchen and walked Fina toward the door. The walls in the living room featured large photographs that were riots of color. Women in saris, heaps of spices, and dark-skinned children with bright white teeth were the subject matter.

"Are those from India?" Fina asked.

"Yes. I go every year. Have you ever been?"

"No."

"It's an amazing place. Very spiritual. My travels in India really set my life on a different path."

Fina followed her to the front door. She gestured at a sleek bike in the foyer. "You bike?" she asked.

"Actually, I'm a triathlete, so swimming, biking, and running."

"That's impressive."

"You look like you're in shape," Juliana said. "You should try it."

"I run occasionally, but generally, I try to do as little as possible. I think that's the opposite of a triathlon."

"Try it," she cajoled. "You'll be hooked."

"It's really a cult, isn't it? You exercise junkies are always trying to recruit innocent souls."

Juliana laughed, and Fina handed her a business card. "If anything else comes to mind, don't hesitate to call."

"Sure."

Fina turned halfway down the stairs. "I hate to ask, but where were you the night Hank was killed?"

"Right here, in bed. All that training makes me sleep like a log."

Fina climbed into her car. She gazed in her rearview mirror and saw Juliana framed in the doorway. From that angle, it looked like she was holding up the house.

Fina drove from Swampscott back to the city, with a quick stop in Revere at Kelly's Roast Beef. Juliana's shake had left her on the full side, but thoroughly unsatisfied; nothing that some fried clams and French fries wouldn't cure. She sat in her car with the windows rolled down and watched the parade of humanity that meandered by. There were sunbathers of every age and shape enjoying the last gasp of summer. Small children fed the seagulls that loitered beneath one of the gaze-bos, much to the dismay of a group of old women gabbing on a bench. Teenage boys leered at girls in string bikinis who seemed to welcome the attention.

Fina dipped a clam in tartar sauce and pondered Hank and Juliana Reardon. Was their divorce really that amicable or was Juliana a terrific actress? Fina knew that she had experienced a spiritual awakening of sorts from her travels and charity work, but it was unusual for people to walk away from money. And it was especially unusual for first wives of wildly successful men to do so. Corporate wives often got little credit for the years of work they put in to further their husbands' careers. When the marriages fell apart, they wanted to be compensated for the time and effort they could never get back; they didn't want their generally younger replacements to reap all that they had sown. But maybe Juliana Reardon really was different. She had her causes, and there was no question that she led a full life. She wasn't sitting around pining for Hank and the way things used to be.

Fina stuffed her trash in the bag and started the car. An old man with drooping, leathery skin ambled by with a metal detector and a large pair of headphones. With his tiny Speedo, he wore more on his head than on his nether regions. Maybe he was European? It was the only possible explanation.

Fina went home to Nanny's and pulled out the letter that Risa had given her. Greta Samuels was the name of the alleged aunt, and she lived in Maine. She claimed that her older sister had given birth to Risa, but she didn't go into any details. Since Risa had never had the urge to find her birth parents, she hadn't done any research of her own, leaving Fina little to go on. She dialed Greta Samuels's number.

"Hello?" a voice answered after two rings. Her inflection rose on the word, as if it were a question, not a statement.

"I'm calling for Greta Samuels. Is she available?"

"This is Greta."

"My name is Fina Ludlow, and I'm an associate of Risa Paquette's."

There was a sharp intake of breath on the other end. "Oh goodness. Is Risa there?"

"I'm afraid not. I'm a friend of hers and a private investigator, and Risa has asked me to speak with you on her behalf."

"But why didn't she call me herself?"

"I'm sure you can understand her hesitation, Ms. Samuels. She hasn't heard from her birth family in forty-six years, and then one day she gets a letter from a woman claiming to be her aunt. Risa wanted to be cautious."

"Of course, I understand. I'm just so anxious to meet her."

"Do you have any documentation regarding her parentage? A copy of her birth certificate, maybe? Or perhaps your sister has something?"

There was a long pause. "Unfortunately, my sister has passed."

"Oh, I'm sorry to hear that. When was that?" Fina doodled on a notepad.

"Six months ago."

"And she didn't leave any paperwork that would be relevant?"

"I'm afraid not. My sister . . . well, she could be difficult."

Fina looked out the window toward Logan. There was a line of planes waiting at the end of the runway. From her vantage point, they were silent, silver birds, but up close, their power would be deafening.

Fina had a sister once. Her picture hung on Nanny's wall, her memory permanently wedged between Fina and her mother. Sisters could be difficult, and Fina hadn't even met hers.

"Hmm. I'm sorry, did you say you have some documentation?" Fina asked again.

"I'm sure I could dig something up."

"If you could e-mail it to me, that would be great."

"Well, I'm not very good with e-mail, but I have a friend who is. I could ask her to help."

"That would be great."

Fina hung up the phone with no more clarity about Greta Samuels and the veracity of her claim. She was left with a gnawing question, though: Why now? Why, six months after her sister died, was Greta suddenly interested in her long-lost niece?

. . .

Walter knew that Ellen would be only too happy to meet with the police, but there was no way he would let her represent the cryobank in
this instance. That's why he dismissed her from his office when the two
detectives were shown in by his assistant, Jenny. Ellen looked annoyed,
which pleased him. If she was irked, he must be doing something right.

"What can I do for you, Detectives?" he asked after dispatching
Jenny to fetch three cappuccinos.

"It's 'Lieutenant,' actually," the woman said, handing her badge to
Walter. "And this is Detective Menendez."

"I stand corrected." He smiled and handed back her ID. She didn't
fit his image of a policewoman, but that's because he was thinking of
the female cops on TV. They always wore dark-colored, figure-hugging
pantsuits, their guns snug against their waists. This Lieutenant Pitney
was short and slightly plump, with ample breasts. Her hair was a mass
of curls, and her outfit looked like wallpaper you'd find in a kindergar-
ten classroom. "What can I do for you?"

"I'm sure you're well aware that Hank Reardon died in the early
hours of Tuesday. We're interested in his relationship with the cryobank."

"'Relationship' makes it sound more involved than it was," Walter said. "He made donations here a long time ago. That was the extent
of it."

Walter gestured to Jenny, who hovered in the doorway with a tray.
She came in and left it on his desk. The detectives took their mugs, and
Walter watched as the lieutenant opened three packets of sweetener,
sprinkling them into the hot liquid. Detective Menendez sipped his
slowly without adding anything to it.

"When was that exactly?" Detective Menendez asked.

"I'd have to check the records." Walter stirred his coffee. "About
eighteen years ago."

"And since then he hasn't had any contact with the cryobank?" Pitney asked.

Walter considered the question. "I couldn't say."

"You can't say?" Pitney peered at him. "Or you don't know?"

"I don't know if he's been in touch. Our organization is quite large; I'm not privy to every conversation and every meeting."

"Of course not. We thought perhaps given the recent publicity that Mr. Reardon had been in touch."

Walter shook his head.

"Is it Heritage's policy to protect a donor's identity?" Detective Menendez asked.

This ping-ponging of questions was annoying and presumably designed to throw him off guard. It wouldn't work.

"Of course, unless the donor has agreed to an open donation, in which case any offspring can be in touch once they reach the age of eighteen."

"So Heritage didn't have anything to do with revealing Hank's identity?"

Walter sighed. "As I've said, we had nothing to do with Hank Reardon's situation."

"Except for the conception of all the kids," Pitney added.

"Yes, Lieutenant, except for that."

"How many kids did he father?" she asked.

"I couldn't tell you."

Pitney smirked. "Because you won't tell me or because you don't know?"

He sipped his coffee. "I don't know."

Cristian sat forward in his seat. "You don't know how many kids he fathered?"

"We're not required to keep track of that information."

"Is there a limit to how many donations a man can make?" Pitney asked.

"How is that possibly relevant to Hank Reardon's demise?"

"Why don't you humor us, Dr. Stiles, and just answer the questions?"

He sighed. "We are in the process of implementing a program that will limit the number of donations. In terms of the number of children that are produced, the mothers will be required to report on their success rate in terms of conception."

"I keep hearing the word 'required,'" Pitney said. "Isn't there an ethical standard somewhere, short of what is required by law?"

Walter tipped his head to the side. "That's rather Pollyannaish, don't you think?"

"I heard about a guy who thinks he has seventy-five kids," Pitney said. "You don't think that's problematic?"

Walter sipped from his mug. "Reproductive technology is on the cutting edge; we are finding our way as we go."

"And finding a way to make as much money as possible," Detective Menendez offered.

Walter leaned back in his chair. "I have to say, I'm surprised at your negative attitudes toward assisted reproduction. Surely you know people who have benefited from it."

"I don't have a problem with assisted reproduction, Dr. Stiles," Pitney clarified. "I have a problem with policies that seem devoid of common sense. You seem quite comfortable offering 'assistance' except for any assistance that might cut into your profit margin."

"You're very cynical, Lieutenant."

Pitney shook her head. "Not really. I'm just looking at the facts."

"Do you have children?" he asked her.

"No," she said impatiently, "and I can't imagine how *that's* relevant."

"And you?" he asked Cristian.

"A three-year-old son."

"Ahh. So you understand that people don't want to encounter road blocks when they're trying to create a family. When you're trying to become a parent, you lead with your heart."

Pitney rolled her eyes. "I don't think making sure that a child doesn't have seventy-four half-siblings—or at the very least keeping track—is a road block, but apparently, my opinion is too theoretical to count."

"Speaking as a parent, Dr. Stiles," Cristian said, "the idea of fathering dozens of kids creeps me out, even if I wasn't raising them."

"Well, then, thank goodness you aren't a donor." Walter smiled. This interview was getting away from him, and he didn't like it.

"You require medical tests of your donors, I assume?" Pitney asked.

"Of course. We have an extensive battery of required tests." He reached into his desk drawer and took out a pamphlet. "They're all listed here."

Cristian took the brochure and tucked it into the breast pocket of his jacket. "Thanks."

Pitney drained her cappuccino and stood up. "Thank you for the coffee, Doctor. It was certainly an improvement from what we're used to."

"My pleasure. Don't hesitate to call if you have any questions." He exchanged cards with the detectives and walked them to his office door.

"And where were you Monday night and early Tuesday morning?" Pitney asked as she tucked his card into her bag.

Walter looked at her. "An alibi, Lieutenant? Why would I want to hurt Hank Reardon? He was the best possible advertisement for Heritage."

"Or its worst possible enemy if he blamed you for the revelations about his donations." She smiled at him and waited.

"I was at home," Walter said. "Now, if you'll excuse me, my assistant will see you out." Jenny jumped up from her desk, and Walter closed his door.

He hoped they were satisfied. He didn't need them poking around.

Fina spent a couple of hours contacting Rosie's friends, to no avail. None of them had heard from her in the last forty-eight hours, and although it was hard to judge their veracity over the phone, they didn't strike her as being overly suspicious.

She decided to deal with one name on the list in person, so after fueling up with Cheetos and a diet soda, Fina made her way to Arlington. There were a few stray reporters on the sidewalk outside Marnie Frasier's house, but they only made a halfhearted attempt to engage her as she climbed the steps. Fina rang the bell and then knocked, but there was no answer. After a moment, she pulled out her phone and dialed Tyler Frasier's number.

"Yeah?"

"Tyler, it's Fina Ludlow, the detective. I'm outside your front door. Do you mind letting me in?"

"My mom's not here."

"I wanted to talk with you, actually."

"I'll be right up."

A minute later, the front door drifted open—as if she'd said "Open sesame"—with no one visible on the other side. Fina quickly stepped into the foyer, closing the door firmly behind her.

"Sorry. I didn't want to end up in any photos," Tyler said. He was standing off to the side, just outside of the sight line of the reporters.

"I understand. Sorry for just dropping by."

"No worries. Come on downstairs."

She followed him into the spotless kitchen and down a steep flight of stairs to the basement. The only natural light in the space was from the window wells. The room was carpeted and divided into two areas by a sectional couch. The couch anchored a seating area with a fireplace and a large TV. The space behind the couch was filled by a round wooden dining table, illuminated by a pendant light. The TV was tuned to ESPN, and preseason football highlights jumped across the screen.

Every available surface was covered with clothes and magazines. Shoes the size of casserole dishes were strewn on the shag carpet, and even a couple of framed pictures on the wall were askew.

Fina swiveled her head to take it all in. "Tyler, this may be the messiest room I've ever seen, and I've seen crime scenes where there have been violent struggles."

Tyler guffawed. "You're just saying that to make me feel special."

"Your mother is okay with this?" Marnie had struck Fina as the type to run a tight ship.

"Oh, she hates it, but it's our compromise."

Fina held up her hands. "What's the compromise? No decomposing bodies?"

Tyler climbed over the back of the sofa and began gathering a pile of clothes in his arms. He cleared a small space and nodded for Fina to take a seat.

"None of my shit is upstairs, plus I cook and keep the kitchen neat." He plopped down onto the couch on the other side of the L.

"You're responsible for the kitchen?" Fina looked toward the ceiling. "It was spotless."

"It has to be. That's a big part of school: keeping your station clean and organized and following health and safety codes."

"But left to your own devices . . ."

Tyler shrugged and smiled. "What can I say, I'm a free spirit."

"I'm here about Rosie Sanchez; her mom can't find her. Any chance she might be under one of these piles?"

Tyler looked around the room, as if doing a quick visual inventory. "She's not here."

Fina held his gaze for a moment. "Do you know where she might be? Renata hasn't seen her since Monday, and she's starting to worry."

"I haven't talked to her."

"So you two haven't been in touch since Hank died? Since yesterday morning?"

"Nope."

Fina adjusted her feet and looked at a sneaker on the floor. Next to her own foot, it looked yeti-sized.

"What are your thoughts about that?" she asked him.

"About what?"

"Hank Reardon's death. I assume your mom discussed your paternity with you before it broke in the papers."

"Yeah, I knew." He ran a hand through his hair. "It's wild, man. I can't believe that guy was my dad."

"Did you want to meet him?"

Tyler smirked. "Does it matter? He made it pretty clear he didn't want to meet us."

Fina watched a wide receiver get clobbered on the screen. "Not exactly the fairy-tale ending that Renata was looking for."

"Yeah, but she'll never admit it. She'll say that it was never about Hank; it was about truth and human rights and all that bullshit." His carefree manner eluded him for a moment. "She's so full of shit."

"Look, I understand if Rosie just needs some time away from her mom, but I'd like to know that she's safe at least."

"I can't help you." He held up his hands in supplication. "I don't know where she is."

"Okay, well, if you hear from her, you know where to find me." Fina pushed herself off the couch and picked her way across the room. Tyler vaulted over the back of the sofa and looked over her shoulder when she paused at the table. What looked like specs and blueprints were spread across the table's surface.

"Is this a school project?"

"Yeah, I'm just working on some stuff before the semester starts."

Fina eyed a fanned stack of color photos of food. "That looks good." She tapped a photo of seared ahi tuna.

"We have to come up with a complete restaurant concept: menu, decor, financial plan, the whole thing."

"A financial plan? That sounds daunting."

"It's part of the business. Doesn't matter how good your food is if you can't pay your suppliers."

Fina climbed the stairs and suspected that Tyler was checking out her ass as he followed. That was okay. It was her job as his elder to school him in the benefits of older women—brains and beauty.

Fina returned to her car and turned the key so she could roll down the windows. She checked her messages and e-mail, but didn't have to wait long. After a few minutes, Tyler came trotting down the front steps, hopped in an old Honda Civic, and took off.

Fina followed Tyler to a triple-decker in Allston and waited outside. No one else showed up during that time, and Fina couldn't very well knock on the door and pretend she was lost. She took down the address and the license plate of the car in the driveway and called a few contacts while she waited. It wasn't strictly legal to run a license plate number through the Registry of Motor Vehicles, but only doing what was strictly legal was so limiting. Tyler came out after an hour and returned to his car. Fina trailed him to Cambridge and the restaurant where he worked.

Renata wasn't picking up her phone, but when she called Cristian, he confirmed that Rosie was still MIA.

"And you better get over here," Cristian said as Fina navigated through Cambridge.

"Where's here?"

"Back Bay. Renata is making trouble at the Reardons' place."

"Oh, Jesus. I'll be right there."

The sun was peeking out through some clouds, and Fina admired the view crossing the BU Bridge. There were small sailboats dotting the Charles and runners on the Esplanade.

Fina pulled into a loading zone on Commonwealth and put on her hazards. Cristian was standing on the sidewalk, deep in conversation with Renata. Two uniformed officers were chatting nearby.

"What's she doing here?" Renata asked as Fina approached.

"I thought maybe she could talk some sense into you," Cristian said.

"Renata, what are you doing?" Fina asked.

"I'm just trying to find Rosie."

"So am I, but that doesn't explain why you're here."

They moved toward the front steps when a cadre of nannies overtook the sidewalk with strollers that resembled small foreign cars. The women spoke a foreign language in a staccato tone while their charges lolled and slept in their rolling pods of luxury.

"I thought maybe she came here to find out about her father." There were dark circles under Renata's eyes and a faint sheen of oil across her face.

"And did she?" Fina asked.

"Not according to her." Renata rolled her eyes toward the house.

"Mrs. Reardon says she's never met Rosie, and as far as she knows, Rosie never came to the house," Cristian said, glancing at his cell phone. "I need to go; can you . . . ?" He looked at Fina.

"Of course."

"I don't need babysitting," Renata protested.

Fina heard a slight commotion and looked to see the uniforms debating with a photographer and a woman she assumed was a journalist.

"Unless you want more bad press, you need to leave now and stay away from the Reardons." Fina put her hand on Renata's elbow and began steering her down the street.

"I'm going crazy with worry, Fina."

"I know, but I think I have a lead. Go to work or go home, whatever, but leave the sleuthing to me."

"Fine," Renata said petulantly.

"Renata, don't give me attitude. I'm doing you a favor."

Renata opened her mouth to speak.

"I don't want to hear it," Fina said, and walked to her car.

. . .

Walter was struggling to get the boxes into the trunk of his car when Ellen appeared at his side.

"Do you need a hand with that, Walter?" she asked.

He prodded it into the space, a task made more difficult under her watchful gaze. "No, thank you. I can manage." He bent the corner of the second box and gave it a final push before slamming the trunk closed.

"Were those cryobank files?" Ellen asked.

"No, no. Just some personal papers from years ago. Decades, in fact."

"Huh." She thought for a moment. "And you kept them at the office?"

"You don't have any personal items floating around your office, Ellen? I find that hard to believe." He smiled at her. "Was there something you needed?"

"I wanted to discuss the visit you had from the police."

Walter walked toward the driver's-side door. "There's nothing to discuss."

"The police are investigating the bank in relation to a murder case. Sounds like something worth discussing. The management team, at the very least, should be brought up to speed."

"There really is nothing to it, and I don't want to worry the team needlessly."

Ellen stood next to him. "I'm sure you're well intentioned, but you don't need to protect the team. They're all professionals."

"If it would make you feel better, I can tell everyone the same thing I've just told you: that it's a nonissue."

"I think that's a good idea. I don't think secrets are good for morale." Her eyes strayed toward the trunk. "They breed mistrust, which can only lead to greater problems."

"If you say so, Ellen. You make it sound much more nefarious than it is."

"Good-bye, Walter."

He watched her walk to her car, wishing that she were fat and ugly.

It would be easier to dismiss her if she were physically unattractive. Her appearance was just one of many weapons in her arsenal.

The next morning, Fina bypassed the front desk at Universum and headed for Hank Reardon's office. The blinds on Dimitri Kask's office were closed, and his assistant wasn't around, but there was a young woman sitting outside the door of Hank's office.

"May I help you?" she asked Fina. She had fair skin and red hair that cascaded down her shoulders in waves. She wasn't traditionally pretty, but her appearance was striking. She was wearing a hunter green blouse and gray trousers. Crystal chandelier earrings hung from her earlobes. A nameplate on her desk said THERESA MCGOVERN.

"I'm Fina Ludlow." She handed the young woman her ID. "Michael Ludlow asked me to stop by and take a look at his father's office."

Theresa studied her. "Really? I don't think anyone is supposed to be in there."

"Really. Michael Reardon asked me to. He's hired me to find his father's killer."

"I thought the police were doing that." Theresa didn't look much older than twenty-five, but it was clear that her youth should not be mistaken for naïveté.

"They are, but Michael hired me, too."

"Huh. I'm not exactly a stickler for the rules, but why should I let you poke around?"

"Do you think Hank had something to hide?"

Theresa opened her top desk drawer and pulled out a compact mirror. She popped it open and examined her face in the tiny mirror. "You ask a lot of questions."

"It is my job. So how about it?"

"I definitely can't let you in there when Dimitri's around." Her movements caused her sleeve to ride up, and Fina caught a glimpse of an elaborate dragon tattoo snaking up her arm.

"Maybe some other time?"

Theresa narrowed her eyes. "You still haven't told me what's in it for me."

"Don't you want to know who killed your boss?"

She snapped the compact shut. "I don't really care, as long as whoever it is doesn't come back and kill me next."

"Oookay. So I'm guessing this isn't your dream job."

"Hardly. I work here to pay the bills and keep my nights free."

"Dare I ask what you do at night?" Fina was flashing back to Melanie's death and the sordid world of escorts Fina's investigation had revealed.

"I'm a DJ. I just do this for the health insurance."

Fina leaned her hands on the desk. "You ever work at Crystal?"

"The huge club near Fenway? I wish."

"I know some people over there; maybe I could put in a good word."

"Seriously? How do I know you're not full of it?"

"You don't. Sometimes you just have to take a chance."

Voices moved toward them from behind Dimitri's closed door. Fina pulled out her card and handed it to Theresa. "We should discuss this someplace else. Call me if you want to take me up on that career advancement."

Theresa dropped the card into her purse and busied herself behind her computer. Fina walked away just as Dimitri's door opened.

When Fina checked her e-mail, the document Greta had promised was sitting in her in-box. The birth certificate from Rockford, Maine, listed the baby's name as Ann Sylvia Patterson, with a birthdate of July 17, 1966, at 3:43 A.M. The mother's name was Elizabeth Hardwick Patterson, but the line for the father was blank. This didn't surprise Fina. Fathers' names weren't compulsory on birth certificates, depending upon the state, and given that Elizabeth had most likely had the child out of wedlock in the late sixties, the family probably kept the whole pregnancy under wraps.

Fina dialed Greta Samuels's number. She was just about to hang up when a woman answered.

"I'm calling for Greta Samuels."

"This is Greta." The voice sounded raspy, like the speaker was under the weather.

"Ms. Samuels, this is Fina Ludlow, the private investigator. We spoke yesterday."

"Oh, of course." She perked up. "Did you get the birth certificate?"

"I did, thank you. Obviously, it's not conclusive, since the two certificates have different names."

"But don't the birthdates match? Rockford is a small town. The population is less than three thousand."

"Yes, the birthdates match, but I still need to authenticate the birth certificate you provided. How did you get it, by the way? Generally original birth certificates of adoptees are sealed."

"Well, like I said, Rockford is a small town. Our family doctor cared for my sister, and she ended up with the birth certificate."

Fina could imagine a scenario in which the certificate got "misplaced" and never ended up in the sealed file. Documents were lost all the time, even in this day and age. "I'd like to have a colleague of mine stop by and look at the original."

There was a long pause.

"Ms. Samuels?"

"Yes, of course. The only thing is that I'm heading out of town for a bit."

"Oh, anyplace fun?"

"Not really. My cousin is ill, and I'm visiting her."

Fina waited for more information, which wasn't forthcoming. "Okay. I do need to verify the birth certificate."

"I'm so sorry I won't be available. I want nothing more than to meet Risa."

"Maybe you could leave it with a neighbor or a friend? It will only take him a few minutes to examine it."

"I suppose I could do that."

"It would be very helpful."

Greta gave her a name and address.

"I hope your cousin feels better," Fina said, and ended the call. She studied the document on her screen. Something felt weird, but she couldn't put her finger on it.

She called a PI in Portland whom she hired on occasion and asked him to go to the friend's house to review the birth certificate. If Greta was running a con, she was going to a lot of trouble.

Juliana and Michael were in Hank's office at Universum Tech. Juliana sat on the couch while Michael sorted through folders in his father's file cabinets.

"Are you sure this is a good idea?" Michael asked his mother.

"Why wouldn't it be? You have every right to go through your father's papers."

"I'm not so sure about that, actually. You *definitely* don't."

"We're not doing anything illegal, Michael." Juliana gestured toward the windowed walls of the office and the assistants perched on the other side of the glass. "We're not sneaking around." She didn't mention the fact that Dimitri was conveniently off-site.

"Danielle wouldn't like it."

"Her feelings are not my concern."

"All this paperwork is going to the attorneys anyway; you'll hear about it eventually."

"I'd rather not wait." Juliana looked at her hands. Now that she was a triathlete—she never got tired of saying that—she wore sunscreen every day, but her hands were still a golden brown tone. She didn't like the idea of wrinkles or, God forbid, skin cancer, but she had to admit, everybody looked better with a tan.

"So I'm looking for something about the center?"

"Yes. It's my center; I have the right to know what your father had in mind."

Michael pushed a drawer closed and swiveled so his chair faced the desk. Juliana scrolled through her e-mails on her phone while she waited. She had a lot of things on her plate these days: the center's annual gala, a trip to India later in the fall, and a race before Halloween.

"I don't see anything, Mom."

She dropped her phone into her large leather satchel. "You're sure?"

Michael looked at her with annoyance. "I looked in all the drawers. There's nothing here."

"Fine." Juliana stood up, and Michael came around the desk. "Thank you for looking, sweetie. I appreciate it."

"Sorry I couldn't find anything."

"It's fine. Any word on the funeral arrangements?"

Michael exhaled sharply. "I'm supposed to meet with Danielle today to finalize them."

"Well, when you do, let me know."

Michael looked at her. "You're not planning on going, are you?"

"Of course. Why wouldn't I?"

"Because you and Danielle aren't exactly bosom buddies?"

"We were married for twenty-four years, and Hank is the father of my child. I'd like to pay my respects."

"I know, I just don't want a scene."

"*I'm* not going to make a scene." Juliana looped her bag over her shoulder. "I can't speak for her."

They walked out of the office and headed toward the elevators. "Do you want to stay with me for a few days?" Juliana asked.

"I don't think so."

"I just thought you might want some company." Michael and his med school girlfriend had broken up six weeks before.

"I'm okay. I'll let you know if I need anything." He pressed the down button. "Are *you* doing okay? Like you said, you were married to him for twenty-four years."

Juliana thought for a moment. "Your father and I had a lot of good years," she said, avoiding the question. She stretched onto her tiptoes and kissed his cheek. "Call me later."

Michael nodded his assent and watched the elevator doors close behind her.

Fina had a message from her contact at the Registry, which she added to the info she'd already dug up. She pulled into a McDonald's parking lot to give the new information her full attention.

The apartment that Tyler had hightailed it to the previous afternoon was owned by a Miriam Goldblum, a name that didn't ring any bells, but the car in the driveway was registered to William Hedquist. Fina looked through the list of contacts provided by Renata.

Bingo.

One of Rosie's coworkers at the shelter was Sam Hedquist. It was too unusual a name for mere coincidence.

Fina ordered medium fries and a diet soda from the drive-thru and went back over the river to Cambridge. She parked in an overpriced garage and sat for a moment licking salt off her fingers. She was fairly sure that Rosie had taken off of her own accord, but she wasn't sure why she took off in the first place. Was she just pissed at Renata or had she done something stupid and panicked?

Twenty minutes later, at the restaurant where Tyler worked, Fina did another do-si-do with the bartender, who finally gave her admittance and directed her to the kitchen. She found Tyler in a line of other white-jacketed men butchering an animal on a stainless-steel counter.

"Hey," Tyler said. He grinned at her, but the smile was muted.

"Hey. Can I borrow you for a minute?"

An older man wearing a toque looked annoyed, but gestured with a huge knife for Tyler to step away from the table.

"Let me take off my gloves," Tyler said when they moved over to a spotless counter.

"Don't bother," Fina said, eyeing his latex-encased hands, which were bloody and greasy-looking. "This will only take a minute."

"What's up?"

"I want you to deliver a message for me."

Tyler looked blank.

"Can you let Rosie and Sam know that if she doesn't get in contact with Renata by eight tonight, I'll have to drag her home myself?"

Tyler's eyes widened, and his mouth formed an O shape.

"I'm a PI, Tyler, remember? I find stuff out."

"Look, I don't know—"

Fina held a hand up in protest. "You don't need to explain. If Renata were my mother, I would have filed for emancipation years ago. I'm not unsympathetic to Rosie's situation." Fina looked at him. "Assuming that's all this is about."

Tyler held up his coated hands in question. "What do you mean?"

Fina detected the smell of raw animal. Something twitched deep in her stomach, and not in a good way.

"I hope Rosie didn't do anything stupid, like confront Hank Reardon."

"What? And kill him? You've got to be kidding."

Fina shrugged. "I'm not saying that's what I believe. But the cops might."

"Fuck." He made a motion to crack his knuckles, but couldn't get purchase on his fingers. "All right. She'll go home."

"If she needs a lawyer—a criminal lawyer—we can find someone for her. Tell her to call me."

"Okay." He glanced over his shoulder. "I should get back."

"Sure. What is that thing anyway?"

"Lamb. It's delicious."

"If you say so. Remember, by eight tonight."

Tyler nodded, and Fina left the kitchen.

On the sidewalk, she called Renata and left a message reassuring her that Rosie would be in touch by eight.

That was one mystery solved.

It was too late for dinner at Frank and Peg's, but Fina found a bowl of potato salad and some sliced ham in the fridge.

"Do you do this at your parents'?" Frank asked when he came into the kitchen. He'd been downstairs working on a leak in the bathroom sink. "Eat all their food?"

"Are you kidding?" She started to help herself. "I'm hungry, not crazy."

Peg sat at the kitchen table sipping a cup of coffee, and Frank walked over to the sink and began to scrub his greasy hands.

"Would you still visit if we didn't have food?" Frank asked, winking at Peg.

Fina considered the question for a moment. "I'd visit Peg."

Frank smiled and poured himself a cup of coffee. "So, Hank Reardon."

"You can't make this stuff up." Fina carried her plate over to the table and popped open a diet soda.

"Those poor kids," Peg said, shaking her head.

"Poor Hank," Frank exclaimed.

"Well, of course poor Hank, but those kids . . . they must be reeling."

"One of them took off," Fina said between bites.

"Which one?" Frank held the mug close to his face and inhaled.

"Renata Sanchez's oldest, Rosie."

"Is she okay?" Peg asked.

"Yeah, I found her, but the timing of her disappearance didn't look good."

"You think she had something to do with Hank's death?" Frank asked.

"It's hard to believe, but I never would have believed that Hank Reardon sold his sperm and fathered cryokids. Who knows?" She took a mouthful of potato salad. Peg's potato salad was the best—rich, but not heavy, with the faint tang of pickles. "This potato salad is amazing, Peg. Thank you."

"You're welcome, sweetie." Peg rotated her mug on the table. "So do you think Rosie was just blowing off steam?"

"Probably. Renata isn't very sensitive. Rosie probably thinks something dramatic was required to get her mother's attention."

"You wouldn't know anything about that," Frank commented, and rolled his eyes.

Fina looked at him. "I'm not dramatic."

"Didn't you once steal your brother's car to teach him a lesson?"

"That was years ago, and he deserved it. He kept on taking my things without asking." Fina had "relocated" her older brother's car when they were teenagers after she got fed up with his loose interpretation of what was his and what was hers. Rand thought nothing of going into her bedroom and claiming her CDs, money, and weed. Carl and Elaine wouldn't step in, so she took matters into her own hands. Despite Carl's punishment, it was worth the trouble; Rand stayed out of her room from then on. Too bad he didn't stay out of other people's rooms in the years to come.

"I'm just saying I don't blame her if she was trying to teach Renata a lesson, or at the very least get her attention," said Fina.

"If you ever have children, I hope they're just like you," Frank said, and grinned.

"I wouldn't hold out too much hope if I were you."

He chuckled. "Just the thought warms my heart."

Cristian wanted her to swing by the station on her way home, but she convinced him to meet her at a nearby diner instead. It wasn't that she didn't like going to the station, but in her experience, the less Pitney saw of her, the better.

Settled in a roomy vinyl booth, Cristian ordered an egg white scramble with wheat toast and a side of fruit. Fina made up for it by requesting a slice of apple pie à la mode and a glass of milk.

"Is this your dinner?" she asked him.

"Yes. Is it yours?"

"Dessert. I had something more substantial at Frank and Peg's."

"How are they?"

"They're good. Healthy and full of spit and vinegar."

The waitress poured a cup of coffee for Cristian. "So I heard that you got Rosie Sanchez to return home."

"Her half-brother was in on it; I strongly suggested she return home and put her mother out of her misery."

"And help the police with their inquiries."

"Well, that goes without saying."

Two plates were brought to their table by a different waitress, who looked like she was pushing seventy-five. Fina couldn't imagine she worked the late shift at the diner for kicks.

Cristian took a bite of fluffy eggs while Fina dissected her slice of pie, allowing the scoop of ice cream to seep into the filling.

"Want a bite?" she asked, working to get the perfect proportion of ice cream, crust, and filling onto her fork.

He shook his head.

They ate in silence for a minute.

"Do you have a theory of the crime you'd like to share?" Fina asked, spearing a chunk of apple with her fork.

Cristian sat back against the vinyl booth and studied her. Some people might assume that their relationship was a one-way street, but Cristian and Pitney knew that Fina could be a valuable source of information if they pointed her in the right direction.

He took a sip of coffee and carefully placed the cup back in its saucer. "Remember, you can't discuss this with anyone. You know we hold back details sometimes."

"I know. My lips are sealed."

"Okay. Hank's car drove into the garage at Universum at eleven forty-five P.M."

"Was he driving?"

"Yes."

"Was anyone else in the car?"

"Not that we can see on the video."

"So either his killer was hiding in the car or snuck into the parking garage but avoided the cameras." Fina took a drink of milk.

"Exactly, and the cameras have blind spots, so it's not as hard as you might think."

"If that's the case, why have the cameras at all?"

"They're a deterrent, and if you aren't familiar with them, you would probably get caught."

"You're looking for someone who has been to the garage before."

"Which is pretty much everyone on the suspect list," Cristian said.

A bell jangled as the door of the diner opened. Three construction workers walked in wearing reflective vests and filthy work clothes.

Fina swallowed a mouthful of pie. "Okay, so the killer is somehow on the scene, and what? Confronts Hank? Surprises him?"

"Either. Both." Cristian took a bite of his crunchy toast. "The blows were to the back of the head; either he had turned away from the murderer or never even saw him or her in the first place."

"There wasn't a struggle?"

"No, which is why 'her' is a viable option."

Fina wrapped her hands around her milk. "Last I heard, the murder weapon was a blunt object, something small and heavy. Anything new on that front?" she asked.

"Nothing, except that it wasn't a traditional hammer."

"You've concluded that because of the pattern of the trauma?"

He nodded. "It didn't leave any round markings. That's good, because it's more specialized, but that's bad, because it's more obscure."

"What markings did it leave?" she asked.

"Squares, about the size of those small Post-it notes. Not the standard size; the little ones."

"I know the ones you're talking about." Fina considered this for a moment. "What about the surface of the weapon? Was it flat or textured?"

"Flat as far as we can tell."

"I saw a bloodstain when I was there, but what about the killer's clothes? How bloody did things get?"

"It wasn't a bloodbath, if that's what you're asking. Hank was hit a few times, hard, but as soon as the heart stops, the blood stops pumping."

"So the killer's clothes may have been stained but not soaked."

"Right. If he was smart, he would have disposed of his clothes or else worn some kind of protective gear, like a boilersuit or Tyvek suit that would be easy to dispose of."

"You didn't find anything useful at the scene?"

"Just hairs and fibers from half the company. It's a parking garage for an office building, and partially exposed to the elements to boot. Not exactly an ideal crime scene."

"Not for *you*, maybe. The killer must have been pleased." She cut through a thick piece of crust, releasing a small flurry of crumbs. "Any news on the Marissa front?"

"She wants Brad to come to Matteo's preschool welcome ceremony."

"What is that exactly? They show them their cubbies and the potty?"

"Basically," Cristian bristled, "but it's a family thing."

"I'm just trying to picture Carl and Elaine attending a preschool welcome ceremony."

"Didn't they just lock you guys out of the house so you could roam and forage all day?"

"Essentially."

The waitress put a folded check on the table, and Fina reached for her wallet. "It's on me."

"Uh-uh. Let's go Dutch. I don't want anyone to think I'm being bought off by the Ludlows."

Fina put a ten on the table, and Cristian put down his share.

They got up from the table and walked to the front door. There was a bowl of white party mints on the hostess stand, one of the few sweets Fina avoided. Aside from their chalklike consistency, she couldn't stomach the thought of all the hands that had already dipped into the bowl.

Cristian held the door open, and Fina walked out of the diner.

"You heading back to the station?" she asked.

"Yup. Duty calls."

They walked in opposite directions.

"Make sure you tell Pitney that I got Rosie to go home," Fina called out over her shoulder.

"Nice try!"

"I do what I can!"

12

There were a few reporters milling around the sidewalk when Fina arrived at the Sanchezes' house the next day. As she started to climb the front stairs, they leapt into action and started volleying questions at her: Was she the private investigator who discovered Hank's identity? Did Renata Sanchez kill Hank Reardon? How did Rosie feel about her father's murder?

Fina gave them the hairy eyeball and rang the doorbell. There was no response, so she came down the stairs and started around back. One of the reporters fell into step next to her.

"This is private property," Fina said. "If you don't get back on the sidewalk, I'm calling the cops."

"I just want to talk to the family, let them tell their side of the story."

"That's so kind of you," Fina said, and moved toward him. "Very altruistic."

He took a step back. "Don't touch me, lady."

Fina took another step toward him. "Go. Away." She stood there until he joined his colleagues on the sidewalk.

Fina climbed the stairs to the back porch and banged on the door. She pressed her face against the kitchen window and thought she saw movement.

"Renata, it's Fina." There was no response. "I need to talk to you. You owe me."

After a moment, a figure came into the kitchen and unlocked the door. It was Rosie.

"Oh, hi, Rosie. Sorry to bug you," Fina said. The young woman had obviously been crying; her eyes were red and slightly swollen. "Is your mom around?"

"No."

"Can I come in?"

Rosie hesitated. "Fine."

Fina came into the kitchen, and Rosie locked the door behind her. The girl continued on to the living room at the front of the house and plopped down on the couch. The blinds were drawn and the room was dark, the only light coming from the TV. Rosie picked up the remote and muted the sound.

"Your mom's not home?" Fina sat down in an easy chair next to the couch.

"She had some conference and then was picking up Alexa."

Fina nodded. "Sorry about dragging you home."

"Whatever."

"No, it's not whatever," Fina said. "I know you're royally pissed at your mom, but she was worried about you."

Rosie pulled a knitted afghan over her lap. "I think she was worried about how it looked."

Fina didn't respond.

Rosie looked at her. "You aren't going to defend her?"

"I think you know who your mother is, Rosie. I'm not going to pretend otherwise. She likes crusades, sometimes at your expense. You're seventeen; you know this."

"But she does it because she loves me," she said sarcastically.

"She does love you, and that's a big motivation for her, I'm sure, but that doesn't excuse the havoc she wreaks."

Rosie picked at the afghan in silence.

"Anyway, I'm sorry I forced you home. Why don't you stay with a friend for a little while if you need some space?"

"Maybe." Rosie stared at the talk show on the TV screen. "Why are you helping her? I thought she fired you guys."

"She did, although she didn't really follow the correct procedures to terminate the relationship."

Rosie snorted. "She never does."

"I wanted to let you know that Michael Reardon has hired me to investigate Hank's death."

Rosie's head swiveled toward her. "Isn't that a conflict of interest?"

Fina shrugged. "Your mom fired us, and then he hired us, and then she kind of rehired us. It's a bit of a mess, but I'm confident I can be objective."

"Let me guess: Michael Reardon thinks my mom killed his father."

"No. He doesn't know who killed him."

"Has it occurred to him that maybe it has nothing to do with my mother? Maybe it has to do with the fact that his father donated sperm to half the state!"

Fina declined to point out that *his* father was, in fact, *her* father. "Michael's definitely pissed at your mom, but I think he's pissed at his dad, too. Lots of people are pissed at other people."

Rosie burrowed farther into the couch. Fina slipped a foot out of her wedge sandal and massaged her instep. She looked at Rosie. "So this is quite a mess."

"Which part?"

"All of it."

Rosie eyed her. "I'm not sure I should be talking to you now that you're working for the enemy."

"Technically I probably shouldn't be speaking with you without your mother present, but I thought maybe we could talk off the record."

"How do I know you're not going to tell the media everything I say to you?"

"You don't know that, but I hate the media. My family is always on their shit list."

"What do you mean?"

Fina filled Rosie in on Melanie's murder and the cloud of suspicion that cloaked the Ludlows.

Rosie nodded. "I remember that from earlier this summer. I didn't realize when my mom hired you guys that you were *those* Ludlows."

"Maybe that's why she hired us. My father doesn't shy away from controversy in legal cases, although he prefers staying out of the limelight when it relates to his own family." Fina slipped her shoe back on. "But even before that we were always being featured for something untoward or scandalous. For example, my father worked for that old lady who killed her grandson."

"Gasser Granny?"

"The very one. Believe me, I grew up with a lot of unwanted attention."

"And it didn't bother you?"

"I hated it, but I didn't have a choice. Luckily, I have brothers, and we've always stuck together." Well, almost always.

Rosie frowned. "Alexa isn't much help."

"Can I give you a piece of advice?"

Rosie looked at her.

"There's always going to be someone, somewhere, saying something nasty. You have to learn to tune it out."

"It's not that easy."

"But it gets easier as you get older. It's one of the few benefits of aging."

Rosie twirled a curl around her finger. "It just sucks."

"I hear ya."

They sat. Outside, bottles could be heard smashing into a recycling truck.

Rosie finally spoke. "He really didn't want anything to do with us, did he?"

"Hank, you mean?"

Rosie avoided her gaze. "Yeah."

"He didn't seem to, but believe me, Rosie, that was about him, not you."

"Did you meet him?"

"A couple of times."

"What was he like?"

"Handsome, well dressed. Obviously he was incredibly smart. And very rich."

"So I've heard."

"Does that matter to you?"

"Doesn't it matter to everyone?" Rosie examined her toenails, which were painted bright purple. "Actually, it doesn't matter to me that much; I mean, not fancy cars and stuff. I'd like money for college, and I don't want my mom to have to work forever, but beyond that, I don't really care."

"Can you explain to me how you ended up at that apartment in Allston?"

"My friend's brother lives there, and my friend is crashing there while his brother is out of town."

"The brother is William Hedquist?"

She nodded. "His brother, Sam, is a friend of mine from work."

"How does Tyler figure into this?"

"I couldn't deal with all the media attention, and Tyler could relate. We hung out, and then Tyler brought me to the apartment."

"When was this exactly?"

"On Monday night."

"The night you told your mother you were staying with your friend Laura?"

"Right."

"And Sam was there with you the whole night? He can vouch for you?"

Rosie looked confused. "He's in a band, and they had a gig. They went out afterward, so he didn't get home until early the next morning."

"So you were there alone when Hank Reardon was killed?"

"I didn't kill Hank Reardon!" Rosie looked aghast at the suggestion.

"I'm not saying you did."

"But you're acting like I need an alibi."

There was a commotion outside, and Rosie sat up abruptly. Fina motioned for her to stay where she was. Peeking around the blinds, she saw Renata and Alexa coming up the stairs.

Renata was threatening to call the cops on the reporters when she pushed open the front door and slammed it shut behind her younger daughter.

"Rosie, turn on some lights in here." She reached over to the switch, and the room was bathed in light. "They already know we're home."

Alexa tossed down her backpack and ran into the kitchen. Renata blinked at Fina.

"Hello, Fina."

"Hello, Renata." The exchange was more challenge than greeting. "I wanted to stop by and make sure Rosie was doing okay."

"She is." She looked past Fina toward the kitchen. "Thank you for your help."

"You're welcome."

They looked at each other. The silence was heavy under the weight of their mutual distrust.

"Was there something else? I did fire your family before Rosie pulled her disappearing act," Renata said, their warm, fuzzy moment having passed in the blink of an eye.

"I know you did, but technically, you have to do it in writing, and then you kind of rehired me when she went missing. Remember?"

Renata rolled her eyes and put her hands on her hips.

"And I'm not here in that capacity anyway," Fina added.

"So why are you here?"

"Michael Reardon has hired me to investigate Hank's death."

Renata's mouth fell open. "You're working for *him* now?"

"Well, per your wishes, I'm not working for *you*."

"Your family is unbelievable."

Fina held up her hand. "Spare me your righteous indignation, Renata. At the moment, you don't have a leg to stand on when it comes to family values."

Rosie looked at the floor and smiled.

"Regardless," Renata sputtered, "you shouldn't be questioning my daughter without me present."

"Oh, right. You're so concerned about my well-being," Rosie muttered.

"I'm always concerned about your well-being."

"We were talking off the record," Fina said.

"That may be, but she's my child. It's unethical. I can't believe your father would sanction this."

Oh, lady. You have no idea.

"If I want to talk to her, that's my business," Rosie said, standing up and putting her hands on her hips just like her mother. "What's left to say, anyway? You've already told everyone our business!"

"That's not true, Rosie."

"Yes, it is! At the shelter, everybody keeps talking about cryokids and donor babies like I'm a freak!" Rosie stomped upstairs.

"Well, thank you very much for that," Renata said, glaring at Fina.

"Oh, come on. You did that all by yourself, Renata."

Renata turned on her heel and walked into the kitchen. Fina followed her and watched as Renata filled a glass with water and took a long drink. Alexa was visible through the doorway, sitting at the dining room table. She was reaching her hand deep into a can of Pringles.

"We can help you or I can put you in touch with people who have different expertise," Fina said. "Crisis managers, a criminal attorney."

"I don't need a criminal attorney! *I* didn't kill Hank Reardon!"

"Your tendency to speak your mind will get you in trouble, and

Rosie might need to explain her whereabouts the night Hank died." Fina reached into her bag and pulled out a small notebook. She wrote down a couple of names and numbers, ripped off the sheet, and handed it to Renata. "I'm trying to keep the kids out of the investigation."

"Why would you care? You get paid either way."

"Like I was telling Rosie, I know what it's like to pay for the alleged sins of the father. It sucks."

Renata glared at her, and the doorbell rang. Footsteps thundered across the floor above their heads.

"I am so sick of these assholes," Rosie yelled, bounding down the stairs.

"Rosie, don't open that door," Renata cautioned, moving toward the living room.

"Oh wait, good news!" Rosie exclaimed. "It's just the cops!"

Renata swallowed and tugged down on the hem of her blazer.

"Renata, you shouldn't speak to them without an attorney," Fina cautioned.

"I don't need an attorney," she scoffed, "and I've already spoken to them."

Fina shook her head. "Well, at the very least, will you let me hang around while you talk to them now?" she asked.

"Fine. Let them in, Rosie."

Fina and Renata avoided each other's gaze and were joined a moment later by Cristian and Pitney. Rosie disappeared as quickly as she'd appeared.

Pitney was decked out in her usual bright attire: a purple pantsuit with a yellow starburst–patterned shirt that was snug across her large breasts. And her breasts weren't *Playboy* playmate–big, but real-life big: oval-shaped and unruly. Her mass of wiry curls was being held back by a pair of oversized sunglasses.

"Ms. Sanchez, it's nice to see you again," Pitney said. Cristian smiled and nodded at Renata and Fina. "We'd like to ask you some more questions."

"I already answered your questions." Renata reached down and pulled off her sensible pumps, which she shoved into the corner.

"I know, but murder investigations are complicated. We often conduct multiple interviews and ask the same questions multiple times."

Renata shrugged.

Pitney turned toward Fina. "Don't you have someplace to be, Fina?"

"You two know each other?" Renata asked.

"Some of my cases have overlapped in the past with Lieutenant Pitney's and Detective Menendez's," Fina said.

"Well, that's very cozy," Renata said, reaching into a cupboard and pulling out an apron. She put it on over her black pantsuit, then turned on the oven.

Pitney looked at Renata and then Fina. "I think we should do this privately."

Renata began opening various cabinets, pulling out dishes and ingredients. She didn't say anything.

"Or we can do it at the station," the lieutenant suggested.

Renata sighed. "Just do it now. It doesn't matter to me if Fina stays."

Pitney glared at Fina.

"I don't have anyplace to be, really," Fina said, and smiled. She leaned her hip against one of the counters. Cristian suppressed a grin.

Pitney scowled at her, then turned her attention to Renata. "We wanted to talk a little more about your interactions with Hank Reardon."

Renata's eyes strayed to the next room, where Alexa was still sitting at the table, writing in a journal.

Cristian nodded toward the girl. "Should she maybe . . . ?"

"It's fine. I don't believe in keeping secrets from my children." Pitney and Cristian exchanged a glance. This open-book approach to parenting was increasingly popular and wildly inappropriate. Some of their work-related conversations were barely suitable for adults, let alone children. "And he wasn't *her* father, anyway."

"That hardly seems the point, Ms. Sanchez," Pitney said. Cristian watched his boss. Pitney was tough, and he was often caught in the middle between her and Fina, but she was forthright and principled. Cristian respected her. "She's a minor. I don't think we should discuss this in front of her."

"I have to agree, Renata," Fina said, earning a raised eyebrow from Pitney.

Cristian looked at Alexa, who peered up at him from beneath her thick bangs. She popped a chip into her mouth.

"I'll decide what's best for my child, not the police." Renata turned to the counter and faced the stack of ingredients she'd gathered there. She peeled the top off a Tupperware container filled with red liquid and dipped a tortilla into it. She spooned meat and cheese onto it, rolled it into a tight parcel, and placed it in the bottom of a casserole dish.

"Had you ever met Hank Reardon before you learned he was your donor?" Pitney asked.

"Not that I can remember. We hardly moved in the same circles."

"No, but you were both active in community events," Pitney commented.

"I don't attend the galas and fund-raisers that people like the Reardons do. I don't have thousands of dollars to spend on buying a table."

Fina knew her father often purchased a table at the events hosted by his favorite charities. Usually, the minimum outlay was ten thousand dollars; that kind of charity required deep pockets.

"So when did you first meet him?"

"At the meeting with them." Renata gestured toward Fina.

"Carl arranged a meeting with Renata and the other SMC, Marnie Frasier," Fina said. "Jules Lindsley and Hank Reardon were there, as well as Danielle Reardon."

"What happened in that meeting?" the lieutenant asked.

"Renata, don't answer that. It's protected by attorney-client privilege." Cristian frowned at Fina.

"I don't have anything to hide, Fina." She filled and rolled another tortilla. "He tried to pay us off."

"How much did he offer?" Cristian asked.

"Five million per child."

Pitney whistled. "That's a lot of money."

"I can't be bought, Lieutenant."

"And it's not really a lot of money when you consider his net worth," Fina added.

"Enough from you," Pitney said, pointing a finger at her. "I'll deal with you later."

Fina tried to look chastened; it was a reach.

"So you were pissed at Hank Reardon," Pitney said to Renata.

"Absolutely, but I didn't kill him."

Fina glanced at Alexa through the doorway. She was pouring crumbs from the Pringles can into her mouth.

Pitney watched Renata. "You used two different donors to conceive your children?" she asked.

"How is that relevant?"

"It's our job to decide what's relevant, and it's your job to provide the information."

"Fine. I used two different donors. By the time I decided to have a second child, donor #575651 was no longer available."

"You didn't bank any when you had Rosie?" Cristian asked. He watched Renata's nimble fingers assemble the enchiladas.

"Someone's done his research."

"Detective Menendez is more than just a pretty face," Pitney offered.

"Indeed," Fina mumbled.

Renata ignored them. "No, I didn't bank any. You have to remember this was almost twenty years ago, and the industry was relatively young. I didn't think to do it, and the bank didn't have an aggressive marketing campaign like they do now."

"But you would have preferred having the same donor," Pitney ventured.

Renata held her hands up in exasperation. They were dripping with chili sauce. "Well, of course, but if there's no sperm, there's no sperm." She nudged the kitchen faucet with her elbow and rinsed her hands.

Pitney and Cristian stepped out of the way as she pulled open the oven door and slid the pan into the heat.

"Anything else?" Renata asked.

"Yes. Where were you on Monday night and Tuesday morning?" Pitney asked.

Renata untied her apron. "I already told you. I was here, asleep."

"Can anyone confirm that?" Cristian asked.

"I don't have a boyfriend, Detective, so no, no one can confirm that."

"Don't you remember, Mommy? You got me a drink of water." Alexa licked her fingers and gazed at her mother. The adults looked at her.

Renata was silent for a moment. "I . . ."

"I had a nightmare and you got me a drink and stayed with me until I fell asleep." The girl looked at them, her round face a blank canvas.

Fina silently implored Renata to shut up.

Renata picked at something on the countertop. "I suppose that's right."

"What time was that?" Cristian asked.

"I don't remember exactly. Maybe four or so." Renata grabbed a sponge and ran it over the countertop.

"Okay. We'll be in touch," Pitney said. "If you think of anything else or if anything changes . . ." She stared at Renata. "Call me. We'd also like to speak with Rosie."

"No. Absolutely not."

"It wasn't a request, Renata. We need to speak with her," Pitney said.

"Do you have a warrant?"

"We're not arresting her, for goodness' sakes."

"Then you're not speaking with her."

"We can compel her to talk to us," Cristian said.

"Then compel away."

Pitney shook her head wearily and left the kitchen.

"Enjoy those enchiladas," Cristian said, walking to the front door. "They smell good."

"Renata," Fina said.

"You need to go, too, Fina. We're having a family dinner before Alexa's soccer game." She shooed the trio out and closed the door behind them. On the front porch, Pitney looked at Cristian.

"That was interesting," she said. They walked down the stairs to the Crown Victoria parked out front.

"Think *you* can get Rosie to talk to us?" Cristian asked Fina from the driver's side.

"I'm happy to try. As long as it's with representation."

Pitney rubbed her eyes with her fingertips. "Oh my God, Fina Ludlow. Go away, please."

"Well, since you asked nicely." Fina started walking away.

Cristian called after her. "Keep in touch and try not to interfere!"

"But I'm so good at it!" Fina said, and climbed into her car.

Twenty minutes later, she was less than a foot away from the curb on Mass Ave, arguably not the safest spot to wait for the light, when a man jostled into her, nearly sending her into the path of an oncoming SUV.

"Shit!" she exclaimed.

Fina regained her footing and retreated a safe distance onto the sidewalk. She scanned in every direction until her eye settled on a man wearing jeans and a black T-shirt. His back was to her as he jogged down the street toward a waiting cab.

"Hey!" she hollered, but before she could catch up to him, he'd hopped into the cab and disappeared in the direction of Harvard Square.

It was time to start paying better attention.

The meeting had been called to order, and Juliana had thanked everyone for giving up their Saturday afternoon. Enough of their board members had demanding jobs that they couldn't pop out in the middle of the day to fulfill a charity commitment. They were halfway through the agenda, but two of the women were stuck on details relating to the boutique proposal. Juliana sipped her water and looked at the other members arrayed around the table. Mary Stevens and Jessica Laramee were arguing about the inventory system that would be implemented if and when the bra boutique opened at the center.

Juliana decided to let them hash it out for a few more minutes. She had learned that some members had to hear themselves speak for a certain amount of time, regardless of the subject matter. She had to balance this need with the other board members' limited patience, but it was a skill she had perfected over time. When she noticed Edith Steagen stifling a yawn, Juliana stepped into the breach.

"Undoubtedly, this is an important issue, but I suggest, Mary and Jessica, that you discuss it outside of the full board meeting. I've no doubt that with Sheila's input"—she nodded at the center's director—"you'll be able to reach a workable solution." Juliana smiled.

Mary and Jessica nodded and scribbled on their notepads.

"Sheila, I understand you have some promising news on the facilities front?"

"Yes, I was able to confirm that the house next door is going on the market." There was a murmur around the table. "Obviously, this would be the perfect opportunity for expansion."

The Reardon Center currently occupied a large Victorian house on a side street in the northern part of Cambridge. The addition of the house next door would nearly double the center's space.

"That sounds wonderful," Edith Steagen said, "but it would be an enormous investment and require a huge outlay of capital. It may be too ambitious."

"Edith! Is there any such thing?" Juliana joked. "This community is counting on us. We need to make this happen."

"Do you know something we don't, Juliana?"

Juliana smiled. "Let's just say that I'm cautiously optimistic."

. . .

Dinner at Scotty and Patty's was a good time. It was occasions like these that reminded Fina why she hadn't left the family fold years ago. True, her parents were challenging, and her oldest brother was a molester, but Scotty and his family and Matthew had a lot to recommend. Being a Ludlow wasn't easy, but it wasn't *all* bad.

The kids had scattered, and Scotty took a phone call while Patty got more wine. Fina and Milloy sat at the table catching up on each other's day.

"A guy tried to push me into the street today, like he wanted me to get run over," Fina said.

"Anyone else told me that, I'd assume they were mistaken, but when it comes to you . . ."

"When it comes to her, what?" Patty asked when she walked into the room with an open bottle of red wine.

"She thinks someone tried to get her run over, and I was saying that when it comes to her, it's completely within the realm of possibility."

"That's a reassuring thought." Patty topped off Milloy's and Fina's glasses.

"The car must have come pretty close." Milloy swirled the liquid before taking a sip.

"Trust me. He came close, and I think there's another guy following me who's giving me the creeps."

"What are you going to do about it?" Milloy asked. Scotty came back into the room and slid into his seat.

"What *can* I do?" Fina asked. "Be more careful?"

"Now what?" Scotty asked.

"Your sister thinks someone tried to run her over." Patty struggled to conceal a grin.

"Oh, honestly, Fina." Scotty looked at her and reached for the wine. "Could we just take a break from the bloodshed?"

"Stop being such a drama queen. Your wife thinks it's funny."

Scotty stared at Patty. "It's not funny."

She curled her fist in front of her mouth. "It's a little funny." Scotty frowned. "Think about it, Scotty. That poor bastard has no idea what he's in for."

"She does have a point," Milloy commented, grinning.

"Stop being such a worrywart. It's all good," Fina said.

"You always say that," Scotty grumbled, and took a large gulp of wine. "And it never is."

13

Sunday was generally a slow day in the realm of private investigation. Most businesses were closed, and people were unavailable and less inclined to shoot the breeze with a stranger when they had family commitments.

On Monday morning, Fina scrolled through her phone messages while the elevator took her down to the garage. She started to exit and bumped into a man who answered her apology with a hand around her neck. Pushing her back into the elevator, he reached up and shattered the security camera with one swift motion.

Fina kicked him hard in the groin, but the doors closed before she could escape. He slammed her up against the wall of the elevator and, after a couple of floors, pulled out the emergency stop button. The car jerked to a halt, and Fina stopped struggling.

"Forget about your gun," he said.

She was quiet. It was good advice. People had this idea that if you had a gun, you had the upper hand, but that was a fallacy. You had to grasp the weapon, release the safety, aim, and get a clear shot, all of which was next to impossible in a small space in fifteen adrenaline-fueled seconds.

"I'm not moving," she croaked as his hand applied more pressure around her neck.

"I think you should take a little trip," he hissed in her ear.

Fina was able to breathe, but just barely. Her head was aching, and her ears were starting to ring. "You're a travel agent?"

He stepped away and backhanded her across the face. Fina tasted blood where one of her teeth had cut her lip. Her cheek stung.

He grabbed her around the neck again and squeezed.

"Either get out of town or I'm going to relocate you myself."

Fina didn't respond.

"Understand?"

She nodded.

He depressed the emergency stop button and the car jerked to life. The doors opened on the fifteenth floor, and he pushed her into the hallway. "You can take the next one."

The doors closed, and Fina doubled over with her hands on her knees. She took a half dozen deep breaths and gingerly probed her cut lip with her fingers. Reaching into her bag, she wrapped her fingers around her gun and then pushed the up button for the elevator.

Back inside Nanny's, she turned the dead bolt, threw down her bag, and went into the bathroom. Her lower lip was starting to swell and split near the corner of her mouth, and a bloom of bruises was appearing around her neck.

This was no time to take a trip.

Fina lay on the couch for half an hour with a bag of frozen peas on her lip. Finally, she took some Advil and willed herself to get up and retrace her steps to the garage. Twenty minutes later, she walked into Carl's office.

"Good," Carl said. "I was just about to call you."

Fina plopped into the chair in front of his desk.

"What happened to you?" He stared at her face.

"I had a little set-to."

Carl sighed. "Are we going to get sued over this?"

"Your concern is touching." Fina went over to the minibar and pulled two diet sodas from the fridge. She popped open one, took a long pull, then pressed the second against her swollen lip.

"How's *he* look?"

"You always ask me that, and whoever he is looks fine." She sat down on the sofa. "I was at a decided disadvantage, being ambushed in the elevator." Her neck was starting to throb. "We should sue the building. Their security is shit."

"We have bigger problems."

"Great. What now?"

"Michael Reardon is on his way in."

"To see you?"

"Yes. He's not pleased with your progress."

Fina screwed up her face in concentration; it hurt. "So he called you? Wouldn't calling me be more to the point?"

Carl shrugged. He was seated in his large leather desk chair and slowly swiveled side to side.

"That's ridiculous," Fina said.

"What's ridiculous is that you aren't on top of this. You should have given him a progress report by now."

"Give me a break. It's been less than a week since he hired me." Fina rotated the cold soda on her face. "Maybe he should hire someone else if he's unhappy."

Carl shook his finger at her. "The Reardons could be a cash cow, so make nice."

Shari tapped on the open door and leaned into the office. "Michael Reardon is here."

Carl nodded, and she ushered him into the room. He was wearing khakis and a checked button-down shirt. His sandy blond hair looked damp and neatly combed. The expression on his face when he saw Fina suggested that he didn't expect the subject of the meeting to actually be in attendance, certainly not looking like a prizefighter.

"Michael," she said. She struggled off the couch, and they both sat down across from Carl. It was like being called to the principal's office.

"What happened?" he asked, giving her a weak smile.

"Occupational hazard."

"Don't worry about her. She's fine," Carl offered.

"I was choked."

"Like choked, your air supply was cut off?" Michael asked.

"Yes, hence the bruises." Fina pointed to her neck.

"You should get that checked out. A lack of oxygen to the brain is no joke. It can cause serious damage."

"How would you tell?" Carl mused.

Fina glared at her father.

"So, Michael," Carl said as he sat back and rested his folded hands on his trim torso. "You sounded unhappy on the phone. I don't want you to be unhappy."

"Well, I don't know about unhappy." He avoided Fina's gaze and looked at Carl. He was seriously off base if he thought Carl would be the friendlier of the two. "More like unsure."

"About?" Fina asked. Carl shot her a warning look.

"The investigation. Where things stand." He glanced at her and looked away.

Fina ran her tongue over her swollen lip and took a moment. The only thing worse than bitching about her was not having the balls to do it to her face.

"I should have called you sooner. I apologize for that." Fina made an attempt at a smile. "I've been busy investigating." She gestured toward her face. "Obviously. But you should never feel that you can't call me directly."

Michael pointed at her face. "That's because of the investigation into my dad's death?"

"It's my primary case right now." True, it wasn't her only case, but Fina had difficulty believing that Greta Samuels had hired some muscle to scare her off.

"Jesus. I'm sorry." He looked at his shoes.

"It's not your fault," Fina said. "I just hope it reassures you that I'm making progress."

"People only beat her up when she's getting close to a breakthrough," Carl said.

"He's right," Fina added, "and I meant what I said. Don't hesitate to call me. Anytime. Day or night."

Carl rolled his eyes as Fina reached into her bag and handed her card to Michael.

"If I don't answer right away, it means I'm busy being beaten or something similar."

He pocketed the card. "I don't want you to get hurt on my account."

"She's tough. Don't worry about her." Carl glanced at his watch and then Fina. "The update?"

Fina took a sip of soda. "I've spoken to Danielle, your mom, Renata Sanchez, Rosie Sanchez, Tyler Frasier, Dimitri Kask, Mickey Hogan, Joseph Skylar, Ellen Alberti, and the cops, of course. I'm making progress, but sometimes you just have to work the leads until something breaks."

Carl tapped a finger on his desk. Fina was familiar with this motion, a metronome of his impatience.

"Wow, okay. I didn't realize you'd done so much."

"When would you like me to provide the next update?" she asked.

He thought for a moment. "How about in a couple of days? Even if you don't have anything concrete to tell me, I'd feel better just hearing from you."

"Of course. I'll be in touch." Fina moved to the edge of her seat. "I meant to ask you, where were you when your dad was killed?"

"Me?" Michael pointed at himself.

"Sorry, but I'd be remiss if I didn't ask."

"I was at home."

"Is there anyone who can confirm that?"

Michael fiddled with the watch on his wrist. "No."

"Great. Thanks." Fina stood up. "There's nothing else you need to tell me, right?"

Michael looked askance. "Like what?"

"Anything your dad said that seems relevant in hindsight. Your conversations with him." She looked him in the eye and gave him the chance to come clean about his fight with Hank.

Michael shook his head.

"Then I'm off," Fina said.

He was unhappy with *her*? Well. She was none too pleased with him at the moment.

"I'm hungry," Fina announced when she walked into Scotty's office. Down the hall from Carl's, her brother's space was a fun version of their father's. It had the same basic elements as Carl's—glass desk, leather sofa, flat-screen TV, private bathroom—but the focal point was a pinball machine, the Magic Genie, which, though muted, flashed in some kind of amusement Morse code.

"Good for you for using your words," Scotty responded, "but now try to do something about it, like a big girl." He looked at her, registering her injuries. "Oh, Christ. Should I even ask?"

"Probably not. Is Michelle around?" she asked, referring to his assistant. "Can we order some lunch?" She plopped down on her brother's couch.

"I already ate, and I have a deposition in fifteen minutes. But she'll get you something if you want. Or you could just buy yourself lunch like most adults in the workforce." He looked up from the documents on his desk and smiled at his little sister.

"Fine."

"How's the Reardon stuff going?" Scotty asked. "Is that"—he pointed at her lip—"because of the case, or did you cut someone off in traffic? Is it the guy from Saturday?"

"I assume it's because of the case, but he didn't introduce himself, and I didn't get a good look at the guy the other day. There are a lot of pissed-off people. It will take some work to narrow down the list."

"Well, you must be making progress if you've got someone spooked."

"That's what Dad said. Speaking of which, Michael Reardon tattled on me to Dad."

"Why? What did you do?"

"It's what I didn't do. I didn't call him in a timely fashion, so he went to the big guy. We just had a little sit-down to clear the air."

"Was it healing?"

"Extremely. I think he might be regretting pulling Dad into it. Dad did his stern-friendly thing."

"Ahh. The stern-friendly can be very effective."

"Exactly. Hey, do you know any plastic surgeons? I want someone to assess the damage."

Scotty called out to his assistant. "Michelle," he said, "will you get Fina in to see Dr. Whitmore?"

"No problem," she responded. The Ludlows were on poor terms with many doctors in the city, but on very good terms with a select group who often testified on their behalf. These doctors were only too happy to keep the family in good fighting form.

"Thank you," Fina said.

"Don't let Dr. Whitmore talk you into anything." Scotty grinned. "Thirty minutes with that guy, and he'll have you scheduled for a hundred thousand bucks' worth of work."

"Don't you worry. I can hold my own with the plastic surgeon."

"So *do* you have anything to report on the Reardon case?" Scotty asked.

"I've talked to a lot of people, and there's a fair amount of animosity, but no one has confessed, if that's what you're asking. It's a stew of money and parenthood—or parentage, I should say." Fina tapped her foot on the carpet as she thought. "Do you think Patty would have had kids if she hadn't met you?"

"With someone else, you mean?"

"No. I mean, if she hadn't gotten married, do you think she would have gone the single motherhood route?"

"I have no idea. You'd have to ask her." Scotty got up from his chair and pulled on his suit coat. "There's still time for you. The man of your dreams may be right around the corner," he said, straightening the stack of papers in front of him.

"That would suggest I dream about such things, and I assure you, I don't."

Scotty walked around the desk and leaned over toward Fina's midriff.

"What are you doing?" she asked.

"Just as I suspected," he said, and patted his sister's stomach. "You might want to have that thing looked at. I think it's broken."

Fina playfully slapped her brother's hand. "Piss off."

Scotty grinned. "Come by the house for dinner again one of these nights."

He walked in the direction of a small conference room, and Fina went the opposite way toward the exit. Something was making noise down there all right, but it was nothing that couldn't be cured with a snack.

At Heritage Cryobank, Ellen Alberti was unavailable, but the bank's director, Dr. Walter Stiles, emerged from the back of the building to speak with Fina.

He strode back out onto the sidewalk, and she had no choice but to follow him.

"Ellen told me about your earlier visit. We have no comment to make, and you need to leave. This is private property."

"Why so jumpy?" Fina asked. Her "meeting" in the elevator and Michael's complaints had put her on edge. This case was starting to annoy her.

Walter was a couple of inches taller than she, dressed in suit pants, a dress shirt and tie, and a white coat. His name was embroidered on his jacket, and an ID badge was clipped to the pocket.

"Ms. Ludlow, Heritage has no involvement in the Hank Reardon situation. We run a business here, and it's paramount that our clients feel comfortable. Your presence has the opposite effect."

Fina put a hand on her hip. "Come on. Those women sitting in there don't know who I am or what I do."

"Leave, or the police will be summoned."

Fina smiled. "Yeah, they love being 'summoned.'"

Walter glared at her. "Do you understand?"

"I do." She started backing away. "But you have to know that this kind of reaction only makes me more curious."

"There's nothing unusual about wanting to protect my organization from harassment."

"Maybe I'll be in touch with Ellen. She seemed less defensive."

"I wouldn't recommend it. Our lawyers will be in touch if you continue this campaign."

"As will mine. Sounds much more complicated than the friendly conversation I was suggesting." She walked to her car and got in.

Walter watched her from the entrance. He didn't return her wave when she pulled out of the parking lot. Fina glanced at him in the rearview mirror, rooted to the spot by the front door.

What was his problem? Anyone that pissy definitely warranted a second look.

Half an hour later, she was sitting in a café in Kendall Square, waiting for a chai latte and Theresa McGovern. Fundamental questions were still unanswered, and these questions weren't going to answer themselves. Did *anyone* have an alibi that could be confirmed? Renata's confirmation was a ten-year-old girl, and Michael didn't have anyone to confirm his whereabouts. Neither did Juliana. Either the killer was smart and had chosen an ideal time for murder or it had been spur of the moment, and he or she had gotten lucky.

And how did the killer get to and from the garage? If you were familiar with a scene, you could dodge the security cameras, but it wasn't easy. She'd have to ask Mickey Hogan if there had been any cars that had entered in the preceding ten hours but hadn't left the garage in a reasonable time frame. Maybe the car was only a way to get to the scene, not flee it. And what about the murder weapon?

Fina was starting to doubt that Theresa was going to show when she breezed in the door. She placed her order at the counter and walked over to join Fina.

"Hey," she said, peeling off a blazer. Underneath she wore a sleeveless shell that exposed the riot of color on her arms.

"That's some ink," Fina commented.

"You like?"

"Not for me, but it looks cool on you."

"You're not too old."

"I didn't think I was, but thanks for the vote of confidence." She inhaled the scent of chai. "Aren't you concerned with how it's going to look when you're old and droopy?"

Theresa shrugged, and a man placed a coffee down in front of her. "Nah, not really." She stirred sugar into the cup. "So how's that gig at Crystal coming?"

"It's coming," Fina said. "I have a call in to someone over there." On the drive over from the office, she'd left a message for Dante Trimonti. He was a pimp and budding entrepreneur who controlled a lot of the business that went in and out of Crystal. As with so many of her relationships, she and Dante had a love-hate thing going, but she'd saved his ass before. She had to imagine that any call in which she didn't threaten to shoot him would be welcome.

"You better not stiff me on this," Theresa said. "If you do, I'll sing like a birdie to Dimitri."

"I'm going to do my best, but I'm not making you any promises. If you can't live with that, I'll get my information some other way."

"I can live with that." Theresa reached into her bag and pulled out a sheaf of papers. "Hank's call log from the two weeks before he died."

Fina took the papers and glanced at them. "Theresa, you rock."

"I'm not sure there's anything in there, and obviously, the police have the same info."

"That's okay. I didn't expect an exclusive." She tucked them into her bag. "Thank you."

Theresa held on to her mug and gazed out the window. Fina studied the serpent on her arm. "So do you have a beef with Universum? Is that why you're doing this?"

Theresa looked at her. "I'm doing it because I want the gig at Crystal. It's not that complicated. I don't want to work as an assistant forever."

Fina nodded. Lots of people were motivated by their own self-interest, pure and simple. It wasn't always about the other guy.

"How'd you get started as a DJ?"

Theresa described her evolution from music-crazed teenager to occasionally paid young adult. Maybe it was something Haley would like. A better reason to be in the clubs than drinking and hooking up.

After draining her coffee, Theresa grabbed her blazer and bag and stood. "I'll hear from you soon?"

"Yes. Thanks." Fina had a last sip of her latte and watched Theresa dodge traffic.

She looked at the phone log peeking out of her bag. She sincerely hoped that Hank Reardon was a Chatty Cathy.

"Are you available tomorrow morning?" Scotty asked Fina later that night. She'd spent the afternoon poring over Hank Reardon's call log. She was trying to eliminate calls that had reasonable explanations and look for any patterns. She had spent hours on it with nothing to show so far.

"Depends on what you want me for."

"I'm doing an interview with Rosie Sanchez at the police station, and I thought it might be helpful if you sat in."

"Why are you handling it? I told Renata you could refer her to someone who practices criminal law."

"She doesn't want to go there. This way she can pretend there's nothing criminal going on."

"Ah."

"I think it would help if you were there."

"You're probably the only one; I don't think Renata or Pitney would appreciate my presence."

"But Rosie would, which is why I think they'll allow it."

"Why not?" She stretched her sore back muscles. "I'm eager to hear what she tells the cops."

"Do you think she's lying about stuff?"

"I'm not sure. Ask me again tomorrow."

Fina spent another hour on the phone log, but reached a point of diminishing returns. All the numbers were starting to look the same, so she took a warm shower and popped some Advil with a few big spoonfuls of chocolate chip ice cream. The smooth iciness of the ice cream felt good against her swollen lip.

The man in the elevator had been in the back of her mind all day. Despite his suggestion, she wasn't going to back off, nor could she walk around with her gun cocked. She was too tired to figure out a plan. Instead, she checked the dead bolt, put her gun on her bedside table, and went to sleep.

14

Getting choked was a great core workout, Fina concluded the next morning. When she rolled over in bed, her midsection ached in a way it hadn't in a long time. She braced herself before looking in the bathroom mirror. Part of her lip was puffy and split as if she could benefit from cleft palate surgery. Her neck was bruised and tender to the touch. Other women might try to camouflage it with a scarf, but looking like a badass wasn't so terrible in her line of work.

With three Advil, a diet soda, and a handful of Oreos on board, Fina made her way to Dr. Whitmore's office. A quick recon of the waiting room suggested that Fina was the only woman there who couldn't use her breasts as flotation devices. Dr. Whitmore examined her face and assured her that ice and anti-inflammatories would do the trick in a matter of weeks. When he started to narrow his eyes and study her nose, Fina knew it was time to leave.

Scotty was waiting for her at the police station when she arrived.

"Where's Rosie?" she asked.

Scotty looked at her, struggling for words. He'd seen her injuries the day before, but his reaction suggested her self-assessment in the mirror had been kind.

"It's not *that* bad," Fina insisted.

"It's not good."

"What do you want me to do about it, Scotty? I just saw Dr. Whitmore, and he prescribed ice and Advil."

He shook his head. "I dunno . . . makeup?"

"Really? You think lipstick is going to fix this?" She gestured at her fat lip.

"Maybe?"

"If you're embarrassed to be seen with me . . ."

"Hardly. I just have to get used to it." Scotty contemplated her. "You ever think that maybe you're not setting a great example for the kids?"

Fina rolled her eyes. "I'm not a battered wife, dumbnuts. I'm in a dangerous line of work. You should be glad they have such a strong female role model in their lives." She spotted Renata and Rosie coming through the front door. Rosie was dressed in black pants and a light blue cap-sleeved shirt. Her hair was pulled back in a bun. Renata was in work attire.

"Is it really a good idea for her to be here?" Renata asked Scotty, nodding at Fina.

"I want her here, Mom," Rosie said, staring at Fina, mesmerized by her appearance.

"Don't ask," Fina said. "It's all good."

A uniformed officer escorted them to the same interview room in which Fina and Pitney had had their friendly chat. Scotty took a seat on one of the couches and gestured for Rosie to join him. Renata sat on the other couch, and Fina studied the framed poster of Monet's *Water Lilies*.

A minute later, Pitney and Cristian walked in.

"Oh, look! The gang's all here!" Pitney said, and glared at Fina.

"Rosie asked me to be here," Fina said, pulling out a chair from the table and sitting down. Pitney sat down across from her, and Cristian took a spot on the couch with Renata. Cristian's eyes widened, and Pitney followed his gaze to Fina's face.

"She doesn't want to talk about it," Scotty said, holding his hand up like a crossing guard. "She's fine, just had a little skirmish."

Fina shrugged innocently.

Renata said something to Cristian in Spanish, looking at Fina.

"Is she talking about me?" Fina asked.

"Nobody's talking about anything in Spanish," Pitney said. "No offense to your mother tongue."

Renata straightened up and looked offended.

"Let's get this show on the road," Scotty said, tapping his watch.

"Fine. Rosie, where were you on Monday night through Tuesday morning?" Pitney asked.

Rosie looked at Scotty. "I was staying at my friend's apartment. Well, actually, it's not his apartment; it belongs to his brother." She scrunched up her toes, which were peeking out of her sandals. Her nails were a bright aquamarine color.

"You're talking about Bill Hedquist's place?" Cristian asked. He had produced a small notebook and pen and was taking notes.

"That's right. Sam's brother."

"And you were there all night?"

"Uh-huh."

"Are we done?" Renata asked, and scooted forward on the couch.

"No, we're not done," Pitney snapped. Today's outfit was a sartorial interpretation of Cinco de Mayo: a blouse with yellow, lime green, and red stripes paired with dark red trousers. "Rosie, tell us about your relationship with Hank Reardon."

"I never met the guy," Rosie said.

"Never spoke to him?" Cristian asked.

"Never."

"You're sure?" Pitney asked.

"Lieutenant." Scotty tipped his head to the side. "Really? She had no contact with the man."

"You didn't have the urge to seek out your father?" Pitney asked.

Rosie looked down at her feet. She touched her bun as if to tame an errant hair that wasn't there. "I wasn't the one who tried to find him in the first place. Remember?"

Renata exhaled loudly. Fina imagined this would be the go-to fight for years to come.

"So you stayed at the apartment all night?"

"Yes. I already told you that."

"Okay," Pitney said. "*Now* we're done."

"Great," Scotty said enthusiastically. "You know how to reach me, Lieutenant." He shook her hand and Cristian's and gave Fina's arm a squeeze on the way out.

Pitney, Cristian, and Fina stayed behind.

"What was that all about?" Fina asked.

Pitney frowned. "Seemed pretty straightforward to me."

Fina looked at Cristian, then back at Pitney. "If you say so."

In the hallway, Fina found Scotty checking his messages. They moved toward the exit. After a moment, he slipped his phone into his pocket.

"Renata and Rosie left already?" Fina asked.

"Yup."

"So what do you think they've got?" she asked, walking with him to a town car that was idling at the curb.

"No idea, but something's up. They were definitely just trying to get her on the record, which usually means they know something we don't."

"Dammit all." Fina slung her bag over her shoulder and leaned her hip against the car.

"Do you think Cristian will give you a hint?" her brother asked.

"Doubt it. I'm going to have to figure it out myself."

"Well, get to it, Sis!" Scotty opened the door. "Do you need a ride?"

"I drove." She thought for a moment.

"What is it?" Scotty asked.

"Nothing," Fina said. "Just a thought."

Scotty looked expectant.

She shook her head. "I don't know. I'll let you know if I come up with anything."

"Let me know either way. I don't want to have to tattle on you to Dad." He climbed into the car, chuckling. "Have him haul you in for a talking-to."

"Very funny. Like you've never been hauled in for a lecture."

"Touché. Keep in touch, and stay safe."

Fina slammed the door and watched the car pull into traffic.

Just a couple of months before, she'd been dredging up the sordid details of her niece's illicit activities, and now she was going to have to start digging around Rosie.

Whatever happened to teenagers going to sock hops and mixers, maybe borrowing their parents' car to "watch the submarine races"? Were all teenagers liars nowadays? Up to no good? Or just the teenagers Fina knew?

Fina went back to Nanny's to catch up on some paperwork. Although she didn't follow rules in general, Fina did follow standard business procedures when it came to her work. She carefully tracked her expenses, regularly generated invoices, and always paid her bills on time. There was always something to do that was more interesting and more pressing, but Frank had taught her that you needed to keep your house in order if you wanted to be taken seriously.

She also spent time reviewing Hank's phone log and ended up with only three numbers she couldn't identify. The reverse number lookups didn't give her any answers, so she put in a call to her contact at the phone company, who was equally unhelpful. Fina called Theresa McGovern, but the numbers were unfamiliar to her. There was a time when Fina would have just called the numbers, but technology complicated things. Even when you blocked your number, there was no guarantee the recipient couldn't ID you, and Fina didn't want to tip her hand. She called Danielle Reardon instead and made a date for later in the day. Risa's was her next stop.

Risa let her in while talking on the phone, and Fina followed her to the kitchen. Risa was doing more listening than talking and rolled her eyes as the other person nattered on.

"Finally!" Risa said five minutes later, putting the phone on the counter. "That Mona can talk." She took a deep breath and looked at Fina. "Did you have an accident?" Risa traced her finger close to Fina's neck. "Those look like bruises."

"A little mishap related to a case."

Risa looked alarmed.

"Not your case." Fina smiled. "I don't think Greta hired someone to rough me up."

"Well, that's reassuring, I guess. What can I do for you?"

"Are the kids around?" Fina asked.

"Nope. Just me."

"Good. I need to get a DNA sample from you."

Risa gently gripped the edge of the granite counter. "Does that mean you've figured something out?"

"The birth certificate that Greta Samuels sent to me is an authentic birth certificate. The baby named Ann Sylvia Patterson—who shares your birthdate and time—was a real person. However, that doesn't confirm that you are Ann Sylvia Patterson or that Greta Samuels is your aunt. The best way to do that is to run a DNA test."

Risa's gaze wandered toward the sliding glass doors overlooking the sizable backyard.

"If you're game, that is," Fina said. "If not, we can leave things as they are."

"But if we do that," Risa said, looking at her, "I won't ever know if she's my aunt."

"No, you won't. You should also know that Greta's sister—possibly your mother—died six months ago."

Risa picked up a glass of iced tea that was sweating on the counter. She took a small sip, then gently placed the glass back down. "So if we're family, there's no chance I'll ever meet my biological mother."

"Right."

The thought and its ramifications hung in the air between them.

"If you decide to go ahead with the test," Fina continued, "you need to prepare yourself for the two possible outcomes."

Risa noticed the glass in her hand. "Sorry, did you want something to drink, Fina?"

Fina always hoped for refreshment at Risa's house, but her friend looked genuinely troubled by the conversation, and it didn't seem right to inquire what was on the menu.

"No, I'm fine."

"I just—sorry, I don't know why I'm having such a tough time with this."

"Because it's a big deal. It would be weird if you weren't having a tough time. You're allowed to feel conflicted, you know." Fina stood. "You don't need to make up your mind right now. Give it some thought. Talk it over with Marty."

"Okay. That's good advice. He always helps me figure things out." Risa and Marty were like Scotty and Patty; they seemed like partners who supported and relied on each other, who had each other's best interests at heart. Witnessing these relationships was always a revelation to Fina, who was used to the Carl-and-Elaine dynamic of two attention seekers wrestling for the upper hand.

"There's no rush," Fina said, and walked to the door. "Call me whenever. I know this is a lot to take in, and if you want to talk, I'm happy to listen."

"Thanks, Fina. I don't know why everyone thinks you're such a hard-ass," Risa said, the hint of a smile curling the edges of her mouth.

"Well, for God's sakes, don't set the record straight."

Fina returned to her car and set off for the nearest fast food drive-thru. All that compassion had generated quite the appetite.

Before quizzing Rosie more about her alibi, Fina decided to quiz Renata at her office. Sometimes interviewing someone at their workplace generated a different reaction, and Renata had her own dubious alibi to explain. Fina didn't know if she would be more truthful in a professional setting, but mixing things up couldn't hurt.

The director of a nonprofit organization dedicated to housing issues, Renata was equally respected and disliked by the various pols in the city, but to the disenfranchised population that she served, she was a hero. There were a lot of people who had a safe place to call home thanks to Renata Sanchez.

The organization was located in a nondescript brick building between the South End and South Boston. A sign on the door asked people not to smoke, loiter, or urinate within twenty-five feet of the entrance, but some of the locals were treating this as a suggestion, not a rule. Nobody was peeing, as far as Fina could tell, but there was a small group of men hanging around, shooting the breeze.

A young woman behind the wood laminate reception desk asked Fina to sign the visitors' log. The waiting area was tightly packed with folding chairs, a couple of cheap side tables, and a few fake plants. The plants were an attempt to brighten up the place, but the effect was actually depressing. There was too little light—and perhaps too little attention—to keep a real plant alive.

"I'm here to see Renata Sanchez," Fina said, showing her PI license. The young woman barely glanced at the ID before picking up the phone and punching in some numbers. She was white, in her early twenties, and had long greasy hair. Her fingernails were easily an inch long and sported intricate nail art. The bed of each nail was painted bright turquoise, and a gold stripe separated that portion from the tip. These were painted in a swirled pattern of pink and purple. It was impressive, yet hideous, all at the same time.

"Wow. I've never seen nails like that," Fina commented when the receptionist hung up the phone. "How long does that take?"

The woman splayed her fingers and admired her talons. "A few hours."

"That's quite a time commitment." Time that could be spent on washing one's hair or other more basic hygiene tasks.

"It's totally worth it, though," the young woman said.

"Definitely."

"Renata says you'll have to wait. She's with a client right now."

"That's fine."

A middle-aged woman sat staring off into space. Fina took a seat on the other side of the room and scanned the reading material. Usually she had a tablet in her bag or could fiddle on her phone, but there was something to be said for checking out the reading material provided for the clientele, whether it was Heritage Cryobank or a nonprofit like this. It might not tell you much about the clients, but it generally told you something about the organization itself.

Here, she found government brochures explaining various housing programs, grants, and guidelines, but little else. A copy of *Woman's Day* from the previous October promised the best recipe for cupcakes that looked like spiders, but instead, Fina grabbed a *Boston Herald*. The Red Sox were in the middle of a meltdown, and a lot of ink was devoted to the personality clashes plaguing the team. Had it been a team composed of women, Fina was sure they would have caught grief for being emotional and sensitive. The men, however, were praised for having integrity and being committed to the game. What bull honky. The whole mess could be solved by paying everyone minimum wage. They'd be too busy trying to make ends meet to bitch endlessly about the respect they weren't getting.

"Fina Ludlow?" A trim black woman scanned the room.

"That's me." Fina left the paper on the chair and followed the woman down a dark hallway to a small office overlooking an alley. Renata was sitting behind the desk, a phone tucked between her shoulder and ear. She was speaking Spanish and gestured for Fina to take a seat. As the conversation continued, Fina took stock of the space. There were three tall gray filing cabinets and a particleboard credenza that was covered with neat stacks of paper. Renata's space was crowded with stuff, but it wasn't messy. On her desk were pictures of Rosie and Alexa at various ages, and behind her on the wall, Renata had prominently displayed a photo of herself with the mayor.

"It's only been a couple of hours. What now?" Renata had hung up the phone and smoothly switched to English.

"I know, but I thought we should chat."

"I have a very busy morning." Renata glanced at a paper diary in front of her.

"As do I, so I'll make it quick. What isn't Rosie telling the cops?"

Renata looked at her. "Nothing. There's nothing she isn't telling them."

"You're sure about that?"

"Yes, I'm sure. Why are you asking me this? She told the police the truth."

"I don't think she did, and I wondered if you had any thoughts about that."

"I know what you know, Fina."

"Which isn't the same thing as knowing the truth."

Renata spread her hands open on the desk. "I know what she told me. Do you want me to give her a polygraph?"

"There's an idea. No, I just thought that, as her mother, you might know if she was lying."

"Does your mother know when you're lying?"

"My mother always thinks I'm lying; we're not a good case study."

Renata's shoulders sagged. She looked small in the desk chair. "I don't know what to do about this."

"Well, maybe I'm wrong."

"But now you've given me one more thing to worry about."

"I'm sorry. That wasn't my intention. I thought you might have some insight."

Fina studied her. It was true that Renata had set this in motion when she started her quest to reveal the donor, but no one could have predicted Hank's death.

"This has turned into a bigger mess than you could have antici-pated," Fina said. "I know it wasn't your intention."

"No," Renata agreed. "It certainly was not."

Fina adjusted in her seat. "What's the story with your alibi?"

"What about it?"

"It seems awfully convenient. Alexa just happens to remember her middle-of-the-night visit when the cops were there?"

"I don't know what to tell you."

"Who do you think killed Hank?"

Renata grabbed a paper clip from a small dish on the desktop. The dish must have been a school project gone awry. It was misshapen and a muddy brown color, a dish only a mother could love. She unbent the paper clip and manipulated it between her fingers. "It's hard to believe that the man didn't have enemies."

"He did. Unfortunately, in the eyes of the cops, you're one of them." Fina grabbed her bag and stood up. "Thanks for taking the time, Renata."

Fina was on the threshold when Renata spoke. "What's going to happen with his estate?"

"What do you mean?"

"I mean, who gets his money?"

"I'm assuming his family."

"What about his other families?"

Fina narrowed her eyes. "I don't think the cryokids qualify as his family."

"But they are," Renata insisted.

"You're going to sue his estate? Were you not listening to our con-versation? You and your daughters are in a mess because you insist on stirring up trouble." The sympathy Fina had felt moments before evaporated.

"So now we should just walk away? After we've come this far?"

"There's no legal precedent of cryokids inheriting from their sperm donors."

"And there was a time when women weren't allowed to vote," Renata countered. "Are you suggesting we should just accept things because that's the way they are? The way they always have been?"

"Renata. Stop trying to bullshit a bullshitter. I'm a female private investigator who carries a gun, and I enjoy nothing more than smashing glass ceilings, but you can't compare suffrage with sperm donations and inheritance law."

Renata was silent.

"And if the law changes, why would any man want to *be* a sperm donor?" Fina asked. "Most wives wouldn't be thrilled at the prospect of sharing their money with these 'other' families."

"Speaking of which, are you investigating the Reardons or does hiring you make them immune?" Renata asked.

"Why would any of them have killed Hank if you were going to sue regardless?"

"Because it's harder for me now that he's dead. We know he was going to give the kids something when he was alive."

"And you think Danielle might try to stop that?"

"Maybe."

"Good-bye, Renata."

Fina left the building, and the small group of men loitering out front parted so she could pass. One of them even complimented her butt. Who said gallantry was dead?

Fina felt decidedly overdressed as she waited in the café of a yoga studio on Beacon Street. The lithe bodies that poured out of the mirrored workout room were all dressed in sports bras and leggings and boy shorts, sweat glistening on bare skin. The bodies may have looked enticing, but the scent of hot sweat that accompanied them was pungent and odoriferous.

Danielle came over to the table where Fina was nursing a freshly squeezed orange juice. She pulled a gauzy T-shirt on over her sports bra and rummaged around in her bag. The large leather satchel was home to a collection of goods, including a pacifier, tiny diaper, paintbrush, and package of molding clay. Once she retrieved a hair elastic from its depths, Danielle pulled her hair back into a bun. Her clear skin and rosy cheeks made her look like a poster girl for yoga.

She lingered a beat too long on Fina's face, but didn't comment on her appearance. "One sec," she said.

Danielle returned a few minutes later with a large cup of steaming liquid.

"Were you doing hot yoga?" Fina asked.

Danielle nodded.

"It looks like torture."

"It's great," Danielle said. "Your muscles get so warmed up, you're able to reach positions you wouldn't otherwise."

Positions your body wasn't intended to reach, Fina thought, but she couldn't argue with the results. There wasn't an extra ounce of fat in the whole place.

Fina slid a piece of paper across the table. "Could you look at these numbers and let me know if you recognize any of them?"

"What's this about?"

"Just following up a lead. Nothing major." Fina had learned over the years that it was never a good idea to give people too much information or context. If you did, the chances were greater that they would tailor their answers to present themselves in the most flattering light, regardless of their guilt or innocence.

Danielle studied them. Her expression was unreadable, but she lingered for an extra moment on one of the numbers. "Nope. They aren't familiar."

"You're sure?"

"I'm sure." She drank some coffee. "Have you made any progress?"

"I have," Fina said, "but nothing I can discuss just yet."

Danielle frowned. "I'm his wife."

"I know, but technically, I don't work for you, and even if I did, I still wouldn't have much to discuss yet."

A man walked up to the counter. He was wearing tiny, skin-tight shorts, and his buttocks looked like two perfectly round spheres. His back was smooth and muscular, and his thighs were ropy. Fina tried to look away, to no avail.

Danielle followed her gaze. "See something you like?"

"No, actually," Fina said quietly. "He looks like he's on leave from Cirque du Soleil."

"Not my type, either. He's freakishly strong."

"I'll bet. He'd come in handy with a stubborn pickle jar, but beyond that, no thanks."

"I guess there's a lid for every pot."

"I guess."

"Was there anything else?" Danielle grabbed her bag. "I need to be someplace."

"Nope." Fina started to follow her to the door. "Actually, I wondered if Jules Lindsley had been in touch with you about Renata Sanchez."

Danielle stopped and stepped to the side, out of the traffic pattern, toward a wall lined with flyers. "What about Renata Sanchez? She's the one who came to my house, right?"

"The very one. I didn't know if there had been any discussion about the cryokids. Things were obviously left up in the air."

"Yeah. A lot of things are up in the air. That's what happens when someone is murdered." Danielle swallowed, struggling to maintain her composure. "Renata Sanchez is not my problem."

"Just checking."

Danielle pushed through the door in a huff, leaving Fina in her wake. Fina looked at the flyers on the wall. If she ever fostered a dog from the shelter who needed doggie yoga, she knew who to call.

15

Back in her car, Fina scrolled through her phone and found Rosie's number.

"When does college start these days? November?" Fina asked her when she answered.

"It starts in late September, but I'm deferring for a year."

"Got it."

"Is that why you called me?" Rosie asked after a moment.

"No, of course not. I need to see you, and it occurred to me that you might be busy with school."

"I'm busy with work. You know, the animal shelter."

"Right. Any chance you could meet me for lunch?"

Rosie was quiet.

"Please?"

"I'm supposed to meet Tyler for lunch."

"Perfect. I need to talk to him also."

"Fine."

Well, it wasn't an enthusiastic response, but she'd take it.

She retrieved a message from Stanley, her doorman, informing her that she had a visitor camped out at her condo building. She didn't recognize his name, and given her recent encounter with a stranger, she decided to meet him in the lobby rather than invite him upstairs.

Fina approached the front desk, and Stanley nodded in the direction of the seating area by the front door. There were a couple of leather chairs facing a gas fireplace that boasted a modest flame year round. Sitting in one of the chairs was a young man, barely out of his teens, wearing baggy black jeans and an oversized T-shirt.

"Him?" Fina asked.

"He insisted on waiting," Stanley said. He made no effort to hide his distaste.

Fina walked over and faced him. "You're waiting for me?"

"Yeah." He stood. "You're Fina Ludlow?"

"Uh-huh." Fina was alert, her muscles tense and ready for whatever he had in mind.

"I'm Brett Linder. I'm one of those kids. You know, the test-tube babies."

"Huh?" Fina narrowed her gaze.

"You know. The guy who died. I'm one of his."

Fina studied him. He had a skinny build and shaggy light brown hair. He was swimming in his T-shirt, and his jeans were belted nearly below his ass. On his feet he wore large canvas sneakers.

"You don't even know his name," Fina stated.

"I know it." His eyes darted around the lobby for a moment. "It's Reardon."

"Well, Brett, I don't know what I can do for you."

"You're the one they keep talking about in the paper."

"What is it that you want?"

"I don't know, I just thought I should talk to some of the other kids. Get to know my family." His eyes kept wandering to the bruises around her neck.

"Don't you have a family?"

He shrugged. "Sure, but we don't see one another much."

"But you suddenly have a burning desire to know your half-siblings."

"Yeah." He smiled. "You got it."

"So money doesn't interest you?"

"Hey, if they wanted to throw some my way, I wouldn't object."

"I bet you wouldn't." She shifted her bag to her other shoulder. "What makes you think Hank Reardon is your biological father?"

"My mom used the same sperm as those other kids."

"Heritage Cryobank?"

"That's the one."

Fina pulled her notebook from her bag. She asked him for his mother's name and his date of birth. She turned to a new page and scribbled something down.

"Here's the info for the detective investigating Hank's murder and for Hank's attorney." Fina tore off the page and handed it to him.

Brett looked at the paper. "What am I supposed to do with this?"

"You're supposed to call them. I'm sure they're interested in potential Reardon kids. The city will be crawling with them before too long."

"I'm not a potential Reardon kid. I *am* a Reardon kid," he said harshly.

"Well, you're going to have to prove it."

Brett shook his head.

"What do you do with yourself, Brett? Do you go to school? Work?"

"I have stuff, projects." He stuffed the phone numbers into his pocket.

"No one is going to give you the time of day until you give a DNA sample to prove that you're related to Hank Reardon. If this is a con, it isn't going to work."

"Fuck you, it's not a con."

Stanley looked up from the desk.

"And you'd better work on your attitude," Fina said.

"Just because I didn't go to some fancy school or shit doesn't mean I couldn't be his kid."

"Of course not. But this"—she gestured at his clothes and general sulkiness—"is not going to help your case. Take a shower, pull up your pants, and call Jules Lindsley. There's nothing I can do for you."

"You don't need to be such a bitch."

"Brett, this is me being nice and giving constructive criticism." Fina turned and walked back over to the front desk.

"We're done, Stanley. Let me know if he shows up again."

"Of course, Ms. Ludlow."

Fina watched Stanley lead Brett to the door and indicate that his visit was over. She waited until he had left her sight line before pushing the button for the elevator. This was exactly what she didn't need, troubled teenagers lining up at her front door.

On the face of it, Walter Stiles was not a particularly interesting man. He didn't have any arrests on his record, didn't owe any enormous sums of money beyond the mortgages on his two homes. Fina couldn't find any record of a marriage or children. He seemed to be active in various professional organizations, including the National Reproductive Medicine Society, and turned up at the occasional charity event related to children. Fina found a couple of pictures of him with a blonde. They were posed with other couples at a Monte Carlo night benefiting a local after-school program.

The online Board of Medicine Registry only provided information for the past ten years and didn't list any disciplinary action against Walter nor malpractice insurance payouts, but ten years was a small portion of a thirty-plus-year career. Fina would have to do more digging.

She was on hold for five minutes, skimming various documents, before Matthew picked up.

"Do you know anything about Dr. Walter Stiles?" she asked between bites of a banana smeared with peanut butter.

"Doesn't ring a bell. Who is he?"

"He's the head of Heritage Cryobank."

Fina heard tapping on the other end. "He's not coming up in our database, but that only means he hasn't crossed our radar."

"Okay. Could you get one of your helpers to dig a little more?"

"One of my helpers? You mean one of my highly paid associates?"

"No matter. Could be the lunch lady as far as I'm concerned, as long as she knows what she's doing."

"What's the case number?"

Every case at Ludlow and Associates was assigned a case number, which was like the Holy Grail. Every minute of work, every photocopy and paper clip associated with the case had to be filed under the case number so that the client was billed for every last dime. If a paralegal did some research for Fina, his or her time had to be billed to Michael Reardon.

"What's going on with you?" Fina asked after giving him the number.

"Work, as usual."

"You can do better than that. Any hot dates?"

"You sound like Mom."

"Mom asks you if you have hot dates?"

"She asks me if there are any serious contenders."

"Well, the sooner you find a future Mrs. Ludlow, the sooner she'll be less focused on me."

"You're deluding yourself. I could have four sister-wives and Mom would still be nosing around your business. You're her daughter; it's her God-given right to butt in."

"That's reassuring. Thanks."

"Happy to be of service. Gotta run."

She met Rosie and Tyler at a Chinese restaurant near Porter Square that boasted a $6.99 lunch special. When Fina arrived, they were already seated, sipping large sodas, their heads bent toward each other.

"Hi, guys," Fina said, pulling out a chair. "Thanks for letting me crash your party."

"I didn't think you'd take no for an answer," Rosie admitted, and sat back in her seat.

"I'm sorry to be pushy, but you are in the middle of a 'situation.'" Fina made air quotes to make her point.

"What happened to your face?" Tyler asked, his expression equal parts repulsion and fascination.

"I was jumped."

"Where?"

"In my condo building. Some goon suggested I take a vacation."

"Because of Hank?" Rosie asked.

"I think so."

Rosie picked at her cuticles. "That's scary."

"It was rather unpleasant, but I survived. I don't have any idea who's responsible, though, which is annoying." Fina picked up the menu and perused the lunch specials. A moment later, a waiter took their orders and refilled Fina's water glass, which she had drained.

"Did Rosie tell you about the conversation at the police station?" Fina asked Tyler.

"Yeah. I heard about it."

"Have you reflected on that little chat, Rosie? Are you ready to come clean?"

Rosie's eyes widened. "About what?"

"About whatever it is you're lying about."

She glanced at Tyler. "I'm not lying about anything."

"Well, let me tell you how I see it. The police asked you some very specific questions to get your responses on the record. That usually suggests they already know the answers to the questions they're asking and are just testing you to see if you're going to lie."

A waiter came to the table and deposited plates in front of each of them. Fina was always suspicious when food was prepared in the blink of an eye; she suspected this was one of those Chinese restaurants that made liberal use of the deep fryer and alternated between two sauces. Not that she was complaining; she loved deep-fried things with sweet, gloppy sauce.

She pulled the paper sleeve off her straw, stuck the straw in her drink, and swallowed some diet soda. "Do you see what I'm saying?"

"That the cops have some proof that contradicts whatever Rosie told them," Tyler offered.

Fina pointed at him. "On the nose, my friend."

Rosie picked up her chopsticks and grasped a broccoli floret. She put it in her mouth and chewed slowly. She took a sip of soda before speaking. "I don't have anything else to say."

"Which is not the same as proclaiming that you spoke the truth," Fina pointed out.

"I'm sick of this whole thing," Rosie said.

Fina looked at Tyler. "What about you? Are you sick of it?"

Tyler shoveled fried rice into his mouth and shrugged. "Sure, but whatever."

"Remind me where you were the night Hank died."

"I dropped Rosie at Sam's apartment and drove home. That's it."

Fina mentally tripped on what he said. Something was bugging her, but she wasn't sure what.

"Has school started for you?" she asked.

"Yup, but I'm still doing some shifts at the restaurant."

They focused on their food for a moment, but then Fina put down her chopsticks. "I'm starting to feel like a broken record; if you guys are lying to the police, you're playing with fire. You need to tell me or Scotty, and we'll help minimize the damage."

Rosie and Tyler looked at each other. Fina studied them, but their expressions didn't give anything away.

Fina speared a piece of sweet-and-sour pork on a chopstick and bit into it. Rosie and Tyler ate in silence.

"How are things with your mom?" Fina asked Rosie.

"We're kind of steering clear of each other."

"That's probably a good idea until things cool down a bit."

"When will that be? When I'm thirty?"

"Maybe, maybe not. It may be a lifelong strategy that you choose to adopt." Fina struggled to pick up some errant grains of rice with her chopsticks. "What about Alexa? Does she get along with your mom?"

Rosie rolled her eyes. "She's a little kiss-ass."

"It probably won't last," Fina said. "Just wait until she's a teenager." Fina had to wonder if being so eager to please was part of the motivation behind Alexa's reclaimed memory of the night of Hank's death. It was a natural instinct, after all, to lie to protect one's parent.

"I hope so," Rosie said. "It's going to piss me off if she ends up getting everything I had to fight for. The oldest kids always have it the hardest."

"Bullshit," Tyler interrupted. "My mother's a lot clingier with me than she was with Jess. The youngest is their last hope. Once you leave the nest, it's downhill from there."

Fina picked up a cube of pineapple. "You're both kidding yourselves. Renata and Marnie have a lot going on; they're going to rejoice when you guys leave the nest for good."

Tyler leaned back in his seat. "I don't buy it. My mom will be totally bummed." He grinned.

"You just keep telling yourself that, Tyler." Fina smiled and reached for the bill when it was deposited on the table. "My treat."

Rosie and Tyler expressed their thanks. Fina dropped some bills on the table and followed them out into the bright sunshine.

"Do either of you know a kid named Brett Linder?" she asked as they started down the sidewalk.

Tyler shook his head. "Never heard of him."

"Me either," Rosie said.

"Well, if his name rings any bells, call me." She walked around to the driver's side of her car. "Or if you decide to tell me the truth, call me. Or if you need legal counsel, call me."

"We get it!" Rosie hollered from a few cars away. "We'll call you!"

"Glad to hear it!" Fina replied, ducking into her car. She started the engine but sat for a moment, provoking an angry horn blast from a car waiting for her space. She watched Rosie and Tyler pause on the sidewalk. Their conversation was heavy with gestures, and although Fina couldn't tell what they were talking about, she doubted it was the beef with black bean sauce.

Fina got Emma Kirwan on the phone as she drove down Mass Ave. Emma Kirwan, her go-to computer whiz, was in her twenties, conservative and uptight yet incongruously good at breaking the law. Fina thought she looked like a right-wing soccer mom, but in Emma's case, looks were incredibly deceiving. Whenever she needed a deep search done that extended beyond financials and the law, Fina called Emma.

"How hard is it to get the info from E-Z Pass cameras?"

"What do you mean?"

"If I want the statement for a particular vehicle, how hard is that?"

"Not your vehicle?"

"Of course not my vehicle!"

"All right. Don't get your knickers in a twist."

"I want to find out the movements of a particular car on a particular night."

"Well, it's not easy, obviously, and it's not exactly legal."

"But is it doable?"

"Of course it's doable."

"Good. I'll e-mail you the tag number as soon as I get it."

"It'll cost you," Emma said.

"It always does."

Fina called her contact at the Registry and put in a request for a tag number. This, too, would cost her money and time, but she'd learned to go with her hunches. Sometimes, they were the only thing she had.

Marnie Frasier agreed to meet Fina after work to answer a few questions. Fina offered to stop by the house, but Marnie gave her the name of a hotel bar in Cambridge instead. When Fina arrived, Marnie was sitting at a small round table in the corner, glancing at the newspaper.

"Am I late?" Fina asked, taking a seat.

"No, I was a few minutes early. I haven't ordered yet."

A man came over with a bowl of mixed nuts and the wine list. Marnie picked up the list after he'd walked away, and Fina dipped her hand into the bowl.

"Oh, they're warm," she said, indicating the nuts. She popped some in her mouth. "That's so good."

Marnie reached over and grabbed some. "Delicious," she pronounced after she'd finished chewing. She ordered a glass of merlot, and Fina jumped on the bandwagon.

"Are you a wine aficionado?" Marnie asked.

"Hardly, but you look like you know what you're doing."

Marnie laughed. "I'm no expert."

"You are in my company." Fina looked around at the other tables. A few of them were occupied by men and women dressed in muted tones and clothing one step below business wear. Fina assumed that many of them were academics or in the sciences. It wasn't hard to imagine that she had the lowest IQ in the room.

"Tyler told me about Rosie," Marnie said.

"Her disappearing act? Yeah, I felt kind of bad forcing her home, but Renata was worried."

"They should have told Renata what was going on. It was crummy to make her worry."

"I think Rosie was at the end of her rope."

The waiter returned with their wine, and Fina watched as Marnie swirled the liquid in her glass and stuck her nose into the opening. She inhaled deeply before taking a sip.

"What's the verdict?" Fina asked.

"It's really nice."

Fina took a sip and held the rich liquid in her mouth. Marnie looked at her expectantly, but Fina just smiled and shrugged. "What you said."

Marnie took another drink. "So Rosie is home now."

"Yes, and she's been questioned by the police."

Marnie raised an eyebrow.

"I don't know if Tyler mentioned it, but I've been hired by Michael Reardon to find his father's killer."

"You're not working for Renata anymore?" She looked surprised.

"We don't seem to be, although with Renata, things seem to change on an hourly basis."

Marnie chewed thoughtfully. "I can't imagine the police like having you over their shoulder."

"They don't, but we manage. Have they questioned Tyler yet?" Fina asked.

Marnie frowned. "I know he's relevant since Hank was his donor, but they can't really imagine he had anything to do with his death."

"I don't know what they think, but I imagine he's on their list."

"Of suspects?"

"Of people they want to talk to."

Marnie reached over and took another small handful of nuts. "Well, obviously he'll cooperate if needed."

"If you want one of my brothers to sit in, that can be arranged."

"But your firm doesn't do criminal defense, right?"

"Right, but for half an hour of questions, it might be easier than finding someone new."

"I'll let you know."

"How's Jess doing?"

Marnie sighed and rested her chin in her hand. "She's okay. I worry sometimes that Tyler is too impulsive, doesn't pay enough attention to things, but occasionally that approach is a blessing."

"Jess is more serious?" Fina asked, holding her wineglass by its skinny stem.

"Yes, and very protective of her brother. They're both good kids."

"The police are probably going to want to know your alibi, and Jess's, too."

"That's fine."

Fina looked at her. "Mind if I ask?"

Marnie looked weary. "Tyler and I were home asleep, and I assume that Jess was at her place. We actually haven't had a family discussion on the topic." She smiled ruefully.

"No need to, it sounds like."

They exchanged pleasantries while emptying their wineglasses and munching on the rest of the nuts.

Outside, Marnie and Fina walked in opposite directions. Fina liked Marnie. She hoped her kids had nothing to do with Hank's murder.

Cristian's phone rang six times before he answered.

"Menendez."

"What took you so long?" Fina asked, her legs propped up on the back of the couch. "You usually answer by the second ring."

"I'm busy. What's up?"

"Nothing. Just wanted to touch base."

"There's nothing I can tell you, Fina." Voices could be heard in the background.

"I'm not asking for any information, actually. I have some for you."

"Hold on a sec." Cristian seemed to cover the phone and came back on a minute later. It was quiet now.

"Are you at work?"

"No." He hesitated. "I'm grabbing something to eat."

"Oh," she said. Cristian sounded funny.

"What did you need to tell me?" he asked.

"I had a conversation in my lobby this afternoon with a kid named Brett Linder. He claims that Hank was his donor."

"Really."

"Yeah, but it might be a scam. I think he's looking for a payday."

"Great. The list grows."

"I told him to contact you guys or Jules Lindsley, but I warned him he wasn't getting anything until he proved he was Hank's kid."

"You think that will scare him off?"

"I don't know, but I wanted to give you a heads-up. Do you hear that, it's me giving you a heads-up?"

"Yes, I hear you. I know that's very hard for you."

"It is. Thank you for recognizing that." She touched her split lip, which was starting to scab. "So, what, are you on a date or something?" she joked.

"Actually, yeah."

"Come on."

He was silent for a moment. "You told me to get a hobby, and I did."

"That's your hobby?"

"Why not? Seems like a good pursuit. Better than fixating on my ex-wife."

"So who's the lucky lady?"

"A speech pathologist named Cindy."

"Hmm."

There was an awkward silence.

"I've gotta go; I'm being rude."

"Cindy better get used to interruptions if she's going to date a cop. Not many women can compete with the job."

"Good night, Fina."

She lay there with the phone in her hand. When she suggested he get a hobby, she meant running or Xbox. It was supposed to be a distraction from Marissa, not from Fina herself.

Milloy answered his phone more quickly, but was unavailable, which only soured her mood more. They made a lunch date for the next day, and Fina had a glass of wine and a 100 Grand bar to offset her annoyance.

Apparently, those two hadn't gotten the memo requesting they be on call 24/7.

16

"I want to give you that sample," Risa said. Fina was fighting her way into the Sumner Tunnel when her phone rang. Matthew had asked her to check something out at the Revere Police Station, and she was coming back into the city.

"Okay. When's a good time for me to stop by?"

Risa's afternoon was booked with fund-raising committee meetings for Grahamson, the private school her kids and Haley attended.

"How about tonight at the club?" Risa asked.

"You want me to take a DNA swab at the club?" Fina was halfway through the tunnel, marveling that it was still standing. The Sumner Tunnel was narrow and dark, and the tiles looked as though they might tumble off the wall at any moment. Fina tried not to think about the ocean that surrounded it, squeezing its aged structure. She wasn't prone to claustrophobia, but she liked to get through it as quickly as possible.

"We could do it in the ladies' room, in one of the changing cabanas," Risa said.

"Okay. It's a little weird, but okay."

"I'm afraid I'll lose my nerve if I put it off."

"That's fine, I just want to make sure you really want to do it."

"I really want to; I'm just scared to death at the same time."

"That's understandable."

"How soon will we get the results?"

"If I put a rush on it, we can get them in twenty-four hours once the lab has both samples."

"Definitely put a rush on it."

"I will get it done ASAP," Fina reassured her.

They made plans to meet later in the day, and Fina drove back to her condo. She took special care when walking through the building's parking garage. Earlier in the summer she'd been jumped there, her wrist broken in the scuffle, which should have put her on alert, but time had a way of making you careless, which helped explain Monday's escapade. Fina wrapped her hand around the gun in her bag and scanned the rows of cars before hightailing it to the elevator.

Once upstairs she wandered into the kitchen, where she peered into the fridge. Fina got groceries delivered from an online grocery service every two weeks. Without the influx of ice cream, diet soda, and Pop-Tarts, she'd probably starve. Her nearly bare cabinets suggested that she was due for a delivery.

A handful of Nutter Butters in hand, she decided to call Greta Samuels. Fina dialed her number and looked out at the harbor while it rang. A tanker was being steered by two tugboats. The two vessels were dwarfed by the boat they were guiding, and Fina was struck by how incongruous the relationship seemed. But babies were little, and they ran their parents' lives; small didn't mean powerless.

"Hello?" a voice answered.

"Ms. Samuels? This is Fina Ludlow, the private investigator in Boston."

"I was worried. I haven't heard from you in days."

"I'm sorry about that, but I've been busy." *And I don't work for you,* Fina thought.

"Did your associate review the birth certificate?"

"He did. How's your cousin?" Fina asked.

Silence.

"Ms. Samuels? How's your cousin? The trip you took?"

"My cousin is fine." She perked up. "Thank you for asking. So do I finally get to meet my niece?"

"Not quite yet."

"I don't understand," she exclaimed. "You verified the birth certificate."

"Yes, but that doesn't prove that Risa is Ann Sylvia Patterson or that the two of you are related. The only way to do that is to run a DNA test."

Silence.

"But I don't know anything about DNA tests."

"You don't have to." Fina wandered into the kitchen and opened the same cabinets she had minutes before. She found a box of graham crackers tucked into the corner and a jar of peanut butter. "I just need a sample from you. I'm getting one from Risa later today. Then we'll send them both to the lab for analysis."

"How do you get the sample?" The stress in Greta's voice suggested she was imagining a six-inch needle.

"It's just a cotton swab from the inside of your cheek. Fast and not the least bit painful."

"Well, that sounds okay, I guess."

"I'd like to have my associate stop by today. It will only take a minute." Fina figured she would hire the same local PI to do the swab and overnight it to her.

"Oh, I don't know. I don't like the idea of a stranger doing it."

Fina dipped a graham cracker into the peanut butter and bit into it. The cracker was slightly stale, but it would do.

"Well, unfortunately, I can't do it. I'm in the middle of a murder investigation here in Massachusetts."

"Oh my. That sounds awful," Greta said.

"So I can send my colleague?"

"Could my doctor do it? I'd feel more comfortable." Her voice was the equivalent of auditory handwringing.

Honestly. It was a cheek swab, not a pelvic exam. This woman was turning out to be a real pain in the ass.

"That would be fine, but I'd need an affidavit swearing that the doctor was the only one who handled the sample. I really do need it today, and I'll pay for a courier to get it to the lab."

"Why is there such a rush?"

"Risa is anxious to get the information. Is that a problem from your perspective?"

"Of course not."

"Good."

"I just never thought this would be so complicated."

"It really isn't. Just a quick trip to the doctor's office. I imagine she's submitted affidavits before."

"She?"

"Your doctor. She or he." Fina put the top back on the peanut butter and walked into the living room.

"Oh goodness, dear. I wouldn't go to a lady doctor."

Fina held the phone away from her ear. Apparently she hadn't just dialed Maine, but Maine in the 1940s. "He, then. I'm sure he's submitted affidavits before."

"I'll call the office as soon as we're done."

"I think we're done," Fina said. "Unless you have more questions?"

"No, no. I'm all set."

"Great. I look forward to getting your sample." Fina ended the call and watched the tugboats race across the harbor, no longer burdened with the tanker. With the DNA samples, Risa would soon have an answer. Although Fina wasn't sure there was any good answer to this particular question.

She changed gears and started a background check on Brett Linder, and what little she found reinforced her wariness about his appearance on the scene. He had two recent arrests that listed his age as nineteen, one for disturbing the peace and the other for felony theft. Fina didn't have access to sealed juvenile records, but she found it hard to believe his life of crime had started at age nineteen. Arrests of young men were often like rats: For every one you saw, there were more lurking in the shadows. The good news was that Brett Linder wasn't really her problem—unless, of course, he had killed Hank.

She put a call in to Hal Boyd, her finance guy, but only got voice mail. Fina had a completely aboveboard financial manager who took care of her own money, but for casework and ethically questionable activities, she employed Hal. Next, she left a message for Emma.

Her phone rang, and she looked at the display. It was Milloy calling; she was late for lunch.

"I'm on my way," she told him, gathering her bag and keys with her other hand.

"You better be."

Fina drove like a madwoman, which wasn't much different from her usual approach, and slid into a booth across from Milloy at Legal Sea Foods ten minutes later. He was sipping an iced tea, and there was a diet soda with a lime at her place. On a small plate in the middle of the table, foil-wrapped butter pats were inserted into the middle of two rolls.

"Oh, you're the best." Fina liked her butter pat to be pre-melted in the warm roll before she peeled back the foil and spread it on the bread.

"I ordered for us," he said.

"Thanks." Fina took a long drink of soda and sat back. "So, what were you up to last night?" She certainly hoped *he* hadn't been on a date. There weren't many things you could count on in life, but Fina had grown used to the idea that Milloy and Cristian would always be available. Clearly, her assumptions were faulty.

"Dinner with Zeke and a couple of other guys." Milloy and Fina had met their freshman year at BU and knew many of the same people. Fina, however, was more of a loner than Milloy, and much of her social energy was put into her family. Who had the time to nurture friendships when they were busy putting out fires on the home front?

"How's the case going?" he asked, spreading butter on his roll.

"It's a mess, but they usually are, right?" Fina unwrapped her butter, but stopped when a man approached the booth.

He pulled a chair away from another table and took a seat at theirs. Dan Rubin was a freelance reporter in his fifties whom Fina had encountered on previous cases. He was wearing dark blue cotton pants and a wrinkled button-down shirt untucked on one side. His hair looked unkempt, and his complexion was ruddy. Over one shoulder, he had a battered leather messenger bag. If you subtracted about thirty-five years, Dan looked like a private-school boy who was late for lacrosse practice.

"I hear you're on the Reardon case," he said, swigging from a bottle of water.

"You're back," Fina noted. "Dan, this is Milloy. Milloy, Dan."

Dan thrust out his hand and shook Milloy's. "I took a little time off."

"I heard," Fina murmured. The waiter set down two steaming bowls of chowder and a few packets of oyster crackers. "I hope it was helpful." Rumor had it that Dan had been in rehab, and although Fina found the man annoying, she didn't wish him ill. She'd seen enough addiction in her work to know it was an evil scourge.

"Time will tell," Dan said, looking around the restaurant. "So *are* you working on the Hank Reardon case?"

"You know I am. What do you want, Dan?"

"I want a scoop."

"And I can't tell you about my clients. Why don't you do some investigative reporting? Like, what's the deal with the ME's report?" Fina already knew what was in it from Stacy, but she was curious if Dan had anything to add to the mix.

"It's being released today. I guess his wife was trying to fight its release, but it's public information."

"Any thoughts on the murder weapon?"

"I came here to ask *you* questions," Dan said, sipping his water.

"And I have nothing to tell you." Fina rolled her eyes at Milloy before dipping her spoon into the chowder. It emerged from the bowl holding a plump clam and a nugget of potato.

"But it's got something to do with the sperm donation, right?" Dan's leg bounced on the floor. Another minute of that and she'd have to punch him in the leg. "Can you imagine waking up and finding out that Hank Reardon was your father?"

"No, I can't." It was bad enough waking up and remembering that Carl Ludlow was.

Dan drained his water. "I think the donor babies are the key."

"Are you basing that on any information or just your reporter's thirst for scandal?"

"It's a good story, Fina."

"Leave the kids alone, Dan."

He leaned closer to her. "Why? What do you know?"

"You should leave us alone," Milloy said. "You're giving me indigestion."

He glanced at Milloy, sizing up his physique. "I will, but just tell me what you know."

"Nothing," Fina said. "I just know that they had nothing to do with the circumstances of their conceptions and births. And most of them are barely legal."

"Didn't stop you from talking to them."

"Good-bye, Dan."

"What do you think about the wives? I heard there was a big brouhaha at the funeral."

"I heard the same thing," Fina said wearily. She'd heard no such thing, but you always got more from people if you pretended you were already in the know.

"Apparently, this town isn't big enough for the two of them. I wonder what's going to happen with the Reardon Center," he mused, watching Fina.

"Your guess is as good as mine." She returned his gaze.

"Does Hank's death open the money taps or close them even tighter?"

"I don't know, but untangling Hank's business interests alone should keep you busy," Fina said before eating a spoonful of chowder.

"What do you know about his waterfront development deal?"

Milloy put down his spoon in annoyance.

Fina shook her head. "Nothing."

"I heard that Dimitri Kask was cut out of it. Care to comment?"

"Good-bye, Dan, and stop following me."

"Just doing my job, Fina."

"Me too. Just FYI, I'm a little jumpy these days, and I carry a gun. I would hate to accidentally shoot you."

"I'm not afraid of you." Dan chuckled.

"You should be," Milloy said, and stared at him.

Dan stood up and pulled out a business card. "If I come up with something, I'll be in touch, and you do the same," he told Fina.

"Um, okay . . . no. Did you have a lobotomy while you were away? We're not buddies or partners."

"Never say never." He stood up and ran his hands through his disheveled hair before hurrying out of the restaurant.

"What a pest," Fina said, and made room for the bubbling seafood casserole that was placed before her.

"Do *you* think Hank's murder is connected to the sperm donation?" Milloy asked.

Fina poked at the top of the dish, releasing steam from the buttery crumbs. "I think it's a strong possibility, but Danielle and Juliana both have a horse in this race, in terms of money."

"So what was he saying about the center? Some of my clients go there." Milloy was a massage therapist and had magic hands. He worked on a range of clients, from professional athletes to cancer survivors.

"Juliana founded the center when she was still married to Hank; it's her baby, but the new Mrs. Reardon has been trying to get a foothold in the city's social and philanthropic circles. Maybe Hank wasn't going to fund both of their interests indefinitely."

"You think he was killed over a charitable donation?"

"Not the donation, but the money in general and everything it provides: luxurious homes, ski vacations, status in the community, respect."

"You live in a dark and twisted world."

"We all do; some of us are just more aware of it."

"What's next?" Milloy asked.

"I need people to start telling me the truth."

Milloy snorted. "Good luck with that. You know, you're not an optimistic person by nature, and yet you always hold out hope that people are going to tell the truth."

Fina sat back in her seat. "You're right. There actually is a small part of me that expects the best of people."

Milloy shook his head. "Wonders never cease."

Michael Reardon suggested that they meet at his home rather than the office when Fina called him after lunch. After the recent intervention, he really wasn't in a position to turn down her request for a meeting. It wouldn't take long before he started pining for the good old days when she hadn't been in touch.

Fina scrolled through her e-mail while waiting for him on the stoop of his South End brick row house. The street was tree-lined and charming, and you'd never know that Copley Square was only a five-minute walk away.

"Hi." Michael lifted his hand in greeting and trotted up the stairs. Inside, Fina followed him up a wide staircase into a bright open space that encompassed the kitchen, living room, and dining area. Most everything in the place was white, with a few dashes of blue and green. The decor was tasteful and reminded Fina of his mother's house in Swampscott. Beachy chic seemed to be a Reardon theme.

"Nice place," Fina said.

"Thanks." Michael rubbed his hands together. He looked nervous. "Your face looks better."

"Eh. No permanent damage. I just have to let time do its thing."

They looked at each other.

"Look, about the other day—" Michael said.

"Don't worry about it. I should have called. It's water under the bridge as far as I'm concerned."

"It's just been so stressful," Michael explained, "and I'm desperate for some information."

"That's understandable."

"Can I get you something to eat or drink?" He opened the large stainless-steel fridge and studied its contents. "I'm afraid all I've got is OJ and diet soda."

"Diet soda? The nectar of the gods? Yes, please."

Michael's shoulders relaxed. "Do you want a glass and some ice?"

"Nah. Thanks."

Fina took the can and followed him to a sofa tucked into the bay window at the front of the town house. She popped the drink open and took a long slug. "I have to tell you, this is so much better than what your mom served me."

Michael laughed. "Oh, God. Was it thick and green?" He opened his can and took a sip.

"It was. I think my intestines still haven't recovered."

"Keeps her young, I guess."

"That's true. She looks amazing." Fina took another sip. "What happened at the funeral? I heard there was some situation."

Michael sighed and shook his head. "We had a small private burial since we're not having the memorial service for a couple of months. It was a mess."

"Let me guess: Your mom and Danielle got into it."

"I told my mom she shouldn't come, but she does what she wants to do."

"So they had a fight?"

"Words were exchanged. It was tense."

"And annoying. It wasn't supposed to be about them."

"Yeah, well, no one told them."

Fina sipped her drink. "I'm sorry. That must have been upsetting."

Michael didn't respond.

"I don't have anything specific to report, but I am making progress," Fina continued. "I do have a question for you, though."

"What's that?" Michael looked at her over his soda.

"Why didn't you tell me that you and your dad had a big fight on the Friday before he died?"

Michael fiddled with the tab on the top of his can before putting the drink down on a coaster on the wooden coffee table. The coaster looked like fabric from a sari, perhaps a gift from his mother.

"I didn't think it was relevant."

Fina cocked her head. "Come on, Michael. That's not going to cut it. I think you were worried that I *would* think it was relevant."

"But it has nothing to do with anything." He fidgeted in his seat.

"It doesn't matter. You still should have told me. Have you told the cops?"

It was faint, but Fina could detect a slight blush creeping out from under the collar of Michael's button-down.

"No, I haven't."

"You need to."

"Why?"

"Because they'll find out—" Michael started to protest. "Not from me, but they will find out, and they'll be pissed. It's just not a smart move."

"It seems pretty dumb to make myself look suspicious."

"Lying makes you look more suspicious. Believe me."

"I don't want to tell them about personal stuff between me and my dad."

"Honestly? Nobody gives a shit. These are seasoned cops. They really don't care about your personal drama unless it screws up their investigation or plays a vital role in it."

Michael picked up his soda and drank some more.

"And that's why I care about it, too," Fina continued.

"But you work for me. I should get to decide what I tell you and what I don't."

Fina sighed. "I know it seems that way to you—and it may be the case in most employer-employee relationships. But if you don't tell me the truth, you're not getting your money's worth."

Michael took a large swallow. "Fine. We had the fight we always have, or a variation of it. I wasn't living up to his expectations."

"At Universum?"

"Yes, and because I was contemplating making a change. I was talking to people in the nonprofit tech sector, and that's the kind of job other people have, not Hank Reardon's kid."

"It seems like the more successful they are, the more they have to control you. My dad and I fight all the time. He drives me crazy."

"But it was just a fight," Michael rushed to clarify. "Sometimes we fought, but we never held grudges."

Fina finished her soda. "Did you speak with him after the fight, before he died?"

"Yeah, we had a brief phone call."

"Well, that's good at least." Fina had had clients whose last contact with the deceased had been hurtful words or accusations; she knew those exchanges could eat away at the survivors.

"I guess." Michael smiled wanly.

"It is. You'd feel worse if your last words had been angry ones. Thanks for the drink." Fina carried her can to the kitchen counter, and Michael walked her downstairs to the front door. "I'll call you tomorrow."

"You can wait a day or two, unless there's something important to report." He leaned against the open door.

"I strongly suggest you tell the cops about the argument; it's in your best interest to come clean."

Michael looked at his shoes. "I'll think about it."

He closed the door as she walked down the steps and headed for her car. Sometimes it was nice to be reminded that the Ludlows weren't the only family with issues.

17

Fina went home for a couple of hours and gathered all the information she could about the Reardon Center, Danielle Reardon's philanthropic efforts, and Dimitri Kask and Hank's waterfront development deal.

As far as Fina could tell, the two Mrs. Reardons were demanding that the city's upper crust choose sides. Photos from major charity events featured either Danielle and Hank or Juliana, but rarely were all three in attendance. Both of the women seemed to be staking a claim, and Fina could imagine that the gossip mills were feverishly at work trying to keep up. The Reardon Center was clearly Juliana's pet project, but there were a few blind gossip column items about the new Mrs. Reardon starting a charity in the Reardon name that might eclipse Juliana's. Philanthropy as a blood sport; it was absurd.

Fina's digging into the waterfront development didn't yield much information, so she called Hal, her finance guy.

"Where are you?" she asked over the thumping bass music emanating from the phone.

"Jiggles," he hollered.

"The strip club? I didn't think you were into that sort of thing."

"I'm not. I'm here with a client. Please tell me you need my immediate assistance."

Fina smiled. "I need your immediate assistance. Get over here or else."

"If you insist. I'll be there in twenty minutes."

Fina tossed her phone onto the couch and sat down at her laptop. Patty had e-mailed her Haley's school calendar, which included holidays, special assemblies, and parent-teacher conferences. She'd also attached the schedule for the JV field hockey team and a plea that Fina attend a game. Patty had started her campaign over the summer to get Haley more involved in school activities, and apparently she'd had some success. Patty may not have been a Ludlow by birth, but her tenacity made her an honorary member of the club. Contrary to people's assumptions that Fina wasn't interested in team sports below the professional level, she had always loved field hockey. There was something incredibly satisfying about striking a heavy ball with an even heavier stick without having to worry about form.

Fina dialed Haley's number.

"Hey," Haley answered.

"You're back at school, right?"

"Yes. School sucks."

"I agree, but you're required to attend by law."

"You're required by law to do lots of things that you blow off."

"Use me as a cautionary tale, then. Aunt Patty sent me your field hockey schedule. The first game's in a couple of weeks?"

"I guess. The first home game."

"You don't sound too enthused."

"I don't know. It seems kind of stupid."

"You know," Fina said, walking over to the windows overlooking the harbor, "there's nothing wrong with enjoying normal, dumb stuff."

"I know."

"Okay, just checking. So do you want me to paint my face or come up with a few cheers? Maybe get some pom-poms?"

"Believe me, if you showed up with pom-poms, the dads would be psyched."

"Okay, scratch that idea."

"I've got to go."

"Bye, Hale."

Fina watched a line of planes snaking around Logan. A field hockey game. It was like a gateway drug to motherhood and domesticity. She'd have to stay on guard.

Her reverie was interrupted by a knock on the door. "It's Hal, Fina."

His face fell when he crossed the threshold. "Wha . . . ? What happened?"

"You know, Hal, you're one of the few people who is truly upset when I get hurt."

Hal plodded over to the couch and dropped onto it. He was short and obese, and usually sweating, regardless of the season. "It *is* upsetting. I don't understand why Milloy and your family aren't more upset."

Fina shrugged. "My family is cold and unfeeling. Milloy doesn't like it, but what can he do?" She sat down on the other end of the couch. "They've probably also gotten used to it at this point. Do you want something to drink?"

"I would love some water, but I can get it." He started to struggle off the couch.

"Let me."

Fina filled a glass with ice water and returned to the living room.

"So, Jiggles?" Fina handed him the water.

"I don't know what's wrong with me, Fina, but those places. I always want to pull the girls aside and give them advice on setting up a 401(k)."

"Nothing's wrong with you. You're a decent guy."

Hal dipped his head and smiled. "What do you need?"

Fina tucked her feet under her on the couch. "What do you know about Hank Reardon's waterfront development deal?"

Hal thought for a moment. "It was a bit of a departure for him. Most of his other projects and investments are in technology."

"I wonder why he was branching out."

"Sometimes the really high achievers get bored in their own fields, so they decide to try something new, like buy a professional sports team. If you've got billions of dollars, what's losing a hundred million on a failed experiment?"

"I suppose. What's the actual proposal?"

"Developing a big plot of land on the waterfront, one of the few left. The proposal includes restaurants, shops, condos, galleries. He pitched it as a destination, a reason for people to go to the neighborhood."

"I've heard that his Universum partner, Dimitri Kask, wasn't part of the deal. Know anything about that?"

Hal leaned toward her. "I only know rumors and gossip."

"That works for me," Fina said.

"I think the deal was too rich for Dimitri's blood, and Hank wasn't willing to negotiate on that point. Hank's older—was older—than Dimitri and had more time to amass his fortune."

"But Dimitri wanted in on the deal?"

"Only when he couldn't get in on it. I think his pride was hurt."

Fina drained her soda. "I need you to do a little digging around to see if there's anything odd about the deal."

"Okay."

"What happens to it now that Hank is dead?"

Hal held up his hands. "I don't know. It has the potential to be a huge mess. He's got a lot of money tied up in it, but I assume Hank had bulletproof estate planning, so maybe it won't be an issue."

"Thanks, Hal." Fina stood and stretched. "Send me the bill and call me when you have some info. One other thing. Two, actually. Can you look into the Reardon Center?"

"The cancer place?"

"Yeah. It's the main charity of Hank Reardon's first wife, Juliana, and I want to know if there's anything hinky or noteworthy in terms of the finances."

"I'll let you know what I find. The other thing?"

"A kid named Brett Linder. I'll e-mail you the basics. I just want to know if there are any red flags."

"Sure. You take care of yourself, Fina," he said, walking to the door. "Every time I hear about a shooting, I think of you."

"Aww, Hal. That's so sweet."

Between Harvard Square and Porter Square, Fina parked around the corner from a large cream-colored house. A picket fence enclosed the yard, and a stone path led to the front door. Green shutters framed the windows, and large terra cotta urns overflowing with plants flanked the front door.

Fina rang the bell and waited. After a moment, a man answered.

"Is Dimitri here?" Fina asked. It was close to dinnertime, and she thought her chances of finding him at home were fifty-fifty. Sometimes it was more interesting when the person you came to see wasn't there.

The man at the door was in his midforties, tall, and carrying just a bit of extra weight around his middle. He had blond hair and a pleasant face. He was dressed in jeans, an untucked light blue polo shirt, and flip-flops.

"No, but I expect him at any moment," he said. "Can I help you with something?" He examined her face.

Fina reached into her bag and handed him her ID. "Michael Reardon hired me to investigate Hank's death. I spoke with Dimitri at the office, but I had a few follow-up questions. And this was from an accident," she added, indicating her face.

"I'm his husband, Andy Collins-Kask. I didn't mean to stare," he said apologetically. They shook hands. "You're welcome to come in if you don't mind waiting."

"No worries." Fina followed him into a beautiful foyer anchored by a staircase with twisted balustrades. The space was bright and light, and the wood floors shone. "Your home is beautiful."

"Thanks. It's a colonial revival. We put a ton of work into it."

"It shows. Is this all original woodwork?"

"Yup. We had to strip everything and refinish it, and when I say 'we,' I mean the contractors, but it was still a huge headache."

"But worth it. This is what people mean when they talk about a house with character."

Fina followed Andy down the hallway to a large modern kitchen with stainless-steel appliances and granite countertops.

"The twins are outside. Let's see what they're up to, and then I'll get you a drink."

They passed through the kitchen onto a sunporch and continued out to a large backyard. The area was fenced in and boasted a patio and large play structure. There was a little boy climbing up the ladder and a little girl swinging, her legs askew, her underpants visible to the world.

"Devin! Anna! This nice lady is here for a visit. Say hello to Ms. Ludlow."

"Fina, please."

They walked over to the kids, who gave her smiles and shy hellos.

Andy consulted his watch. "How about a mojito?"

"That's the best offer I've had all day. Can I give you a hand?"

"Nope. Just make sure nobody falls on their head."

Shit. She'd rather mix the cocktails.

"Push me," Anna demanded once Andy had gone toward the house. Fina walked behind her and gave a gentle push on her small back.

"Guess how old I am," Anna said.

"Hmm. Forty."

"What!" She giggled, as did her brother.

"No? Okay. Sixteen?"

"I'm not that old!" Anna hollered. Devin paused at the top of the slide.

"Okay," Fina said. "One last guess. Four and a half."

Anna twisted around in her swing, wide-eyed. "How did you know?"

Fina smiled. "I know lots of things."

Devin came careening down the slide, and Fina pushed and listened to the stream of chatter from the little girl.

"Are you two twins?" Fina asked.

"We are, but Devin's older!" She giggled, clearly tickled by the notion.

A minute later, Andy emerged from the house, his arms full. Fina walked over to the patio and sat down on one of the outdoor couches. On a tray, a pitcher of mojitos was sweating, the very sight of it increasing her thirst. There was a plate of cheese and crackers and a large bunch of plump grapes. Cocktail napkins were fanned out next to small glass swizzle sticks. Andy poured their drinks into heavy tumblers filled with crushed mint and raised his in a toast.

"Your kids are very sweet," Fina said.

"Thank you." He smiled.

"Did you know Hank well?" Fina asked.

"I knew him socially, from company events, that sort of thing."

"What did you think of him?"

"He was a nice guy. Very bright, obviously."

"What about the two Mrs. Reardons? I got the sense from Dimitri that he was a bigger fan of Juliana."

"He's known Juliana longer; I think he feels some loyalty to her. Dimitri always does favor the underdog."

"You mean the discarded first wife?"

"Exactly."

"And do you have a preference?"

"They're apples and oranges, but I'm partial to Danielle."

"Why's that?"

"She's more fun. These dinners and conferences we go to can be a complete bore. Having a fun buddy makes all the difference, and I can't let down my hair with just anyone—it wouldn't reflect well on Dimitri." Fina knew that being married to the president or CEO of an organization could be isolating. If you're married to the head honcho, you have an image to maintain.

"There was a meeting in Vegas last year; we had a ball." Andy popped a grape in his mouth.

"You and Dimitri?"

"Me and Danielle. Dimitri has no time on those trips. I see him when we check in at the hotel and a couple of days later when we check out. Danielle and I did a spa day and went to some shows. It was great."

"So you two get along; did Dimitri and Hank?"

Andy refilled his glass. "You want me to tell tales out of school?" He narrowed his gaze.

Fina shrugged and grinned.

"They were business partners, and sometimes they disagreed, but they'd compromise and move on."

Devin ran over and put his little hands on Andy's large knees. "Daddy, when's Papa coming home?" Pieces of his hair were plastered to his face with sweat. Playing was hard work.

"Soon, sweetie, soon." He stroked his son's back. Andy's lip was slightly curled, and Fina wondered if Dimitri's schedule was a source of friction.

"My dad worked crazy hours when I was growing up," she said, stabbing at the mint with a swizzle stick.

"Things were supposed to change once the babies were born, but that didn't really happen." He glanced at his watch.

"I don't envy parents trying to figure all that stuff out."

Andy didn't respond, just stared into his drink.

"I'm hungry!" Anna hollered from the swing set.

"Have some grapes," Andy suggested.

Anna hopped off the swing and ran over. She studied the grapes but instead reached for a piece of cheese, which she picked up and examined. After handling it, she put it back down on the plate and chose another. When she started the routine with a third piece, Andy interceded. "Anna, peach, you can't touch all the food. No one else will want to eat it if you've put germs on it."

Anna look surprised. "I don't have germs," she insisted, wiping her nose with her bare arm.

"What about the waterfront development deal?" Fina asked once the twins had taken their spoils over to the table.

He frowned. "Did you ask Dimitri about it?"

"Not yet. That's why I'm here."

Andy considered for a moment. "It was a bone of contention. I don't think it was Hank's finest moment."

"Because he cut Dimitri out of the deal?"

"I can't be specific."

"Sure." Fina nodded. "I assume the police asked Dimitri for an alibi."

"Yes, and he was here with me, asleep, all night."

Of course. Wasn't everybody tucked safely into bed on the night of Hank's murder?

"Papa!" Devin slid off his chair and ran to the doorway. Dimitri was standing there in his work clothes, his phone in his hand.

"Hey, buddy!"

Anna joined her brother, and Dimitri kneeled down and gathered the kids into a bear hug. "I missed you guys." Fina smiled at the scene. She supposed that's why some people had dogs, so they could be slobbered with love when they walked in the door.

"Hey." Dimitri walked over and gave Andy a peck on the cheek. Andy poured him a drink. Dimitri took a gulp and sat down next to his husband. He looked at Fina and seemed to register her banged-up appearance, but was either too polite or too disinterested to comment.

"What happened to five o'clock?" Andy asked reproachfully.

"What always happens," Dimitri said, and avoided his gaze.

Andy studied him for a moment, then sat up straighter, a physical indication that he was done with that subject for now. "Fina was asking some questions about Hank."

"I introduced myself when I arrived. There hasn't been any subterfuge," she assured Dimitri. "You have a beautiful home and children. Under other circumstances, I'd ask you two to adopt me."

Dimitri let a small smile crack his face. "Andy deserves the credit for that. He's very welcoming."

"Fina was asking about the waterfront development deal," Andy said. A look passed between the two men, the kind of brief look that spoke volumes to the two people who spoke the language.

"There's not much to say about it," Dimitri said.

"I got the sense that it generated some bad blood between you and Hank," Fina said.

"I wasn't happy about it," he admitted, "but we moved on." Anna came over and climbed onto Dimitri's lap. Devin stayed at the table, overseeing a race between a slice of cheese and a club cracker.

"Got it." Fina drained her drink and moved forward on the couch. "Thank you for your hospitality and for answering my questions."

The two men stood up, Anna in Dimitri's arms, and followed her to the front door. They exchanged pleasantries, and Fina walked around the corner to her car. Over the fence, she could see the two men engaged in what looked to be a heated exchange. Maybe they were discussing Dimitri's tardiness—or maybe her questions had ignited a spark.

"Is anyone coming?" Risa asked.

Fina looked around the changing room. "It's just us. Open your mouth."

Risa did as she was told, and Fina ran the cotton swab along the inside of her cheek. She popped it into a plastic tube, pushed on the top, and sealed it with a sticker.

"I feel like this should be a bigger deal, more of a process," Risa commented.

"You mean like the procedure should match the gravity of the situation?"

"Something like that."

The women emerged from the clubhouse and walked over to the patio. Elaine was sitting at a table with Patty. The table had been cleared of plates and glasses, and the boys were back in the pool.

"Did you eat?" Patty asked Fina and Risa.

"I'm waiting for Marty," Risa said.

"What were you two doing in there?" Elaine asked.

Fina looked at her mother. "Peeing."

Patty gave Fina the hairy eyeball. Fina knew she antagonized her mother, but her questions were nosy and stupid. She got the answers she deserved.

"Oh, I see Marty," Risa said, and pushed back her chair. "I'm going to round up the kids for dinner." She exchanged good-byes with the other women.

A waitress appeared and took Fina's order for a diet soda, and Elaine asked for a refill on her gin and tonic. Patty was nursing a glass of white wine.

"You're not eating?" Elaine asked.

"I'm not hungry, Mom."

"You should eat."

Fina ignored her and accepted the glass from the waitress brimming with ice and diet soda. "Where's Scotty?"

"He and your dad had a business dinner," Patty said. "Your mom was just telling me about the work they're having done on the kitchen."

"What's wrong with the kitchen?"

"It's outdated," Elaine said.

In an ideal world, Fina would ask about the updates, gush about paint colors and fixtures, and offer to shop for backsplash tile, but that wasn't the world she lived in. As it was, she thought it demonstrated tremendous restraint not to remind her mother that the kitchen was two years old. Fina felt that her silence was a gracious response. Elaine didn't feel the same way.

"You could at least pretend to be interested," Elaine said.

"I am interested," Fina said. "I'm just surprised. I didn't think the kitchen was that old."

"Well, it is." Elaine pouted.

"Two years is old?"

Chandler, Patty's youngest, hollered from the pool, requiring some adult assistance. Patty started to rise, but Elaine stopped her. "I have to use the ladies' room anyway." She got up and walked toward the shallow end.

Patty stared at Fina.

"What?" Fina asked.

"Why do you care how old her kitchen is?"

"Because it's ridiculous. It's completely wasteful and just shows how out of touch she is with the real world."

"That's bull. It's because it's her. If I were redoing my kitchen, you wouldn't have such a strong reaction."

"First of all, you wouldn't redo a brand-new kitchen. Second of all, I could tell you what I think and you wouldn't pout."

"Fina, you are never going to change who she is. Your disapproval serves no purpose except to keep the two of you angry with each other."

Fina shrugged. "I can live with that."

Patty shook her head. They sipped their drinks in silence.

"What was the problem?" Patty asked when Elaine returned.

"He just needed the tie on his bathing suit retied," her mother said, slipping into her chair.

"Thanks."

"Have you spoken with your brother?" Elaine asked.

"Which one?" Fina replied between sips.

"You know which one."

Fina traded looks with Patty.

"What? Are you two in cahoots about this?" Elaine asked.

"No, Mom," Patty said. "But I share Fina's feelings on this one." Fina was always taken aback when Patty referred to Elaine as "Mom." Why would you claim this woman as your own if you weren't legally obligated to?

"Well, he's her brother."

When Fina uncovered Rand's crimes, the decision had been made to keep Elaine in the dark. Sometimes Fina wondered if that had been the right decision.

"I know you've had a falling out," Elaine said, "but—"

"It's a little more serious than that, Mom."

"Fina . . ." Patty warned.

"I'm just not sure why we're doing this," Fina insisted.

"Doing what?" Elaine narrowed her eyes.

"Not now, Fina. Just stop," Patty said.

Fina took a swig of soda and avoided her mother's gaze.

"You listen to her but not me." Elaine drained her glass. "I'm going home." She stood up and gathered her bag. It was ugly and expensive, Elaine's signature style.

"Mom, you don't need to go," Patty said, but Elaine left anyway.

"Don't stop her," Fina said, "and please don't act like this is the same as our kitchen issues. Maybe we should tell her the truth about her precious son."

Patty rotated her glass on the tabletop. "I don't know. It's all a big mess."

"No argument here."

"Finally," Patty said, and smiled at Fina.

Milloy called her during the drive home, offering to swing by with Chinese food since he was in the neighborhood. Miraculously, her appetite reappeared.

After a meal eaten off actual plates (Milloy insisted), they took their usual positions on the couch: Fina lying on her side, her feet bumping up against Milloy's thigh. Before long, Milloy pulled her feet onto his lap and began kneading her insteps.

"Easy, easy," Fina instructed. "You don't know your own strength."

Milloy eased up on the pressure. The circular pattern he made with his thumbs felt good.

"Are you feeling frisky?" Fina asked.

Milloy raised an eyebrow. "Maybe."

"Don't be coy," Fina said, sitting up. "But remember, I'm not one hundred percent." She leaned toward him and made a poor attempt to pucker her lips.

"You've got other body parts," Milloy reminded her, and was pulling her toward him when there was a knock on the door.

"Seriously?" Milloy asked. "For someone who doesn't like people, you have an awful lot of visitors."

"I know." Fina padded over to the door in her bare feet and looked through the peephole.

"It's work. I can't blow it off," she said, opening the door.

Cristian stood on her threshold when she opened the door. He looked pleased to see her, until he noticed Milloy in the background.

"Sorry. Is this a bad time?" he asked.

"It's fine."

"Hey," Cristian said to Milloy.

"Hey," Milloy responded.

The two men knew they had similarly ambiguous roles in Fina's life. Neither wanted clarification of his own role, but wished the other's status were more explicit.

"Wow. That was an emotional moment," Fina commented.

"I'm going to take off," Milloy said, rising from the couch.

"You don't have to," Fina said. Cristian was silent.

"Nah. I'll catch up with you tomorrow." Once Milloy had pulled the door closed behind him, Cristian took his spot on the couch.

"Did I interrupt something?" he asked.

"Kind of."

"Are you two an item?"

"What decade are you from? Next you're going to ask if he's pinned me, and I don't mean sexually."

"I'm just curious."

"Are *we* an item?" She pointed at him. "Probably not, since you're dating."

Cristian squirmed on the sofa.

"Exactly." Fina sat down next to him.

"You told me to get a hobby and stop obsessing about Marissa," Cristian said.

"That wasn't exactly what I had in mind. Anyway, I assume you aren't here to talk about your feelings or the speech pathologist. What's up?"

"I had a visit from Michael Reardon this afternoon. He told me about a fight he had with Hank a few days before his death."

"Did he, now?"

"He said that you told him to come clean."

Fina smiled at him. "I did. Is Pitney going to give me brownie points for that?"

"I told her that you had encouraged Michael to be in touch."

"And I bet she said, 'That's what she should have told him.'"

"Something like that."

Fina looked at Cristian. He was handsome in a completely different way from Milloy, but appealing nonetheless. Variety really was the spice of life.

"I think Pitney holds me to a higher standard than she does most people."

"Actually"—Cristian scratched his five o'clock shadow—"she pretty much expects everyone to obey the law."

"It's a little dramatic to suggest that Michael was breaking the law by keeping quiet."

"Ever heard of obstruction?"

"Practically every day of my life. It's your favorite topic; Pitney's, too."

"Any other updates I can pass along?" Cristian asked.

Fina pulled her feet up onto the couch. "Not really. I've just been talking to people, but there haven't been any smoking guns. Any thoughts on the murder weapon?"

Cristian shook his head.

She grinned at him. "Liar. You know who was bugging me today? Dan Rubin."

"The reporter? I thought he was in rehab."

"He was, but he's back."

"What did he want?"

"I don't know. Yet another person who wants me to do his job for him?" She grinned at Cristian, who looked annoyed. "I'm kidding. I know you work hard."

Cristian leaned forward and took her chin in his hand. He studied her face. "It's looking better."

"The plastic surgeon assures me I'll make a full recovery."

"You're the only woman I know who has regular fistfights and consults a plastic surgeon afterward."

"I'm one of a kind, Cristian." She looked into his eyes. For a moment, they teetered on the precipice.

"I've gotta go," Cristian said suddenly, and stood up.

"It's early. What's the rush?"

"I'm taking Matteo to preschool in the morning, and I need to be sharp."

"The next time you have him, you guys should come to the club. Enjoy the last gasp of summer."

"And be mistaken for the help?"

Fina followed him to the door. "As if they hire Hispanics."

Cristian rolled his eyes. "Bring him to a place where he's an outcast?"

"I know, it's not ideal, but I bet he'd have fun. He'd be like a tiny little Rosa Parks."

"You're appalling."

"We could hang out with Scotty's boys. They'd take good care of him."

"I'll think about it." He turned to her at the door. "Let me know if anything comes up with the case."

"Of course. Don't forget, I sent Michael Reardon your way."

"You won't let me forget."

"At least not until my next good deed."

Cristian left, and Fina wandered into the kitchen and rooted through the cabinets. She found a Swiss chocolate bar and took it back to the couch, where she sat watching TV and sucking on the rich squares. It was a poor substitute for Milloy's magic hands and Cristian's dreamy eyes, but it would have to do.

18

Juliana put the phone on speaker and climbed onto her training bicycle in the bedroom she'd remade into an exercise studio. Short of a swimming pool, the room had everything Juliana needed to train: a bike, a treadmill, free weights, and a weight-lifting station. She preferred to do all her training outside in real-world conditions, but sometimes she fit in an extra session while doing other things, liking being on hold.

She was waiting to talk to Edith Steagen, her fellow board member and key ally. Edith was an attorney by trade, but had made a name for herself bringing her father's medical equipment company into the twenty-first century. Edith was also in her late fifties, and the mother of two daughters. Unlike Juliana's, her marriage had remained intact.

"Edith Steagen." The voice materialized out of the ether.

"It's Juliana, Edith. How are you?" Juliana downshifted her bike and reached for her phone on a nearby shelf.

"I'm fine. How was the funeral?"

Juliana took the phone off speaker and used her other hand to wipe her brow with a towel. She didn't stop pedaling. "What have you heard?"

"That you were ill-behaved."

"Well, I wasn't. Maybe you could get that word out."

"No, thank you, my dear. I only heard because Susan Wickens cornered me at the institute cocktail party last night. You know I'm not interested in gossip."

"Danielle thinks I was 'ill-behaved' because I was in attendance. But for goodness' sakes, Hank was my husband a lot longer than she had him, and I wanted to be supportive of Michael."

"How is he?" Edith asked.

"How should I know? I'm only his mother."

Edith chuckled on the other end. "I assume you're calling about center business?" Edith had been an early supporter of the Reardon Center, and her financial contributions and business acumen were tremendous assets to the board. Juliana knew that Edith's support was critical to the success of any initiatives she might propose.

"Yes, I wanted to convene a committee regarding the expansion into Forty-four Oak Street." Forty-four Oak Street was the house next door to the center that had recently come on the market.

"Fine, let's do it at the next board meeting."

"I don't think we should wait. I've spoken to the agent representing the sellers, and there's a lot of interest."

Edith paused. "Juliana, this seems rather impulsive."

"We've always said that if the possibility for expansion presented itself, we would be interested."

"Of course, but you can't just jump into something."

"That's exactly what we need to do. It could be the difference between getting Forty-four Oak Street and losing it."

"And how will we be financing this purchase?"

Juliana changed gears on the bike. "Various sources. We have money in the endowment, and we can get a good interest rate. I also hoped that you might consider giving a bit more this year; I'm planning to make a sizable contribution—more than double last year's."

Edith made a sound as if she were sipping something. "Does this have something to do with Hank's death?"

"What do you mean?"

"I mean, will his estate continue to provide for the center in a mean-ingful way?"

"Of course, but that's always been the case."

"Oh."

Juliana stopped pedaling. "What is it, Edith?"

"Nothing, really. I'd just heard that Hank was going to pull back in his support of the center."

"The Reardon Center? The place that bears his name? That is a phil-anthropic beacon in the city?"

"Okay, okay. I'd heard that Danielle has some cause she wants to support. That's all."

"For someone who doesn't like to gossip, you seem to have heard a lot."

"Juliana, I'm just trying to do what's best for the center."

"As am I, obviously, and I think expansion is what's best. Think of all the people we'd be able to serve in the additional space."

"I don't disagree with the concept; I just want to make sure there are no problems with the execution."

"As do I, and I appreciate your being forthright, Edith. I rely on your frankness."

Edith laughed. "If you say so."

"So would you think about a committee? We could e-mail everyone and see who's interested."

"Fine. Why don't you send something out, and I'll make some calls in the meantime."

"Wonderful. I'll do it right after my swim."

"In the ocean?"

"Of course in the ocean. That's where triathlons take place. If King's Beach isn't too stinky, I'm going to head in that direction." The large sandy beach just south of Juliana's house was lovely but plagued by red tide, which often prompted drivers to roll up their windows even on the nicest day.

"Isn't it freezing?" Edith asked.

"I wear a wetsuit."

"That sounds miserable. Enjoy and be safe."

"I will be. I don't want to make my child an orphan."

They ended the call, and Juliana hopped off the bike and walked to the windows overlooking the beach.

She would definitely be careful. This was the start of something big.

Fina wasn't getting any traction with the mystery numbers from Hank's call log, so she decided to just bite the bullet and make the calls. She blocked her number and dialed the first mystery entry. It was an inn in Newport, Rhode Island. The second number had been disconnected, but the third was picked up by voice mail.

"Leave a message, and I'll return your call as soon as possible." The speaker didn't identify himself, but the voice was familiar. Fina called it again and stared out at the water. She struggled to pull a name from the recesses of her brain, but came up empty. Focusing on something else usually helped her subconscious loosen up, allowing the information to float to the surface. In order for that to happen, she needed to switch gears completely.

She dialed the Crystal nightclub and tricked a bartender into revealing a home address for Dante, and fifteen minutes later she pulled into a lot near Downtown Crossing. Fina looked around before exiting her car. She could have walked from her place, but her recent run-in had made her more cautious. In her car, she could lock the doors and exercise some control over her environment; on the street, she was a walking target.

Fina pulled out her phone and punched in a number.

"The Waterstone Building, how may I help you?"

"I've got a delivery for Dante Trimonti in unit 802, but my guy says he tried to deliver it and it's the wrong unit. Sometimes he flips his numbers, so I thought it might be 208, but I don't want to send someone out there if I don't even have the right building."

"Hold on a second." Fina studied her cuticles as she waited. "You've got the right building, but they were wrong about the unit. He's in 1103."

"Christ! How hard is it to get an apartment number right? You're a lifesaver."

"Happy to help."

Fina retrieved a reusable shopping bag from her trunk and filled it with some clothing items she kept on hand, topped off with a package of toilet paper. Nobody questioned your motives when you were carrying toilet paper.

She walked over to the front door of the Waterstone and made a fuss rummaging through her bag. In less than two minutes, some poor sap took pity on her and held the door open behind him. Fina strode to the elevators, flashing a bright smile at the man behind the desk, and dove into some chitchat with her unknowing accomplice. Clearly, she was a tenant. Who else would walk in so brazenly with a bag of groceries?

Her new friend got off on the sixth floor, and Fina continued on to eleven. Loud music emanated from 1103. Fina stood to the side so she wasn't visible through the peephole and knocked on the door. After a moment, she banged on the door.

"I'm coming. I'm coming. Who is it?"

"Golden Pagoda!"

"I think you've—" The door opened. "Oh, hell no!" Dante exclaimed when he caught sight of Fina.

"You aren't happy to see me?" she asked, wedging her foot in the door.

"I'm never happy to see you."

"Let me in, Dante. I come in peace." She tried to look doleful.

"Do you have a gun on you?"

"Always, but I promise not to use it."

He stepped back from the door and walked into the apartment. Dante Trimonti was in his early twenties, handsome, but sleazy. His hair was slicked back and his skin was golden. He was wearing a tight T-shirt and well-fitted jeans, both of which showcased his impressive body.

Fina followed him past an open kitchen/living room area that had a view over the Common. He picked up a remote, and the throbbing bass line receded in the background.

"Very nice view," Fina said, gazing out over the park below. "Now, this is what I was talking about." Fina punched him lightly on the arm, which was solid. "Oww. That's like brick."

Dante flexed his arm and nodded at her. "Feel it."

Fina squeezed. "Very impressive, and so is the apartment." When they'd met earlier in the summer, Dante's surroundings hadn't positively reflected his career aspirations. He was gaining traction in Boston's criminal world but lived in a dumpy three-family in Allston. "You took my advice: Live and dress for the job you want, not the job you have."

"Yeah, it's all because of you. Is there anything you don't take credit for?" Dante padded into the kitchen in his bare feet and grabbed two bottled waters from the fridge. He threw one at Fina, who caught it one-handed.

"What happened to your face?" he asked. "Piss off someone else?" He leaned on the kitchen counter and unscrewed the top of the bottle.

Fina sat down on a black leather sectional and unscrewed her bottle cap, then took a sip. "Apparently. You wouldn't know anything about it, would you?"

"You're accusing me?"

"No, I'm not accusing you. Don't be so defensive! I thought you might have heard something."

Dante shook his head. "What else do you want? You always want something."

"Just a couple of questions. You ever heard of a kid named Brett Linder?"

He walked over and sat down in a black leather chair next to her. The apartment was the prototype of a bachelor pad: black leather furniture, glass accent tables, an enormous flat-screen TV, an Xbox, and piles of games.

"No. Should I?"

"Not necessarily. I just thought I'd ask." Fina put the water on the coffee table. "How's business?"

Dante leaned back and put his bare feet on the table. Generally, Fina found men's feet to be disgusting, but Dante's were smooth, his nails trimmed and neat.

Fina leaned forward, examining his toes. "Do you get pedicures?"

Dante shrugged. "Maybe."

"They look good. That must make you a hit with the ladies. Nice feet are a bonus."

He puffed up his chest. "Believe me, the ladies have nothing to complain about."

Fina rolled her eyes. "I'm sure. So, business? It's good?"

"Business is good."

"I guess having Bev Duprey out of the way has been a positive development?" Bev Duprey had been the owner of the city's most exclusive escort agency and had also overseen a successful porn business. Her physician son had been decimated by a Ludlow and Associates lawsuit, and when she'd taken revenge on Rand and Haley, Bev had wandered into Fina's crosshairs. With Bev out of play, Dante's business opportunities had multiplied.

"You want credit for that, too?" Dante asked.

She gestured at him with her water. "I've earned the credit for that."

"And now you're here to collect."

"I want you to keep your ears open. I want some info on Brett Linder and the mystery man who threatened me." She gestured toward her face.

"Why's this kid so important?"

"He may not be. He could just be a nuisance, or he could be a murder suspect. The more I know, the better. Also, I need you to get a DJ a set at Crystal."

"What do I look like to you? A temp agency?"

"She's good. You'll like her." Wow, she made lots of stuff up. "Give me your e-mail address, and I'll send you her info."

Dante recited it, and Fina entered it into her phone. "Is she hot?" he asked.

"Look her up and decide for yourself." Fina stood and walked to the door.

"When do you start owing me?" Dante asked.

"I don't think of it as owing each other. I think of it as scratching each other's backs."

Dante smirked. "I bet you'd love that."

Fina leaned toward him. "I like men, Dante, not boys." She punched him again in the arm before walking down the hall toward the elevator. "Keep in touch!"

He slammed the door, and a moment later, the music blasted from his unit.

His neighbors must love him.

Fina popped into a coffee shop around the corner from Dante's and ordered a diet soda. She claimed an empty overstuffed chair and checked her e-mail. Her contact at the Registry had come through with the car registration info, which Fina forwarded to Emma. She was contemplating her next move when Carl showed up on her caller ID.

"Yes, Father?"

Carl snorted. "I want an update."

"Why? Has Michael Reardon been telling on me again?"

"Come to the club at six thirty."

"I'm not having dinner at the club. I can update you right now."

"I don't want an update over the phone. Why won't you have dinner at the club?"

"I was there last night with Mom and Patty." A homeless man sat down across from her. He rummaged through a plastic bag and took out a small collection of Tupperware, which he proceeded to sort.

"So?"

"I've had my fill of Mom for the week."

"Don't talk about your mother like that."

"How many nights a week do you have dinner with her?"

"Don't be a smart-ass."

"You didn't answer the question."

Carl was silent. Left to their own devices, the two of them could stay on the line all day trying to outlast the other.

"I'm not going to the club for dinner," Fina finally said. "I have work to do, but I'll try to stop by and give you an update. Happy?"

"Ecstatic," Carl said, and ended the call.

Fina stared at the phone for a moment, and something clicked.

An impatient, bossy man.

That's why that voice mail had sounded so familiar.

A moment later, her ringing phone snapped her out of her musings. The homeless man glared at her, the sound seemingly disturbing his work.

"I e-mailed you that E-Z Pass statement," Emma said when Fina picked up.

"That's great, thanks. I'll take a look right now."

Fina toggled over to her e-mail and scanned the list of transactions from Emma, quickly at first, then more slowly a second time.

Dammit.

There was nothing there.

Walter Stiles had left the office for the day, and Fina decided to approach him away from the cryobank. Catching him off guard seemed like a good idea, and he might be less cagey if his professional reputation wasn't foremost on his mind. This was more likely to happen at his home in Framingham.

Five minutes after exiting Route 9, Fina was winding along sparsely populated roads that tucked in and out of the woods. She didn't understand the appeal of living out in the sticks, even if you were really only ten minutes from the nearest mall. Some people found it peaceful, but it felt creepy to her.

She turned into a road marked by two stone columns and followed Walter's driveway to a moderate-sized contemporary house. The exterior was shingled in dark wood that blended in with the large forest it abutted. The doorbell didn't sound like a standard chime, more like the first few notes of a classical piece. As she waited, Fina peeked in through the glass bordering the door. The space was full of light and wood and looked expensive and custom-built. Walter had done all right for himself.

A woman opened the door. She was in her fifties, wearing a velour tracksuit, her dyed blond hair pulled back in a loose ponytail. Fina recognized her as Walter's companion at various charity events that had been featured in the *Globe*. "Yes?"

"I'm here to see Walter. Ellen said he'd left for the day."

"Is he expecting you?"

"He should be."

"He's back there," she said, and led Fina through the living room with its white walls and high ceilings. The doors were framed with intricate moldings, and the wood floors were polished to a sheen. They walked through a modern kitchen, which featured a corner of windows overlooking the woods. The accoutrements of dinner preparations were laid out on the counter, and a small TV was broadcasting the news. "Do you work at the bank?" the woman asked over her shoulder.

"No, just consulting. I'm Fina."

The woman turned and offered her hand. "Lucy. Walter hasn't mentioned you."

"Our work hasn't overlapped much."

"Walter, Fina is here." Lucy poked her head around the door frame into a smaller room.

Walter sat at a wooden desk, his back to a wall of windows. He was reading something on the desk and glanced up after a moment. He peered at Fina and scowled.

"Why are you here?" He started to rise from his seat.

Lucy looked confused.

"I was telling Lucy that I'm consulting with the bank on the Reardon situation." Fina stared at him. It was a game of chicken, but Fina couldn't really lose; if he kicked her out, that just confirmed that she was onto something.

"Should I not have . . . ?" Lucy glanced between the two of them.

"It's fine. I'll take care of it." He pointed to a love seat perpendicular to the fireplace, and Fina sat down. The room must have been cozy in winter, but without a roaring fire and autumn colors outside the window, it seemed oddly barren. Walter glared at Fina, and Lucy padded down the hallway.

"Is that your housekeeper or your wife?" Fina asked before he could speak.

"Neither. What are you doing at my home?"

"Short workday for you today, or do you always leave before three?" He didn't answer. "Okeydoke. I have some questions I want to ask you."

"I'm calling the police. This is harassment." He picked up the phone on the desk.

"Please do. They can fill me in on your interactions with Hank Reardon. I'm assuming you've already told them about that?" Walter stopped dialing. "I don't actually care about your baby-making empire. I've been hired by Michael Reardon to find his father's killer. That's my only concern."

Walter was quiet. He moved his jaw as if he were actually chewing on this notion. He sat down in his large desk chair. "There's nothing to tell."

"So the police know you had contact with Hank shortly before his murder?"

"The police are aware of details that are relevant to the case." He folded his hands on the desk.

Fina smiled. "Nice try, Walter. I'm from a family of attorneys, remember? I'm fluent in evasion."

"Any conversations I had with Hank Reardon are covered by doctor-patient confidentiality."

"What? That's bogus. You weren't his doctor."

"I have nothing to say on the matter."

"Obviously you and Hank knew one another, but I can't figure out why you and his widow don't want anyone to know that he was in touch. What's the big secret?"

"You've never heard of privacy?"

"I think the fear of bad publicity trumps privacy." Fina stood and looked at the bookshelves. A couple of shelves were filled with medical journals and some awards. There were a few pictures of Walter receiving the awards, smiling proudly while holding a crystal bowl or a shiny plaque. The other shelves were crammed full of books—the classics, from the looks of the spines—but Fina would have bet money that they had been acquired by a decorator, not a voracious reader. A couple of banker's boxes were on the ground next to a basket of firewood.

"Do you want to hear my theory?" Fina asked.

"No, and would you kindly sit down? I don't want you pawing at my things."

"Walter, I haven't touched anything, but if it makes you feel better." She reclaimed her place on the love seat. "I think that Hank Reardon was incensed and was coming after the cryobank."

Walter gave her a pitying look. "That's preposterous, and why are you so sure he was angry? Maybe he wanted to champion the work of the cryobank."

"You make it sound like you've cured cancer. I know reproductive medicine is a big deal, but you're not Jonas Salk or Mother Teresa in a lab coat."

"You shouldn't assume donating sperm was a source of shame or unhappiness to Mr. Reardon."

"I didn't say it was, but I know that he didn't want the publicity. Trying to convince me that he wanted to be the next poster child for the cryobank is going to be a hard sell."

Walter waved his hand. "Your theories aren't of any consequence. It's time for you to leave."

"Okeydoke." Fina rose once again. "Take care, Walter."

She walked back through the kitchen, where Lucy stood at the sink. "Nice to meet you, Lucy."

"Bye."

Fina saw herself out and sat in her car for a moment before turning the key. There was some issue or bone of contention between Walter and Hank, she was sure of it. If Hank had just threatened legal action, he would have sent Jules Lindsley as his emissary, but he'd contacted Walter directly.

Walter and the widow Reardon could stonewall her all they wanted. It just made her more curious.

This time, Danielle Reardon's maid didn't make her wait on the doorstep, but she did leave her in the foyer for ten minutes. Fina took a seat in an elaborate chair that was probably from some French monarchy. It had a scrolled back, and the arms were oversized and curvy. Covered in striped silk, it probably cost more than Fina's car.

"She's in her study," the maid announced.

"I can find it if you tell me where it is," Fina said, rising from the chair.

The maid gave her a withering look. "I'll take you." The security at the Reardons' was certainly better than that at Heritage Cryobank.

They rode the elevator to the fourth floor. Fina was directed a few doors down the hallway into a room overlooking Commonwealth Ave. There was a large couch, a fireplace, bookshelves, and a flat-screen TV mounted on the wall. Danielle was on the phone, pacing by the window.

"But he assured me that he would take care of the permits," she said, gesturing for Fina to come in. "Uh-huh, uh-huh. Would you? Thanks." She hung up a moment later.

"What's going on?" Danielle asked. She was wearing a wrap dress that hugged her figure perfectly, and her hair was down. It was shiny and glossy, like she'd just stepped out of a shampoo commercial. She wore a couple of necklaces of varying lengths. Her feet were bare, with manicured toenails. Fina could see a pair of three-inch heels kicked off in front of the couch.

"Do you have a minute?"

"Sure." Danielle shrugged and walked over to a wall cabinet. She pushed on a panel, which opened to reveal a wet bar. "Do you want a drink?"

"Sounds good. What do you have?"

Danielle stood back to show off an incredibly well-stocked bar. "I'm partial to vodka myself. Vodka martini? Vodka and cranberry? Vodka tonic?"

"Vodka and cranberry." Fina sat down on the couch. The room retained the feeling of a men's club, but there were touches indicating this was Danielle's space. There were framed black-and-white photographs on the shelves, and the coffee table books were all art-related. The couch was covered in a cranberry-colored fabric, and the room was accented with deep reds and silvers. "I didn't know if you'd be busy with baby stuff right now," Fina said.

"No." Danielle glanced at a crystal clock on the wall. "She's having a bath."

Not on her own, presumably, since she couldn't sit up unassisted.

Fina's understanding was that, unless you had a catlike baby who didn't like water, bath time was one of the highlights of having an infant. Patty and Scotty always loved bathing their babies.

Danielle mixed the drinks and brought them over to the couch. Fina took a sip and fought the urge to wince. She wasn't kidding about liking vodka.

Danielle took a long draw from what Fina guessed was a vodka tonic. Her shoulders visibly relaxed.

"I heard the funeral was a bit of a scene," Fina said.

"I told Michael she shouldn't come," Danielle said with a sigh, "but he's never been very good at standing up to his mother."

"Most men aren't," Fina commented. Her brothers crushed opponents in court but tiptoed around Elaine. It was ridiculous to see grown men act like such pussies.

"I'm surprised your security didn't deal with her."

"And create even more of a scene? There were press there. They would have had a field day if I'd thrown her out." Danielle drank some more.

"Why did you lie to me about that phone number?" Fina asked.

Danielle swallowed and looked at Fina. "I don't know what you mean."

"The phone number I showed you on Tuesday. You recognized it. Why was Hank calling Walter Stiles?"

Danielle sat back against the cushions and fiddled with her engagement ring. "Who's that?"

Fina put her glass down on the coffee table with more force than was required. Danielle started. "Please don't waste my time and Michael's money."

Danielle met her gaze. "Fine," she said after a moment. "I don't know why Hank was calling him."

"But you do know who he is?"

"The sperm dealer? Yes, I know who he is."

"So why lie about it?"

"Because it's nobody's business. Whatever Hank was discussing with him was a private matter."

"Danielle, nothing is private when it comes to murder, and little is private when you're a public figure. You know that."

"Well, it should be. Hank made those donations when he was young and stupid, but he made them believing that his identity would be kept confidential. He didn't do anything wrong."

"I agree."

"That's rich, coming from you. You're the one who outed him."

"I did what anyone could have done."

"So you're not responsible?"

Fina tipped her head to the side. "I'm responsible for the role I played, yes. But the revelation of Hank's identity was a matter of when, not if."

"It's still just an excuse."

"Maybe." Fina picked up her glass and took another drink. "What was Hank's reaction when the news broke?"

"He was bullshit. It was a complete invasion of his privacy, and it couldn't have come at a worse time."

"Because of the waterfront development deal?"

"Yes, and bad publicity is never good for Universum."

"Did you know about the sperm donations before we identified him?"

Danielle tapped her glass with a perfectly manicured fingernail. "Of course I knew. I was his wife." She looked at Fina. Most people avoided eye contact when they were lying, but there was a smaller subset who looked you straight in the eye, defied you to call their bluff. Fina wondered if Danielle was a member of that subset.

"And did it bother you? The possibility that he had fathered other children?"

"He *had* fathered another child—Michael. It wasn't like I thought I was getting first crack at him."

"A child from a previous marriage is quite different from multiple children from assisted reproduction."

"I'm Hank's wife, and Aubrey is his legitimate daughter. That's all that matters."

"So you really have no idea why Hank contacted Walter Stiles?" Fina asked. She finished her drink and placed the glass on the coffee table.

Danielle shrugged. "Nope."

There was a light tap on the door, and a different maid entered the room. She carried a tray on which sat a plate of sashimi and a small bowl of wilted spinach.

"Your dinner, Mrs. Reardon."

Danielle checked her watch. "Thank you, Marie." The maid put the tray down and picked up Fina's empty glass, which she spirited away.

Fina stood. "You don't like to cook?"

"Nah, and I never needed to. When Hank was alive, either we went out or he was out, and I'd have the cook make me something or order in. I didn't want to cook for two people, let alone one."

"I don't cook, either. My mother thinks it's a character flaw, although she doesn't cook much anymore."

"Mine thinks the same thing, but I think she's just jealous." She picked up a pair of lacquered chopsticks.

"If you think of anything, like why Hank was in touch with Walter, let me know."

Danielle shook her head. "I won't think of anything. Can you find your way out?"

"Yup. The elevator and down. Take care."

Fina glanced back on her way out. Danielle had reached for a remote, and the large TV screen sprang to life. She had the chopsticks in her hand as she flipped through the channels. It was a picture of wealth and privilege and downright loneliness.

19

Fina stopped at a diner in Allston and ordered a BLT and fries. Walter Stiles had been on her list since their confrontation outside the cryobank, but he'd vaulted to the top. Hank Reardon was pissed that he'd been outed and had contacted Heritage's director; did he blame Walter for the release of the information even though it hadn't come from the cryobank directly? She couldn't compel Walter to talk to her, but she could be a pest. Oftentimes, people would talk if they thought it would make you go away.

When she pulled into the parking lot at the club it was after seven, safely beyond the dinner hour. She bumped into Patty and the kids walking through the parking lot. Fina exchanged kisses and hugs.

"I'm pumped for that field hockey game, Hale," she said to her niece.

Haley rolled her eyes. "Don't embarrass me. Seriously, you'll be disinvited if you don't behave."

Patty laughed as she corralled the boys into the car.

"Of course I'm going to behave," Fina protested. "Aunt Patty will keep me in line."

"I will," Patty said. "It's Pap we need to worry about."

"My dad's going to a game?" Fina asked. Carl wasn't exactly a hands-on grandfather. He loved the kids and spoiled them in many ways, but rarely with his time.

"That's what he says."

"That should be a hoot. Is my mom here?"

"I plead the fifth." Patty climbed into the front seat.

"Shit."

"Aunt Fina!" Teddy scolded her. "You owe Mommy a quarter!" The other boys giggled. Fina reached into her wallet and pulled out a five-dollar bill. She handed it to Patty, who had rolled down her window.

"Let's run a tab."

Patty shook her head. "It doesn't work that way."

"Bye."

Fina walked through the lot and up the path to the pool area. The light was waning, and there were only a handful of people around. Schools had started back, and summer schedules were giving way to the demands of September. In a couple of weeks, the pool would close for the season, and the socializing would move indoors.

Fina spotted her parents sitting at a table with Matthew and Scotty. There was an unfinished bowl of ice cream melting into a puddle and a plate with half a slice of cheesecake. Other empty bowls suggested other, larger appetites.

"I thought you said you couldn't make it," Carl said.

"I couldn't, but I told you I'd stop by with an update."

"Are you going to eat something?" Elaine asked. Most mothers would be poised to order her something, but Fina knew her mother would only do that if she could offer color commentary on Fina's choices. Eating was always an opportunity for a critique, in Elaine's book.

"No, Mom."

"What? You don't like the food here all of a sudden?"

"Did you dig anything up on the good doctor?" Fina asked Matthew.

"Nothing. I'll let you know if I do."

"I gotta go." Scotty stood up and stretched. "Any word on our young interviewee?"

"I had lunch with her a couple of days ago. I think I'm on to something. I'll let you know."

"You always talk in code," Elaine commented, and pushed back her own seat.

"Just trying to maintain confidentiality, Mom," Scotty said.

"Humph." Only her mother would interpret a law as a personal affront.

"I'm going, too." Matthew downed the rest of his drink and pushed back his chair.

Fina and Carl watched the threesome circumvent the pool and disappear behind the hedges. A young waitress came over and cleared away the remaining dishes. Once she left, Fina turned to her father.

"Rosie Sanchez was questioned by the police regarding her whereabouts the night Hank was killed. Scotty and I both think she's lying, and I'm trying to get to the bottom of it. Hank's business partner was angry about being cut out of a land development deal, and Hank's former and current wives are battling over money for their respective charities. And not long before Hank was killed, he contacted the head of the cryobank, regarding what specifically, I don't know."

"That sounds like a lot of ifs and maybes," Carl said.

"Yes, and ifs and maybes lead to theories and facts. You know that." Fina picked up a fork and cut off a bite of cheesecake. "Also, our client had a big fight with his father a couple of days before the murder."

Carl's eyebrows climbed his forehead. "He told you that?"

"Of course not. I detected it. Have you heard from Renata? I think she wants to hire you again."

"Christ, that woman is a pain in the ass."

Fina ate another bite and wiped her hands on a stray napkin. "So we're good?"

"For now." Carl stood, and Fina followed his lead.

They walked to the parking lot together in silence.

When they didn't talk to each other, they got on like gangbusters.

"Now, don't be mad," Fina said, sliding into a booth at Dunkin' Donuts the next morning.

"So that's why I haven't heard from you." Frank gave her a stern look. Her lip and neck were looking better each day, but it was still obvious there had been fisticuffs. "When is this going to stop?"

"What?" Fina reached across the table toward his cruller. He lightly slapped away her hand.

"If you're old enough to get in fights, you're old enough to buy your own donut."

"Ouch. That's just mean. Hold that chastising thought for a second."

Fina went to the counter and ordered a honey-glazed and an OJ. She brought them back to the table and offered part of the donut to Frank.

He declined. "I shouldn't even be having this one. Peg would kill me. Ice cream is supposed to be my only indulgence."

"I won't tell her. Back to your question. I don't know when 'this'"—she pointed to her face—"is going to stop."

"I never got into scrapes the way you do."

"I think our investigative techniques differ somewhat." She took a bite of donut. The thick sugary coating smeared across her tongue.

"Meaning you break the law more often."

"You make it sound like the police do this to me."

"No, but you get mixed up in things you shouldn't, maybe because you're breaking the law."

Fina took another bite. "That's one theory. Another is that the world is just a more dangerous place than it used to be."

Frank grunted. "So what are you doing to get to the bottom of this?"

"I'm just trying to solve the case. I've put some feelers out, but haven't come up with much. I could use Mark Lamont right about now."

"Oh my God. The last thing you need is Mark Lamont or whoever has taken his place."

Mark Lamont was a high school friend who had risen in the ranks of wealth and status along with the Ludlows. He'd also been heavily involved in Boston's crime world, thereby serving as a good source of information. Unfortunately, he'd landed in hot water a few months back, largely thanks to Fina's detective work. They were no longer on speaking terms.

"Are you still friends with that guy, the one who owns the gas station on Route Nine?"

One of the keys to being a good PI was cultivating relationships with people from all walks of life, all over the city. Medical malpractice, class action, and the other sorts of cases taken on by Ludlow and Associates brought a wide variety of people in the door.

"You mean Korfa?"

"He owns the chain, right?" Five years before, Korfa Mahad's daughter had fallen off a play structure and suffered serious injuries. The Ludlows had helped them sue the manufacturer, which paid her medical expenses and footed the bill for a few Pump n' Pantries.

"Yes." Frank sipped his coffee. "What do you need from him?"

"Does he have security cameras? That actually work and record things?"

Frank nodded. "I would assume so. He takes his security seriously, but nobody keeps that stuff for very long."

"Would you mind calling him and letting him know I'll be in touch?"

"Of course, but you have to be polite and return the favor to him one of these days."

"I promise, and I'm not impolite."

"Is that what I implied? I'm sorry, sweetie, I meant focused."

"I can live with focused." She licked sugar off the webbing between her thumb and finger.

"But sometimes when you're focused you can forget your manners."

"Me?"

"Are you going to give me the details of this case?" Frank asked.

"I'd rather wait until I have more to report. I want to make you proud."

"I'm always proud, but I'm ecstatic when you stay in one piece."

"I'll keep that in mind," Fina said, and got up from the booth. "Give Peg my love." She leaned over and gave Frank a peck on the cheek. "I'll come by soon for dinner."

Fina walked back to her car and saw she had a message from Hal.

Maybe one of the seeds she'd planted was actually starting to grow.

Fina decided her next stop should be Swampscott, via Kelly's on Revere Beach. She didn't make the trip north solely for the purpose of procuring fried clams, but it was a tasty incentive nonetheless and a nice chaser to her donut.

She finished her meal and drove to Juliana Reardon's house, but her knocks on the door were met with silence. Fina noticed a man kneeling in the yard next door and decided to introduce herself.

"Do you know if Juliana is around?" she asked the man. He paused with a pair of garden shears in his hand. He looked to be in his eighties, wearing khaki pants and a polo shirt. His bare feet were wedged into boat shoes, and a hat protected his face from the sun.

"She was out for her swim, but then she came home and left in the car."

"A swim in the ocean?" Fina asked incredulously.

"It's part of that racing thing she does."

Fina looked toward the beach. "It must be freezing. That sounds awful."

"She wears a wetsuit." He put down the shears and began to struggle up from his knees. Fina gave him her hand and helped pull him up to a standing position. "Thank you, young lady." He brushed dirt off his knees. "I'm her de facto lifeguard. She lets me know when she's headed out, and if I'm around, I keep an eye on her."

"That's nice of you."

"Bud Mariano." He took off his gardening gloves and hat and offered Fina his hand.

"Fina Ludlow. I'm a private investigator, and I've been hired by Michael Reardon to investigate his father's death."

"A private investigator? Well, isn't that something!" He peered at her fading bruises. He had thinning white hair on the top of his head and piercing blue eyes. When he smiled, his eyes crinkled at the corners.

"I spoke with Juliana last week and have some additional questions for her."

"If you want to wait a bit, I've got some lemonade inside."

"That sounds great. Thanks."

Fina followed Bud into a two-story white stucco house with black shutters. The kitchen was tidy, with oak cabinets and a farmhouse sink, and opened onto a dining room with a view of the beach. While Bud poured two glasses of lemonade, Fina wandered toward the glass dining room table, where a stack of brochures was fanned out next to a laptop and a wall calendar. Fina tilted her head to read some of the titles. They featured the Caribbean, with a few from Belize thrown in the mix.

"Planning a vacation?" Fina asked.

Bud brought in their glasses and pulled out a seat for Fina. He sat down at the end of the table next to her and reached for one of the brochures.

"I need to do the open-water portion of my scuba certification. I'm trying to decide where to go."

Fina must have done a poor job of hiding her surprise.

"It's completely safe," Bud assured her. "I got checked out by my doctor, and he gave me the go-ahead."

"I think it's fantastic," Fina said. "I wish my parents would learn how to scuba dive." Because when you're underwater, breathing out of a tank, you can't talk.

"My children disagree."

"I'm sure they just worry about you."

"They do. Too much. They think since their mother is gone, I'm completely incapable of taking care of myself."

"Do your kids live nearby?"

"I've got a daughter in Marblehead, a son in Sudbury, and another daughter in Connecticut. What about you? You live in this neck of the woods?"

"I grew up mostly in Newton, but I live in the city now." She gestured toward the window, where the skyline could be seen in the distance. "My family is still in the MetroWest area." Fina nodded at the brochures. "Have you narrowed it down?"

"I think Grand Cayman and Bonaire are at the top of the list. Are you a scuba diver?"

"God, no. I don't want to know what's down there. I don't even like opening my eyes in pools."

"Ever snorkeled?"

"No. I don't like to share the same space or perspective as the shark in *Jaws*."

Bud guffawed. "Shark attacks are extremely rare in the Caribbean."

"You know where they're really rare? On land."

"How can you be a private investigator and be such a scaredy-cat?"

"It's easy. I never take any cases that require scuba diving. And I'm not a scaredy-cat on land."

"I would hope not. You wouldn't have much of a business."

Fina sipped her lemonade. "So how long have you lived here, next to Juliana?"

"My wife and I moved into the house forty-three years ago. My kids think it's too big for me now," Bud said.

Fina shook her head. "You're just disappointing them left and right."

"Indeed I am, young lady. I feel like a teenager—struggling for my independence, but well aware I may need them in the not-too-distant future."

"When did your wife die? Assuming she did."

"Sadie died just under a year ago."

"I'm sorry. I'm sure that must be very difficult."

"It is."

Neither spoke for a moment. Bud was stuck in his head with his wife, and Fina didn't want to interrupt.

"Now, Juliana moved in about three years ago," he said, picking up the thread. "She's a good neighbor. I don't know her well, but she was kind when Sadie died. She's enthusiastic about my scuba diving."

"I would expect she would be; she's had to reinvent herself in recent years." Fina caught a drip rolling down her glass with her fingertip. "Do you know her son, Michael?"

"We've been introduced. He seems like a nice young man."

"Does he come around much, as far as you know?"

"Not really, but his father made the occasional visit." He fiddled with the corner of a brochure.

"Hank?"

"The very one."

"I guess I shouldn't be surprised. He and Juliana seemed to have a decent relationship, for exes at least."

Bud's laptop pinged, indicating he had new e-mail. Bud was obviously more active and engaged in life than some people half his age. He clicked the mouse a few times to mute the machine. "I think Juliana deserves the credit for that."

"Why's that?" Fina asked.

"She obviously took the high road. Hank's current wife is young enough to be his daughter. I don't understand my peers, replacing their wives with younger versions. What are they thinking?"

Fina grinned. "I'm guessing that you and Sadie had the real thing."

Bud nodded emphatically. "We did."

"So you think Juliana was accepting of Hank's remarriage?"

"In general, although their last visit didn't go so well."

"In what way?" Fina asked.

"I wasn't snooping," Bud insisted.

"I'm sure you weren't, but sometimes it's hard not to hear your neighbors."

"That's right." Bud took a drink of lemonade. "I was working in the bushes in the yard, and they probably didn't see me. They were fighting about money."

Fina nodded knowingly. "The Reardon Center."

"Exactly." Bud tapped his nose. "They had a big argument about the endowment for the center."

"I wonder if Hank was going to pull some of the funding," Fina said. "It would be too bad if the center suffered because of their divorce or his remarriage. It provides a great service to the community."

"Indeed it does."

"I have read, however, that his new wife, Danielle, has her own charitable causes."

"And there isn't enough to go around?" Bud asked incredulously.

Fina laughed. "Good point."

"It's ridiculous."

Fina finished her drink, but stayed and chatted with Bud for another twenty minutes. He was funny, smart, and handsome, and had an opinion about everything—just her type.

They brought their glasses into the kitchen and left them in the sink. Bud walked her to the door but stopped her before she left.

"Are you related to those attorneys? The ones I see on TV?"

Fina leaned her head toward him. "Promise you won't hold it against me?" she said under her breath.

Bud held his hand up as if taking an oath. "Never. It's been a delight."

"For me, too, Bud. If you were younger, I'd ask you on a date."

"Oh, young lady. Go, before I have a heart attack."

"Shoot me an e-mail and let me know how your trip goes." Fina handed him her business card.

"And you let me know when you've worked up the courage to open your eyes underwater."

"Will do."

Fina walked to her car with a smile on her face.

She dealt with a lot of douchebags in her line of work, but every once in a while, she uncovered a gem.

Fina was zipping past Suffolk Downs, mulling over this newest piece of the puzzle. It seemed that Juliana Reardon wasn't completely Zen when it came to Hank and their split. If Hank had threatened to pull funding from the center, Juliana would see that as a serious threat—to the center, certainly, but also to her reputation as the peaceful philanthropist. But was it reason enough to kill him? And what impact would killing Hank actually have on the financial situation?

She drove through Back Bay and got on Huntington Ave. A few minutes later, she pulled into a large gas station with eight pumps and a convenience store.

"Is Mr. Mahad in?" she asked the old man behind the register. He looked Somali, which made sense, given that the Mahad family had emigrated from that African nation.

"Korfa! There is lady to see you." The man remained on his stool, his eyes jumping between the security monitor trained on the back of the store and a small TV tuned to the local cable station.

A younger man poked his head around a doorway at the back of the store. He was close to forty, wearing trousers, a short-sleeved button-down, and reading glasses.

Fina approached him. "I'm Fina Ludlow, Carl Ludlow's daughter. I think Frank Gillis was going to give you a call."

The man beamed. "Of course, Ms. Ludlow, please come in." He beckoned her into the office. The room was small and windowless, but neat. A computer sat on the desk next to a stack of paperwork. There was a file cabinet in the corner, as well as a safe. Off to the side were stacked cases of diet soda and Reese's peanut butter cups. It was like visiting the Promised Land.

"Please, sit." Korfa gestured at a chair facing the desk.

"I can't remember if we met when my father was handling your case."

"I don't believe so, but I met your brothers, and your father spoke highly of you." Korfa removed his glasses and placed them on the desk.

"Really?"

Korfa nodded. "The case concerned my daughter, so he told me about his."

"Good enough." Fina assumed that Carl thought she did a good job, but he was stingy with praise in general. She rarely heard any. "How is your daughter, Mr. Mahad?"

"Amina is wonderful." When he smiled, his eyes sparkled and his pearly white teeth popped in contrast to his dark skin. "She is healthy and very successful in school. I owe your father and Frank a great deal."

"Well, you and your wife should take credit for Amina. Carl and Frank had nothing to do with it."

"But she would not have received such excellent care if your father had not prevailed. She saw the best doctors and nurses at Children's, and thanks to them, she is wonderful."

"I'm so glad." Fina looked at a framed photo hanging on the wall. It was next to a business license and numerous inspection reports from the state. In it, Korfa posed with a woman in a hijab. In front of them there were three children: a tween, whom Fina assumed was Amina, another young girl, and a fat baby boy. They all smiled widely for the camera.

"Did Frank mention my reason for stopping by?"

"He said you were interested in my surveillance video."

"That's right. I'm trying to determine if a car passed this station or the station on Washington Street overnight, the Monday before last."

"Is this a case for your father?"

"Sort of. It's a murder case, actually." Korfa's eyes widened. "But I'm not asking you for anything that's illegal or dangerous," Fina was quick to reassure him. "No one has an expectation of privacy from cameras owned by private businesses on private property."

He nodded emphatically. "I would be honored to be of assistance."

Fina gave him the date, and he tapped at his computer keyboard. "Could I e-mail you the files?"

"That would be great. I'm surprised you still have them. A lot of places get rid of film every few days."

"We used to, but with digital, there's no need. It has been a good investment. When a customer claims he slipped in my parking lot, I can produce the tape, which proves him wrong."

"My father would be impressed, Mr. Mahad." Fina pulled out a business card and handed it across the desk. "If you or your family ever need anything, don't hesitate to call."

"Thank you, and let me know if I can be of further service to you."

She wouldn't mind a case of peanut butter cups, but stopped herself from asking. When you started consuming something—anything—by the case, it wasn't a good sign.

20

Fina made a quick call to see if Walter Stiles was at Heritage Cryobank. According to the receptionist, he was out, which made it the perfect time to pay a visit to Ellen Alberti.

The cryobank was busy when Fina arrived. She rushed into the reception area and interrupted as another woman was conferring with the receptionist. It was a different receptionist than last time, thankfully. Presumably, the original was basking in the glow of new motherhood.

"I'm so sorry I'm late, but my sister is back there." Fina gestured toward the door leading to the rest of the bank. "She's going to kill me if her appointment has already started."

The other client glared at her, and the receptionist waved her in. Fina gave her a big smile and walked through the door. Wow. Still not locked. These people were idiots.

Fina wound her way through the hallways and knocked on Ellen Alberti's open door. The associate director looked up from her lunch, momentarily confused.

"Do we have an appointment?" She had carved out a small square of space on her desk, which was occupied by a salad in a Tupperware container, a diet soda, and a shiny red apple.

"No. I don't know if you remember me or not."

"Wait." Ellen pointed at her. "You're the private investigator." Ellen was wearing tweed pants with a blue sweater set. Peeking out from her medium blond hair were large gold earrings, and on her wrist was an assortment of bracelets.

"Fina Ludlow." Fina looked at the chair in front of the desk and dipped her head in question.

"Just put that stuff on the floor," Ellen responded.

Fina transferred the stack of files to the industrial carpet and took a seat.

"You just waltzed back here again?" Ellen asked. She stared for a beat too long at Fina's neck.

"I told you that your security is horrible. Aside from people wandering around where they shouldn't, someone could walk in with a gun and take over the entire place. You can't think this is a good setup, and your insurance provider definitely can't."

Ellen dropped her fork into her salad and leaned back in her chair. She put her hands up and shrugged. "I think it's terrible."

"So call your insurance company and tell them you'd like them to do a security audit."

"Which will end up costing us more money."

"You don't think it's going to cost you money when someone sues you?"

Ellen tipped her head to the side.

"I'm not talking about Renata Sanchez," Fina said. "I'm talking about some other mother who claims her eggs or the sperm were interfered with. You can't guarantee that your supplies are secure."

"They're under lock and key," Ellen insisted.

"Trust me. Any good attorney would have a field day with your lax security. It's just a matter of time."

"Is that why you're here, to give me security advice, save me from a lawsuit?" She speared a cherry tomato with her fork.

"No, that's just a bonus. I was wondering if Hank Reardon had been in touch with you before his death."

Ellen considered the question for a few seconds. "No, he wasn't in touch with me."

"You took a long time to think about that."

She took a sip of her drink. "I wanted to be sure. I was searching my memory."

"Do you know if he was in touch with Walter?"

"You and Walter are on a first-name basis?"

"Actually, I visited Walter yesterday at his home."

"I'm sure he was thrilled to see you." Ellen grinned.

"'Thrilled' might be a bit of an overstatement. But back to my question: Was Hank Reardon in touch with Walter?" Her hand drifted up to her lip; it was almost completely scabbed over.

"What happened to your face?"

"Accident. No biggie. Hank and Walter?"

"I don't know if they were in touch."

"Huh." Fina gazed out the window. It was coming up on her favorite time of year. She loved fall, when the leaves were blazing with color and the air was crisp but not too cold.

"You're suggesting that Hank was in touch with Walter?" Ellen asked. "Not Hank's attorney?"

"I'm not suggesting anything."

Ellen chewed a mouthful of lettuce. "You're very cryptic."

"Just trying to make sense of all the bits and pieces of information. You don't seem surprised that perhaps Walter was up to something."

"Oh, I *know* that Walter was up to something," Ellen said, looking Fina in the eye.

"Really? What's that?"

"I don't know exactly what, but I don't trust him, and neither should you."

"And you're telling me this because . . . ?"

"I'm feeling charitable." She snapped the top onto the Tupperware.

Fina brushed a loose hair back from her face. "Maybe, or maybe you think it's time for Walter to move on."

"Speaking of moving," Ellen said, "I wonder why he removed a couple of file boxes from the cryobank last week. He claimed they were personal files, but that's hard to believe. But why would he remove cryobank files? It's curious, and obviously against policy."

"Ellen, you are just full of interesting tidbits."

She blotted her lips with a napkin. "I just want to do the right thing."

"Who knew the world of assisted reproduction was so cutthroat?" Fina stood and put her bag over her shoulder. "I appreciate your time, Ellen. Good luck with your coup d'état, and let me know if I can do anything." Fina pushed her card across the desk. "And for Pete's sake, do something about your security."

Ellen looked at the card and slid it under her blotter. "Take care, Fina."

In the reception area, Fina smiled at the receptionist and gave her two thumbs up. The woman beamed back at her.

Somehow, Fina didn't think they were celebrating the same thing.

Fina called the medical lab from her car. She waited on hold for a couple of minutes, forced to listen to a Muzak version of a Rolling Stones song. Finally, a surly lab tech came on the line and informed Fina that the second sample for her test had not yet arrived.

She hung up and dialed Greta Samuels's number. After six rings, someone finally picked up the phone.

"Hello?"

"Greta Samuels, please?" Fina asked.

"She's not available at the moment. May I take a message?"

"Could you tell her that Fina Ludlow called and ask her to call me back?"

"Fina Ludlow," the woman said slowly, as if writing it down at the same time. There was a small commotion in the background, and the woman whispered to someone else before coming back on the line. "Could you hold on for one moment?"

"Ah . . . sure," Fina said to the empty line. She could hear more conversation in the background and what sounded like the phone being put down and picked up again.

"Fina?"

"Greta?"

"Yes, it's me."

"I thought you weren't available."

"My friend was mistaken."

"Okay. What's going on? I just called the lab, and they haven't received your sample."

"Oh, things have been very busy."

"I don't understand. When we spoke on Wednesday, you were going to stop by the doctor's office that day."

"Well, they didn't have an appointment available."

"Greta, you contacted Risa, remember? It's not really fair for you to approach her and then drag your feet over the test."

"I'm not dragging my feet," she responded snappily.

"If you're getting cold feet, I suggest we stop things now, before we go any further down this road."

"I promise I'm going today," Greta insisted. "The doctor's going to do the procedure and fill out whatever that legal form is that you require."

"Procedure" seemed a little dramatic for a DNA swab, and the legal form was a standard affidavit. Greta seemed on edge.

"That's terrific, and I'll let you know as soon as I have the results," Fina said, wanting to end the call on a high note.

"Well, good, then. I'll talk to you soon."

Greta hung up, and Fina slipped her phone into her bag. What had

that been about? First, Greta couldn't wait to claim Risa as family, and now she was stalling. Greta was asking a lot of Risa; she should be grateful that Risa was entertaining this whole notion in the first place, not giving Fina attitude.

She had teenagers for that.

Fina called Jules Lindsley's office to determine if he was around—no need to spring for parking if he was out of the office. The melodious voice on the other end of the line assured Fina that Mr. Lindsley was present, so she drove to the parking structure below his office and prepared to pay a king's ransom for the privilege.

She sat in the waiting area of his office, sipping water and leafing through *Boston* magazine. Fifteen minutes later, Jules came down the hallway, his briefcase in hand. As long as Fina had known him, Jules had had white hair, but he never struck her as old. Instead, with his understated but well-tailored suits and shiny loafers, he struck her as timeless.

"I can talk if you walk with me, Fina, but I don't have time to stop." He offered his hand. Fina jumped up and shook it.

"That works for me." She followed him to the elevators.

"What happened to your face?" he asked. The two businessmen who shared the car stole glances at her.

"On-the-job injury, but I'm on the mend."

"I don't know how your father manages. I'd be a wreck if my daughter were in your line of work."

Fina swatted away the comment. "Well, you have a heart, Jules. That would make it difficult."

He laughed heartily, and they exchanged more pleasantries until they reached the sidewalk.

"So what's this about?" he asked as they dodged the pedestrian traffic.

"I know you have privilege and all that," Fina started, "but I'm trying to get a handle on Hank's estate. Who gets what—that sort of thing."

"If you know about privilege, then why are you even asking? I can't tell you anything."

"You're aware that Michael Reardon hired me, right?"

"Yes, I am, but I still can't tell you his father's business."

"There's *nothing* you can tell me? Even about the funding for the center?"

"Why would you ask about that?" Jules looked at her as they waited for the light to change.

"Because sources have told me that changes were afoot that were causing friction between Hank and Juliana."

They'd arrived at the entrance of a large office building across from South Station. Commuters were streaming in and out of the doors of the old station, the daily influx and exodus under way.

"I can't comment."

"Ugh. This is so frustrating." Fina put her hands on her hips, but realized that the posture made her look like a four-year-old. Jules smiled at her. She dropped her hands to her side.

"Okay. One last question," Fina said.

"Quickly, so I'm not late for my meeting."

"I had a visit a few days ago from a kid named Brett Linder."

Jules looked at her but showed no reaction.

"He claimed that Hank is his biological father."

"Why did he approach you?"

"Apparently, he'd seen my name in the news. I told him that he should contact you or the cops."

Jules rolled his eyes. "I haven't heard from him, but that doesn't mean I won't."

"I also told him that he'd have to prove that Hank was his biological father."

"Yes, he will. What was his response?"

"He wasn't thrilled at the prospect of a DNA test. Maybe he's telling the truth, but it seemed kind of convenient."

"I can't imagine he'll be the last to crawl out of the woodwork—or the petri dish, as it were."

"I wouldn't think so. Also, Renata Sanchez is interested in what Hank's death means for her."

"She should get in line. Everyone wants to know what Hank's death means for them. I need to go."

"Of course. Thanks for talking to me." Fina started walking.

She was ten feet away when he called after her. "Fina!"

"I don't know if any of the Ludlows are in the market for a house," Jules said when she stood next to him again, "but I hear there's a lovely place in Cambridge that's just come on the market."

"Is that so?" Fina pulled out her notebook and a pen. "Well, you know us. We're always looking for a good investment."

"The address is Forty-four Oak Street."

"Thanks for the tip, Jules."

Frank had taught Fina early in her training that she should take any clue in stride, no matter how cryptic. Act like information was un-expected and the messenger might get cold feet. If Jules had suggested she buy an orangutan, she would have dutifully noted the details and looked into purchasing a giant jungle gym.

It sounded like she needed to take a drive over the river.

Forty-four Oak Street was lovely and—surprise, surprise—it was smack-dab next to the Reardon Center. Fina pulled over to the curb and gazed at the two buildings. The center was in a large Victorian that looked freshly painted and had attractive landscaping in the front yard. There was a driveway that ran along the building's side and led to a parking lot out back. A couple of women, one of whom wore a scarf over her bald head, were standing on the front steps, deep in conversa-tion. The house next door was of equal size, but not quite as well maintained. There was no For Sale sign out front, but Fina didn't doubt the intel; Jules had good sources.

Just what was Juliana up to?

Fina grabbed her mail from the condo lobby and started sorting it in the elevator. Bills, catalogs, and junk mail made up the majority of the pile, not to mention an offer from a company interested in recycling her remains and using them as compost. A couple of years earlier, Fina had noticed that she was getting a lot of mail from AARP and other businesses targeted to those closer to the end of their lifespan than the beginning. She'd had her financial planner do some digging to determine that she wasn't a victim of identity theft or a mix-up on her credit report. He came back empty-handed, and they determined that on some list out in cyberspace, she was an octogenarian interested in things like long-term care insurance, seated motor scooters, and burial alternatives. Fina had seen the future, and it wasn't pretty.

A nine-by-twelve mailing envelope with no return address was the only thing of interest. Fina waited until she was inside the condo before ripping open the top and pulling out the contents.

It stopped her in her tracks.

There were half a dozen photographs, all of which featured Haley from a distance. The first two showed her with a group of friends outside her school. Another featured her on a field hockey field wearing athletic gear. The remainders were shots of sidewalks and parking lots. Fina felt her stomach lurch and a light sweat appear at her hairline. The envelope didn't contain a note, but the message was clear.

Someone had Haley in his sights.

Fina scooted into the lobby of Cristian's apartment building behind a young woman who was on the phone. The woman paused in her conversation and glared at Fina.

"I'm visiting Detective Menendez in 4F," Fina insisted. "You can follow me up there if you like."

The tenant returned to her conversation, and Fina sprinted up the stairs rather than wait for the painfully slow elevator. She knocked on his door and heard murmurs behind it.

"Fina, what are you doing here?" Cristian asked. He was wearing jeans and an untucked T-shirt, holding a beer. She peered around him but didn't see anyone, just heard noises emanating from the kitchen.

"I need to talk to you."

He took a step out into the hall. "This isn't a good time."

"I'm sorry. I can tell you're busy, but it's urgent."

Cristian exhaled loudly. "It's always urgent with you."

"Just look." Fina handed him the envelope. He gave her his beer, and she took a long pull from it.

Cristian flipped through the photos, frowning. "I assume she's okay."

"I spoke with Patty on the way over here. I didn't want to alarm her so I didn't say anything specific, but Haley seems to be fine."

"Cristian! I think the chilies are done roasting." A woman appeared on the threshold. She was young—in her late twenties—and very pretty. Her long hair was shiny and wavy, her complexion olive-tinged. She looked wholesome, with her bright eyes and smooth skin, not like the kind of woman who'd get choked in an elevator or throw any punches.

Cristian stood awkwardly between the two women.

"I'm Fina, a friend of Cristian's," Fina finally said, extending her hand.

"Cindy," the young woman answered. Her grip was firm and warm.

"I'm really sorry to interrupt," Fina said. "It's a family crisis."

"That's okay. You guys don't need to stand in the hallway." Cindy beckoned them in.

"Right," Cristian said reluctantly. "Come on in."

Fina followed them into the kitchen. "Do you have any thoughts?"

She nodded at the photos in Cristian's hands. Cindy stirred a pot on the stove. Fina took another drink of Cristian's beer, a motion Cindy followed with her gaze.

"You're not going to get anything from these." He put the photos back in the envelope. "No return address. I doubt there are any prints."

"Do you and Pitney have any leads that might point me in the right direction?"

Cristian shook his head. "Nope, and I'd be on it already if there were a credible threat."

Fina nodded. "I know. Shit. I've got nothing."

"The list of people you're annoying can't be exhaustive."

"You'd be surprised." Fina drained the beer and put the empty on the kitchen table. Cindy picked up hers and sipped it delicately.

"Keep an eye on Haley and work it from the other end," Cristian suggested. "That's all I can tell you."

"Maybe I need to draw this guy out again. I'm assuming it's the same one I met in the elevator."

"That's a terrible idea." Cristian reached into the fridge and pulled out a fresh beer. He popped off the top and took a swig. "Do not do that."

Cindy moved the pot off the stove. She pulled on a pair of oven mitts and took a pan out of the oven.

"That smells amazing," Fina said, sniffing the air.

"You're welcome to stay for dinner," Cindy offered.

Cristian did not look pleased at the invitation.

"No, thank you. I've barged in enough. I just wanted you to know what's going on," she said to Cristian.

"I wish I could do more."

"It was nice meeting you, Cindy." Fina walked back to the front door with Cristian trailing behind her. He handed her the envelope.

"Look, I know this scares you, but the chances of anyone actually doing anything to Haley are slim."

"But not nonexistent. I can't believe we went through all that shit over the summer and I might have put her right back in the middle of things."

"It's not your fault, Fina."

Fina rubbed her eyes with her palms. "I hate this. I hate this feeling."

"I know." Cristian pulled her toward him and hugged her. "Calm down, and don't do anything stupid. Haley will be upset if you get yourself killed."

Fina pulled back a few inches and looked at him. "What about you? Will you be upset if I get myself killed?"

He looked at her with a sad smile. "Go home. Maybe Milloy should come over and keep you company."

Fina stepped back. "Pushing me into the arms of the enemy? You must really like her."

Cristian shrugged.

Fina walked back to the stairwell and slowly made her way down the four flights to the lobby.

Back at Nanny's, she opened her computer and contemplated watching the surveillance footage provided by Korfa Mahad, but her heart wasn't in it. Reviewing surveillance footage was tedious and time-consuming, but you had to pay attention. Space out at the wrong moment and you might miss the very thing you'd waited hours to see. Fina knew she should rally and watch, but she was tired and grumpy. Once in a while she just couldn't rally, not unless her life depended on it, and tonight, it didn't.

Instead, she took a long, warm shower, put on her cozies—as her young nephew referred to loungewear—made herself a fluffernutter, and poured a tall glass of milk. She curled up on the couch, eating and watching reality TV.

Things weren't going the way she wanted them to, and quite frankly, it was pissing her off.

21

After a quick shower and a few Oreos the next morning, Fina sat down at her laptop and started reviewing Korfa's footage. She was able to fast-forward through it, but it would still be time-consuming reviewing the tapes from both gas stations.

She hadn't slept well the night before. Her mind kept ricocheting between thoughts of Haley, which scared her, and Cindy, which annoyed her. Now she had to fight to stay focused on the images in front of her. Half an hour in, there was a knock on her door.

Fina peeked through the peephole and unlocked the door for Hal. He was dressed in his typical uniform of dress pants and a button-down shirt that appeared to be made from a synthetic fabric.

"You look better than last time," he commented, lowering himself into one of Nanny's chairs.

"Thanks. I feel better." Fina went into the kitchen and got him a glass of ice water, which she placed on the side table next to him.

"Thank you."

Fina settled back onto the sofa. "So, what do you have for me?"

Hal popped open his briefcase and removed a file. He did most of his work electronically, but it wasn't unusual for him to provide a paper copy, which Fina was then instructed to shred.

"I can understand why Dimitri Kask would be bitter about the waterfront deal."

"Why's that?" Fina took the proffered file. She looked inside, but the columns of numbers were a foreign language.

"It has the potential to be incredibly lucrative." Hal had some water. "Not only that, it could be a landmark, one of those iconic places that people associate with a city. Not right away, of course, but over time."

"I wonder why Hank didn't want him involved."

"That I can't tell you, but depending upon Mr. Kask's personality, being left out could be quite a blow," Hal said.

"He seems like a decent guy, but who knows. I'm sure his ego is oversize."

"It usually has to be to attain the level of success he has."

"Any thoughts about the future of the project now that Hank is dead?" Fina tossed the folder onto the coffee table.

"So far, all systems go."

"Hmm. Okay. What about the other thing? The charities?"

"Now, that's rather interesting." Hal sat up straighter in his seat. Hal loved to investigate things, but he also loved reporting his findings to Fina. Occasionally, she tried to move things along, but he was such a nice guy that she didn't like to spoil his fun.

"So, you know that Juliana Reardon is essentially the patron of the Reardon Center?"

Fina nodded.

"Apparently, Danielle Reardon is in the process of establishing the Hank Reardon *House*. It was going to just be the Reardon House, but since he died . . ." Hal gave her a knowing look.

"What's that exactly?"

"It's like the Ronald McDonald House, except not just for kids. A place for families to stay when their loved ones are in the hospital."

"How far along is the process?"

"They haven't announced any formal plans yet, but all signs point to it. The sale for the land is about to go through."

"I imagine that requires a lot of cash."

"Millions, over a long period of time. Eventually, you want something like that to be self-sustaining."

"I've been wondering if Hank got tired of funding the Reardon Center, especially if Danielle had her own project that required his checkbook."

Hal shrugged. "Both places seem like worthy causes. It's too bad he couldn't do both."

"I agree. Can you look into a piece of property for me?"

"Sure." Hal pulled out his phone and prepared to type in the details.

"Forty-four Oak Street in Cambridge. It's next to the Reardon Center. I'm wondering if Juliana is looking to expand."

"That's got to be expensive," Hal said, tucking his phone into his pocket.

He got himself unwedged from Nanny's chair, and Fina walked with him to the front door. "Make sure you shred those documents when you're done with them," he told her.

"I promise," Fina said. "Keep in touch."

Hal left, and she returned to her laptop.

Another hour watching traffic on Korfa's surveillance tapes confirmed the hunch she'd had all along.

Generally, she believed it was better to know something than not, but in this case, ignorance had been bliss.

Fina spent Saturday afternoon confirming her suspicions with multiple viewings of the security tape and treated Sunday as a day of rest. If the good Lord got a day off, why shouldn't she?

"You wanted to speak with me?" Juliana Reardon said on the other end of the phone on Monday morning.

"Yes." Fina pulled herself away from the computer screen, where she had queued up the critical footage once more.

"Well, I just finished up some meetings at the center. We could grab a quick lunch," Juliana suggested.

"That would be great."

They made a plan to meet in ninety minutes.

Fina skipped the footage back thirty seconds and watched it again.

There it was, clear as day.

Rosie and Tyler in Tyler's car, driving by Korfa's gas station at one in the morning—when they'd claimed to be snug in their beds. She cursed them under her breath. This was probably what the police had on Rosie.

Fina grabbed her bag and headed out the door. On the way down to the parking garage, she wrapped her hand securely around her gun. She'd told Cristian she wanted to draw out her nemesis, but in reality, she wasn't looking forward to the encounter and wasn't sure how she'd do it. She breathed a sigh of relief once the car door was securely locked behind her and she was on her way to Ludlow and Associates.

Scotty wasn't in his office, but his assistant told her to wait; he was due back any minute. Fina was smashing buttons on the Magic Genie when he came through the door, a legal pad under one arm and a bottle of water in the other hand.

"Hey. What's up?" he asked as he dropped into his expensive leather desk chair.

"Those little stinkers were lying to us."

"Which ones?"

"Rosie Sanchez and Tyler Frasier."

Scotty nodded his head and started thumbing through a pile of file folders on his desk. "Go on," he said.

Fina grabbed a diet soda from his wet bar and sat down in the chair across from his desk. "They both claimed that they were asleep in bed when Hank was killed, but I have proof that they were gallivanting around town."

Scotty found the file he wanted and spread it open. "Gallivanting? Tell me more."

"I don't know more, but I know neither was where they claimed to be, and they both have possible motives for killing Hank."

"We only represent Rosie."

"I know, but we may end up representing Tyler."

"I can't worry about a non-client."

"Fine. Let's focus on Rosie. What are we going to do?"

Scotty sat back in his chair and twirled a ballpoint pen between his fingers. He frowned. "This isn't good."

"Do your clients really pay you eight hundred dollars an hour for that kind of pronouncement?"

"Hey, 'I don't get paid unless you get paid,' remember?"

"*Some* of them pay you up front," Fina grumbled.

"Easy, killer."

"Sorry, I'm just disappointed that they didn't tell us—me—the truth."

"Don't take it personally. They're teenagers, and even adults do stupid things when the police are involved."

"So what should we do?"

"Let's get Rosie in here to discuss this."

"Are you going to advise her to come clean?"

Scotty considered for a moment. "I don't know. I assume the police already know; why else the little chat at the station? But if that's all they've got, it's obviously not enough. Why help their investigation?"

Fina scratched her lip. The healing was coming along nicely, but it was itching a little. "We'll have to include Renata in the meeting. Technically, Rosie's a minor."

"Do you think Renata knows about this already?"

"No, actually. I think Rosie has been lying to her, too." Fina had a swig of her drink. "I'll call Rosie and set something up."

"Sounds good. Talk to Michelle to coordinate our schedules."

"Okay." Fina continued to sit, picking at the tab on the soda can.

"Yes?" Scotty asked after a moment. "Do you want to discuss something else?"

"Not really, but I think I should."

"Those feelings you're having, they're natural. It's all part of puberty." Scotty suppressed a smile.

Fina rolled her eyes. "Wait until you have to have that talk with the boys. And I don't think 'Insert tab A into slot B' qualifies."

He laughed. "So what's bothering you?"

Fina gestured toward her neck. "So you know how I was . . ."

"Attacked?"

"That sounds so violent."

"It was violent!"

"Okay, fine. See, you're getting upset already, and I haven't even told you anything yet."

"Fina, spit it out. I have a meeting in five minutes."

"I think the guy who did it is trying a different angle. He sent me photos of Haley."

"What kind of photos?" Scotty asked, leaning forward.

"Nothing like that. Photos like she's being watched."

Scotty shook his head. "Please tell me you're not serious."

"I'm serious." Fina looked down at her feet.

Scotty tapped his fingers on the desk blotter. He was very different in temperament from Carl, but they shared some behavioral tics. "What are you going to do about this?"

"I'm not sure, but I'm working on a plan."

"That's it?"

"I didn't think I should wait until I had a plan to tell you."

"Well, what? Do you think she needs protection?"

"No, but I want you and Patty to keep an eye out."

"And what about the boys?"

"They weren't in any of the photos. Clearly, the guy is just fucking with me, Scotty."

"Except it's not just you. Have you told Dad?"

"No, and I don't want to, not yet at least."

"You're saying that Haley may be in danger, but you don't know who is threatening her or how to stop him."

"In a nutshell."

"This has been a great visit."

"Look, I'll call you later and we can decide if we need to take extra precautions."

"Fine, but don't forget to call me. If I don't hear from you, I'll have to assume that you've been the victim of another violent attack."

"Stop being so dramatic."

"Stop getting beaten up."

Fina left the office and took the elevator down to the Prudential Center. She checked her messages and picked up one from Dante and another from Theresa. She'd deal with them later.

In the fifteen minutes she had to kill before meeting Juliana, she browsed the clothing stores. Fina liked clothes but hated shopping. Her usual routine was to grab a bunch of items off the racks, buy them, try them on at home, and eventually give the rejects to Haley or Patty. Returning stuff was never a priority on her to-do list. Before lunch she quickly chose two dresses, three tops, and a pair of pants. Something was bound to fit someone.

The café that Juliana had selected was the sort where you order your meal at the counter and they bring it to your table. Fina spent the moments waiting for Juliana studying the completely vegan menu. Her approach to good nutrition was simple: Avoid it at all costs. A quick metabolism and lack of chronic illnesses had so far enabled Fina to eat a diet consisting mostly of preservatives and processed foodstuffs. Maybe she'd feel physically better if she adopted better eating habits, but maybe she'd be hit by a bus on the way home, in which case her arteries wouldn't get a vote. Why not revel in the food industry's manipulative marketing and taste-altering campaigns in the meantime?

Clearly the diners at this café wouldn't agree, since most of the offerings were gluten-free in addition to being free of animal products. Fina understood that eating animal flesh was distasteful to some people, but what did butter ever do to you? She was trying to decide between the BLT made with tempeh bacon or the Reuben made with shaved seitan when Juliana breezed in. Fina shared her quandary with her.

"Definitely have the BLT. It's delicious."

"If you say so."

"Don't be so skeptical, Fina. You'll miss out on so much in life."

Fina wasn't in the mood to be lectured, but bit her tongue. She needed to stay focused.

They found a table at the window overlooking Huntington Ave and uncapped their drinks. Fina had opted for seltzer, but Juliana chose carrot beet juice.

"How are things at the center?" Fina asked.

"They're terrific. Very busy, but that's the way I like it." Juliana brushed a lock of hair behind her ear. She was wearing a fitted pantsuit and short boots, both of which were flattering and expensive-looking.

"I met your neighbor Bud Mariano," Fina said. "He's a hoot."

"He's such a sweet man. Did he tell you about his scuba diving?"

"Yes, he showed me some of the brochures for his trip."

"I think it's fantastic. He's eighty-two and starting on a new adventure."

"He's obviously impressed by your triathlon training."

Juliana shook off the compliment and didn't have a chance to respond before a young man brought their sandwiches to the table. He was cute, but there was not an ounce of fat on him. His clothes seemed to wear him rather than the other way around, and Fina fought the urge to pick him up, toss him over her shoulder, and find an ice-cream sundae, *stat*.

"So you have more questions for me?" Juliana asked after taking her first bite of sandwich.

"One of the things I run up against in most investigations is that people don't necessarily lie to me, but they leave a lot of things out."

Juliana looked at her with a guileless expression. "Such as?"

"Such as your fight with Hank about the funding for the Reardon Center."

Juliana put down her sandwich and wiped her fingers on her napkin. "Did Bud tell you we had a fight? You know, his hearing isn't great."

Fina chewed her bite. It was taking an unreasonable amount of time and effort.

"I, respectfully, call bullshit on that," Fina said once she'd finally swallowed her mouthful. "His hearing is just fine. And I didn't just hear this from Bud; I've heard from other sources that your funding was in jeopardy."

"What other sources?"

"I'm not going to say, so let's move on. Did you have a fight with Hank?"

"I'm not going to discuss this with you."

Fina pulled open her sandwich and removed the offending tempeh. She put the slices of bread back together and took a bite of her newly constructed LT sandwich.

"Did you know that your son also had a fight with his father just days before his death?"

Juliana looked annoyed. "And who told you that?"

"Michael did."

"Well, that's his business, not mine."

"Okay, but I work for Michael, and presumably, you don't want to be an obstacle in this investigation."

Juliana leaned toward Fina and lowered her voice. "I didn't kill Hank, so I couldn't possibly be an obstacle to anything. You shouldn't be focusing on me. You should be focusing on other people."

"Such as?"

"Oh, I don't know. His wife? His business partner? His illegitimate children? Their mothers?"

Fina took a swig of seltzer and tried to swallow her annoyance at the same time. "I told Michael when I took the case that I was going to investigate everyone—even you—and he agreed to that."

"Well, I don't think he really thought it through."

"Be that as it may . . ."

Juliana reached down and picked up her designer handbag. "I think we're done. If you have any real questions to ask me, then please, don't hesitate to be in touch." She pushed back her chair and took off, her half-eaten sandwich left behind.

Fina loaded their plates onto a tray and spent what felt like an hour separating out the various components of their trash. She wasn't opposed to recycling or composting; she just never remembered to build it into her schedule.

Back in the Prudential Center, she set off in the direction of the food court, one of America's most inspired inventions.

Whew. She was famished.

22

Dante spent most of his nights at Crystal, overseeing his burgeoning criminal empire, but his days were spent in an office at the Hercules Body Shop in Somerville. Fina didn't doubt that there was some legitimate work done at the shop, but she didn't think it was the main source of income.

Fina was openly ogled when she walked through the garage and asked for Dante. She was directed to the second floor of the building. The upstairs hallway was dominated by a trophy case that held wrestling and boxing awards. One of the two rooms at the top of the stairs was closed off with a child gate, behind which were three kids ranging in age from one to four. Two middle-aged women were tending them, and a TV mounted overhead was playing a cartoon.

In the room next door, Dante sat behind one of two desks. The space was overstuffed with the desks, chairs, and file cabinets, and large slatted venetian blinds hung over the two windows. Dante was on the phone, leaning back in his chair with his feet on the desk. He looked surprised to see Fina and irked when she sat down in the chair behind the other desk.

"I'll call you back." Dante hung up and looked at her.

"I got your message and I thought I'd just stop by," Fina said.

"A call would have been fine."

"I like to see you in your various elements."

"It's a wasted trip. Like I said on the phone, I don't have much to tell." A calendar featuring a naked woman on a tractor hung on the wall next to him. The photo looked like an accident waiting to happen.

"Who puts out a naked tractor calendar?" Fina asked.

Dante hunched up his shoulders. "Who cares?"

"I'm just curious. What's up with the day-care center next door?" She nodded toward the room with the children.

"Your questions are annoying."

"Again, just curious. So, what do you have to tell me?" She swiveled the chair on its base.

"That kid? Brett Linder? I couldn't get anything on him. I think he's just a white kid pretending to be a gangster."

Fina looked at Dante and tried not to smile. "He has a record, though."

"Mostly chickenshit stuff."

"Okay, what else?"

Dante leaned forward in his seat and looked at her. "It hurts me to say this, but that chick, Theresa McGovern? She's awesome."

"Really?" Fina asked, arresting the swiveling of her chair. "Not that I'm shocked, but I'm glad you think so, too."

"She's cool. I thought she was going to be all proper and shit, but she's got a wild side." Dante smirked.

"I'm not sure I want to hear this," Fina said, rising to her feet. "Did you hear anything about the guy who's after me?"

He shook his head. "Sorry."

"He's threatening my niece now, which is totally uncool."

He held up his hands. "I got nothing for you."

"I'm a little disappointed in your lack of information, but in general, I like this new relationship we're forming, Dante. It feels very congenial."

"If that means I'm scared of you, then that's about right."

"Keep in touch!" Fina said, and retraced her steps out of the body shop.

Fina tilted her face up to the sun. She was sitting on a bench outside the Universum Tech headquarters, waiting for Theresa. Rather than call, Fina decided to stop on her way back over the river. Theresa's message had been cryptic and definitely warranted a follow-up.

"Hey," Theresa said, sitting down next to her. She had a coffee in one hand and a waxed bag in the other. She pulled a scone out of the bag. "Want a bite?"

"No, thanks. What's going on? Your message was mysterious."

"First of all, I wanted to thank you. I did a set at Crystal, and it was awesome."

"Those were Dante's exact words."

"You spoke to Dante?"

"Just came from seeing him. He seemed really pleased."

Theresa smiled. "Good."

"You may not be aware of this, but Dante is a criminal. He's a pimp and involved in a variety of illegal activities."

"What's your point?" Theresa took a bite.

"He's not boyfriend material."

"Where's your sense of adventure?"

"There's a difference between adventure and destruction, but hey, do what you want. You've been warned."

"You're kind of a worrywart under that tough exterior, aren't you?"

Fina snorted.

"Anyway," Theresa continued, "thanks for the gig. I'm working on a little something for you in return."

"Meaning?"

A group of young men walked by them on the way to Universum's front door. They looked to be in their early twenties, wearing cargo shorts, T-shirts, and a variety of casual footwear, including flip-flops. A couple of them didn't look old enough to shave, and they were sporting various body types: reedy, round, bony, pillowy. They had to be engineers.

"It means that I was going through some of Hank's papers, and there was something off about his most recent physical."

Fina straightened up on the bench. "What do you mean specifically?"

"I haven't figured that out yet, but it aroused my suspicions."

"Can you give me more to go on?"

"I'm working on it, but I have to be careful. I can't screw around with his medical records."

"I'm not asking you to, but I can only get so far on supposition."

"I'll let you know."

"Sounds good."

Theresa balled up her bag and tossed it into the trash can next to the bench. "Do you have contacts any other place where I could get a gig?"

Theresa could give assertiveness training to a bull in a bullfight.

"Not off the top of my head, but I'll think about it and let you know." A shadow fell across Fina.

"Hi, Dimitri," Theresa said, and stood.

"Theresa. I didn't realize you knew Fina." He looked at the two of them.

"We have a mutual friend," Fina said. "It's nice to see you, Dimitri."

"I'm heading in," Theresa said, nodding toward the building. "See you up there." She walked away.

Dimitri shoved his hands into his pockets. "You don't really expect me to buy that, do you? The mutual friend bit?" he asked.

"It's the truth, but it doesn't really matter if you believe it or not." Even with sunglasses, Fina had to shield her eyes to look up at him. He was backlit, making his expression hard to read and putting her at a decided disadvantage. "Have a seat."

Dimitri looked around, as if worried about being seen with her, before sinking down onto the bench.

"Is there an end in sight to your hanging around?" he asked.

"Most definitely. Once the case is solved."

Dimitri crossed one ankle over his other knee. "Of course."

"I haven't been *that* disruptive. Andy and the kids seemed to like me."

"Andy's taste can be dubious, and my children love Barney."

Clouds darted in front of the sun, and Fina shivered. "Did you attend Hank's funeral? I heard that Juliana and Danielle got into it."

"It wasn't pretty. Andy was upset about the whole thing."

Fina nodded. "Right. More Team Danielle than Team Juliana." Fina rose from the bench. "Give my regards to Andy."

"What? No other questions for me?"

"Not really. Everything I hear says you were extremely angry about being left out of the waterfront development deal. Was that reason enough to kill Hank? Maybe."

"I didn't kill him."

"So you say. See ya."

Fina walked back to her car, mulling over Theresa's suspicions about Hank's health.

It raised a big question. She had to find a lead in the question.

Fina decided to head home and formulate her next steps. Under other circumstances, she would have found a place for a snack, but given the threats hanging over her, home seemed like the best place to relax and regroup.

She was reaching into a bag of tortilla chips when there was a knock on her door. A glance into the peephole revealed Cristian and, unfortunately, Pitney.

"I know you're in there," Pitney said when Fina didn't respond right away. "The doorman told me."

"Remind me to dock his Christmas bonus," Fina said, unlocking the dead bolt and opening the door.

Pitney walked in, and Fina glared at Cristian. He was always welcome in her home, but she wasn't in the mood for Pitney. He gave Fina an apologetic look.

"So this is where you spend your time when you aren't making the streets of Boston more dangerous," Pitney said.

"It's my grandmother's place," Fina said, following Pitney into the living room with Cristian bringing up the rear.

"You live with your grandmother?" Pitney took in the view of the harbor.

"My grandmother's dead. It was her place when she was alive."

"Well, that explains the decor." So said the woman wearing a plum-colored pantsuit with a clashing chevron-patterned shirt underneath.

"Interior design isn't a priority. Is that why you're here? To critique my home?"

"No." Pitney walked over to one of the armchairs. "May I?"

"Knock yourself out."

Fina took a seat on the couch, and Cristian joined her, but kept his distance.

"I hear you have a Haley situation," Pitney said.

Fina looked at Cristian. "Do you have something?"

"No, but we wanted to follow up," he said.

Fina felt the brief surge of adrenaline subside. "I don't have anything new to report."

"Can I see the photos?" Pitney asked.

They were tucked under a pile of papers on the coffee table, which Fina pushed aside. She handed the envelope to Pitney, who examined them.

"Are you working on another case that could inspire this reaction?" Pitney asked.

Fina shook her head. "Not really. The Reardon case is definitely the most likely."

"We heard there was quite the dustup at Hank's funeral," Cristian said.

"I wasn't there."

"No, but what did you hear about it?" Pitney asked.

"Probably the same thing you did, that Juliana and Danielle got into it."

"What more can you tell us about them?" she asked.

"About the wives?" Fina asked. "Nothing."

"So you're doing all this investigating and haven't turned up anything of interest about the two of them?" Pitney asked. "You're a better investigator than that."

Fina smiled. "Really? You think you can flatter me into telling you something?"

"Worth a shot."

"I don't have anything to tell you except that they both seemed interested in his money." Fina adjusted on the couch. "What do you think about Walter Stiles?" she asked.

Pitney looked at her. "The clinic director? Nothing in particular. Why?"

"He just seems fishy to me."

"Fishy?" Cristian asked.

"There's something off about him and the cryobank, and no, I don't have anything specific to back that up." Fina didn't see the need to share Ellen Alberti's musings with them, not until she knew what was in those files.

"I'll put that in my pipe and smoke it," Pitney replied, rising from her chair.

"Well, that was a thoroughly unproductive visit," Fina said.

"How's Haley doing?" Pitney asked as they approached the door. Pitney didn't know the extent of Rand's crimes, but she knew that Haley had been through a difficult few months, and she'd done what she could to protect her.

"She's okay. She's playing field hockey and getting more involved in school stuff. My sister-in-law, Patty, is a great influence."

"I'm glad to hear it. I'll make a call over to Newton and ask them to keep an eye on things in their neighborhood—suspicious cars, that sort of thing."

"I would appreciate that, and it will reassure Patty and Scotty. Thank you." She looked at Pitney.

"You're welcome, Fina."

Fina poked Cristian in the shoulder. "I'll talk to *you* later."

"Sounds like you're in trouble, Menendez," Pitney teased.

"Great." Cristian frowned. "Something to look forward to."

"Don't forget that you're legally obligated to share relevant information with the police," Pitney said once in the hallway.

"How could I forget? You're constantly reminding me," Fina said. "Good-bye, Boston's Finest." She closed the door behind them.

Rosie and Renata agreed to meet at Scotty's office later that afternoon. Scotty was squeezing them in between a client meeting and a client dinner, so Fina got right to it.

"We know that you lied about your whereabouts the night Hank died."

Renata pivoted in her seat and stared at Rosie. "What is she talking about?"

Rosie looked down at her hands and picked at her cuticles. They were sitting in the conversational seating area separate from Scotty's desk. Michelle had offered beverages; Fina and Scotty were nursing diet sodas, but Renata and Rosie had declined the offer.

"Actually, can I get a bottle of water?" Rosie asked. Fina got one from the bar and handed it to her. Rosie took her time unscrewing the cap, had a sip, and screwed the cap back on.

"Rosie. Stop stalling," Renata said. "What is this about?"

Rosie blinked back tears. Fina and Scotty exchanged a look.

"There's surveillance video that shows Rosie in a car at one A.M. the night Hank was killed," Fina said. "We suspect this is what the cops had when they were so keen on hearing her alibi."

"Is this true?" Renata asked.

Rosie swallowed another gulp of water. "Yes."

"How could you be so—" Renata started.

"Don't lecture me, Mom!"

"We're not here to fight about this," Fina interceded. "We're here to make a plan."

"Whose car was it?" Renata demanded.

Rosie looked at Fina, who remained silent.

"It was Tyler's," Rosie admitted.

Renata looked at Scotty and Fina. "Does Marnie know about this?"

"One thing at a time," Scotty said. "Right now, I'm going to counsel you not to discuss this with anyone else, especially not Tyler and his mother."

Renata opened her mouth to speak.

"Do you understand that?" Scotty said. "You cannot discuss it with anyone, and if anyone asks, you refer them to me."

Renata pressed her lips together.

"I don't want you speaking to the police—either of you—without me present. Okay?" Scotty asked. Obviously, Renata's choice to reveal Hank's identity to the press was fresh in his mind.

Rosie and Renata nodded. Scotty looked to Fina.

"Where did you go that night, Rosie?" she asked.

Rosie squeezed her half-filled water bottle, which produced a crunching sound. "Mostly, we just drove around."

"Mostly? And what about the small part when you weren't driving around?"

There was a long pause. "We went to Hank Reardon's house."

Renata gripped her armrests tightly.

"For what purpose?" Scotty asked.

"No purpose. We just were talking about him and decided to check out where he lived."

"You went to the man's house?" Renata couldn't control herself.

"We went to our *father's* house," Rosie said. "Remember that whole thing, Mom?"

"Were you drinking or on any drugs?" Fina asked.

Rosie avoided her gaze. "We'd smoked a little pot."

Renata looked like her head might rotate on her neck, like a maternal version of the girl in *The Exorcist*.

"Did you do anything when you got to the Reardons'?" Scotty asked.

"No, it was the middle of the night. We sat on the front step and talked."

"So you have no idea if he was home?" Fina said.

Rosie shook her head.

"Did anyone see you hanging around?"

"I don't think so." She drained her water bottle.

"How long were you there?" Scotty jotted notes on a legal pad.

"I don't know, fifteen, twenty minutes, maybe."

"And then where did you go?"

"Tyler dropped me back at Sam's, and I went to bed. I assume that Tyler went home."

Scotty finished writing something and put his pen down. "I'm not a criminal defense attorney, so if this gets any more involved, I'll have to refer you to someone else. I can put you in touch with some top people."

"You're abandoning us?" Renata asked.

Fina was annoyed. "That's not what he said, Renata. Would you please listen and stop adding your dramatic interpretation to everything?"

"Exactly! This is what I have to deal with every day!" Rosie interjected.

"Don't speak to anyone about this, and be in touch if something else happens," said Scotty, staring at mother and daughter. "It's that simple. The lying and the pot is something you two need to figure out."

"We will, believe me." Renata rose from her chair and pointed Rosie in the direction of the door. "Thank you. We'll be in touch," she said formally before striding out of the office.

"That's going to be a fun ride home," Fina commented. She stretched her arms over her head and gently moved her neck from side to side.

"Any progress on the Haley front?" Scotty asked.

"I only told you a few hours ago. I need a little more time."

Scotty sighed.

"Stop acting like Dad," Fina said. "Seriously. You are not allowed to turn into him."

He stood and walked around from behind his desk. "If anyone is going to turn into him, it's you."

Fina winced. "Ouch."

Her brother grinned. "Hurts, doesn't it?"

"Touché. I'll call you later, and thanks for squeezing this in."

"No problem."

Fina left Ludlow and Associates and sat in her car with the doors securely locked.

Scotty's anxiety was reasonable. What the hell was she going to do about the Haley situation?

23

Tyler and Jess Frasier's conceptions may have been atypical, but the family dinner Fina interrupted was all-American.

The mysterious Jess answered the door and reluctantly introduced herself. The young woman was whippet thin but muscular. Her hair was brown and short, her face free of makeup. In her shorts and a BU track-and-field T-shirt, she could have passed for a high school student.

She led Fina into the kitchen, where Marnie sat at the table and Tyler was prepping plates at the counter.

"I can come back later," Fina said, turning toward the front hallway. "You look like you're having a real family dinner."

Marnie smiled. "As opposed to a fake family dinner? This is how we have dinner in our house. You didn't?"

"Hardly. People ate and ran. But seriously, I'll come back."

"Stay," Tyler said. "There's plenty, and you can give an unbiased opinion of my latest."

Fina looked at Marnie, who nodded. Only Jess seemed less than enthused, avoiding Fina's gaze.

"Thanks." Fina took a seat, and Tyler handed her a glass of water. Marnie offered her wine, and Jess sat down, while Tyler went to the stove. After a moment, he returned bearing a plate in each hand. He lowered one in front of his mother and the other in front of Fina.

"Roasted salmon with lentils and bacon," he declared, and came back with two more plates. Fina looked at it. A perfectly sized salmon fillet was nestled on a bed of beans and small flecks of bacon. She inhaled deeply while Jess passed her a small plate of salad.

"This looks and smells amazing, Tyler. Is this a homework assignment or just for fun?"

"Homework." He sat down and pulled a napkin into his lap. "We're doing a unit on fish right now."

The first five minutes of the meal were dominated by the sounds of cutlery and appreciative noises, especially from Fina. People assumed that, given her usual diet, Fina was opposed to healthy foods like fish and beans, but it wasn't the flavor she minded; it was the preparation. She was lazy. If someone wanted to cook for her like this, she'd have no objection.

"I think the bacon is a little too smoky," Jess commented after a minute, washing a mouthful down with some water.

"Ya think?" Tyler asked.

"Just a touch. I feel like it's overwhelming the cleanness of the salmon."

"Mom?" He looked to Marnie for her opinion.

"I agree. Just a touch."

"You're a tough crowd," Fina commented.

"Per his request," Marnie said.

"Yeah, it isn't helpful if they don't tell me the truth," Tyler said between mouthfuls. "Only gets me in trouble with my professors."

Everyone knew that Fina was there for a reason—not just an outstanding meal—but they seemed to reach an unspoken agreement that they wouldn't sully dinner with talk of murder or scandal. Instead they talked about the kids' studies, Jess's involvement on the BU cross-country team, Marnie's job, and a proposed family trip over Christmas. Fina's job was a drudge sometimes, but it was also a privilege to be invited into the homes and lives of strangers. And anyone who thought that a traditional nuclear family was the right kind of family needed to spend time with the Ludlows, the Frasiers, and the Collins-Kask families. The two-parent, heterosexual-led Ludlows were by far the most dysfunctional in the group.

Fina cleared the plates while Jess stacked the dishes. Marnie lingered at the table with Tyler, discussing the next day's schedule. Fina tried to engage Jess in small talk, but the young woman wasn't interested.

"I assume there's business you need to discuss, Fina?" Marnie asked her after the counters were wiped clean.

"Actually, it's Tyler I need to talk to."

Jess frowned, and Marnie looked at Tyler. She hesitated, but then got up from the table. "I have some phone calls to make, unless you need me, Tyler?"

He wiped his hands on his pants. "No, I'm good."

Jess leaned against the kitchen counter. Her short-sleeved T-shirt showcased her taut arms and well-defined muscles.

"We'll go out back," Tyler said, standing up from the table. His sister shook her head and dropped the sponge into the sink. She walked out of the room.

"Was it something I said?" Fina asked as she followed Tyler down the stairs into the backyard.

"Nah. She's just protective of me. So, what's up?" he asked, sitting on a patio chair.

She claimed the chair next to him. "Well, if I didn't like you so much—and if you hadn't fed me so well—I'd be really pissed at you."

Tyler's eyes widened into a "Who, me?" expression. Girls probably found his innocent charm irresistible.

"I just came from a meeting with Rosie and her mother and my brother, who is acting as Rosie's attorney." Tyler's face lost some of its expression. "I know all about your visit to Hank's house on the night of his death."

"Rosie told you that?"

"No, I did this thing I do called 'detecting' and found video of you two dumbnuts driving around when you said you were at home in bed."

Tyler chuckled.

"It isn't funny," Fina chastised him.

"It's a little funny. You don't actually think that either of us killed Hank, do you?"

"It doesn't matter what I think; it matters what the police think."

"They think we killed Hank?"

"Have they asked you for an alibi?"

"Yes."

"And you told them you dropped Rosie at the apartment and were home all night?"

Tyler's face clouded. "Yes."

"So they have you on record lying to them."

Tyler leaned forward in his chair. He proceeded to crack every knuckle and joint in both hands. It set Fina's teeth on edge.

"So what do you want from me?" he asked.

"Tell me the truth, for starters." She held his gaze.

"We smoked a little pot, went for a drive, and ended up at Hank's."

"Did you try to go in?"

"Like break in? No way. That place is like Fort Knox. We hung out on the sidewalk. We didn't ring the bell or anything."

"And then?"

"I dropped Rosie at Sam's and came home. I went to bed. That's it."

"Does your mom know about your little escapade?"

"No."

A lawn mower started up a few yards away.

"I won't tell her," Fina said, "but you might have to if the police get more involved."

"I thought *you* were going to solve Hank's murder."

"I'm trying, but I've been wasting my time figuring out the lies you and Rosie have been spinning. It's hard for me to concentrate on other suspects if I'm spending all my time on you two."

"Sorry," Tyler said, and actually looked sheepish.

"Apology accepted, but stop doing it. All right?"

"Scout's honor." Tyler raised his fingers in a pledge.

"Like you were ever a Boy Scout."

"Briefly. They didn't appreciate my energy."

"I'll bet." Fina rose from her seat. "Thanks for dinner. I was impressed."

"You should come again. I always welcome appreciative diners."

"Say bye to your mom and Jess for me." Fina stood.

"I really am sorry. Maybe I can make it up to you."

"I can't imagine how."

Tyler mimicked smoking a joint.

"Oh, honestly. Your poor mother."

He broke into a huge grin and laughed.

Fina walked through the side yard to her car. She couldn't believe that Rosie or Tyler had done anything to harm Hank, but they'd lied. Just because you lied didn't mean you were a murderer, but she'd yet to meet a murderer who wasn't a liar.

Michael Reardon was home when Fina stopped by, although he didn't look thrilled to see her.

"Is this a bad time?" She glanced behind him. Maybe he had company.

"No, it's fine. I was just hanging out." He was wearing jeans and a faded T-shirt, and his feet were bare. Fina followed him inside and up the stairs to the main living space. The TV was on, the screen frozen on a military scene in the crosshairs of a weapon.

"You play?" Michael asked.

"What is that, Call of Duty?"

Michael nodded. "Do you want a beer?" He padded over to the kitchen.

"Yeah, thanks. My brothers play this stuff sometimes, but I've never really gotten into those games." She had a gun in real life; she didn't need one in her fantasies.

Michael brought over a large can and a glass into which he poured the dark liquid. Fina took a sip, expecting a heavy, bitter flavor, but was surprised by its sweetness.

"That's not what I expected."

"It's Czech." They both took a seat on the overstuffed couch. "What can I do for you?"

"I had a very unsatisfying conversation with your mother earlier today."

"Really?"

Fina detected a faint twitch in Michael's neck.

"I'm trying to understand what's going on with the funding for the Reardon Center, but she isn't being forthcoming."

Michael took a long pull from his drink. "What does funding for the Reardon Center have to do with anything?"

Fina looked at him. She leaned back into the couch and took another sip of beer. She was silent.

Michael glanced around the room. "What? You're not going to say anything?"

"I'm adopting a new policy of not answering stupid questions."

"How is that a stupid question?"

Fina put down her beer and rubbed her face with her hands. "We're really going to do this? This charade where you pretend that nobody you know could possibly be responsible for your father's death?"

"It's not a charade. I *don't* know anyone who could be responsible, especially not my mother."

"I told you when you hired me that everyone was fair game."

"I know, but I expected you to follow the evidence, not investigate us just to make a point."

"What point would that be?"

"Equal treatment. That we're not immune just because we're his family and have money."

"Seriously?"

"You don't think maybe you're going easy on the cryokids because they're the underdogs?"

Fina shook her head. "No, I don't think I'm going easy on them."

Michael's cell phone rang, and he looked at the display. "I have to take this." He wandered into the kitchen and answered the call.

Fina was willing to admit to herself that she didn't want Tyler or Rosie to be responsible for Hank's death, but was that hope clouding her judgment? Was Scotty's representation of Rosie a conflict of interest? Was she being easy on them because they hadn't had as many breaks in life as Michael, Juliana, and Danielle? There was no question that Tyler was a more likable guy than Michael, but Fina felt confident that if the evidence led to him, she wouldn't have a problem busting him.

Michael's comments put her on notice, which wasn't necessarily a bad thing. When you worked as an investigator by yourself—for yourself—you didn't have the checks and balances that the cops did. Cristian and Pitney worked on behalf of the citizens of the Common-wealth; they were bound by an oath. Fina wasn't, and sometimes that made things more complicated.

"Sorry about that." Michael returned to the couch and sat down.

"No worries. Michael, I hear what you're saying, and I will keep it in mind. I don't think that I'm favoring anyone in this investigation, but I also can't favor you or your mom. If she doesn't want to discuss things with me, you can't force her, but that will be an obstacle."

"I understand."

"What do you know about the plans for the Hank Reardon House?"

He looked genuinely befuddled. "I don't know what that is."

Fina had another sip of beer. She wasn't going to say more about the mysterious Reardon House, not until she knew more herself.

"What about Heritage Cryobank? Did your father talk about them at all?"

Michael shook his head. "No. He didn't discuss that with me. Why? What's going on?"

"It seems that your father was in touch with the director of the cryo-bank shortly before his death."

He shrugged. "I don't know anything about that."

"That's what Danielle said."

Michael drained his beer. "Do you have anything to report, or are you only here to ask me questions?"

"I can tell you that I'm making progress. However, I would love to know more about the fight your parents had over the Reardon Center funding. Seeking information from your mom doesn't mean that I'm targeting her. It just means that I need more information."

He sighed. "I'll talk to her, but I can't make any promises."

"I would appreciate that." Fina brought her glass to the kitchen sink. "Sorry to interrupt your game."

"No problem."

"I'll be in touch as soon as I have something concrete to report."

"Hope that's soon," he said, standing on the front door threshold, rocking back and forth on his feet.

He closed the door, and Fina returned to her car. She looked up toward his bay window, and after a moment, lights flashed behind the glass. His battle had apparently picked up right where he'd stopped it. Those were very considerate enemies.

Back at Nanny's, Fina dialed Scotty's number.

"I don't have a plan yet," she told him as she stripped off her clothes and climbed into bed.

"That's all you have to say?"

"You told me to call you, and I'm calling you."

"Okeydoke."

"I'm on it, Scotty. I'll figure something out. Is Haley home?"

"Everyone's here, and the alarm is set."

"Good."

"Well, thanks for calling, at least. Now I don't have to worry that you've been beaten to a bloody pulp and left in a ditch."

"You'd be the only one worrying, but thanks. That's sweet."

Fina put her phone on the bedside table and turned off the light.

For the next eight hours, worry could take a backseat.

24

The next morning, Fina's alarm woke her at seven A.M., and she couldn't remember why on earth she'd set it in the first place. She rolled over onto her back and stared at the ceiling, willing the neurons and synapses to start firing and help her recall.

Frank. That's right. One of the few people for whom she'd set an alarm.

She called him to be sure he wasn't headed out for the day, and then showered. Fina skipped breakfast, hopeful that Peg would have something on offer, and at eight A.M. she was not disappointed by the aromas that greeted her when she came in through the Gillises' front door.

"That smells good," she said, walking into the kitchen.

Frank and Peg were both wearing sweatsuits, presumably having already completed their morning constitutional.

"You chose the right morning to visit," Frank said. "She's taken pity on me."

Peg put a plate of iced cinnamon rolls on the table. "Want some juice, hon?" she asked Fina.

"Yes, please. What's the occasion, Peg?"

"His numbers from his checkup were good, and I know I shouldn't reward him with food, but he was getting kind of cranky."

Frank had had a heart scare a few years before, and as a nurse, Peg took it upon herself to ensure he followed a healthy diet.

"I'm the same way," Fina said, pulling one large roll apart from another.

"You get cranky if you haven't had sugar or fat for two hours!" Frank exclaimed. "I'm talking about months—years—of watching what I eat."

"Wow. You *are* cranky," Fina said before taking a bite.

Peg placed a glass of juice in front of Fina and topped off Frank's coffee. She joined them at the table and claimed a roll for herself.

"Delicious, right?" Frank asked his wife.

Peg chewed slowly and wiped a smudge of icing off her finger. "It's almost too sweet for me."

Frank and Fina exchanged eye rolls.

"So, what brings you over here so early?" he asked.

"I just wanted to bounce the case off you and get your advice."

"Shoot."

Fina updated him on the recent developments: the video footage from Korfa disproving Rosie's and Tyler's alibis, Ellen's claims that Walter had stolen files, Juliana's alleged expansion plans and fight with Hank, and Danielle's subterfuge regarding Hank's calls to Walter Stiles. She finished with the photos of Haley.

"That poor girl," Peg said, shaking her head.

"Trust me. I feel terrible." Fina looked at Frank. "But what am I supposed to do about it? I don't know who's making the threats."

"Did you report it to the police?"

"I told Cristian and his boss, but I haven't done anything official yet."

"Why not?"

"Because I haven't told Haley about it."

"You haven't?" Peg frowned.

"I didn't want to needlessly freak her out."

"But if she isn't aware of it, she might not be careful," Peg said.

"Scotty knows," Fina said, "and we discussed hiring protection for her, but only as a last resort."

Frank sipped his coffee. "How close are you to wrapping up the case?"

Fina raised her hands in a question mark. "Pretty close, I think, but you know how this works. I could be on the threshold or barking up the wrong tree completely."

"Maybe you should pull her out of school for a few days. At least at home someone could keep an eye on her," Frank said.

"I wish I could just draw the guy out somehow," Fina mused. She ran her finger along a hillock of icing on the plate.

He shook his head. "That sounds like a terrible idea."

"That's what Cristian said."

"I've always liked that young man," Peg said. "Do you two date?"

"Can we please focus on one crisis at a time?" Fina asked.

"Unfortunately, I think you have to remain on the defensive," Frank concluded. "Be alert and solve the case."

"Oh, that's all? Well, then."

Peg offered her half-eaten cinnamon roll to Fina, who happily scarfed it down. The three of them sat in companionable silence for a moment.

"Do you think I have a bias against rich people?" Fina asked finally.

"I don't understand the question," Frank said, leaning back in his chair, his hands folded over his stomach.

"Michael Reardon claims that I'm giving the cryokids a free pass since they're less privileged than he is, and that I'm holding his family up to more scrutiny."

Frank considered for a moment. "I think if you have any bias— well, we all have biases—it's in reaction to your upbringing. At times you *are* more sympathetic to the underprivileged, but I don't think you've demonstrated a bias in this case. It sounds like you're following the evidence."

"That would suggest that she favors people who have experienced fewer benefits in life," Peg said. "Is that really a bias? Sounds like a correction of sorts."

"It's a bias if she turns a blind eye to evidence or gives the poor guy the benefit of the doubt that she wouldn't give the rich guy. I don't think that's happening here. I wouldn't worry about it."

"Okay," Fina said. "I wanted to be sure. I think he assumes that he and his family are beyond reproach, that they shouldn't have to answer my questions or explain their behavior."

"Because that's probably how they've lived their whole lives," Frank said.

"Probably." Fina finished her orange juice. "Thanks, you guys. You're the best, you know that? Good food and good advice."

"How are your folks?" Peg asked as she cleared the dishes from the table.

"What about good food and good advice brought Carl and Elaine to mind?" Fina asked, rising from the table.

"You're very hard on them," Peg said.

"They taught me well! Gotta run."

Fina checked her messages, and since no one was demanding her attention, she drove out to Worcester to run some records checks at city hall. There were often items on Fina's to-do list that weren't particularly urgent but certainly inconvenient. She attended to these tasks when her schedule permitted, thereby killing two birds with one stone: crossing something off her list and distracting herself while waiting for a more pressing case to break.

Lunch was a plastic sleeve of powdered donuts from a gas station, and her phone rang as she licked her fingers clean. It was the private lab in Longwood. The caller refused to release test results over the phone, so Fina hopped on the Pike and headed east.

She cooled her heels in the medical area traffic that seemed prevalent no matter the time of day. Parking was another headache, so by the time she'd signed the various release forms, the suspense was killing her. She sat down on a couch in a waiting area smelling of antiseptic and floor polish and ripped open the envelope. Inside was a small sheaf of papers; it took a moment for her to find the pertinent data.

Well, I'll be damned.

At least she was making progress on one of her cases.

Fina spoke to Risa's housekeeper and tracked her down at Grahamson, the private school that her kids and Haley attended. After checking in with the front desk and getting lost in a warren of hallways, she was led to the gymnasium by a girl with patrician bone structure wearing a school uniform blazer and kilt. She looked like she'd just finished a session of dressage.

Inside the gym, a gaggle of tweens and teens in shorts and T-shirts bounced basketballs while being corralled by two coaches. Fina scouted the stands and found Risa sitting on one of the top risers in the corner. She trotted up the stairs and sidestepped to her spot.

Risa looked taken aback to see her.

"Is this some kind of punishment?" Fina asked, sitting down next to her. The constant thumping of the balls and their echoes thundered through the gym. "How can you even hear yourself think?"

"Jordan asked me to come for his scrimmage since I can't make his game tomorrow." On the court below, the boys had broken into two teams, one of which was pulling on red pinnies. A student was gathering the extra balls and putting them in a large bin.

"Got it. I can catch up with you later. I don't want to distract you."

"Like I'd be able to concentrate now if you left? I assume you have some news for me?" Risa chewed on her bottom lip. It was an uncharacteristic display of anxiety, which convinced Fina that she should put her out of her misery.

"I do have news. Greta finally got her DNA test done, and it's a match."

Risa was silent. Her eyes followed the progress of the ball across the court. She took a deep breath. "Okay, well, I guess now I know."

"You do. I haven't spoken with Greta. I wanted to tell you first."

"Do we know for sure that she's my aunt?"

"We know that the two of you are related, separated by one generation."

Risa's features slackened. "Could she be my mother?"

"No," Fina assured her. "She's definitely not your mother."

With the scrimmage under way, there was only one ball echoing through the space, but it was coupled with the squeaks of ten pairs of expensive basketball sneakers, a whole new sensory torture.

"Now what?" Risa asked.

"That's up to you. I'll handle it however you want. I think we should tell her the results, but whether you want to have contact with her is your call."

"I don't know. I— Good shot, Jordan!" she hollered toward the court. "I don't know what to do."

"You don't have to decide right away. Why don't you take a little time to digest the news, talk to Marty? Greta hasn't been in your life for forty-six years; a week or a month isn't going to make a difference."

Risa inhaled. "You're right. Just because she wants to be in touch doesn't mean I have to be."

"And you can figure out what kind of relationship you want, if any." A loud buzzer rang over their heads. "Maybe you and Greta talk on the phone or just send letters to each other. Maybe you meet, but you don't have to. There are no rules even though she's a blood relative."

"No? You don't think so?"

"No. I know it feels like there are, but believe me, I'm up to my eyeballs in a case that's all about nature versus nurture, and the rules are just theoretical."

They watched the action on the court for a few minutes. Fina had never understood the appeal of watching basketball. Why watch the whole game when it was often decided in the last two minutes?

"I heard that Haley's playing field hockey," Risa said.

"Yes, I'm actually going to her first home game."

"I think that's good for her."

"So do I. Patty and Scotty are taking good care of her."

"I'm so glad. I know her mom's death and Rand's absence have been really difficult."

"I'm sure she misses her mom a lot. How about you?" Fina asked, anxious to steer the conversation away from her brother. "Melanie was your best friend. How are you doing?"

"Actually, a lot of the time I can't quite believe she's gone. I'll have a conversation with someone or read the paper and think, 'I need to tell Mel about this,' and then it will dawn on me: she's dead."

Fina nodded.

"Your neck looks better," Risa commented, peering at Fina's skin.

"I'm definitely on the mend."

"Good. You need to be careful, you know. The last thing Haley needs is another family crisis."

"Believe me, I know." *Like being the victim of a crime herself.* Fina shook off the thought. "I'll be in touch in a couple of days, but until then, I won't update Greta."

"You think that's okay?"

Fina stood. "She dragged her feet getting the test; you're entitled to your own foot-dragging."

"Thanks, Fina."

"Of course. And Risa, this isn't bad news or good news; it's just news."

"I'll try to keep that in mind."

Fina climbed down the bleachers and escaped into the hallway, where she was greeted by silence and a distinct lack of musty teenage boy smell. She took a deep breath of clean air and walked back out to her car.

The last thing Fina expected to find on her phone was a message from Juliana Reardon. Their lunch hadn't ended well, and Michael didn't seem optimistic about changing his mother's attitude. Fina couldn't imagine what she wanted.

"Hi, Fina," Juliana said when she picked up the phone.

"Juliana. How are you?" Fina gazed out at the Grahamson grounds. The school looked more like a country estate than a school, with its rolling hills, looming stone buildings, and winding paths.

"I'm good. I was wondering if you would grant me a do-over?"

"I would be happy to. Just give me a time and place."

"How about a drink at the Four Seasons in an hour?"

"Works for me."

Fina wended her way through Newton and arrived at Scotty and Patty's house a few minutes later. She was pleased to find the front door locked and knocked before letting herself in with her key.

"Patty? Anyone home?" Fina called into the large foyer.

"We're upstairs," a voice responded from above.

Fina climbed the wide staircase and collided with Teddy as he raced down the carpeted hallway.

"Hi, Aunt Fina!"

"Hey, buddy! Where's your mum?"

"In Haley's room!" he called over his shoulder, disappearing into one of the boys' bedrooms.

Fina walked down the hall and into Haley's bedroom. Since she'd moved in a couple months before, Patty and Scotty had made every effort to make the space her own. The walls were painted lilac with shiny white trim. The queen-sized bed was covered in a duvet with a turquoise geometric pattern. Clothes were strewn across the floor, and various cords took up real estate on her desk. There was a bulletin board filled with pictures of hugging teens making goofy faces, and a framed photo of Haley with her mother was prominent on the bedside table.

Fina splayed across the bed next to her niece as Patty did an inventory of the closet. "They say you need a white button-down or blouse."

"Hey, Aunt Fina," Haley said. "I think I have one."

Patty poked her head out of the roomy closet. "Hey."

"Hey. What do you need a white shirt for?"

Haley rolled her eyes. "School chorus."

"You have a nice voice; why are you rolling your eyes?"

"Because it's dorky."

"It's not dorky," Patty said. She held up two shirts. "Do either of these still fit?"

"I don't know."

"Well, then, try them on."

Haley struggled off the bed and took the shirts from Patty. She stepped into the en suite bathroom, and Patty claimed her spot.

Patty looked at Fina. "Scotty told me about the photos."

"Good. I don't have anything new to report, but the Newton PD is going to keep an eye out."

"What are you guys whispering about?" Haley asked from the bathroom. "This one doesn't fit." She tossed a shirt back into the room.

"We're whispering about you, of course," Fina said. "What else is there to talk about?"

"Very funny. This looks too preppy. Seriously." Haley stepped into the room wearing a button-down that was too short in the sleeves and looked like it came from an L.L.Bean catalog circa 1989.

Patty studied her. "You're right. We'll have to get you something new."

Haley returned to the bathroom and emerged a moment later with her T-shirt back on.

"So you just came by to say hi?" Patty asked.

"And to borrow some clothes. I'm having drinks at the Four Seasons, and I don't want to look like too much of a bum," she said, gesturing at her dark-wash jeans, T-shirt, and flats. "I was in the neighborhood and didn't want to drive all the way home. Could you hook a girl up?"

"Sure. Let's go into my room."

Fifteen minutes later, Fina was headed out the door wearing a purple silk top, chunky earrings with amethysts, and wedge sandals. She cleaned up good.

Juliana was waiting for her at the bar wearing a deep orange shift dress that showed off her tan and toned body to maximum effect.

Fina climbed up onto the bar stool next to her and asked the bartender for a mojito. Juliana was sipping a martini.

"Is that allowed in your training regimen?" Fina asked, nodding toward the glass.

"You bet. There are some things I'm unwilling to give up."

The bar was filled with hushed conversation, and more than half the cocktail tables were occupied. A couple got up from one by a window, and Juliana picked up her drink. "Let's go over there. We'll have a little more privacy."

The bartender acknowledged their move, and Fina followed Juliana. They sat down in large upholstered chairs that looked out onto Boylston Street. Across the street in the Public Garden, Fina could see men in suits and women in business attire heading home for the day.

"I think I owe you an apology," Juliana said, sitting back in her seat. Fina was quiet. "I'm very protective of Michael and even Hank. I know we were divorced, but you don't just shut those feelings off after twenty-four years."

"Of course not. I wouldn't expect you to."

A waiter came over and placed a mojito on the table in front of Fina. It was swimming with crushed mint and ice. He also set down a plate. "These are seared ahi tuna bites with Oriental dipping sauce."

"Thank you," Juliana said, and waited for him to walk away. "I was having a bad day yesterday. I don't want you to take that out on Michael."

Fina narrowed her gaze. "I don't follow. Why would I take anything out on Michael? And how?"

"Well, he mentioned that you were upset with me and, therefore, upset with him."

Wow. That guy could be a real brat.

"No," Fina said. "I just reiterated that it was hard to investigate if you two are anything less than forthcoming. I don't understand why he would hire me, only to tie my hands behind my back." Fina stirred her drink and took a sip with the straw. It was like summer in a glass.

"That wasn't his intent. He's just protective of me and his father. You can understand that."

"Sure." Fina took another sip. "So does a do-over mean you're willing to answer some more questions?"

"If I have anything to add, I'd be happy to."

Fina didn't understand where this was going. That was hardly an offer to spill the beans, and yet it seemed important to Juliana that Fina view her as being helpful.

"The fight you had with Hank?"

"That was a misunderstanding, compounded by Bud's lack of context. We weren't arguing about the funding itself but rather the distribution of it."

"So the center was going to get the same amount it usually does?"

Juliana reached over and plucked one of the ahi bites off the plate. "Essentially." She popped it into her mouth.

"Does that mean it was the same amount or it wasn't?"

"It was."

Fina didn't believe her, but sometimes you learned more by keeping up the charade. She was curious to hear what Juliana wanted her to.

"So there wasn't going to be any disruption to the center or its services?"

"Nope. Have one of these; they're delicious." She pushed the plate toward Fina.

"What about Forty-four Oak Street?" Fina asked before eating the ahi.

Juliana was bringing her drink to her mouth, and there was the slightest hiccup in the motion. "What do you mean?"

"Buying a big house in Cambridge is extremely expensive. I would think you would need significantly more cash than usual to make a purchase of that size."

"Expansion has always been part of our plan. I believe in dreaming big; your only limit should be your imagination."

Fina sucked on her drink and mentally bit her tongue. It was like happy hour in the Hallmark store.

"Did Hank have any health issues that you were aware of?"

Juliana looked surprised. "Not to my knowledge. Why? Was he sick?"

"No, I just wondered if there was anything that might not be obvious or a family history."

"His dad died of a heart attack, but that was part of the reason he took good care of himself. He didn't want to drop dead prematurely." When the words were out of her mouth, she gaped as if trying to give them a place to return to. "That came out wrong."

"I know what you meant," Fina said. "He didn't want to die from something that could be avoided."

Juliana nodded and drained her drink.

"Have you ever heard of a young man named Brett Linder?" Fina asked.

Juliana shook her head. "Doesn't ring a bell. Why?"

"He claims he's one of Hank's."

Juliana rolled her eyes. "I always told him the shit would hit the fan one of these days."

"What do you mean?" Fina asked, trying to free the crushed mint embedded in her straw.

"The sperm donations. I told him it would come back to haunt him."

"When did you have this conversation?"

"I don't know. Twenty years ago?"

"Wait—so you knew about the sperm bank?"

"Not when it happened, but he told me a few years into our marriage. We were having fertility issues, and it came up."

"You weren't upset?"

"Of course I was upset, but we'd been broken up at the time. There was nothing I could do about it."

"But Michael never knew?"

"No. There's really no good time to tell your child he might have dozens of half-siblings, and until one of them materialized, there didn't seem to be any point." Juliana stood and grasped an expensive leather handbag by its handles. "I'm glad we were able to clear the air."

"Me too," Fina said, standing and offering her hand.

"Don't hesitate to contact me if I can answer more questions." She strode out of the bar, and Fina dropped down into her seat.

More questions?

That would suggest she'd answered any.

She and Milloy ordered Greek takeout later that night and sat on the couch eating and watching *I Didn't Know I Was Pregnant*.

"I don't buy it," Fina said, popping a stuffed grape leaf into her mouth. "How do you not know?"

"Don't ask me."

"But, seriously: Ask any pregnant woman, and she'll tell you it's like having an alien onboard. If you mistake that for indigestion, you should be seeing a lot of specialists, not just an ob-gyn."

As the credits rolled, Fina muted the TV. "I think I might need to hire some protection for Haley."

Milloy dipped a triangle of pita into some taramosalata. "But you're on the fence?"

"Completely. If I do, then I have to tell her and tell my dad and on and on."

"But it would probably keep her safe."

"Safer than not having protection." Fina munched on a corner of pita bread. "How is this kid ever going to have a normal life?"

"Her life is never going to be *normal*, and unless you're willing to get a new job, there's not much you can do." Milloy stretched his arms over his head. "Has anyone considered boarding school for her?"

"It came up briefly, but she wasn't enthusiastic, and we all have high hopes for the Patty and Scotty arrangement."

"Which seems to be going well."

"It is. It's the threats to her personal safety that are posing a problem."

"You don't have to figure it out this minute. Sleep on it," Milloy suggested.

Fina looked at him. "You wanna stay over?"

Milloy raised an eyebrow.

"For company," Fina clarified. "No promises on the nooky front."

"Company's good," he said, and stood up. He reached out his hand and pulled her off the couch.

Nestling next to Milloy in bed felt good. She breathed deeply and inhaled his scent, which was a mélange of soap, clean cotton, and a hint of sweat. He fell asleep quickly, and the rhythm of his quiet breathing soon helped her do the same.

25

They parted company the next morning in the garage. Milloy backed out of a visitor parking space as Fina ducked into her car. She was putting the key into the ignition when her door was flung open and she was pulled out and tossed onto the cement floor. Before she could formulate a cogent thought, her assailant punched her in the face. Fina kneed him in the groin, and as he pulled back in pain, she punched him in his windpipe. This bought her enough time to roll over and start scrambling away, but not enough time to cover much distance. He was on her again, and they grappled, a maelstrom of nails, fists, and elbows.

It felt like they spent an eternity in this violent embrace before he miraculously pulled away from her. Fina crab-walked away from him, her palms scraping the rough surface of the garage, before realizing it wasn't a miracle at all. Milloy had the man in a headlock and proceeded to punch him in the face and body until he succumbed and collapsed into a heap.

Fina fought to slow her breathing and looked at Milloy. He massaged his knuckles.

"I forgot my phone," he told her.

"Good," Fina said in a daze. "That's good."

.   .   .

Fina sat in the open bay of the ambulance, an ice pack pressed to her face. She watched Cristian and Milloy engaged in conversation in the alley behind the building. Fina's assailant was getting medical care in a second ambulance.

The blow to her face had caught the edge of her eye and her temple, and there was dirt and blood matted in her hair. Fina's palms were cut and bleeding, and she'd torn through the leg of her pants. She plucked off a small stone that was stuck to her bloody knee.

Pitney strolled over and climbed into the ambulance beside her.

"What's the verdict?" Pitney asked the young EMT who was tending to Fina. JOE was stitched onto his uniform shirt.

"She'll live," he said. "We're going to take her in, though. They'll want to run some tests." He hopped out of the ambulance and started conferring with a colleague.

"I'm surprised you agreed to that," Pitney commented. She was wearing a pantsuit the color of cranberries with a green top. Fina must have sustained a head injury since her impression of the outfit wasn't one of total visual dissonance.

"Documentation," Fina said, and pulled the ice away from her face. "It's the Ludlow holy grail."

"Of course." Pitney nodded. "And if they think you need to go"—she gestured at the EMTs—"you should."

"Is he saying anything?" Fina sat back against the bench seat. The EMT had tried to convince her to lie down on the gurney, but she wasn't *that* injured.

"Not yet. We'll get him back to the station. That might make him more talkative."

Fina and Pitney were quiet. They watched Cristian and Milloy across the street.

"Can you imagine the conversation?" Pitney mused, grinning.

Fina glared at her.

The two men walked across the alley toward them.

"We're all set," Cristian said.

"Do you want me to ride with you?" Milloy asked.

"No, and you don't need to come. It's just routine stuff. I'm fine."

Milloy tilted his head in question. "Okay," he said after a moment. "I called the office, though."

"Thanks."

Pitney climbed out of the back of the ambulance, accepting Milloy's helping hand in the process. "We're headed back to the station. I assume you'll keep her updated?" she asked Cristian.

"I'll call you," he said to Fina.

The EMT returned, climbed up next to her, and pointed at the gurney. "Now you have to let me strap you in. It's the law."

"That's not a compelling argument to her," Cristian said.

"But I'm happy to do it for you, Joe," Fina said, shifting over to the gurney and allowing the young man to fasten the seat belt low and snug around her hips.

Cristian slammed the back doors shut and pounded twice on the ambulance, which the driver interpreted as a signal to leave.

Fina rested her head against the thin pillow and closed her eyes.

It wasn't the ideal way to get a catnap, but beggars couldn't be choosers.

"I didn't expect to see you," Fina told Matthew when he strode into her curtained nook in the ER an hour later.

"Dad and Scotty were tied up." Matthew pulled a chair over to the side of the bed and sat down. "So they got the guy?"

"Milloy got the guy. He was coming back to get his phone, thankfully."

"You couldn't have handled him?" Matthew grinned.

"I'm not bionic, Matthew, but thanks for the vote of confidence."

"Are they going to keep you here?"

"I doubt it. I had a CAT scan and some X-rays. I'm waiting for the results, but you don't have to wait. I know you're busy."

Matthew looked at his watch. "I have an hour before a meeting. I'll stay until then."

They killed the next half hour watching *The Price Is Right*, a game at which Matthew proved to be surprisingly adept.

"How do you know the price of a baker's rack or a ten-person hot tub?" Fina asked him.

He grinned.

Fina tried to concentrate on the show, but her head was throbbing, and in the hallway outside, a phone rang incessantly.

"If someone doesn't answer that goddamn phone, I'm going to rip it out of the wall," Fina said, squeezing her fists in frustration.

"Take it easy, killer, and focus on the Showcase Showdown."

Mary from Tulsa was overbidding on a trip to Japan when the curtain was thrown open and a young man in a white coat walked over to Fina's bedside.

"Your films all look clear. You can go; just take it easy for a few days. We'll give you some pain pills, so no alcohol."

"Have we met?" Fina asked. "That's a lot of directives from someone I don't know."

"Dr. Carlson," he said.

"Right. Of course."

"So nothing permanent?" Matthew asked.

"Nope. If she takes care of herself, she'll be good as new in no time."

"Clearly, they didn't take a complete history," Matthew said under his breath. Fina sat up and nudged him with her foot. "My clothes, please?" She nodded toward a plastic bag hanging on a hook on the wall.

"The discharge nurse will bring in the instructions and your prescription," Dr. Carlson said before taking his leave.

Matthew waited in the hall while she got dressed, and Fina chased down a nurse to get her paperwork. She knew her situation was minor compared to her fellow patients, and it was a waste of time and a bed if she had to wait around to be told not to OD and to take it easy.

"So what should I report to Dad?" Matthew asked after ten minutes in the car, sitting in traffic.

Fina knew without asking that Matthew was referring to the case, not her health. "That obviously I'm making progress. Nobody beats you up if you're on the wrong track."

Matthew pulled over in front of the Boston PD headquarters. "I'll pass that on."

"Thanks for the company at the hospital." Fina put one foot out of the car and winced when she stood.

"You really should take it easy," Matthew said, frowning.

"I have a few things to take care of, then I promise I'll go home and lie down."

He pulled away, and Fina climbed the building steps. She checked in with the desk sergeant and was fetched a few minutes later by a woman in uniform, who took her upstairs to the Major Crimes squad room.

Pitney beckoned to her, and Fina followed her into a space the size of a walk-in closet with a one-way mirror that looked into a second room. The man from the garage sat handcuffed to the table.

"I thought he'd look worse," Fina commented. She settled down into a chair and gazed at the man on the other side of the glass.

"You should see his torso. Milloy did a job on him."

Fina glared at Pitney. "He was just protecting me."

"I know. Don't be so defensive."

"Sorry! I'm feeling a little touchy today," Fina said sarcastically.

The man squirmed in his seat, searching for comfort that wouldn't be found in the metal chair he occupied. He looked at the clock on the wall.

"Is this the one you had trouble with before?" Pitney asked. "Cristian said something about the elevator in your building."

Fina leaned toward the glass and peered at him. His eyes seemed to rest on her for a moment, even though he couldn't possibly see her through the glass.

"He's the one. He may be the one from the street also, but I can't be sure."

"What are you talking about?"

Fina waved her off with a bandaged hand. "Nothing."

"Well, he's really got the hots for you," Pitney commented. There was a knock on the door, and Cristian came in holding two cups of coffee with a folder tucked under his arm. He handed one to Pitney.

"Do you want a soda?" he asked Fina. "I didn't realize you were here."

"Just some water. I have to take some pills." She reached into her bag and pulled out a bottle, which she shook.

"Great," Pitney said. "Narcotics."

"Legally prescribed narcotics."

Cristian ducked out of the room and spoke to someone. He stepped back in and closed the door behind him.

"So has he given you guys *anything*?" Fina asked.

"Quiet as a church mouse," Pitney said, then sipped her coffee.

A light tap on the door produced a cup of water, which Fina used to wash down a pill. "What's his name?" she asked.

Cristian opened the folder. "Denny Calder." He looked at her expectantly.

Fina shook her head. "Nope. Did you ask him about the pictures of Haley?"

"He lawyered up," Pitney commented, glancing at her phone.

"He has a lawyer? His own lawyer?" Fina asked.

"No," Cristian said. "Public defender."

"I wish I felt more optimistic about this," Fina said, standing.

"No reason to," Pitney said. "He's not going to give us anything."

"Well, let me know if he does," Fina said as Cristian opened the door. He followed her into the squad room and toward the stairs.

"What did the doctor say?"

"Surprisingly little. His bedside manner was slim to nonexistent."

"But you didn't leave AMA, did you?" Cristian asked.

"Against medical advice? That's an offense worthy of disinheritance in the Ludlow clan." Fina took the stairs slowly. "I got a clean bill of health. I feel like shit, and that wouldn't bother me so much if I knew Haley was safe."

"I would still keep an eye on her if I were you."

"I was all set to get her some protection, but I'd rather not if it's not necessary."

"That's your call," Cristian said. They were standing outside the front door of the station. Cops and other members of the public floated by. An old woman came up the stairs, bumping a metal grocery cart behind her. She was wearing a hat with a plastic daisy stuck in the brim.

"Young man," she said, gripping Cristian's arm, "I need to report a crime."

"They'll help you inside, ma'am," Cristian said, offering her a pleasant smile.

"But I like the look of you," she said to him.

"Everybody likes the look of him," Fina said. The woman stared at her and curled her lip at Fina's appearance. She returned her attention to Cristian. "President Kennedy has been stealing my *People* magazines."

Cristian glanced at Fina, who suppressed a smile. "Inside, ma'am. The desk sergeant would be happy to help."

The woman snuck another look at Fina and pulled her cart behind her into the station.

"Wow. I'm so sorry I'm not a cop," Fina said, rolling her eyes.

Cristian grinned. "I'll let you know if we get anything out of Denny Calder."

"Thanks." She started down the stairs. "How's Cindy?" she called back to him.

Cristian shook his head and went back inside. Fina hailed a cab and headed back to Nanny's.

.   .   .

Danielle Reardon answered her phone after two rings. "Are you making any progress?" she asked Fina.

Jeez. Fina had many masters on this case.

"Yes, and you could help me make some more."

"Okay."

"Do you have surveillance cameras outside your home?"

"Of course."

"Good. I wonder if I could get the tapes from the night Hank was
killed."

"Why? You think his killer was *here*?"

"I just need to check something, and the tape would be helpful."
Fina didn't feel like arguing or explaining; she just wanted the damn
tapes.

"You'll have to speak with Mickey Hogan at Universum. He over-
sees all our security."

"Okay. I'll give him a call. Thanks. How are you holding up?"

Danielle sighed on the other end of the line. "I'm okay. One of my
sisters is here visiting."

"How's Aubrey?"

"She's good," Danielle said. There was some hesitancy in her voice.
"She's just doing her baby thing."

"Well, it must be nice to have your sister around."

"It is. In fact, we're on our way out."

"Well, don't let me keep you. Thanks, Danielle."

Fina dropped the phone onto the coffee table and rolled over onto
her side. What she wanted to do, more than anything, was pop another
pill and curl up under Nanny's afghan, but that wasn't how cases got
solved. The detecting fairy didn't flit by, sprinkling fairy dust in your
hair while you slumbered.

Calling Mickey Hogan was an option, but she'd learned that in certain circumstances, a battered appearance could work to her advan-

tage. Contusions and lacerations indicated a level of seriousness that mere words couldn't begin to convey.

Fina changed into jeans that weren't torn and bloodstained and a lightweight V-neck sweater. The bruises on her neck were faint shadows compared to the discolorations blooming around her eye and temple. She pulled her gun out of her bag and tossed a light jacket over her hand. If someone else was waiting for her downstairs, he was in for it.

At Universum, the young receptionist, Tony, drew back at her appearance. She asked for Mickey Hogan and was ushered to the seating area to wait.

"Can I get you anything?" Tony asked her in a hushed tone.

Fina couldn't imagine what might be on offer. "I'm good, thanks."

Tony returned to his desk and launched into an animated conversation with his desk mate. His frequent glances in Fina's direction made her wonder if she was the topic of conversation.

Ten minutes later, a beefy man in a dark suit led her back to Mickey Hogan's office. Mickey was sitting behind his desk, flipping through a stack of papers.

"Thanks for seeing me on short notice," Fina said, taking a seat across the desk.

"Christ." He studied her face. "That looks painful."

"It was. Is."

"What happened?" Mickey turned the papers over and gave her his full attention.

"I was jumped by some guy who's been trying to warn me off."

"The investigation into Hank's death?"

"I think. He's never that specific in his threats, just wants me to leave town for a bit."

"Did he take off?"

"No. Luckily a friend of mine happened upon us and clobbered the guy. He's at Boston PD right now. Denny Calder. You ever heard of him?"

Mickey thought for a moment and then shook his head. He tapped a few keys on his computer.

"Nope. We don't have anything on him."

"They're going to interview him, but so far, he's not saying much."

"So what can I do for you?" Mickey leaned back in his chair.

"I just spoke with Danielle about video footage from the house on Commonwealth."

Mickey nodded, but didn't say anything.

"She said you would have it for the night of Hank's murder and I could take a look."

"Okay. Give me a minute." Mickey picked up the phone and dialed a number. "Mickey Hogan calling for Mrs. Reardon." He looked at Fina and shrugged. "Trust, but verify."

"Of course." Fina rested her chin on her fist. The pain from her injuries was muted, but she felt just a tiny bit dopey from the pills. It was tough to find the sweet spot between being pain-free and completely loopy.

Mickey had a conversation with Danielle that involved mostly nods and a few "Yes, ma'ams." He hung up and tapped on his keyboard.

"Did you ever determine if there were any unaccounted-for cars in the garage before or after Hank's death?"

"There weren't any. We were able to match each car to its owner, and all visitors and guests were accounted for. Here it is," he said, turning the monitor toward Fina. Video of the Reardon front door started running in a new window. "Do you have a time frame?"

"Let's try eleven P.M. onward."

Mickey clicked the mouse. "What are you looking for?"

"I assume the police asked you for this footage?" Fina countered.

"Yup. What are you looking for?" he repeated, not willing to leave his question unanswered.

"A couple of kids who claim they were camped out on the doorstep for about twenty minutes that night. Not doing anything, but hanging around when they should have been tucked up in bed."

Mickey maneuvered the mouse and jumped the video forward an hour. He set it to advance at eight times the usual speed, and they watched the frame stay virtually the same for a few minutes.

"Wait. Stop," Fina said.

Mickey backed up the recording and started playback on normal speed. After ten seconds, Tyler came into the frame. He was followed by Rosie a moment later. The two of them sat down on the front steps and began talking.

"Who are they?" Mickey asked.

"Those are two knuckleheads who were fathered by Hank Reardon. Mum's the word, by the way."

"Cryokids?"

"Yup. They were recorded on a surveillance video driving around town, and when I confronted the girl, she admitted that they'd gone to Hank's to hang out."

"Do you believe them?"

Fina shrugged. "That's all they seem to be doing."

"Do you think that was their intent?"

"I don't know, Detective Hogan." Fina grinned. "But what else would it be? There's not much they could get away with, given your security measures."

They kept watching the footage.

"And that," Fina said, pointing at Tyler lighting up a joint.

Mickey nodded.

Rosie and Tyler smoked for five minutes, seemed to have a conversation with someone out of frame on the sidewalk, and left seventeen minutes after they'd appeared.

"Looks like they were telling the truth, at least about that," Mickey said, pulling the monitor back to his side of the desk.

"That's something, at least."

"Anything else?"

"The Reardons have other cameras, right? What about their movements the night of Hank's murder?"

"The cameras for the rear entrance didn't record anything of note."

"Got it." Fina stood. "Thanks for taking the time."

"Be careful."

"Will do." Fina walked to the door. "One last thing," she said, turning back to Mickey. "Do you think any of the Reardons are capable of murder?"

Mickey looked impassive.

"You can't answer, right?" Fina said. "Because you work for them. I get it."

Mickey sighed. "You and I both know that most people are capable of murder under the right circumstances."

"I suppose," Fina conceded. "Not a very reassuring thought."

"Luckily, the circumstances aren't often right," he said before ushering her out.

Fina returned to the lobby area and asked to see Theresa McGovern. After making a call, Tony escorted her to the seventh floor, where the assistant was sitting at her desk, a phone receiver tucked under one ear. Fina took a seat in the chair next to her desk and glanced into Dimitri's office. He was at his conference table with three men and two women, engaged in a discussion. It took a moment, but he did a double take when his eyes skittered across her features.

"I understand, but the machine has been broken for almost a week. It needs to be fixed by Friday." Theresa rolled her eyes. Her hair was pulled back in a chignon, her lips bright red next to her alabaster skin. "Uh-huh. Uh-huh. Good. Thank you." She put down the phone.

"There's a machine you guys can't fix?" Fina asked.

"It's the frosty Slurpee thingamajig." Theresa gestured down the hallway. "We use it for happy hours and parties, and something's screwed up with the piña colada side."

"That must be a blow to productivity."

"It is. No joke." Theresa straightened some papers on her desk. "So why are you here? You got another gig for me? And what happened to your face?"

"I was in a fight, and no, I don't have a gig for you. I had a meeting with Mickey Hogan and thought I'd stop by to see if you have any other info for me."

Theresa picked up a plastic cup half-filled with iced coffee and took a sip. "Oooh, so you want something from me."

"I think we want things from each other. Nothing wrong with a mutually beneficial relationship."

"I haven't made a lot of progress." Theresa patted a stack of folders. "Dimitri's got me working on a ton of extra stuff."

"Really?" Fina glanced through the glass again. What looked to be blueprints had been unrolled on the table.

"Yes. Like making a gazillion copies for those people."

"Isn't making copies part of your job?"

"Yeah, but this isn't strictly Universum business; they're talking about the waterfront development."

Fina looked at Dimitri. If he felt her gaze on him, he wasn't letting on. "I thought Dimitri wasn't involved in that?"

"He wasn't." Theresa jabbed at the ice in her cup. "But now he is."

Fina considered this bit of news. A slight throbbing had emerged on the side of her face, but she blinked and tried to ignore it. "Back to the part where you help me out; any new info about Hank's medical records?"

Theresa sorted through some folders on her desk. She opened one and pulled out a Post-it note.

"Normally, Hank would have an annual physical for insurance purposes. It's always been straightforward—just another appointment on his schedule—but this year, he had three appointments."

"Do you know why?"

"No, just that it was different from the past three years, and Dimitri had his regular single appointment."

"But Hank didn't seem sick?"

"Nope."

"And he didn't give any indication about what was going on?"

"Nope, but there also were more calls to certain people around the same time."

"What people?"

Theresa consulted her notes. "Jules Lindsley, his college roommate, and his wife. His ex-wife, I mean."

Fina looked at Theresa. "Something was wonky with his physical, and he started calling Juliana more often?"

"I'm not saying it's cause and effect. Maybe it's just a coincidence."

"Maybe," Fina said, rising from the chair. "Why don't you get Dante to find you a gig?"

"He's working on it, but I still expect a little quid pro quo from you." Theresa wagged her finger at Fina.

"I'll do my best," Fina said.

"Did you need to speak with Dimitri?" Theresa asked.

"Nah. I think he already got my message." She locked eyes with him before making her exit.

26

Fina drove to Heritage and pulled into a space in the parking lot. A quick phone call established that Walter Stiles was still in the building, and she decided to wait. She knew that he'd kick her off the property, so following him to a more neutral location was her best bet.

After half an hour—during which Fina listened to a story about food safety related to produce, which only confirmed that her diet of processed foods was the safest option—Walter came ambling out of the building. He swung his briefcase in one hand and clicked his car open with the other. Fina pulled into traffic behind him and tailed him to an athletic club in Newton. Once there, he grabbed a duffel bag from the backseat and started toward the entrance.

"Walter!" Fina called across the parking lot. "Fancy meeting you here!"

Walter shook his head.

"No worries, I'm not going to make you late for your Zumba class. I just have a quick question."

Walter grimaced. "I don't do Zumba, and I don't have any answers for you, Ms. Ludlow. Any questions you have should be directed to the bank's attorneys."

"Do you know a guy named Denny Calder?"

Walter shifted his bag to the other hand. "I'll tell you what I told the police: no."

"So they questioned you already."

"Yes." He turned and walked away.

"I know you've got secrets, Walter. I'm guessing they're humdingers."

He moved a few steps back toward Fina. "You know nothing, Ms. Ludlow, and frankly, I'm shocked that anyone would pay for your 'expertise.' You seem to have a talent for getting beaten up and not much else."

"Well, I can't take *all* the credit for that. Denny Calder deserves some." Fina smiled at him. "We're not done, Walter. You're kind of like a bee in my bonnet at this point."

"Lucky me," he said in a tone that could only be described as withering. Fina watched him walk through the front door of the club and disappear from view.

Intellectually speaking, likability and guilt had nothing to do with each other, but Fina couldn't help but hope that her suspicions about Walter would pan out.

Fina went home and took a nap. When she rolled over and checked her phone two hours later, there was a message from Cristian and one from Carl. She dialed Cristian's number and left a message, but she couldn't stomach calling Carl; she didn't have enough drugs in her system.

Her bandaged hands posed a problem in terms of bathing, so Fina gave herself a modified sponge bath and got back into her clothes. She repeated the trip down to her car with her gun once again in hand. With the car door securely locked, she returned the gun to her bag and took a deep breath. This was no way to live. Fina didn't long for a white picket fence, 1.86 kids, or a dog playing fetch, but grasping a gun in her own condo building, looking like Sugar Ray Leonard? There had to be a better way.

It took thirty minutes to get to Somerville and another ten minutes to find a parking space near the Sanchezes' house. Rosie answered Fina's knock, and they sat down on the couch after Rosie got two sodas from the kitchen. A large open bag of tortilla chips sat on the coffee table next to a bowl of guacamole.

"Help yourself." Rosie pushed the bag in her direction. "You don't look so hot, Fina."

"I know. It really hasn't been my day." She scooped up a chipful of the green dip and put it in her mouth. The salt of the chips and the tang of the avocado were the perfect mix. "That's so good."

Rosie chewed and nodded. "I could eat this stuff all day."

They snacked, and Fina asked about her work at the shelter. Rosie was enthusiastic when she described the animals under her care.

"So am I in more trouble?" Rosie finally asked. She adjusted her position on the couch so her bare feet were tucked under her. Her wavy hair was loose and framed her face.

"Actually, you're in less trouble than you were. I saw the surveillance footage from Hank's house, and you and Tyler were doing what you said."

Rosie cringed. "There's more surveillance footage?"

"Yep. Hank was a billionaire. He had a lot of security."

"Not enough, apparently," Rosie noted.

"True." Fina sipped her soda. "Anyway, you guys made for very boring viewing. Thankfully."

Rosie nodded.

"It looks like things have calmed down around here. No press outside, at least," Fina said.

Rosie shrugged. "For now."

"I'm assuming your mom isn't here or else we'd have heard her."

The girl smiled. "I expect her home any minute."

Fina unconsciously touched a fingertip to her temple, but moved it away when Rosie's gaze settled on her injuries.

"I've been meaning to ask you," Fina said, "did your mom say something to you about the night Hank died?"

"What do you mean?" Rosie pushed the guacamole toward the center of the coffee table, out of her own reach.

"Well, she told the cops that she was here all night. Alexa said that your mom helped her in the middle of the night when she had a bad dream. She said your mom got her a glass of water."

"I wasn't here that night, remember?"

"I know, I'm just wondering what you think. Does that sound like Alexa?"

Rosie stared at her. "You think I'm going to tell you if it doesn't?"

Fina sighed. "No, of course not. Sorry."

"My mom can be a pain in the ass, but I don't think that she would ever kill anyone."

"Sorry." Fina held her hands up. "I'm just trying to figure stuff out."

"You weren't supposed to eat that!" Alexa came barging in the front door and stood with her hands on her hips, staring at the guacamole.

"Why not?" Rosie asked. "It was in the refrigerator. What's your problem?"

"Mom! Rosie ate the guac I made for the overnight!"

"Alexa! Stop yelling; I'm right here." Renata came in the front door, laden with a tote, briefcase, and grocery bag.

"Hi, Renata," Fina said, rising from the couch and taking the grocery bag from her arms, placing it on the coffee table.

"Hello, Fina. This is a surprise." Renata stared at her face, but Fina was tired of explaining.

"I was just telling Rosie that I was able to confirm her whereabouts with Tyler on the night in question." Fina glanced at Alexa, who was overloading a tortilla chip with guacamole.

"The night Hank was murdered, you mean?" Renata plopped down in a chair.

"Yes," Fina replied, remembering that discretion wasn't in Renata's toolbox.

"How did you confirm this?"

"There's surveillance footage from outside the Reardon house."

"You mean there's video of Rosie and Tyler trespassing in the middle of the night and doing drugs?" Renata asked.

Rosie snorted.

"I think that's a little dramatic," Fina said. "There's video of them sitting on the front step, smoking a joint. Pretty minor stuff."

"Not to a college admissions committee."

"Renata, nobody is going to see the tape, and frankly, if you think that teenagers don't regularly get stoned, you're living in a dream world."

"I don't care what most teenagers are doing, just *my* teenager."

"And I applaud your parenting, but on the scale of misbehavior, this barely registers."

Renata's phone rang, and she answered. She said little and hung up. "CVS doesn't have the inhaler you need, Alexa. They need to order it from a different pharmacy."

"But I need it for my soccer game," the girl protested. "I don't want to miss my game!"

"I know, sweetie, but you can't play without it."

"Allergies?" Fina asked.

"And asthma," Renata said. "Treatable, but the attacks can be very scary."

"I bet." Fina rose. "I should be going."

"You look like you've been in another accident, Fina," Renata said.

Fina shrugged and opened the front door. "What can I say? I'm a trouble magnet."

"Did you talk to her?" Michael Reardon asked. He was watching his mother toss vegetables in the wok. She put down the bamboo spatula for a moment and cut chunks of tofu off a brick. "Can't you leave that out?"

"All this good protein?" Juliana asked. "Of course not. You can eat around it if you find it so distasteful."

"That's the problem," Michael mumbled. "It doesn't taste like anything."

"It's an acquired taste, and it takes on the flavor of the other ingredients."

"Great. Broccoli-flavored mush."

Juliana looked at him. "I said we could go out, but you didn't want to, remember? Stop complaining."

Michael sipped from a can of beer and hooked his feet around the bar stool's footrest. Some people might flash back to childhood memories at a moment like this, sitting in the kitchen while their moms cooked dinner, but for Michael, this scenario was relatively new. He and his mother had often eaten dinner together when he was young, but she hadn't taken much interest in cooking until after the divorce. She'd decided that a cook was an unnecessary extravagance, and every human should be able to feed themselves. Cooking also allowed her to keep track of exactly what she was eating, a necessary component of her triathlon training.

"So did you talk to her?" Michael asked again.

"Yes, I met Fina for a drink at the Four Seasons."

"And? How did it go?"

"It was fine. We had a drink. I answered her questions. It was very friendly."

"Good."

Juliana doled the stir-fry out into two large bowls and carried them over to the table. Michael brought their drinks, and they got settled.

"Are you sure you really want to keep this up? Fina's investigation?" she asked.

"Of course. Why wouldn't I?"

"It seems like a waste of money. Why pay her to do what the police are going to do anyway?"

Michael pushed a floret of broccoli around with his chopsticks. "I don't understand why it bothers you so much. It's not a lot of money in the scheme of things."

"It doesn't *bother* me, but I don't think you need the extra stress." Juliana took a sip of wine.

"I can handle it, Mom." He rotated his beer on the table. "I had a message today from Jules, something about signing some papers related to stock holdings? He said it had to do with you."

"Uh-huh. I'm freeing up some cash to make a purchase for the center."

Michael avoided her gaze. "Do you think that makes sense right now? Shouldn't we wait to see what happens with the will?"

Juliana put her chopsticks down. "We can't wait, Michael. The property next to the center will be scooped up if we don't make an offer, and a good offer at that."

"I'm not sure I want to sell that stock, Mom."

Juliana looked taken aback. "It's a tiny percentage of the portfolio. Why would that be a problem?"

Michael fiddled with the tab on his beer can. "I don't think it looks good spending a lot of money so soon after Dad died, and I want to make sure we're spending it on the right things."

Juliana swallowed. "Your father was one hundred percent committed to the center."

Michael looked at her. "Was he?"

"Of course he was. What are you suggesting? Wait." Juliana held up her hand. "Let me guess: Danielle is putting ideas into your head."

"This isn't about Danielle," Michael insisted. He put a piece of tofu in his mouth and chewed. "This is about my taking more responsibility for the money."

"The money your father and I accumulated."

"Yes, that money, but it isn't all yours, Mom."

"*Most* of it isn't mine! But I'd like to use what I do have to support a good cause."

"I'm sure Danielle feels her causes are equally deserving."

Juliana squeezed her eyes shut. "I don't want to talk about her, and the only cause she's interested in is herself. She can't even be bothered with her own child."

"That's not fair."

"But it's true." Juliana reached over and squeezed his hand. "Michael, please. I am asking you to sign the papers so we can purchase the house and expand the center. I wouldn't be asking if it weren't critical."

Michael put down his chopsticks. "Fine, yeah, I'll sign the papers. I just wish you would have talked to me first. It's embarrassing hearing things from other people. I found out about the sperm bank from a reporter, and Jules called me about the stock. You could talk to me directly."

"You're right, and I'm sorry. I've been so caught up in the idea that I didn't think things through. Do you accept my apology?"

"Of course, Mom."

Juliana smiled over her wineglass. "We can name the new space after you: the Michael Reardon House."

Michael blushed. "That isn't necessary."

But secretly, the idea did hold some appeal.

"What? You were hoping I'd be gone for the day?"

"Such a negative outlook, Dad," Fina said, lowering herself to the couch in her father's office. "Maybe you should talk to someone about that."

"That's your solution for everything these days: therapy."

"Oh, right. I can't stop yammering away about therapy." Her outrageous insistence that Haley see a therapist had been met with much derision by Carl and Elaine. Problems were managed—or not, as the case might be—within the family. There was no reason to bring a stranger into the mix. Fina rubbed her forehead. Maybe stopping by Ludlow and Associates wasn't such a great idea.

"I have a question for you," Fina said.

Carl stood up from his desk and walked over to the wet bar. He took a heavy crystal tumbler off the shelf and poured himself a finger of scotch. The fridge opened with a gentle popping sound, and he pulled out a cold can of diet soda, which he handed to Fina.

"Thanks." Fina accepted the offering with wariness. Her father didn't usually serve her, literally or figuratively.

"You can put it on your face if you don't want to drink it. You look like you went ten rounds."

Fina pressed the can to her temple, but then popped the tab and took a sip. "Did Matthew fill you in?"

"Just the broad strokes," her father said.

"Those are the only strokes at this point."

Carl stood over her. "You had a question?"

"Do you get a regular insurance physical?"

Carl peered at her. "Why do you ask? You have plans for me?"

"Maybe. Depends how this conversation goes."

Carl snorted. "Yes, a yearly physical."

"Is it like a typical physical?"

"It used to be. When we first got the insurance it was an hour, tops. Just like a regular checkup, but now . . ." He waved his hand in the air.

"What does it entail now?"

Carl swallowed the last of his scotch. He sat back down behind his desk. "It's ridiculous. A day, sometimes more. Every test you can imagine and one of those Holter monitors."

"What's that?"

"It's one of those portable monitors that you're supposed to wear for days at a time to monitor your heart and your brain."

"You wore that?" Fina asked, surprised.

"Of course not. Always delegate when possible."

"Wait. You delegated part of your physical?"

"I didn't say that exactly."

"Hypothetically speaking, you outsourced part of your physical? Some poor junior associate wore a monitor for you?"

Carl raised an eyebrow, but remained silent. Fina always felt better about herself when she spent time with her father; he really was beyond the pale.

"Okay, you don't have to answer," Fina said. "But the upshot is that you have all these fancy tests and try to prevent any potential problems, thereby minimizing the insurance payout."

"Exactly. They look for even the hint of a problem, monitor you, and treat the hell out of it. It's ridiculous."

"You don't want to know if you might get sick down the road?"

"'Might' and 'down the road' being the operative words. It makes people feel in control when they aren't."

Fina glanced at her watch. Her head was pounding, but she wasn't supposed to take another pill for a couple of hours.

"Can I see the report?" she asked.

"You want to see the report from my insurance physical?"

Fina nodded.

"No, you cannot see the report."

"It's for a case, Dad. Trust me when I say I have no interest in knowing the details of your health."

Carl shook his head. "No way."

"Why not? You've already admitted half of the numbers are false."

"Then why look at it?"

"Because I'm not interested in the particulars of your test, just what you were tested for."

Carl cracked his knuckles. "Is this about Hank Reardon?"

"Yes, and it will help me make progress. If you don't help me, it's like you're obstructing."

"Bullshit on that, but fine; I'll have Shari send you the report. But then destroy it and don't discuss it with anyone."

"I won't. I promise." Fina stood and walked to the door. "I'll be in touch."

"And I'll expect a quick result, given my assistance."

"Bullshit on *that*," Fina said, with one foot out the door. "You always expect a quick result."

"Wait." Carl looked at her. "We need to discuss your brother."

"Which one?"

"You know which one."

Fina walked back toward his desk. "There's nothing to discuss."

"Rand is coming back, whether you like it or not."

"I don't like it, and I'm not going to welcome him back into the fold. I can't believe that you're willing to."

"There aren't a lot of options."

Fina shook her head. "I don't buy it."

"He's family, Fina."

"He's a pervert, and you're going to do irreparable harm to Haley if you act like his behavior is acceptable."

"So what do you suggest?"

"You know what I think should happen, but it's not up to me."

Carl leaned back in his chair. "You're right, it isn't. I expect you to get on board."

Fina squeezed her fists closed. "Please don't make me fight you on this."

"I'm not making you do anything."

"I will fight to keep him away."

Carl steepled his fingers together. "Don't start a fight you can't win."

"You should follow your own advice, Dad."

Carl shrugged and picked up his phone.

Fina needed to get home and get some pain relief.

She was pretty sure that the recommended dosage only applied if you were operating heavy machinery.

27

Fina felt crappy the next morning when her alarm went off. She rolled around in bed for a little bit, willing herself to get up and face the day.

Cristian had left a couple of messages, which she'd yet to return. She punched in his number, knowing he would not be pleased.

"I was getting ready to call for a welfare check," he said.

"I'm sorry. I got caught up in stuff yesterday, and then I came home and just crashed."

"How many pain pills did you take?"

"More than the recommended dosage."

"That's what I thought. You might want to ease up on that. People do OD accidentally, you know."

"I didn't take *that* many, but your concern is duly noted."

"'Duly noted' usually means 'heard and ignored.'"

"Well, 'heard' is a start, right? Did you really call me to check on my pill consumption?"

"I wanted an update from you."

"You first. Did Denny Calder start singing like a canary?"

"Hardly. He hasn't given us anything."

"Dammit. That gets me nowhere."

"It gets you one less creep who's trying to beat you up."

"True. I love that about you, Cristian; you always look on the bright side."

"That's me." There was a ruckus in the background. Just another day at the Boston PD. "So what do you have for me?"

Fina palpated her temple. "Oh, I don't know. Nothing really. Was Hank Reardon sick, as far as you know?"

"You have such trouble with this concept; you asking me questions isn't helpful to me."

"Really? It seems to me that sometimes I ask you questions that prompt you to investigate certain avenues you might not have, had I not raised the subject."

Cristian didn't respond.

"Aha! See, I'm not as unhelpful as you like to pretend."

"You still want more than you're ever willing to give."

"I don't like where this conversation is going. It's sounding very Oprah to me."

"Fine. So you have nothing for me."

"Not yet, but I am making progress. I will share something as soon as I deem it prudent."

"I look forward to that, and don't OD in the meantime. It's not a classy way to go."

"Hold on a sec," Fina said, and was quiet for a moment. "Okay, great. I just added 'Don't OD' to the top of my to-do list."

"Piss off, Ludlow."

"Hugs to you too, Detective Menendez."

The call ended, and Fina felt energized.

Sparring with Cristian always put a spring in her step.

Fina took off her bandages and showered, a rookie mistake that she paid for. The water and soap made her palms sing in pain and prevented her from doing much washing. She ended up with stinging hands and poorly cleansed hair. Her attempts to reapply the bandages to her hands were amateurish. It looked like a toddler had been playing doctor or wrapping her up like a mummy, ill-prepared for burial.

A Pop-Tart served as breakfast, and Fina drove to Arlington, hopeful that Tyler Frasier would be home. On the way, she got an update from Hal regarding Brett Linder. There was practically no financial record of the kid, which wasn't a surprise. He was too young to have created much of a paper trail. Hal promised to set his sights on Denny Calder next.

She called Emma, who had found the same information as Fina regarding Brett Linder's arrests. He had been raised by a single mother, but that didn't mean he was the product of Hank Reardon or even Heritage Cryobank.

"Okay. I need you to look into a guy named Denny Calder next."

"All right. Fina, you don't happen to have any tickets for the Pats-Jets game, do you?"

Fina sighed. Her family had season tickets to all of Boston's professional sports teams, and they were constantly doling out tickets to keep their contacts happy.

"How many do you need?"

"Just two."

"New boyfriend?"

"No comment."

"I'll see what I can do." She hung up and her mind wandered, trying to imagine her computer genius on a date. Either she'd spend the evening debating algorithms or having hot, freaky sex. Emma truly was an enigma.

In Arlington, Marnie opened the door and brought her into the kitchen. She was dressed for work, in pants and a short-sleeved sweater, and a bowl of cereal sat on the table.

"Is this a bad time?" Fina asked.

"No, it's fine. I have a meeting downtown in a bit, so I've had a leisurely morning." Marnie sat down and nodded for Fina to join her. "Do you want some coffee?"

"No, thanks. Is Tyler around?" Fina asked, taking a seat.

Marnie shook her head and lingered a moment too long on Fina's face. "He's in class this morning and then work this afternoon. I don't expect him back until late tonight." She dipped her spoon into the cereal.

"I'd leave a message, but it's probably better to speak with him in person."

"Is this about the night of Hank's death? The field trip to the Reardons'?"

"He told you about that?"

"Yes. Tyler doesn't have great impulse control, obviously, and sometimes that means he admits things to me that other children might keep to themselves."

"Well, since you already know about it, you can pass on a message. I watched some surveillance tapes that back up his story. It shows him and Rosie hanging around, smoking."

Marnie nodded. "Of course there's video. I imagine they have a sophisticated security system." She used her spoon to chase an oat cluster around the bowl.

"They do, but I wouldn't worry about the tape. Danielle Reardon doesn't have any plans to disseminate it in any way."

"I'm not worried, actually, but I can guess who is." She grinned slyly.

Fina smiled. "You are correct."

"Renata can create more drama than anyone I've ever met. It must be exhausting being her."

"Being her and living with her, I suspect."

Marnie sipped her coffee. "So does this put Tyler in the clear?"

"We're moving in the right direction, but I'll have to check with the cops to see exactly where he stands."

The front door banged open, and Marnie cocked her head to the side. "Hello?"

"It's me, Mom," a female voice called from the front hall. "I forgot something!"

Marnie and Fina listened as Jess trotted up the stairs.

"I thought she lived in Brighton," Fina said.

"She does, but she stays here occasionally."

Jess's footsteps echoed overhead, and a moment later she appeared in the kitchen.

"Oh," she said, eyeing Fina. "I thought you were alone."

"Fina stopped by to give us some good news. It seems that Tyler is slowly getting out of trouble."

"That's good," Jess said. She shifted a stack of papers and a few other items around on the kitchen counter. "I can't find my Clarinex, and we have a long run this afternoon. It's going to be a killer."

"Did you look in my bathroom?" Marnie asked.

Jess pivoted and ran back up the stairs.

"Allergies," Marnie said, responding to Fina's unasked question. "They always flare up in the fall, and she spends a lot of time outside running in all that pollen."

"I assume you don't suffer or your gardening would be torture."

"Thankfully, I don't. I would hate to give up my garden."

Jess came back into the room. "Found it!"

"I was right?" Marnie asked with a grin.

"You're always right, Mom." Jess leaned down and gave her mother a peck on the cheek. "I've gotta run. See ya." She gave a limp wave to Fina and banged back out the front door.

"So you'll let Tyler know I stopped by?" Fina asked as Marnie carried her cereal bowl over to the sink.

"He'll be sorry he missed you. I think he has a bit of a crush on you."

"That's very flattering, but let's hope his tastes change as he gets older. He should look for a nice librarian or pediatrician in the making. Private investigators don't exactly live staid lives."

"I wasn't sure if I should mention it," Marnie said, gesturing toward her face and bandaged hands.

"A work mishap. Nothing permanent. Tell Tyler I said hi."

Fina sat in her car for five minutes, recent conversations rolling through her mind like waves at the beach. Something was stirring in the recesses of her brain, but she couldn't put her finger on it. Patience was not a virtue Fina had much of, but she'd learned that her brain would make the connections when it was good and ready.

Risa had left her a voice mail, so Fina called back and they planned to meet at her house in an hour. Fina drove to Newton and spent twenty minutes making phone calls and checking e-mails. Shari had sent over the report for Carl's insurance physical as promised; Carl hadn't been exaggerating about its breadth. Fina was marveling over her father's 16 percent body fat, wondering if he'd outsourced the appointment with the fat calipers, when Risa drove up.

Outfitted in a white tennis dress and zippered top, Risa hauled two bags of groceries out of the car before Fina took one from her. She tossed a carryall holding her racquet over her shoulder and unlocked the front door. In the kitchen, they placed the grocery bags on the counter, and Risa dropped her sports gear in the mudroom.

"I'm so thirsty," Risa said, opening the refrigerator door. "Iced tea?"

"Yes, please. Good match?" Fina asked, climbing onto one of the stools at the granite counter.

Risa waved her hand in the air. "It was fine. Doubles, and I had to play with Terry Livingstone. Melanie used to call her Tweety because the woman doesn't shut up. Ever."

"That must be distracting."

"It is, but if I asked for another partner it would create a scandal of epic proportions at the club. I can't be bothered." She placed a glass of iced tea down in front of Fina. "I'm not even going to ask about your face. Are you hungry?"

Fina smiled and took a sip. "Depends on what you have."

"Because you can always make room for certain things?"

"Exactly. I don't understand people who say otherwise."

Risa opened the fridge and took stock. "Oh! I know. I have to make something for a Grahamson meeting, so I tried a new recipe." She pulled out a large glass bowl. "Grand Marnier chocolate mousse."

"Bless you, Risa."

Fina watched as she doled out a large helping of mousse and topped it with fresh whipped cream. She slid the bowl in front of Fina and took a long drink from her glass of tea before unloading some perishables from the grocery bags and putting them away.

Fina dipped the spoon in and took a bite. "This is sublime." She scooped another spoonful and dredged it through the whipped cream. "I assume you're going to make it for the meeting?"

Risa scrunched up her face. "I don't know. It's just chocolate mousse, and they're a pretty tough crowd."

"There is nothing 'just' about this. There's a reason some recipes are classic. Everybody loves them."

"It depends how inspired I feel in the next couple of days."

Fina licked the spoon. "I doubt you asked me here to weigh in on the dessert."

"No, although I do like feeding you, Fina. You're always an appreciative eater."

"Tell my mother that."

"Oh, that's not about food, sweetie. That's about control."

"Yes, her infinite need for it."

Risa smirked.

"Okay, so maybe I have control issues, too," Fina said. "Moving on . . ."

Risa leaned her elbows on the counter. "I've decided to be in touch with Greta Samuels."

Fina relished the delicate flavor of chocolate and orange in her mouth. "Okay. Sounds good."

"Do you have an opinion about it?"

"No."

Risa looked at her, tilting her head.

"Really, I don't," Fina insisted. "It's your decision. I assume you talked to Marty about it?"

"I did, and we agreed that I would proceed, but if at any point I don't like where things are going, I can call the whole thing off."

"That's reasonable. How do you want to proceed?"

"You haven't told her the results yet, right?"

"Nope."

Risa retrieved the glass pitcher of iced tea from the refrigerator. She refilled her glass and topped off Fina's.

"I think we should meet," Risa said decisively.

"You don't want to ease into it with some letters or phone calls?"

"I thought about that, but what's the point?"

"Well, sometimes people like to take baby steps. It helps them get used to the idea of having a relative they didn't know about before." She ate another spoonful.

Risa considered this for a moment and shook her head. "I don't think baby steps will help. It's like ripping off a Band-Aid: I'd rather just get the thing done."

"Great. Sounds like you're really looking forward to it."

Risa smiled. "I don't mean to suggest that it's going to be awful, but I think the initial contacts will be awkward. I'd like to bite the bullet and get through that phase as quickly as possible."

"Okay." Fina scraped her spoon around the sides of the bowl. She licked the last smears of mousse off her spoon.

"I can give you a doggie bag if you'd like. There's plenty."

"No, thank you. This stuff is dangerous." Fina brought the bowl and her glass over to the sink and ran them under the water. "Where do you want to meet her?"

Risa leaned with one hip against the counter. She was in terrific shape, her legs lean and tan. "You said it was about an hour and a half to her place?" Fina nodded. "How about halfway?"

"I'm sure there's a restaurant or a diner that would work. Let me figure something out," Fina said.

They walked to the front door and exchanged a hug.

"I'll let you know as soon as I've been in touch with Greta," Fina said.

"I hope I'm doing the right thing," Risa said.

"Like you said, you can change your mind at any point."

"It's not that I'm not happy with the family I have, but I guess I'm a little curious."

"That's natural."

"Given the chance to learn something about my biological relatives, I feel like I should take it," Risa added.

"Are you trying to convince me or yourself?"

"Neither. I'm comfortable with my decision, it's just hard to articulate something that feels so primal, if that makes any sense."

"I understand. Follow your instincts. You never know; this could be the start of something wonderful."

"You must be on pain pills. Let me know when you talk to her."

Fina returned to her car and made a note to call Greta Samuels. She was anxious to facilitate the meeting between aunt and niece, but there was another meeting that was more pressing.

Fina had more questions for Juliana, but couldn't imagine she'd be more forthcoming than she was at their last meeting. Divide and conquer was a popular strategy, but occasionally unite and conquer could be equally effective. This was the thinking behind her meeting with Juliana and Michael. She'd planned on seeing them on neutral territory, but when Juliana suggested the Reardon Center, Fina agreed. It might be interesting to see Juliana work the home field advantage.

The parking lot behind the center was like a brainteaser; there were a couple of available spaces, but getting her car into one seemed to require math and a PhD-level understanding of angles. One shouldn't break a sweat while parking, but by the time Fina emerged from her car, she felt like she'd had a mini-workout.

The center was in what had originally been a single-family Victorian-style home. The front door opened into a large foyer with high ceilings and a wide staircase leading to the second floor. The space was flooded with natural light, the walls painted a light eggshell color, which provided a backdrop for the original artwork lining the walls.

Fina checked in at the front desk and took a seat in a comfortable upholstered chair. There were a few women scattered around the waiting room, a couple without hair.

A young woman appeared before Fina. "Can I get you something to drink? We have a selection of teas and water flavored with cucumber or lemon."

Water flavored with cucumber? Really?

"I'll try the cucumber water, please."

Fina perused the stack of magazines on the side table next to her. *Health, Natural Health, Holistic Health, Yoga Journal*—slim pickings for a junk food devotee. Where was the waiting room that was geared toward her interests? Journals devoted to sugar, fat, and lounging on the couch?

She picked up a copy of *Yoga* magazine and started paging through it. There were men and women with perfect, sculpted bodies in pretzel-like poses. Fina felt like a child staring at *Playboy*, turning the magazine this way and that in an attempt to make sense of the body parts on display.

"Ms. Ludlow? I have your water, and Juliana and Michael are ready to see you."

Fina followed the woman up the stairs to a room at the front of the building, overlooking the street. There was a small Parsons table in the corner, but most of the room was dominated by two couches that looked soft and inviting. Juliana was sitting in the corner of one, with Michael seated at the other end. They were deep in conversation when Fina walked in and claimed a spot on the other couch.

"Fina, how are you?" Juliana asked, and reached for a mug on the coffee table. "You look like you were in an accident." She was wearing a fitted sheath dress in navy blue topped with a blazer in a small silvery blue pattern. Her short blond hair was tucked behind her ears. Fina may not have been a fan of Juliana's, but she couldn't deny that she was a stellar role model in terms of embracing life after fifty. When she grew up, Fina wanted to look like her.

"Something like that. How are you two doing?"

"I'm fine," Michael said. "Mom nearly killed herself on her bike."

"Really? What happened?" Fina had a sip of her cucumber water; it was surprisingly tasty.

"It's not a big deal. A guy opened his car door, and I took a tumble."

"Show her your arm," Michael urged.

"She doesn't care about my bruises," Juliana said, but Fina suspected that Juliana welcomed the opportunity to show off her war wounds. Fina's brothers were that way. It was some macho code that proved how tough you were. She never had to contemplate showing her injuries; they were usually as plain as day on her face.

"Show me," Fina said.

Juliana stood up and slipped out of her jacket. One shoulder and upper arm were a mottled purple.

"That looks painful," Fina said, wincing.

"But not as painful as your injuries," Juliana said, slipping her jacket back on and crossing her legs as she took a seat. She smiled at Fina, but there was a hint of something sour under her expression.

"Actually," Fina said, "I was attacked. It's the second time I've been assaulted in the course of this investigation." She looked at Juliana and Michael.

"That's horrible," Juliana said. Michael squirmed on the couch.

"It hasn't been fun." Fina didn't say anything more. She knew that

Juliana wasn't unnerved by her silence, but she didn't think Michael could withstand her Jedi mind tricks.

"Are you going to be okay?" he asked.

"Absolutely, but as you can imagine, it makes me even more anxious to get to the bottom of Hank's murder. Do either of you know a man named Denny Calder?"

Juliana and Michael looked at each other.

"The name isn't familiar," Juliana said.

Michael shook his head. "Is he the one who attacked you?"

"Yes. He's in police custody, but he isn't talking. *I* don't know him, so I suspect he's working for someone else."

Juliana dipped her head down and studied the hem of her dress.

"What can we do?" Michael asked.

"Well, Juliana, you could explain why there was an increase in your communication with Hank in May."

Juliana looked puzzled. "I don't know what you mean."

"I've learned that he contacted you"—Fina consulted her notebook, which she'd pulled from her bag—"four times the third week of May, then an additional three times the next week."

Juliana gave her a pitying smile. "We share a child. Even though he's an adult, we still have things to talk about."

"Understood, but it's the uptick in calls that interests me."

Michael looked at his mother. Fina sipped her water and waited.

"I don't know what to tell you, Fina. I'll have to look at my calendar and let you know if there was anything in particular happening, but nothing comes to mind."

"That's fine. Why don't you take a look? I assume you keep your calendar on your phone."

Juliana let out a short exhalation and reached for the purse at her feet. Michael picked at one of his cuticles while she tapped on the screen and scrolled through various apps.

"I don't see anything of particular importance," Juliana said, slipping her phone back into her bag.

"I don't understand," Michael said, looking at his mother and Fina. "What's going on? Were you and Dad having an affair?"

"Goodness, no! That's a ridiculous idea." Juliana brushed her bangs to the side. "Although I'm not sure it's an affair when your former husband is involved," she said, almost under her breath.

"It is if he has a new wife," Fina said.

Juliana smiled and patted Michael's hand. "I was not having an affair with your father. I'm sure there's an innocent explanation for the extra phone calls. Let me check with a few people and see if anything was going on here during that time."

"That would be helpful," Fina said. "As far as you knew, Michael, your dad was in good health?"

Michael looked at his mother. "He was in great shape. Right, Mom?"

"Yes." Juliana frowned. "I thought we covered this the other day, Fina."

A woman poked her head into the room before Fina could answer and broke into a wide smile when she saw Juliana.

"Jennifer! You look wonderful," Juliana exclaimed. She leapt up from the couch and pulled the woman into a warm embrace.

"I feel better," Jennifer replied.

"Jennifer has been participating in our new Health 360° program," Juliana said. "This is my son, Michael, and our acquaintance Fina Ludlow."

Hellos and handshakes were exchanged with Jennifer, who looked thin but not frail. Her hair was shorn close to her head, but it had crossed over from a chemotherapy marker to a fashion-forward pixie.

Juliana and the woman made promises to be in touch, and Jennifer left. They took their places on the couch.

"Her recovery has been so inspiring," Juliana said. "She was given a terrible prognosis."

"You wouldn't know it. She definitely looks like she's more well than sick," Fina commented.

"She is, and it wouldn't be happening if not for the Reardon Center." Juliana smiled and turned toward Michael. "Tell Fina the good news."

Michael scooted forward on the couch. "The center is buying the property next door and expanding."

Fina blinked and looked at Michael. "That's exciting."

"Very," Juliana said. "We couldn't be more pleased. This acquisition is going to have a huge impact on our ability to serve the community. People like Jennifer won't sit on waiting lists for months on end."

Juliana's sales pitches were starting to tire Fina out. "Congratulations. It sounds like you're taking a more hands-on role at the center," she commented to Michael.

"I just want to continue to make a contribution to the community in the Reardon name."

"So Hank would have supported this purchase?"

"Absolutely," Juliana said.

"Have the particulars of the will been discussed?" Fina looked at mother and son.

"That's a very personal question," Juliana said.

Fina looked at her. "It is."

"We've spoken with Jules in general terms," Michael said.

"Any surprises?" Fina asked.

Michael shrugged. "Not as far as I can tell."

"Well, I'm glad the center is thriving. It seems like a wonderful resource." Fina stood and grabbed her bag.

"We're having a gala after the first of the year," Juliana said, standing and smoothing her dress. "Can we count on your support?"

"Sure. Better yet, send it to my father. He can buy a whole table." Fina grinned. She always got a warm and fuzzy feeling when she helped spend Carl's money.

"Wonderful."

Michael and Juliana walked into the hall with her. Sunlight was streaming in a bay window, making the space bright and toasty.

"Juliana, if you could follow up with your contacts and try to determine what was going on during those two weeks, I would really appreciate it," Fina said. "The sooner I wrap this up, the better it will be for everyone."

"Well, we can't do your job for you, Fina," Michael said, as if he'd just grown a pair.

"You're right, Michael." Fina smiled and shook her head. "You couldn't possibly."

She walked down the stairs and outside to the sunshine and the rustling leaves.

28

Once again, the Reardon maid left Fina waiting in the foyer while she went to locate the mistress of the house. Fina spent a few minutes studying the intricate carvings on the banister of the opulent staircase. It was hard to fathom the time and work that went into creating such a detailed work of art, and she was glad that people like the Reardons took care of it. The public might scoff at their enormous wealth, but it was people like the Reardons—and the Ludlows—who helped maintain community treasures like libraries, parks, and historical buildings.

Fina's patience was reaching its limit when the maid returned and led her to the elevator. The mirrored capsule carried them to the fifth floor and Danielle's art studio. Fina followed the maid across the paint-splattered floor, navigating the maze of canvases and easels. Danielle was sitting on the overstuffed sofa in the farthest corner of the room, flipping through the pages of a heavy hardback art book. On a table underneath the window, there was a collection of what looked to be ceramics in various stages of completion and stacks of black-and-white photographs.

"Hi, Danielle." Fina took a seat at the other end of the couch.

"Hey." She struggled to close the large book and place it on the floor by her feet. It was a book about Michelangelo and the Medici Chapel.

"Getting inspired?" Fina asked.

"Trying to." Danielle was wearing tight jeans and a paint-stained oxford shirt over a tank top. Her hair was in a messy bun, her face devoid of makeup. She looked tired and seemed to sense Fina's assessment. "I look awful. I know."

"You look gorgeous, which is pretty amazing. Newly widowed and a new baby? Sounds exhausting to me."

Danielle nodded. "It is." She fiddled with a button on her shirt. "Aubrey had a bad night."

"Babies are so inconsiderate." Fina shifted on the couch. "Thanks for giving Mickey Hogan the okay to show me the surveillance tapes."

"Sure. Was it helpful?"

"It was, actually." Fina decided to hold back the details. No need to stir up Danielle's feelings about the cryokids. "I have another question to ask."

"What's that?" Danielle asked. She got up from the couch and walked over to the table with the ceramics. She picked up an object that looked like a decanter. Danielle examined it from various angles, its surface a beautiful mélange of shades of blue.

"Do you remember anything in particular about the third week of May?"

Danielle's fingers stilled. She thought for a moment. "No. Why?"

"Hank had some weird phone traffic around that time."

She turned to face Fina. "What do you mean?"

"What about his insurance physical?"

"What about it?"

"Were the results unusual this year?"

Danielle looked annoyed. "I can't discuss his medical record with you."

Fina matched her expression. "Of course you can. You're his widow. You can tell me whatever you want. You're not bound by HIPAA," she said, referring to the federal act barring the disclosure of personal health information.

"Well, there's nothing to discuss anyway. Hank was completely healthy. I thought you knew that from his autopsy." Danielle carefully placed the decanter back on the table and perched on the arm of the couch farthest from Fina.

"I'm not suggesting he wasn't healthy. I wondered if the results were unusual in any way."

Danielle shook her head.

"Did he suffer from allergies?" Fina asked.

"Yeah, but so does everyone I know."

"Bad ones?"

"He took a prescription for seasonal allergies."

Fina thought for a moment. "The increased phone calls seemed to coincide with the physical—or physicals, I should say. He had a couple of follow-ups."

"How do you know all this?"

"I have my sources."

"Who was he calling?" Danielle asked, twisting her engagement ring on her thin, tanned ring finger.

"Jules Lindsley, his college roommate, and Juliana."

Danielle shrugged. "He and his roommate were serving on some alumni committee. I'm sure he had his reasons for the others."

Not the reaction Fina was expecting. "Do you know what those reasons might have been?" she pressed.

"It was probably something about Michael. Why don't you ask Jules or Juliana?"

"Jules won't tell me anything, and I spoke with Juliana, but she didn't have anything to offer."

Danielle held up her hands. "I wish I could help, but I don't know what to tell you."

"So it really doesn't bother you that your husband was spending time chatting with his ex?"

Danielle smirked. "Believe me, Hank had no interest in starting things up again with Juliana. She held no appeal for him, despite their history." She stood. "I need to go."

"Sure. Thanks for taking the time."

They walked to the elevator, and Fina stepped off on the ground floor. "I hope Aubrey sleeps better tonight."

"Me too," Danielle said, leaning against the mirrored wall as the elevator door slid shut.

Fina found a drive-thru and got a diet soda and a large order of French fries. Salty fries probably weren't the best choice; her shoddy bandaging allowed some of the salt particles onto her palms, which made her hands sting. From the depths of her bag, Fina dug out a pill and washed it down with the soda. She needed to transition to over-the-counter pain relievers soon. Soon, but not yet.

After cleaning the grease and salt off, Fina pulled out her phone and dialed Greta Samuels's number. She assumed that Greta would be pleased with the news, but she also knew that assumptions were dicey propositions in her line of work.

"Hello?" Greta always sounded surprised when she answered the phone, as if she didn't quite believe there would be someone on the other end.

"Greta? It's Fina Ludlow."

"Hello. I assume my sample arrived."

"It did. Thank you."

"And?"

"And I got the lab results back, and it appears that you and Risa are related."

"Well, of course we're related. I've been telling you that all along."

"Sure you have, but you can't imagine the things people tell me, Greta. I mean, the things they expect me to believe! It would blow your mind!"

"*I* certainly wasn't lying, if that's what you're implying. The test proves that."

"No, you weren't, but I wouldn't be very good at my job if I didn't verify things independently."

Greta didn't respond. They'd reached an impasse, both annoyed with the other.

"So, can you give me Risa's number?" Greta asked after another moment of awkward silence. "I'm anxious to speak with my niece."

"And she's anxious to speak with you, but she would prefer to meet in person."

"Oh."

Fina watched a bunch of teenagers horsing around in the parking lot. They were jumping onto one another's backs and shoving one another playfully. They piled into a small rusty car and backed out of their space.

"You don't sound pleased," Fina said.

"I'm . . . I'm just surprised. I thought she'd want to speak on the phone first, get to know each other a bit before meeting in person."

"Risa doesn't see the point in delaying things. She'd like to meet and see how things go. If you two hit it off, then you can figure out the relationship moving forward."

"And if we don't?"

"Then you don't need to be in each other's lives."

"But we're family. We have to be in each other's lives."

Fina swallowed some soda. "You haven't been for the last forty-six years, and you've both managed okay."

"Only because we didn't know about each other. The idea that we would know and not have a relationship doesn't make any sense."

"Greta, I would caution you to proceed carefully. If you are needy or demanding, that might spook Risa."

"I don't understand."

Fina sighed. "What was your expectation, exactly? What did you think would happen if—"

Greta made a sound of protest.

"Fine," Fina continued, "*when* the test came back a match?"

A timer dinged in the background. "I need to put the phone down a minute. I need to take something out of the oven."

"Go ahead." Fina heard banging and rustling in the background. She was still hungry, but going through the drive-thru a second time seemed sad, even for her.

"I'm back. I didn't want my blueberry buckle to burn. Now, what was the question?"

"What was your expectation regarding the outcome of the DNA test? What did you think would happen?" This was like déjà vu.

"I assumed Risa and I would be in touch on the phone and get to know each other better. Before too long, we'd meet and establish a real relationship, as aunts and nieces do."

Clearly, Greta had a limited view of the aunt-niece relationship. She probably couldn't imagine pulling her niece out of a nightclub, having her puke at her feet, or uncovering her job as an escort. True, these weren't typical aunt-niece interactions, but they had happened. Fina didn't want to give Greta apoplexy, so she chose not to share.

"Well, Risa would like to meet in person," Fina reiterated.

"That's fine, I suppose."

"It's going to have to be, Greta. Risa is interested in exploring this relationship, but she wants to do it on her terms."

Greta sniffed. "I don't see why my preferences shouldn't count."

Fina massaged her temple gently and closed her eyes. This woman was a pain in the ass. "They do, but a meeting is what Risa is offering. Take it or leave it. It's your choice."

"Fine. I need to look at my calendar and will call you back."

"Greta, I have to ask you again; you were so anxious to get this test done, but you've been dragging your feet. What gives?"

"Nothing. Nothing gives."

Fina unpeeled a damp napkin from around her sweating drink and dropped it into the center console. "Okay. Why don't you give me a call once you've checked your schedule?" Honestly, what would she have to check? That she didn't have a quilting bee to attend or a porch to sweep?

"I'll be in touch, Fina. Thank you for calling." Greta ended the call, and Fina was left holding the phone.

Was this just nerves? Anxiety about meeting a long-lost family member? Fina didn't doubt that the whole endeavor was stressful, but Greta needed to put on her big-girl pants and get a grip.

"Oww! That hurts!" Fina lay facedown on Milloy's portable massage table. He moved his hands down her back and focused on a different spot.

"That's better," she said.

"So any update on the guy who did this?"

"His name is Denny Calder," Fina said from the face cradle. "He's not talking, and last I heard, they hadn't uncovered anything useful."

"That's frustrating," Milloy said, kneading her flesh.

Milloy was one of the few people Fina knew who could identify a thought or feeling and sit with it. Unlike her, he wasn't constantly trying to banish discomfort or pain. He acknowledged it, let it play out, and moved on when the time was right. It was extremely Zen, and sometimes annoying.

"It *is* frustrating," Fina agreed.

"You're all set," he said after a moment. Fina pulled the sheet around her and walked into the bedroom. She emerged a few minutes later wearing a T-shirt and sweats. The massage table was folded, leaning against the wall, and Milloy emerged from the kitchen, his hands just washed.

"I never thanked you for yesterday," Fina said, plopping down on the couch.

"For?" He joined her.

"Saving my ass."

"You're welcome."

"I really appreciate it, Milloy. It wasn't going well from my perspective."

"I kind of noticed." He grinned. "I know you don't like people fussing or worrying, but one of these days . . ."

"Actually, I don't mind if you fuss a little." She adjusted her position on the couch. "Finish your thought: One of these days . . ."

"One of these days, I won't be around, Cristian won't be, either, you won't be able to reach your gun, or you'll just be outmatched. You could end up seriously hurt."

"I know. The thought has occurred to me." Fina picked at the nail polish on one of her toenails. Haley had convinced her to paint them bright orange a couple of weeks before, and now they just looked like the late stages of a skin disease.

"And?" he asked.

"And that's it. I hadn't gotten any further than the thought itself."

"Well, that's something, at least." He stretched his arms along the back of the couch. Milloy's arms were nicely muscled. They looked like they could take care of things and people. "What's on the menu, little lady?"

"Hmm. Thai, Greek, Chinese, Italian, or Ben and Jerry's?"

"Thai sounds good."

They ordered and settled down to watch an episode of a show where first dates took place in unconventional locations, like night court and sunrise boot camp workouts.

"Maybe arranged marriage isn't such a bad idea," Fina said, watching a couple attempt to flirt between arraignments.

"Really? So you want Carl and Elaine to choose your spouse?"

"Good point. I'd rather marry one of the accused," she said, pointing at the men in orange jumpsuits.

The doorbell rang, and Milloy answered while Fina fetched utensils and plates from the kitchen. He placed the brown bag on the coffee table and handed her a manila envelope. "The concierge asked the delivery guy to bring it up."

Fina looked at the envelope, her name neatly printed on the front. She tore it open and, with a hint of dread, pulled out the contents.

Photographs. Of Haley.

Fina sank down onto the couch, the photos hanging loosely from her hand.

She'd lost her appetite.

Fina's first instinct was to hop in her car and drive to Scotty's, but Milloy reminded her there wasn't much she could do at that moment. Instead, she called her brother with much trepidation.

"How are you feeling?" he asked.

"Eh, not so great, but that's not why I'm calling."

"What's up?"

"So I assumed—or, more accurately, was hoping—that the guy who jumped me was also responsible for the photos of Haley."

"Yeah, I was hoping the same thing."

"Well, he's still in jail, and I just got more photos."

"Dammit."

"I know."

"Do you think whoever hired him to jump you could still be sending you the pictures?"

"Maybe. Or someone else is sending the pictures."

"So that means two people are after you."

"I don't know. I'm doing my best to figure it out, but I think we need to get some protection for Haley."

"Fina, she's gonna hate that."

"I know, but what else can we do?"

"Have you talked to the cops about it?"

"Not about the most recent photos, but I know what Cristian is going to say; he'll tell me to file a report and do what I think is best in terms of protection."

"Great."

"Look, I'm going to make some calls and arrange for a guard."

"More unwanted attention; just what she needs."

"I know, but she doesn't have a choice. I'll hire a woman, someone who won't be too conspicuous."

"There are female bodyguards?"

"Of course there are female bodyguards. I have a contact who worked a detail for the royal family of Saudi Arabia. They don't want Western men guarding their women."

"Somehow that doesn't make me feel better."

"Can you or Patty talk to the school? I don't think the guard needs to be in the classroom with her, just on the premises."

"I'll talk to them. This has to stop."

"I know."

"Does Dad know?"

"No, I'll call him."

"Do it now. He's probably tired and has had some wine. He'll be mellower."

"He hasn't been mellow a day in his life."

"Well, it's better than him being energized, which he will be after his workout tomorrow morning."

"Good point. I'll be in touch."

Fina hung up and looked at Milloy. He'd cleaned up the takeout leftovers while she'd been on the phone.

"Here," he said, handing her a bar of Swiss milk chocolate. "I found it in the cabinet. You need to eat something."

"Thanks." Fina opened the package and peeled back the foil. She broke off a square and put it in her mouth. "You don't need to stay, you know. I have to call my dad and Cristian. I don't think I'm going to be very good company."

"Is it safe for you to be on your own? I know the photos show Haley, but the threat is directed at you, too."

"I'm not that worried about my safety. I have good locks and a gun."

"I don't mind staying." Milloy flopped down on the sofa and switched the TV to a baseball game. He turned the volume down low as Fina picked up her phone, walking over to the expanse of windows that overlooked the harbor. The runway lights at Logan twinkled in the dark, and the outline of a tanker was visible on the water.

First, Fina left a message for Cristian, making no attempt to hide her distress at the situation and her inability to reach him. Then she called Dennis Kozlowski, a PI with whom she occasionally worked who was plugged in to the investigative community in the city. He promised to send a man over to Scotty's right away who would be replaced by a woman in time for school the next morning. Twenty-four-hour protection carried a high price tag, yet another incentive to get things resolved quickly.

Carl answered the phone after two rings.

"What's wrong?" he asked.

"I just wanted to let you know that I've hired some temporary protection for Haley."

"Why?" he asked sharply.

"Because there's been a threat to her safety. I thought it was handled, but it's not, and we need to take care of it."

"We? You want me to pay for this?"

"Yes, you. First of all because the threat is a direct result of the Reardon case, and second of all, because you're her grandfather."

Carl didn't answer.

"Dad? Are you still there?" A faint cheer erupted from the screen behind her. "It's just temporary. I'll have this thing wrapped up soon."

"You still think that you're better for her than her father?"

Fina gaped. Blood rushed to her head, and she blinked back tears of anger. "Are you fucking kidding me? I'm trying to keep her safe!"

Milloy looked up from his place on the couch.

"She wouldn't be in danger if not for you!" Carl yelled.

"This is not my fault! Sometimes our work is dangerous!"

"So now it's *our* work? Now you're all about the family?"

Fina leaned her head against the cool glass of the window and took the phone away from her ear. She could hear Carl still yelling. She depressed the end button and disconnected the call.

"Did you just hang up on Carl?" Milloy asked.

"Yes."

"Wow," Milloy said softly.

Fina walked over to the couch and lay down, her feet in Milloy's lap. She closed her eyes and tried to think of nothing but the balls and strikes being counted on the TV.

29

The next morning, Fina woke up pissed.

She was far from perfect, but every day she tried to work in her family's best interests, particularly those of the youngest family members. For her father to suggest otherwise was untrue and just plain mean.

But instead of avoiding Ludlow and Associates, which was her first instinct, she decided to enter the lion's den. In her experience, the best way to deal with a bully was to stand up to him, even if—especially if—the prospect of doing so was unnerving.

She gave herself a quick sponge bath, threw on jeans, a light sweater, and ankle boots, and downed half a fluffernutter and a pain pill. Fina gripped her gun and strode down to her car, itching for a fight.

At the office, Carl's door was ajar, and Fina pushed through it, much to the consternation of his assistant.

Carl was on the phone and glared at her. She sat down in a chair in front of his desk and glared back until he cut the conversation short.

"What is it?" he asked.

"Don't ever compare me to Rand again."

"Or else?"

Fina stared at him.

He studied her. After a moment, he spoke. "You need to calm down."

"Maybe, but you need to stop antagonizing me."

They looked at each other.

Finally, Carl broke the impasse. "This is a waste of time. Let's move on."

It was what Fina wanted, but it also irked her. She knew the error was her own; she always rose to the bait that Carl reeled out before her. She got worked up, and then deflated when he was done with the exercise. It was all about control, and Fina realized that, once again, Carl had way too much influence over her. She could have ignored his harsh words the night before, gotten a good night's sleep, and been on her merry way. Instead, her father had taken up prime real estate in her head for the last twelve hours.

"Let's." Fina stood and left the office.

She spotted a familiar face when she walked by one of the small conference rooms.

"Hi, Renata. I'm surprised to see you here," she said, popping her head into the room.

Renata looked up from the document she was reading. "Hello, Fina. I have a meeting with an associate to discuss my case against Heritage."

"So you're going ahead with it?" Fina came into the room and leaned her butt against the table.

"I'm seriously considering it."

Fina nodded. "How are the girls?"

"They're fine. Busy. I'll be relieved when this murder is solved."

That was ironic, coming from the original pot stirrer.

"So will I," Fina said.

Renata's phone beeped. She looked at the screen and shook her head.

"Something wrong?"

"I'm fighting with our health insurance, trying to get an appointment with a new allergist for Alexa. I hate insurance companies."

"You and my father both. Good luck with that." She left Renata tapping furiously on her phone and bumped into Matthew on the way out.

"Do you have a sec?" he asked.

"Sure. What's going on?" She followed him down the hallway to

Scotty's office, where he was gabbing on the phone, his feet propped on the desk. Matthew walked over to the Magic Genie pinball machine and pulled back on the plunger, releasing a ball into play. Fina watched as the ball ricocheted around the bright-pink-and-turquoise playfield and celebrated bonus points with flashing lights. The sound had been muted on the machine—it was a place of business, after all—and Matthew swore under his breath thirty seconds later when the ball slipped through the flippers.

"Guys," Fina said, tapping her watch.

Scotty wrapped up his call, and her brothers glanced at her nervously.

"What's going on?"

"Rand's coming back," Scotty said, and cracked his knuckles.

"When?"

"I don't know the details," Scotty said.

Fina folded her arms across her chest. "And you two are in favor of this?" She glared at them.

"No, of course not," Scotty said. "But what can we do about it?"

"Something," she insisted. "We have do *something.*"

"I'm staying out of it," Matthew said, raising his hands in a gesture of surrender.

"You don't get to stay out of it," Fina said. "That's not an option."

Matthew shrugged.

Fina could feel the blood creeping up her neck. "No, seriously. It's not an option."

"What are you suggesting, Fina?" asked Scotty.

She moved her hands to her hips. "That he be banned from the family."

"How would we even do that? And what about Mom and Dad? There has to be another way, some way to keep the peace."

"Do you think Haley has much peace when he's around?" Her brothers were silent. "Please, support me on this." They didn't protest, which Fina decided to accept as tacit agreement. She walked to the door and turned to look at them. "Our family may be more fucked up than most, and you can feel bad about that, but don't let your sadness cloud your judgment. The next generation is counting on us not to fuck things up even more."

Fina fumed in the elevator down to the garage. All you had to do was pick up the paper or turn on the news to find examples of collective denial and the destruction it wrought, but she couldn't stomach it when it came to her own family. Sure, it was heart-wrenching to admit that your sibling was a monster, but it was even more terrifying to pretend otherwise.

Heritage Cryobank's Miracle Ball was unquestionably Walter's favorite event of the year. Although the children themselves didn't attend, their grateful parents did and spent much of the evening lavishing him with praise. The staff created an elaborate photo display of the cryokids, and the event gave their clients an opportunity to interact with one another. When they'd first started the ball twenty years before, attendance had been small; people weren't yet comfortable associating themselves with a cryobank, but that had changed. It was no longer a source of shame or embarrassment. The bank partnered with a local children's charity, thereby raising their standing in the community. And who didn't like the chance to dress up in fancy clothes and get a night off from their kids?

"It doesn't make sense, Walter."

"I don't understand what you're saying, Ellen." He sipped his cappuccino and looked at her.

Ellen took a deep breath, presumably to tamp down her irritation. Good. Walter was glad that he got to her.

"The Miracle Ball doesn't fit with our mission. We don't make any real money from it, the charity doesn't make much, and frankly, I think it's weird."

Walter put down his mug and leaned over his desk. "What is that supposed to mean?"

"Reproduction and conception are supposed to be private matters. I think it's weird to throw ourselves a party and invite the press. It's very self-congratulatory."

"It's a celebration of the families we've created. I'm stunned that you find fault with that."

Ellen crossed her legs. She looked tan, as if she'd recently returned from a tropical isle. "There are others who share my concerns."

"Really? Who are these 'others'?"

"Other members of management."

"Well, they should bring me those concerns directly."

"You don't generally welcome dissent."

Walter threw his hands up. "I have an open-door policy, Ellen. You know that."

"I do." *But not an open-mind policy,* she thought.

"I know you want to put your stamp on the bank, and I appreciate your enthusiasm, but we won't be making any changes to the ball. Not this year." He picked up a pen and began to write.

"Not this year. Okay." Ellen stood and left his office.

After Fina left her brothers, some questions occurred to her that required immediate attention. She circled the streets near Renata's office and finally wedged her car into a too-tight space. Just like on her last visit, there was a small gaggle of men loitering by the front door. They were laughing and gabbing, but parted like the Red Sea when Fina approached.

The same stringy-haired young woman was manning the front desk. She held up an elaborately decorated talon to Fina as she wrapped up a call on her cell phone.

"Did you turn it off and then on again?" she asked, rolling her eyes at Fina. "Uh-huh. Uh-huh. Dad, I've gotta go. I'll stop by tonight and see if I can fix it."

Fina smiled. The younger generation used to help their parents in the fields; now their job was to troubleshoot their electronics for them.

"So it just came back on?" she said. "What did you press?" Fina could hear animated chatter on the other end. "Dad, I'll talk to you later. Bye."

She ended the call and looked at Fina. "Sorry about that. My father is lost without his *Ellen*. How can I help?"

"I'm here to see Renata." Fina handed over her ID.

"Let me see if she's available."

The young woman tapped the phone keys with nails painted with a chevron pattern of orange, black, and blue. Fina couldn't imagine getting daily tasks done with them, not to mention personal care. One wrong move doing her business and she'd look like a crime victim. Fina cringed at the thought.

After a brief conversation, the receptionist hung up the phone. "Renata says go right back."

"Thanks."

Fina wound her way through the hallway to Renata's office, where she was sitting behind the desk, writing something on a notepad.

"I have to leave in a few minutes for a meeting," Renata announced when Fina crossed the threshold.

"That's all right. This won't take long." Fina stood across from her desk.

Renata looked at her expectantly.

"Do you suffer from allergies?" Fina asked.

Renata raised an eyebrow. "I don't understand."

Leave it to Renata to make things more complicated than need be. "It's not a trick question. Do you suffer from allergies or asthma?"

"No."

"So Alexa doesn't get her allergies from you."

"No, that's one thing I can't be blamed for."

"Does Rosie have allergies or asthma?"

"No." She put down her pen. "Why all these questions?"

"When you chose your donors, did you get to see a medical history?"

"A very limited one. Nothing like they provide nowadays."

"So you wouldn't have known about those particular conditions at the time of conception?"

"No. What does this have to do with Hank?"

"That's what I'm figuring out."

Renata stood and began putting folders into her soft-sided briefcase. Fina waited as she grabbed her coat from a hook on the back of the door and followed her to the lobby.

"I'll be back in a couple of hours," she told the young receptionist.

Fina held the door open for her and listened as Renata conversed in rapid-fire Spanish with a couple of the men near the door. She laughed at their responses.

"See you, Renata. Thanks." Fina started down the sidewalk in the opposite direction.

"I want to know what you find out!" Renata called after her.

Why did everyone think she worked for them?

Fina met Cristian at a café close to the police station, where he was getting a coffee to go.

"You want anything?" he asked.

"Nah." French toast with a side of bacon appealed, but it was tough to eat on the go.

"You're calmer than I expected," Cristian said. A waitress handed him a cup, which he carried over to a side counter. He popped on a plastic cover. "You sounded stressed last night in your message."

"I was a little worked up, but I'm calmer now because I've taken action."

"Oh God."

"Nothing illegal."

"I'll take your word for it. So, what's up?"

"I got more pictures of Haley last night."

Cristian looked at her. He motioned to a table in the window that offered a little more privacy. "I guess our friend Denny Calder isn't behind it, then?"

"He's still locked up, right?"

"Yeah. He had a couple of outstanding warrants."

Fina brushed some sugar granules off the tabletop. "So either his employer is sending them to me or it's somebody else."

"And the action you alluded to?"

"I went ahead and hired protection for Haley. It seemed stupid not to take precautions."

"I would agree with that. Who'd you get?" He wiped the corner of his mouth with a napkin.

"Robin Dwyer. You know her?"

He shook his head. "The name's not familiar."

"She does a lot of high-level protection gigs. She's good, and discreet." Fina looked at him. "One of us needs to solve this case. Soon."

Cristian nodded. "I know."

"How's Cindy?" Fina asked.

The corner of Cristian's mouth twitched into a grin.

"What? You're being secretive all of a sudden?" she asked.

"No. She's good."

"Well, good."

"I wasn't sure how you'd feel about Cindy," he admitted.

"Why not?"

They got up from the table and walked out. On the sidewalk, a woman was gripped in the momentary paralysis leading up to a big sneeze, which she then released into the nook of her elbow.

"Gesundheit!" Fina offered.

"Thank you," the woman said, and walked through the door that Cristian held open.

"I thought you might have an issue with Cindy," he said, catching up to Fina, "because sometimes you and I have a thing."

Fina shrugged. "I feel fine about it."

But sitting in her car a few moments later, she had to wonder: Did she really feel fine about it?

Fina called Ellen Alberti and arranged to meet her for lunch at the CambridgeSide Galleria. She had some time to kill, so she called Patty to ask about the bodyguard situation and thank her for her patience. Raising someone else's kid—a challenging kid at that—was no small task, but Patty took Haley's addition to the family in stride. If you could judge a man by his choice of wife, then Scotty was a star.

Inside the food court, Fina found Ellen by the Middle Eastern counter. They ordered gyros and hummus, and Ellen insisted on sharing a small Greek salad. They carried their trays to a table and waited as a short elderly Asian woman wiped it off.

Ellen looked great, lightly tanned and bright-eyed. Her shift dress flattered her toned body, and a collection of bracelets showed off her delicate wrists.

"How are things at Heritage?" Fina asked.

"The usual, which I'm not pleased about."

"Sorry to hear that. Walter still reigning over his kingdom?"

"Yes, and I thought you were going to help with that situation." Ellen put some salad on her plate and nudged the rest toward Fina. Fina didn't take the hint.

"Well, if Walter is up to something illegal or unethical, I'm happy to help, but I can't get him booted just because he's impeding your professional development."

"He's doing something, believe me." Ellen unscrewed the cap on her mineral water.

"You didn't really give me much to go on."

"Is that why you wanted to meet?"

"Sort of. Tell me about the testing that the bank does on donors. Both now and when Hank Reardon donated."

A few drops of sauce from the gyro dribbled down Fina's arm, and she dabbed at it with a napkin. A gyro was one of those things in which the whole was better than the sum of its parts. Taken individually, the lamb, tomatoes, onions, and tzatziki were all okay, but together, they achieved a new level of deliciousness.

"Seriously? We do a lot of tests."

"Just give me some examples."

"HPV, herpes, HIV, chromosome testing, cystic fibrosis, CMV, spinal muscular atrophy. And then there are tests geared to specific donors based on their backgrounds."

"Like?" Fina dipped a triangle of pita into the hummus. She liked hummus, despite its nutritional benefits.

"Jewish donors are tested for a specific kind of anemia, Niemann-Pick Type A, Bloom syndrome, Tay-Sachs. African-Americans for sickle cell. That sort of thing."

"It sounds pretty thorough."

Ellen picked an olive pit out of her mouth and placed it on a napkin. "Trust me. There are a lot of tests."

Fina had a sip of her soda. "It's a wonder that anyone makes the cut."

"Less than five percent do."

"Really?"

Ellen grinned. "Don't look so surprised."

"It's just more rigorous than I thought," Fina said.

"I would deny ever saying this," Ellen said, leaning toward her, "but it's bad business if people take home a bum baby."

"You mean one who's sick or predisposed to a health problem down the road."

"Right. Nobody wants a sick baby, if they're being honest."

Fina took a bite of her gyro and chewed for a moment. "But you didn't always do these tests," she said after swallowing her mouthful.

"No. The technology didn't exist, plus they're expensive."

"What about things like allergies and asthma?"

"We don't test the donors for those, since they're not considered life-threatening or severely debilitating. The donors are supposed to report it if they suffer from either."

"But that's just self-reporting, right?"

"Sure, but if they aren't forthcoming, it's not disastrous."

"Kids can die from asthma and allergies," Fina noted.

Ellen put down her gyro. "Is this a friendly hypothetical conversation or have I misunderstood something?"

Fina held up her hand. "It's a completely friendly hypothetical conversation. I'm just trying to figure stuff out."

"Yes, people can die from asthma and allergies, but it's rare." Ellen shook her head. "You know what's really frustrating? When it comes to donor sperm, people have much higher standards than they do when it comes to procreating with a spouse."

"What do you mean?"

"My husband is a wonderful man, but heart disease runs in his family, he's an incredibly picky eater, and he's allergic to grass, for crying out loud. He might make it through the donor-screening process, but no one would pick him. Everybody wants the perfect donor."

"But you know that your husband is a wonderful man," Fina said. "You know that his assets outweigh all that other stuff. SMCs or anyone else weighing the options don't have as much to go on."

Ellen took a sip of water. "I suppose, but it just seems like people think they're owed a perfect baby to make up for the fact that they couldn't get one the old-fashioned way."

"I can understand that. They probably think that something should go their way."

Ellen nodded. She forked a slice of cucumber and popped it in her mouth.

"What kind of reports are generated from all the tests?" Fina asked.

"What do you mean?"

"How detailed are they? Who sees them?"

"They aren't *too* detailed—unless you have a scientific background, it doesn't take long for your eyes to glaze over reading that kind of data. Obviously, the donors see their results, and a medical profile and history are made available to prospective parents."

"Is the testing done in-house?"

"Some of it. Some of the samples are sent out to specialty labs."

"That sounds expensive."

"It is, and it's only going to get worse. Prospective parents clamor for every new diagnostic, but they don't want to pay for it."

Fina contemplated her half of the salad, then thought better of it. "How'd you end up in this field?"

"I stumbled into it after grad school, but it's been a good fit. It's a nice marriage of science and business, and who can argue with the end result? Who can resist a cute baby?"

"Not me, as long as I can give it back."

They dumped their trash in a barrel and headed to the exit. During the walk to the parking lot, Fina and Ellen chatted about nothing in particular and parted company when Ellen reached her car.

"I hope this helped," she said, unlocking her car with a beep.

"It did," Fina said. "The wheels are turning."

"Talk to you later." Ellen climbed into her expensive SUV, and Fina wandered back to her less-conspicuous vehicle.

Her head was starting to feel crammed with information, and she massaged her temples with her fingertips. She hadn't had a pain pill since first thing in the morning. She put one in her mouth and washed it down with a swig of warm water.

That would help. She'd been known to do some of her best thinking while medicated.

30

She was crawling through the clogged streets of East Cambridge when her phone rang. Fina answered using the hands-free option; she hated talking on speaker, but having both hands on the wheel was generally a good idea, especially in Boston.

"I cannot believe you!" Haley exclaimed.

"I know you're mad, and I'm sorry."

"Do you know how embarrassing it is going to school with a bodyguard?"

"Yes, actually, I do. We had them for a spell in middle school because Pap was hired by some goons."

"And you did it anyway, knowing how miserable it would be?"

"It seemed better than the alternative."

"My getting killed or kidnapped?" her niece asked.

"I don't think either is very likely, but why take the chance?"

"So I have this woman who looks like a Secret Service agent following me around all day. She acts like she's trying to be inconspicuous, but that's a joke."

"That is the idea—that she would follow you around and try to be inconspicuous."

Haley sighed. "For how long?"

"Hopefully, not long at all."

"You're being evasive."

"Thank you, counselor. Is there anything else I can do for you this fine day?"

Haley was quiet for a moment. "I'd feel better if I had some new clothes."

"You're such a little stinker."

"You owe me, Aunt Fina."

Fina was halfway through an intersection when the light turned red. She tried to ignore the bus driver who was gesticulating wildly at her, critiquing her driving. "I love you, so yes, I'll take you shopping, but not because you're owed anything."

"Good. I'm busy today, but maybe tomorrow?"

"Text me and we'll figure something out. And Haley? Don't try to pull a fast one with the bodyguard."

"I won't. Scout's honor."

Fina disconnected the call and pulled over into an illegal parking space. She needed to think for a moment before making her next call. An idea was taking shape in her head, but it was still vague. Sometimes, talking to someone on her list would jar her brain and knock something loose or into place. First, though, she wanted to give Haley an unexpected present.

Fina dialed Dennis's number. "I have a request," she said when he answered.

"What do you need?"

"I'd like to swap someone in for Robin on my niece's detail."

"Is there a problem?"

"Yes. Robin isn't a strong, handsome man. Do you have someone who looks like a movie star with a pro athlete's physique?" Fina asked. "The whole inconspicuous thing isn't working; let's go full-on conspicuous and enviable."

Dennis laughed. "Sounds like Milloy."

"He would be great, actually, but he has a job, and not enough professional distance from the subject."

"I'll make a swap."

"And tell Robin I'll use her some other time."

"Will do."

She pulled back into traffic and contemplated Haley's frustration. Unfortunately, there was nothing to be done about it. Fina drove by a neighborhood playground that had seen better days. The basketball nets were missing, and the intended green space was devoid of grass. The ground beneath the deserted monkey bars was crumbling concrete, not the fancy, spongy layer that cushioned kids in other zip codes. Even if the children who played here were relatively safe, they didn't have the toys and distractions that Haley and her peers usually took for granted. Maybe Haley needed to start thinking about her bodyguard as an unusual tax on her privileged lifestyle.

Everybody paid. Only the currency differed.

Juliana pulled a thick towel from the clean stack next to the shower and wrapped herself in it. Her muscles emitted a faint ache, but she welcomed the sensation, which proved that she'd pushed herself. That feeling of depletion was one of Juliana's favorites, something she strove for at the end of every swim, bike ride, and run.

She patted her skin dry with the towel and reached for a bottle of body lotion she'd picked up on her last trip to India. The formula included the Indian butter plant, and Juliana loved the feel of it on her skin. Maybe she could import it and make it available at the Reardon Center. She slathered it over her skin and hung her towel on the towel bar. She walked into her bedroom naked and glanced out the window overlooking the beach to make sure she didn't have an audience before cracking the window and letting the cool breeze fan over her.

When she was younger, Juliana had been in good shape, but not like she was now. Her muscles were smooth and solid, her stomach flat, and her ass firm and lifted. She felt a sense of pride in her body and reveled in its strength. Some people were naturally thin or naturally strong, but it was rare that a trim, sculpted physique was purely the result of genetics. Her body proclaimed that she was tough and disciplined. Juliana wasn't declining with age; she was just hitting her stride.

She pushed a button on the remote, and the TV sprang to life. Flicking through the channels, she settled on the local cable channel before walking into her closet and choosing an outfit. There was a subcommittee meeting later on at the center, but before that a lunch date with a potential donor. She wanted to look classy, but not too rich, which might prompt her donor to question why she needed his help.

Juliana plucked a navy blue sheath from its hanger and laid it across the bed. She was hooking her bra when the news anchor got her attention. Coming up after the break was a segment about a new charitable organization in the city with deep roots and big plans. The screen cut to a shot of two women in the "chat" area of the news set. The tease was brief, but Juliana took a seat on the end of the bed, her blood pressure creeping up. She waited through two and a half minutes of commercials for cleaning products and butter, her mind a choppy mess of conflicting thoughts.

The anchor returned to the screen and introduced her guests, a chirpy PR flack and Danielle Reardon, Hank Reardon's heartbroken widow, new mother, and philanthropist. Juliana curled her fists into balls as she watched her replacement unveil plans for a new home to support the families of patients who were forced to temporarily relocate to Boston for medical treatment. The Hank Reardon House—or Hank's House, as Danielle referred to it—was going to be built in the Longwood Medical Area and would be a homey environment that would provide not only support services but also living quarters free of charge for qualifying families.

The rational part of Juliana's brain knew it was a wonderful addition to the city, fulfilling a need that certainly existed.

But the other part of her brain?

It was furious.

.   .   .

Theresa McGovern had left a voice mail for Fina asking for a call back, so Fina left her a message, frustrated at the prospect of playing phone tag. She also sent pleading texts to Hal and Emma asking for something, anything, on Denny Calder. In the meantime, she decided to head to Harvard Square on the off chance that Marnie Frasier was available at work.

Marnie was high up in the student affairs office at a small university, her office tucked into a collection of colonial-style houses in Cambridge that were connected by additions built in recent decades. Fina parked in a visitor parking spot and walked into a yellow house where the ceilings were low and the scarred wooden floors creaked. An eager student sat behind a desk in the small front room. In contrast to Renata's receptionist, her hair was shiny and bouncy, and her nails were short and polished a pale pink.

"Can I help you?" she asked sweetly.

"I'm here to see Marnie Frasier. I'm afraid I don't have an appointment. My name's Fina Ludlow."

"One moment." She dialed the phone and had a brief conversation. "She's available."

Fina followed her through a succession of narrow hallways, but rather than feeling cramped, the space felt cozy. Marnie's office was on the first floor, with large windows overlooking the Cambridge Common. Wood was stacked in the unlit fireplace, and the floor was covered by an Oriental rug. Marnie sat behind a large desk, but directed Fina to a seating area next to the fireplace. The office was tidy but lived-in, with plants on various surfaces and framed prints showing Cambridge in the good old days.

"I'm sorry for dropping in unannounced," Fina said.

Marnie sat down in a club chair next to her and rotated her wrists. "No, it's good. I'm working on some budget stuff, and I could use the break." She plucked a piece of lint off her black pants.

"I'm interested in getting your nonscientific opinion on something."

"All of my opinions are nonscientific," Marnie said, smiling. "What's on your mind?"

"You've always been pretty involved with the SMC group, right?"

"That's right."

"Do you have any sense that the offspring have a lot of allergies or incidences of asthma?"

"Well, Jess has allergies, as you know, and Alexa has them." Marnie gazed out the window, thinking. "I know of a few others, but I don't think the occurrence is any more frequent than the general population. Why?"

Fina shook her head. "I'm not sure. Since you don't suffer from allergies, did you assume when she first developed them that Jess's donor did?"

"That's what her doctor thought." Her fingers played with a small button at the neck of her lilac cardigan sweater. "There isn't a definitive genetic link between parents and kids when it comes to allergies, but my understanding is that there is some predisposition if one of your parents suffers from them."

"But Rosie and Tyler don't."

"No, but that doesn't mean that Hank didn't."

"No, in fact, I know he had seasonal allergies. But that wasn't disclosed in the donor history, right?"

"No. Even nowadays I don't think they run allergy tests."

"When you selected your donor you got a medical history from the cryobank that included test results?"

"That's right."

Fina rubbed her temple. The discomfort from the attack had subsided, but she felt like something else was brewing in her brain.

"How did you know it was accurate?" she asked after a minute.

"What do you mean?" Marnie asked, looking puzzled. She brushed a stray hair from her face.

"The report and the history."

Marnie considered that for a moment. "I didn't. No more than you know the tests from your doctor's office are accurate. When you get your cholesterol tested, do you ask for a retest?"

"No, but that sounds like something my father would do. Send any unacceptable results back for reconsideration."

"I did have a friend who was a doctor review the report for me at the time. He thought everything looked straightforward."

Fina didn't say anything.

"Should I be worried about something?" Marnie asked.

"No. It's all good. It's all history, anyway."

"Okay." Marnie didn't sound convinced.

"Seriously." Fina stood and walked to the door. "I bet this office is really cozy in the winter."

"It is. I build a fire. Have some cocoa. Watch the snow fall on the Common."

"It must make winter more palatable."

"It does." Marnie took a seat behind her desk. "You'll let me know if you learn something relevant?"

"Of course. Thanks for seeing me."

Outside, Fina walked over the uneven brick sidewalk back to her car.

She felt like a kid the week before Christmas, full of excitement and energy without a clear sense of what was really coming.

Fina had missed the appointed dinner hour at Frank and Peg's, but she had no trouble pulling together her version of dinner in their kitchen.

"I don't think Peg would approve," Frank commented. He was sitting in his chair in the living room, the local cable news station on in the background.

Fina dipped a spoon into a bowl of Brigham's chocolate chip ice cream, which she'd smothered in hot fudge sauce and whipped cream from a can.

"Well, *I'm* not going to tell her. Are you?" she asked. Peg volunteered a few nights a month at a low-income health clinic a couple of towns over, which explained her absence.

"I don't like having to hear about your escapades from a third party," Frank said, looking at her head.

"I knew you wouldn't be pleased. I was trying to avoid your disapproval."

"That's a very mature approach."

"Who told you about it, anyway?" She ate a spoonful.

"Scotty. He called me to ask about an old case."

Fina sighed. "Well, Frank, I don't know what to tell you."

They turned their attention to the news and a story about a drunk driver who killed two people while driving the wrong way on the highway. The driver had walked away without a scratch.

"Why do the drunks always survive?" Fina wondered.

"I've heard it's because they're relaxed. They don't tense up before the moment of impact, but don't quote me on that."

They watched stories about a fire in an ice-cream parlor, and then one about a local boy trying to break the Guinness World Record for the largest ball of plastic wrap, and then Danielle Reardon's face popped up on the screen.

"Can you turn it up a notch?" Fina asked.

"Is that the widow?" Frank asked.

"Yup." The story described Hank's tragic death and the charity that he and Danielle had been working to establish for almost a year. According to Danielle, it would now serve as a tribute to Hank's commitment to the community, aptly called Hank's House. Danielle didn't seem completely at ease during the segment, but she did a good job of pitching the cause and certainly appeared sympathetic.

Fina finished her ice cream, brought the bowl out to the kitchen, and stacked it in the dishwasher. Back in the living room, she perused the family photos proudly displayed on the wall. There were photos of

Frank and Peg and their two sons in a variety of settings, as well as snaps with members of the extended Gillis family.

"Have I seen this one before?" Fina asked Frank, pointing at an eight-by-ten photo of a new baby nestled on a blanket. He—she guessed it was a he—looked like a tiny old man: wizened skin, sparse hair, grumpy expression.

"That's our niece's new baby, Oliver."

"He looks adorable but angry."

"He's two weeks old. He has a lot on his mind."

"Apparently."

Fina stayed through the end of the newscast and gave Peg a quick hug when they passed at the front door, taking a rain check on a longer visit.

Fina needed to go home, stare out the window, and think.

Back at Nanny's, she checked her messages and e-mail before going to bed. Theresa McGovern had left another message, which Fina returned, but the game of phone tag continued. A quick scroll through her e-mail didn't produce much of interest until she got to one from Greta Samuels. She wanted Fina to pass it on to Risa, and it rivaled *War and Peace* in its length and drama. By the end she was skimming it, irked by Greta's bid for kinship and a close familial relationship. Wasn't this exactly what she'd told her not to do? Did the woman ever listen?

Fina pulled up a map program and entered Greta's address. It estimated a one-hour-and-seven-minute drive to Rockford, Maine. If it were another client, Fina would be willing to let things play out, but Risa wasn't just any client. She was a friend, and there was something fishy about Greta Samuels even if her DNA matched.

31

Fina slept most of the weekend and climbed into her car on Monday morning with renewed energy. After grabbing a hot chocolate and chocolate croissant from the café around the corner, she set off at seven. She had forgotten how great it felt to get in the car and just drive. Confident that Haley was being looked after, Fina could relax and watch the scenery go by. She had the radio turned low and let her thoughts drift from one place to the next. This was often how cases got solved, by allowing her subconscious to take over. People didn't generally think of detectives—private or police—as being creative thinkers, but they were and had to be. Wearing a rut in the same thought processes and being unwilling to let your mind roam free were guaranteed to get you nowhere fast in an investigation.

The town of Rockford, Maine, wasn't especially memorable. There was a small town center that consisted of a gas station, a mom-and-pop grocery store, a volunteer fire station, and a smattering of small businesses in renovated houses. The streets didn't have sidewalks, just pavement that crumbled into gravel and dirt and overgrown bushes. Fina crossed a small river where two men dangled fishing rods into the water. The people out weren't in any hurry; Rockford seemed to run on its own time, and Fina wondered how the residents spent that time. She got a clue as she drove farther out from the center and spotted large satellite dishes on the smattering of houses. A mile out, the houses sparsely dotted the landscape and the driveways were longer. Most of them were small, with piles of stacked wood in yards sheltered by towering trees.

After a couple of wrong turns, Fina drove up to 37 Beech Creek Drive and turned off the engine. It was eight thirty, and there were no signs of life. The house was painted a light minty green with white shutters and front porch. It was two stories, but the upper story was topped with a slanted roof and no dormers; it looked more like an attic with windows than inhabitable space. The front grass was yellowing, and tall pine trees lined the property. Uneven pavers created a path to the porch, and upon closer inspection, Fina could see that the white paint on the shutters and porch was flaking and peeling. The house didn't look run-down, but it could use a little TLC.

Fina rang the doorbell and tried to peek through the glass panel in the door, which was covered with a lacy curtain. She could see movement and shadows and was about to ring the bell again when the door was pulled open. A woman looked at her blankly. She was short, and not overweight, but bloated-looking. Her hair was gray and reminded Fina of Nanny's hair, which she had set once a week at the hair salon. She was wearing pants and a shirt with a flowered pattern, topped with a gray cardigan. Her most striking feature was the slightly yellow tinge of her dry skin. Fina studied her with a growing sense of unease.

"Yes?" the woman asked.

"Greta?"

The woman looked behind Fina as if looking for some kind of backup.

"Yes. Didn't you see the sign?" She pointed at a NO SOLICITORS sign hanging in a window near the door.

"I'm not selling anything."

"This isn't a good time. I'm on my way out," Greta said, and stepped back into the house.

"I'm Fina Ludlow. Risa's friend."

Greta's mouth formed a silent O, and she stared at her shoes. She started to close the door on Fina.

What the hell was going on?

Juliana stared at the racks of designer clothes in her closet. She always took care with her appearance, but today felt different. One of the lessons she'd gleaned from her triathlon training was the importance of focus and stamina. It wasn't always the fastest athlete who won the race but the one who wouldn't give up, who moved through the pain— embraced it, even—to triumph on the other side. She was adopting this approach in her training, and it occurred to her that she needed to do the same in her life.

Danielle was making a play, but Juliana had time on her side. Her long marriage to Hank and her charitable activities would stand the test of time, whereas Danielle would soon be written off as a footnote, the young wife Hank would have divorced eventually. She'd remarry, find some other old sap to use, and in a few years, she might not even be Danielle Reardon anymore.

Juliana could wait. She could persevere. She had to keep her head down and focus on the work, which was why she was moving forward with the center's expansion plans. Jules had hinted that the money was there, and if it wasn't, Juliana would find it somewhere else.

She chose a fitted black dress, high heels, a butter-soft leather jacket, and a voluminous designer purse. Examining herself in the mirror, Juliana was pleased. She looked strong and powerful, like a woman with a plan. Her vision would come to fruition. There was no other possible outcome.

"Greta!" Fina pressed her palm against the door. "What is going on?"

"I told you, Fina. I'm on my way out. It's not a good time."

"Uh-uh. I drove up here to talk to you, and I'm not leaving until I do."

Greta's shoulders slumped, and she released the door. She walked slowly through the modest house to a kitchen at the back. The floor was covered in yellow speckled linoleum, and the white wooden cabinets had forged-iron knobs and pulls. The appliances were dated, and even the microwave looked like it hailed from the 1980s. Beneath the wall-mounted mustard yellow phone, a calendar was held up by a thumb-tack. It advertised a local insurance company and featured a photo of a covered bridge surrounded by glorious foliage. The front of the refrigerator was bare except for a schedule from the local Methodist church and a flyer announcing lawn and leaf services.

"I really am on my way out," Greta said, lowering herself onto a plastic cushioned chair at the small dinette table. "I expect my ride any minute."

Fina looked at Greta's hands, folded on the table. They were dry and jaundiced-looking. Greta pulled her sweater tight around her middle.

"You're sick," Fina said, standing over her.

Greta was silent.

"Are you dying? Is that why you got in touch with Risa?"

"Would you sit down?" Greta asked. "You're making me nervous."

"You're nervous because you're hiding something, but sure, I'll sit." Fina pulled out the chair next to her and sat. Greta kneaded her puffy hands as if they were two balls of dough. "If you're dying, why the reluctance to meet Risa?" Fina asked.

Greta glanced at the clock on the wall. It was a black cat with eyes that moved side to side with each second. She took a deep breath. "It's complicated."

"It always is," Fina said, sighing. "Why don't you just tell me so you can get on with your busy day?"

Greta avoided her gaze. "I have kidney disease. I can't talk now because I'm going to dialysis."

Fina looked at her and, for a moment, was speechless. She got up from the chair and paced the small space.

"So you've been using me as an organ trafficker."

Greta began to sputter. "I . . . I . . ."

"You need a kidney, and the fastest and best way to get one is from a relative. That letter was your attempt to gain favor before the big ask."

"That's not the only reason I contacted my niece."

"Really? What's the other reason? Your strong sense of family?"

"I've always wanted to know her."

"Right." Fina strode to the front door with Greta in slow pursuit.

"You have to understand. I'm desperate. Risa could function on one good kidney; both of mine are worthless."

Fina opened the front door just as a late-model Chevy sedan pulled up out front. The large older woman behind the wheel tooted her horn and waved at Greta.

"Looks like your ride is here," Fina said, trotting down the front steps.

"I'm begging you, Fina. Please don't punish me for being sick."

Fina turned to look at Greta. "What if she doesn't want to give you her kidney? Is she still family then?"

"Yes, yes. I want to know my niece, no matter what." Greta slowly descended the stairs while her companion in the car looked on with concern. "What are you going to tell her?"

Fina unlocked her door and considered the question. "Honestly? I have no idea."

She spent the first twenty minutes of the drive fuming and ruing the day she'd agreed to take Risa's case. Of course, hindsight was twenty-twenty—she had no reason *not* to take the case at the time, and better her than a stranger—but that didn't temper her regret.

What was she going to tell Risa? That her aunt was thrilled to meet her, and oh, by the way, how about handing over a kidney? She dreaded that conversation, but she couldn't not tell her. And what if Risa really was Greta's best chance for survival? Was she obligated to help her because they were related?

Fina used one of her bandaged hands to rummage through her purse. She was hoping for a prescription pain pill, but an over-the-counter pill was her only option. That was probably a good thing. She'd seen enough people who grew too fond of prescription drugs legitimately prescribed in the first place. She didn't have time to be an addict, not to mention that it wreaked havoc on your looks.

She swallowed the pill with some musty-tasting water from a half-empty bottle and tried to put Greta out of her head, a battle she fought unsuccessfully until her phone rang.

"What?" she said, her patience and nerves shot.

"Well, that's not very friendly. It's Theresa McGovern."

"Sorry. Someone else is irritating me, not you."

"Please. I work for CEOs. I never take anything personally."

"What's going on?" Fina asked. She could hear someone talking in the background.

"So, I came across a name that might be of interest to you."

"Who?"

"Dr. Janet Pally."

"And she is?" When had Fina's every conversation turned into a guessing game?

"A pulmonologist. Apparently, Hank had a number of phone calls with her around the same time he was calling Juliana, his college roommate, and Jules Lindsley."

"How'd you find this out?"

"I looked at the phone bill for his cell and saw a bunch of calls to the same number not logged on his call sheet, so I called and got Dr. Pally's office." There was a noise in the background.

"That's fantastic. Have you ever thought about becoming a PI?"

"One sec," Theresa said. Fina could hear muffled conversation and a man's voice before Theresa came back on the line. "Don't you get beaten up a lot? No, thanks."

"Not all investigative work is done in the field. You'd be safe behind a desk."

"As far as I'm concerned, Universum better be my last desk job."

"So you can DJ full-time?"

"You got it. Speaking of which, how's that other gig coming along?"

Fina tapped her fingertips on the steering wheel while she thought. "Do you do private gigs? Parties and stuff?"

"Sure, but bar mitzvahs and sweet sixteens aren't really my style."

"Nor mine. I was thinking more adult parties or charity events."

"Maybe."

"All right. I'll give it some thought. Thanks, Theresa."

"Sure. Oh, and Dante says hi!" Theresa said, giggling with the man in the background.

Fina shook her head and disconnected the call.

Kids today.

Fina drove to Ludlow and Associates and waited outside Scotty's office until he was available.

"Very nice move with the bodyguard," he said when she took a seat across from him. "I think Patty might claim *she's* in danger."

She smiled. "He's that hot? I'm glad to hear it."

"I don't have a lot of time, but I can talk while I eat. Do you want something?" He moved over to the conference table.

"What are you having?" She grabbed two diet sodas from the wet bar, gave one to him, and took a seat.

"Veggie stir-fry with tofu and brown rice."

Fina frowned. "Really?"

"Really. It's delicious. Trust me."

"Fine."

"Michelle!" Scotty hollered toward the outer office. "Can you bring enough for Fina?"

"And Matthew," Fina added.

"Got it," Michelle answered.

"I didn't realize he was joining us," Scotty said.

"Well, two legal minds are better than one, right?"

"Sure."

A minute later, Matthew breezed into the room carrying a bottle of iced tea and a tablet computer. The siblings exchanged pleasantries, and then Fina stood up and walked over to a wall-mounted whiteboard. She uncapped a dry-erase marker and started writing.

"I'm going to put some words up, and I want you guys to do some free association. Okay?"

"Whatever comes to mind?" Matthew asked.

"Whatever comes to mind."

Fina made a list: *reproduction, genetics, serious, pulmonologist, specialist, sperm donation, crisis, physical, insurance, tests.*

She put the cap back on the pen and stepped back from the board. Her brothers studied the list in silence. Michelle came into the room bearing a tray with three beautifully arranged plates of food. She unloaded them along with napkins, chopsticks, and utensils and floated back out of the room like an adult-sized Tinker Bell with treats.

"You want something that relates to all those categories?" Scotty asked.

"I just want to know what pops into your heads."

The brothers looked at each other as Fina took her seat.

"Well, there's the obvious," Scotty said, digging into his lunch. Matthew nodded.

Fina glanced between the two. "Which is?"

"CF," Matthew said between chews.

"Exactly," Scotty said, shaking extra soy sauce onto his stir-fry.

"Wait. Cystic fibrosis?"

"We have taught you something," Scotty said.

Fina sat back in her seat and looked at the board. "How'd you come up with that?"

Matthew pointed at the board with a chopstick. "It's a serious genetic disease that requires a lot of specialist care, mostly from pulmonologists. Parents can be tested for the gene, and fetuses can be tested for the disease. They also test newborns now. People know within the first day of birth if a child has it."

"So you've had cases that dealt with CF?" she asked.

"Yup. Although I imagine they're going to become less frequent given all the testing options nowadays."

Fina picked up a fork and took a bite of stir-fry. "What flavor am I supposed to be getting?"

"Soy and veggies. You know, the flavor of fresh produce," Scotty said.

"That's what I thought." She put down her fork. "I need to go."

"You just got here," Matthew said.

"I know, but you guys have given me a huge lead. I've got to get on it."

"Hold up," Scotty said.

"What?" Fina asked, pushing back her chair and grabbing her bag.

Matthew and Scotty exchanged a look.

"I know that look, and I don't like it."

"I spoke to Dad and Rand, but I don't think it made a difference," Scotty said, and took a swallow of soda.

Fina dropped her bag onto the chair. "Meaning?"

"Meaning we can't stop him from coming back," Scotty said.

Fina started to protest.

"Seriously, Fina, what do you want us to do?"

"Something. I want you guys to do something."

"You can't make him or anyone else behave a certain way," Matthew said, stabbing a piece of tofu with his chopstick.

"Since when? You two spend every waking moment getting people to do what you want."

Her brothers were silent.

Fina threw her bag over her shoulder. "Fine. Thanks for the heads-up."

"I don't get what you want us to do," Scotty said.

"I don't want you to do anything."

"Don't leave pissed," Matthew implored.

"Don't worry. I'll get over it. We get over everything, don't we? Act like it never even happened? Isn't that the Ludlow way?"

Fina hurried out of the room, not trusting herself to remain in their presence and behave. She took a detour by the vending machines on her way out and deposited enough change for some peanut butter cups and a package of M&M's.

Today was not the day to revamp her eating habits.

Fina made a quick call to Renata with a request and then drove over to the Sanchez home in Somerville. When she knocked on the front door, Rosie opened it and handed a thick file folder to Fina.

"Is that what you want?" Rosie asked.

Fina flipped through it. "Perfect. How are you doing, Rosie?"

"I'm okay. Do you want to come in?"

"Another time," Fina said, trotting down the stairs. "I need to take care of something."

"You go, Magnum, P.I.," Rosie called after her.

Fina shook the file in the air in response and returned to her car.

She needed both hands to extricate her car from its parking space, but once she was back on Mass Ave, she punched in the number for Heritage Cryobank on her phone. She was pleased to hear that Walter Stiles was out of the office and was transferred to Ellen Alberti's line.

"I'm in the middle of something, Fina," Ellen said, sounding mildly irked.

"Consider it a brief session of career counseling. How to climb the ladder."

There was a pause on the other end of the line. "How soon can you get here?"

"Fifteen minutes."

Fina sped to Cambridge with her window rolled down, the crisp breeze against her face. She loved this feeling—the moment when solving a case seemed not only possible but inevitable.

32

"Tell me about cystic fibrosis," Fina said to Ellen.

Ellen looked at her. "You didn't really come here to ask me something you could find out online, did you?"

"No, but let's start there."

Half a turkey sandwich sat unwrapped on Ellen's desk next to a plastic bag of baby carrots. She took a bite of carrot and chewed thoughtfully. "It's a genetic disease caused by a mutation. The most serious symptoms are related to the lungs; patients have to contend with a thick mucus that they have trouble clearing, which makes them prone to infections. This is just an overview," Ellen cautioned.

"That's all I want."

"It's chronic and difficult to manage, although the life expectancy of patients has increased drastically in recent decades. People used to die from it as children, but now they can live into their thirties with a good quality of life."

"Is it passed through the mother or father?" Fina asked.

"Both. It's a recessive gene, and the child needs to inherit a copy of the defective gene from both parents to develop the disease."

"But you test for this?"

"Absolutely." Ellen picked up her sandwich and took a bite.

"When did you start testing for it?"

"I think the first test was developed in 1989, 1990, but let me check." She turned to her computer and started typing. "Looks like we started using it in 1992."

"On newly donated sperm or all of the sperm?"

"All of it."

"So sperm used to conceive a child in 1994 would have been subject to CF testing?"

"Yes. Where are you going with this?"

Fina reached into her bag and pulled out Renata's file. She scanned it until she found the pages detailing donor medical history and testing. "Show me where the CF test is." She handed the pages to Ellen.

She studied the page and pointed to a line. "Right here. It was negative."

"You said yesterday that this report is a condensed version of the testing that's performed. Does Heritage keep all of the documentation in its files?"

"Yes, we keep all the documentation."

"What kind of documentation are we talking about?"

"Notes from the doctor, receipts from lab tests that are done off-site. Keep in mind, files that are twenty years old are still in hard copy, not on the computer."

"Can we take a look at Renata Sanchez's complete file?"

Ellen wrinkled her nose. "I'm not supposed to show you a patient's file."

"What if she gives her permission?"

Ellen bit off a piece of carrot. "I'd need it in writing."

"I'll have it faxed over by the time you find the file," Fina said, pulling out her phone.

Ellen got up from her desk. Fina started dialing as she left the room.

"I don't understand why you need this, Fina. Didn't you just pick up the rest of the file from the house?" Renata asked after Fina had made her request.

"Oh my God, Renata! Just do it!" Fina exclaimed.

"You don't need to be short with me," she said.

"Apparently, I do! Please just fax over a release right away." Fina gave her the number, and two minutes later, Ellen's fax machine started purring. Fina retrieved the hastily penned release from the tray and placed it in the middle of Ellen's desk, happy she had made good on her promise.

After five minutes, she began to wonder what had become of Ellen. Ten minutes went by, and Fina stuck her head out of the office and looked down the hallway. She was about to find the receptionist when Ellen came back into the room with an odd look on her face. She picked up the release and studied it, then sat back in her chair.

"I can't find the file," she said. Frown lines had emerged on her forehead.

"Could it have been misfiled? Lost someplace?"

"Sure, but we had an intern here over the summer, and she did an amazing job organizing the files."

Fina thought for a moment, the wheels turning. "Can you look for another? I don't need to look in the file itself. I just want to know if you have it."

Ellen looked puzzled, but got up once more. "What's the name?"

"Marnie Frasier."

Ten minutes later, she was back, empty-handed.

Fina called Renata and asked for the names of women from the SMC group who had used Heritage sperm around the same time as she and Marnie. She handed Ellen a list of eight names, and Ellen returned to the file room.

Ten minutes later, she was back.

"I can't find any of those files, Fina," Ellen reported.

Fina looked at her and then out the window, contemplating. "How big were the boxes you saw Walter putting in his car?"

"They were standard banker's boxes. But why would he take those particular files?"

"Do me a favor, don't tell anyone about this. Not yet."

There was a glint of excitement in Ellen's eyes. "Tell me what you're thinking."

"I'm not sure yet. Promise me you'll keep a lid on our file search?"

"Yes. I promise."

Fina took back Renata's file and slipped it into her bag.

"But don't keep me waiting too long," Ellen said. "The anticipation might kill me."

Fina grinned and left the office.

She knew she should go see Risa, but Fina couldn't muster the courage for that conversation, not yet. Instead, she decided to head home to recharge and regroup.

Her hands had healed enough that a shower wasn't a completely masochistic exercise. The energy she got from being clean outweighed the discomfort. She put on some jeans and a V-neck sweater and pulled her hair into a bun. Her reflection in the mirror was thoroughly unsatisfactory; the area between her eye and her temple was a slice of the spectrum from purple to yellow, although most of the swelling had gone down. Time might heal all wounds, but it never worked fast enough for her taste.

Fina called down to the concierge, hoping there was a package from Emma or Hal. Nothing had been delivered, so she put calls in to both of them, and they promised her updates on Denny Calder and anything new on Brett Linder by the end of the day. Great. More waiting.

Some people cleaned when they had time to kill, but Fina didn't see the point. Everything just got dirty again. There was a service that came in every couple of weeks to keep the place from degrading into frat house conditions, but she never felt the need to supplement their work. Instead, she sat down at her computer and got her paperwork up to date. There were receipts to scan and file, time sheets to update, and invoices to generate. Any small business owner or independent contractor knew that if you didn't stay on top of your paperwork, it would come back to bite you.

Plus, the rote tasks freed up her mind to wander, which never hurt a case. Fina was fairly certain what Walter Stiles had been up to, but she wasn't sure that it was motive for murder. She needed a little more information before reaching a conclusion.

She was searching through her bag, looking for a receipt, when there was a knock on the door. Still wary after her beat-down, Fina grabbed her gun and padded over to the door. She looked through the peephole and gripped her gun tighter when she saw who was on the other side.

"I know you're in there, so you may as well let me in so we can get this over with."

Fina unlocked the dead bolt and opened the door, gun in hand.

"You're going to shoot me?" Rand asked.

Fina shrugged. "You said we should get this over with."

Her oldest brother was handsome like all of the Ludlow men, but he didn't have Scotty or Matthew's warmth. Standing five feet eleven with thick, wavy hair, he had full lips, like the other Ludlows, but didn't smile often.

Rand walked into the room and looked around as if he owned the place. He examined the pictures on the wall and ambled over to the windows overlooking the harbor. Fina stayed close to the door.

"What do you want, Rand?" Her pulse had quickened and her stomach flip-flopped.

"Why don't you redecorate the place? It looks the same as when Nanny was alive." He was wearing a light gray suit and a dress shirt, but no tie. He was tan, his dark skin contrasting with his straight white teeth.

"What do you want, Rand?"

"I want to come back. I want my life back. Miami has been fun, but

I'm getting a little tired of the sun. I miss the seasons. I love New England in the fall."

"You're lucky you're not in prison."

He glared at her. "I was never going to prison."

"Well, you need to go back to Miami."

Rand chuckled. "No, I don't think so. I talked to Dad, and he wants me back in the firm up here. I'm being wasted on our clients down south."

"You don't like the satellite Ludlow and Associates that Dad created for you?"

"I want to be here."

"I don't care what you want. I don't want you anywhere near Haley—or any child, for that matter, but right now I can only take care of Haley."

Rand walked over to her. He stood so close, she could feel his breath on her face. "Looks like you got in another fight."

For an instant, she thought she might actually throw up on him, so intense were her feelings of anger, disgust, even fear. She took a deep breath and leaned closer to him.

"Go back to the beach."

He stepped around her and reached for the doorknob. "I don't know what trick you have up your sleeve, but it's not going to work." He opened the door and was gone before she could respond.

Fina dead-bolted the door, walked to the couch, and dropped down onto the cushions. She wiped at the sheen of sweat that had broken out along her hairline, and after a moment, she placed the gun on the coffee table.

Now all she needed to do was conjure up a trick.

Fina pushed Rand to the back of her mind, to the compartment labeled *Nasty, Immoral Criminals,* and pored over the materials from Emma and Hal, which arrived shortly after Rand's departure. She could only hope that the information might yield a lead, and after almost two hours of reading, her efforts were rewarded.

"Can you meet me somewhere?" she asked Cristian over the phone.

"I'm in the middle of something."

"It's important, and it won't take long."

"Is Haley okay?" There was giggling in the background.

"Yes, she's fine. This is about Denny Calder."

"Why don't you give Pitney a call? I think she's at the office."

Fina held the phone away from her face and took a moment to try to swallow her annoyance. It didn't work.

"I don't want to talk to Pitney," she said loudly into the phone. "I want to talk to you. Since when has a woman gotten in the way of your job? You never let Marissa do that."

There was a bumping noise on the other end and a pause before Cristian came back on the line. "Calm down."

"I'm calm, but I have a lead on the guy who attacked me, and I'd appreciate a little more interest on your part."

"I know this is an adjustment for you, as much as you deny it."

"What? You're changing the subject."

"I know you like having my full attention, but maybe things are changing."

"I can't have this conversation with you right now," Fina said.

"Fine. Tell me about the lead. Either that or we can meet up later."

Fina exhaled loudly and rested her head against the back of the couch. "I can't meet up later. Denny Calder's sister-in-law used to work for MetroWest Janitorial Services."

"And?"

"And up until eighteen months ago, MetroWest held the contract with Heritage Cryobank."

Cristian was quiet for a moment. "How'd you get this?"

"I just did a really deep background on Denny and his nearest and dearest."

"You know we don't have the resources. Not on an assault case."

"I know, I know, but now that you know, could you look into it? Maybe do something about it?"

"Yes, of course."

"Thank you."

"What are you going to do in the meantime?" Cristian asked.

"Nothing you need to worry about," she said. "Go back to enjoying your afternoon delight."

He snorted. "Bye."

"Bye."

Fina disconnected the call. What was her problem? Did she want Cristian for herself? Or maybe she just didn't want anyone else to have him. Christ, she was turning into a Lifetime movie.

She stowed the files from Emma and Hal in her bag, grabbed her shoes, and rummaged in the kitchen for a snack. A cold soda paired with a couple of Nutter Butters would hit the spot.

Her to-do list seemed to be packed with possible confrontations, and she wasn't looking forward to crossing them off her list.

Fina was tired of driving, but she didn't have a choice. Things were unraveling—or falling into place, depending upon your point of view—and she couldn't afford to take a break.

It was around dinnertime when she got to Juliana's house in Swamp-scott. Fina rang the bell and rocked from one foot to the other while waiting.

"I'm surprised to see you," Juliana said, leaning on the door. She was dressed down in jeans and a fitted T-shirt. Her bare feet showed off her pedicure.

"Can I come in? I'll be brief."

Juliana shrugged. "Sure."

Fina followed her to the kitchen, where some vegetables sat on the counter, a peeled cucumber on a cutting board. Juliana picked up a large glass of white wine and took a sip. She didn't offer Fina a glass.

"I assume you've heard Danielle's announcement," Fina said.

"Haven't we all?" Juliana chopped the cucumber quickly and efficiently into thin rounds.

"You don't want her to be a philanthropist? It will be great for the city."

Juliana used her knife to guide the cucumber pieces into a bowl. She picked up a red pepper and ran it under the faucet. "I would like her to show a little respect. That's what I would like."

"To whom?"

"To me, and to the other women who have been running the charities in this city for years."

"Why does that matter?"

The knife made a crunching noise as it dug in around the stem of the pepper. "I don't know," Juliana said softly.

Fina watched her work for a moment.

"I know that Hank was calling you to tell you about his insurance physical and the genetic tests that were done," Fina said.

Juliana stopped midchop.

"I'm not sure why he'd be talking to you instead of his current wife, but I think he got some alarming news and was confiding in you." Fina tapped her fingernails on the countertop. "How am I doing?"

Juliana put down the knife and took a long pull from her wine. "I don't know as much as you think I do."

"Tell me what you do know. He had the routine physical and what?"

"He got back test results and he thought they were wrong, so he had the tests run again."

"And got the same results?" Fina asked.

"Yes."

"What tests?"

"He didn't tell me."

"C'mon, Juliana."

"I swear. He did not give me the details. He was upset, though, and had scheduled appointments with some specialists. And he was extremely angry."

"Why angry?"

"I don't know, but my sense was that heads were going to roll."

"Why would he tell you some things and be so evasive about others?"

"I don't know, and who says I wanted the details?" She shrugged.

"But why listen at all?"

"Because you can't be married for twenty-four years, share a child, and then just detach from each other. We were entangled. We always will be."

"And you probably didn't mind that he was confiding in you instead of Danielle."

A smile emerged at the corners of Juliana's mouth. "I can't lie. It was satisfying to think about the smug look on her face and knowing that he was telling me his troubles on the side."

"Right. Well, thanks for the information." Fina walked to the front door. "Good night, Juliana."

Fina walked to her car and inhaled deeply, drawing the salty tang of the air into her lungs. She liked the taste of the ocean on the breeze, and she needed it; this case was leaving a bad taste in her mouth.

Fina pulled up to Risa's house an hour later and turned off the engine. She'd had a lot of weird conversations in her life, but this promised to be one of the strangest. And the saddest. Nobody liked to think that their spare parts were their best assets.

Risa opened the door wearing what looked like cashmere loungewear topped with a long cashmere sweater with a drape collar. She looked surprised. "Hey, Fina. Is everything okay? It's kind of late."

"Yeah, but I wanted to talk to you if you can spare a few minutes."

"Sure. I was just losing brain cells in front of the TV."

They walked into the family room attached to the kitchen, and Risa steered her toward one of the couches. The TV was turned to a real estate reality show. "Marty's not around?" Fina asked.

"No. He's in New York on business."

Fina *really* didn't want to have this conversation without Marty around to pick up the pieces, but it was a little late to change course.

"Do you want a drink or a snack?" Risa asked.

"No, thanks."

"Okay, now I know something is wrong." Risa sat down next to her on the couch.

Fina smiled and turned to face Risa. "I went to see Greta Samuels yesterday."

"In Maine?"

"Yes. I took a little road trip because something was bugging me about the situation."

"Are you telling me we're not related?" Risa's forehead wrinkled with concern.

"No, no, you're related, but her motives aren't as pure as we'd hoped."

"She wants money," Risa said, her shoulders drooping.

"Actually . . ." Fina winced. "She wants your kidney." She braced herself as if expecting a blow.

Risa's eyes widened. "I'm sorry, what?"

"Greta has kidney disease, and she needs a kidney."

Risa opened her mouth to speak, then closed it. She opened it again, but nothing came out.

"That was my reaction," Fina said. She reached over and squeezed Risa's hand. "I feel terrible about this."

"Why would *you* feel terrible? Do you want my liver?"

"No, but I feel like an organ broker. I never would have pursued this had I known her endgame."

Risa sat back against the couch cushions. "I can't even wrap my head around this."

"To be fair, she claims that she wants to have a relationship with you regardless of the kidney situation."

"Do you believe her?"

"I don't know what to believe. She may want both: a relationship and a kidney."

"How sick is she?"

"She's on dialysis. She looks crummy, but from what I understand, dialysis can keep her alive for a while."

"Dialysis is supposed to be miserable," Risa said, looking into space.

"Maybe, but that's not your problem."

"But I could possibly save her life."

"Possibly, or you might not even be a match. Or you might decide that you want to keep your spare kidney for yourself."

"Or for my kids. What if one of my kids needs a kidney someday and I've already given mine away?"

"That's a valid consideration."

Risa pulled her sweater tight around her middle and was silent.

"I think you need time to digest this," Fina said. "You don't have to make any decisions right away."

Risa nodded. "This is surreal."

"You have to do whatever works for you and your family."

Risa looked at her with a wry smile. "Which family?"

"This family," Fina said, looking around the room. "The family you've built with Marty."

"But she's my blood relative, too."

Fina waved her hand in the air. "I'm finding that argument less compelling these days." She stood. "Whatever I can do, just let me know."

Risa walked her to the door and gave her a big hug. "Thanks, Fina."

"I'm not sure why you're thanking me."

"You're a cool head when I need one. I appreciate your support."

"Of course. Keep in touch."

Fina returned to her car but didn't feel relieved.

It was a sad state of affairs when the easiest thing on your to-do list was a conversation about organ donation.

. . .

Was it wrong to break in to her parents' house? Was it even breaking in? She was related to the owners, after all, generally welcome there if she was willing to pay the entrance fee of unrelenting criticism from Elaine. Fina could have walked in like it was a regular visit and tried to run her covert op right under her father's nose, but Carl was suspicious. He wouldn't believe she was just coming by to say hello.

Fina sat out in her car for a couple of hours, leeching off the neighbors' Wi-Fi, waiting for her parents to turn in for the night. She didn't even need them to be asleep; once they were ensconced in the master suite upstairs, there was no need to venture down to the first floor. They had a wet bar in their sitting room along with a giant TV. Elaine would probably get in bed and read a trashy book, and Carl would stay up watching a game, too distracted to pay much attention to anything else.

Honestly, it was breaking and entering for dummies. Fina silently closed her car door, snuck up to the side door, and spent a few minutes picking the lock. The tricky part would be disarming the alarm, but she was fairly certain that Elaine only cycled through a few codes; she claimed she couldn't remember them if they changed too often. Truly a burglar's dream house.

Once inside, Fina punched Haley's birthday into the alarm pad, which elicited a blinking red light. Ryan was next, but equally unsuccessful. Worried she'd only get three tries, she decided to skip Teddy and go for Chandler. She had a fifty-fifty chance, and if she was wrong, she'd have to make up a story that would satisfy Carl. Her hand hovered over the keypad and then punched in her youngest nephew's birthdate. The pad flashed green.

Fina tiptoed to her father's office at the other end of the house and took stock. She knew the safe was a lost cause; unlike Elaine, Carl changed the combination frequently and didn't share it with anyone. Instead, Fina took out a penlight and started quietly rummaging through the file cabinets. There had to be something that wouldn't appeal to the average thief but would hold value within the family.

Fina was surprised how little time it took to find a suitable candidate. She slipped out the way she had come in after resetting the alarm.

That wasn't so hard.

She should do it more often.

33

A good night's sleep eluded Fina, and the drive to Framingham the next morning was too long; it gave her too much time to ruminate. Haley still required a bodyguard, but that risk was insignificant compared to the damage Rand's return might cause. Fina needed to neutralize Rand while not completely antagonizing Carl. And what was the deal with Cristian? Was he really serious about this woman? Fina had assumed that he was done with traditional marriage after his own imploded, but maybe she'd misread him all this time.

Fina drove through the pillars and parked. She pulled Renata's folder out of her bag before climbing the stairs to the front door. The living room was empty, but she could hear loud classical music through the door. It took a few tries of the doorbell before Walter appeared in the room. Fina stepped to the side so as not to spoil the surprise.

He was wearing a pair of khaki pants and a sweater that had patches on the elbows. He looked professorial with a book in his hand as he answered the door.

"I told you I wasn't done with you," Fina said, stepping forward.

Walter sneered and started to close the door.

"You'll want to hear what I have to say." She held up Renata's file. "Trust me."

"I should call the police. This is harassment."

"Harassment, tenacity. It's so hard to tell the difference, but by all means, do whatever you feel is necessary. I'm a fan of law enforcement."

Walter folded his arms so the book was tucked under one armpit. He studied the elaborate stone pattern under his feet before casting the door open. Fina followed him to his office, where he sat down behind his desk, rigid as a sentry.

"Where's Lucy?"

"Not here," Walter responded tersely.

"This will be brief, because you don't need to say anything," Fina said. "I think you're a fraud."

Walter scoffed.

"Please, act indignant. I find it entertaining." Fina made a tour of the room, gazing at the bookshelves and peeking behind the love seat. "Even if you got rid of the files, you're screwed. The proof is in the pudding, so to speak. You know, the offspring."

"I haven't the foggiest idea what you're talking about."

"You told donors and prospective parents that you ran tests for which you were paid handsomely. But you didn't run the tests. You pocketed the money and falsified the results instead, and maybe it would have stayed your little secret, but then Hank Reardon had to come along with his fancy insurance physical."

Walter nudged a letter opener on his desk with his fingertip. The handle was shiny and black with a mother-of-pearl inlay, the blade long and tapered. Fina went over and picked it up. A stab wound would be a fitting end to this case, but she just didn't have the energy to staunch her own bleeding.

She pointed the letter opener at Walter. "Hank found out that he had something you told him he didn't, and I think he was going to make your life miserable. What was it exactly that he had?"

Walter swallowed. "I can't possibly divulge patient information to you."

"But that's why you took those files from the clinic, right? So that no one could prove that the tests weren't actually run?"

"Missing files are hardly proof of anything."

"Oh, but Walter, that's the beauty of my job. I'm not a prosecutor; I don't need proof. I'm like a defense attorney; I just need doubt. What do you think would happen if the mothers from 1994 sat down and compared notes?"

Walter grimaced.

"Or a reporter? What if a reporter got a tip that the region's most successful cryobank was built on lies and false data?"

Walter leaned forward and glared at her. "There are thousands of babies, thousands of happy families, who wouldn't exist if not for Heritage. You're just being spiteful if you try to tarnish that."

"Was Hank spiteful when he found out he was a carrier for the cystic fibrosis gene?"

Walter flinched. "You don't know what you're talking about."

Fina shrugged. "Maybe I don't, but does that even matter nowadays?" She walked to the door and put the letter opener on a shelf. "You're a creep, Walter, with a God complex, and you prey on people's vulnerability. Shame on you."

Fina strode out of the house, slamming the front door in her wake. On the drive back to the city, she contemplated who would make Walter's life more miserable: Renata or the reporter, Dan Rubin. It was a wonderful quandary that delighted her all the way to the city.

She was starting to feel like she was besties with the Reardons' maid. Fina stood in her usual spot in the foyer as the maid went to find the lady of the house, but Fina soon decided that she'd done enough waiting. No one else was around, so she got into the elevator and pushed the button for the top floor. A minute later, the doors drew open and she picked her way across Danielle's art studio. Most of the space looked the same, except for a now empty corner that had been littered with canvases during her last visit.

She perused the room, not sure exactly what she was looking for, but certain that she'd find something. On the table near the couch, Fina picked up a stack of photographs and flipped through them. They were mostly landscape shots, some buildings, and children playing. Fina stopped at one, certain the setting was familiar but unable to place it.

"What are you doing up here?" the maid asked. Her speech was hurried, as if she was flustered.

"I'm waiting for Danielle."

"Mrs. Reardon isn't here, and you were supposed to wait in the foyer."

Fina gazed at the photos again. "Oh, sorry. I misunderstood."

"Put those down." The woman strode over and took the photos from Fina's hand. She placed them facedown on the table. "You need to leave."

"When will Danielle be back? We had a meeting scheduled."

"She has a benefit tonight at the Saveena Gallery for Hank's House. I don't know why she scheduled a meeting. She won't be home all day." The maid gestured toward the elevator.

Fina didn't take the hint, so the maid walked back to the elevator and picked up the phone mounted on the wall. "Could you please send Mike up to Mrs. Reardon's studio? There's an intruder."

"That's a little dramatic. I'm leaving." Fina walked over to the elevator.

The maid punched the down button and gave Fina a nudge into the elevator when it arrived. She stood next to her, glaring during the brief ride down.

The doors opened onto the first floor, where they were met by a large man in a dark suit. He was wearing an earpiece like a Secret Service agent, his legs firmly planted like two enormous tree trunks.

"Please remove her," the maid said.

The man took hold of Fina's elbow and guided her to the front door.

"Thank you, kind sir," Fina said as he reached for the doorknob.

He opened the door and steered her out before slamming it behind her.

She really wasn't having much luck with the fellas lately.

Fina called Theresa McGovern from the road and asked for a brief meeting with Dimitri. He was leaving in a couple of hours for San Jose, but Theresa could squeeze her in if she hurried. When Fina arrived half an hour later, Dimitri was at his desk, tapping away at his laptop.

"Fina."

"Dimitri. How's the waterfront development deal going? The one you didn't care about?"

He smirked. "Fine. Thank you for asking."

Fina sat down in a chair facing his desk. "Have you ever seen Aubrey Reardon?"

"The baby?"

"Yeah."

"I'm sure I have." He looked puzzled. "Why?"

"You're sure?"

Dimitri shrugged. "Well, actually, I don't know."

"It's important. Try to remember."

"I know that Danielle and Andy are always trying to set something up."

"But has that something ever happened?"

Dimitri pinched his lower lip between two fingers. He shook his head.

"Don't you find that odd?"

"A bit, but Hank lived in the spotlight, and maybe he didn't want his daughter to be scrutinized."

"But I can't even find a picture of this child. Did you get a birth announcement?"

"I don't know. Andy handles that kind of stuff." Dimitri leaned back in his chair. "What are you suggesting? That she doesn't exist?"

"No, no. I think she exists."

"So what then?"

"I'll let you know." Fina rose and left the office, waving good-bye to Theresa.

Cristian had left her a message, so she called him from Nanny's.

"I'm working on that lead," he told her, "connecting Denny Calder to Walter Stiles."

"Good. Here's a juicy tidbit: I'm pretty sure that Walter committed fraud, which explains why he didn't want me poking around."

"What are you talking about?"

"Pretending to run tests on sperm donations that he actually didn't. For all I know, he's still doing it today. I'll tell you more later."

"Why not now?"

"Because I don't have proof."

"When has that ever stopped you?"

"Maybe I'm turning over a new leaf, growing more cautious."

"Uh-huh."

"And I think I know who sent the photos of Haley."

"Who?" There was a bang on the other end of the line, as if Cristian had dropped the feet of his chair onto the floor.

"I don't want to say."

"Of course you don't. Do you have any proof to support this theory?"

"Nothing that would make a DA happy, but I'm working on it." She sucked on a square of chocolate she'd found on the coffee table. "Rand's in town."

"That's not good."

"No, it's not."

"Is he here to stay?"

"So he says."

"I'm betting you say otherwise."

"If I have anything to do with it."

"Be careful, Fina. Your brother is dangerous," he reminded her.

"That's exactly why I'm trying to do something about it."

"Anything I can do? That's legal?"

"No, but thank you for asking."

"Want to get some dinner later?"

"Like a date?" she asked.

"Do you want to have dinner or not?"

"I'd like to, but I have a previous engagement."

"A date?"

"A party, but it's work-related, so don't get jealous. I'd bring you, but you'd cramp my style."

"I bet."

"How about a rain check?"

"Sure."

"Talk to you later."

She disconnected and called Milloy, asking if he wanted to go to a party. He was game, and they made a plan to meet later.

Fina spent the next couple of hours watching videos on YouTube—videos that made her cringe and made her heart ache.

But was it motive enough for murder?

34

The Saveena Gallery was in Fort Point, not far from Nanny's condo. In recent years, the area had been revitalized by the Big Dig and the rehab of old factories into lofts and restaurants. It was a neighborhood that attracted artists and start-ups, the second population promising to squeeze out the first before too long.

They left Milloy's car with the valet and walked into the minimally decorated space. The walls were white, and the ceilings rose fifteen feet. The floor was scarred, dark-stained wood, and beams crisscrossed overhead. Art of various sorts was displayed throughout, including sculptures, photographs, ceramics, and some of Danielle's paintings. The space was crowded with a well-dressed forty-something crowd.

Fina and Milloy got drinks and did a circuit of the room, checking out the art.

"What's this all about?" she asked Milloy quietly as they studied a sculpture made of empty boxes of Kraft macaroni and cheese.

He looked at her. "You really want to hear my theory?"

She squeezed his arm. "Eh. Not so much."

"That's what I thought."

They moved on to an abstract painting featuring shades of brown, listening while a hipster in square glasses expounded on its "visual fluency and cultural dissonance."

"Rand is back in town," Fina said while staring at a photograph of a turkey.

"I thought he'd been exiled to Miami."

"He was. Carl shipped him off, gave him some clients down there. I thought it was permanent, but apparently it was only until the dust settled."

"I assume he's never going to be prosecuted for the abuse?"

Fina gave him a withering look. "Over Carl's dead body, and frankly, the publicity would destroy Haley. I guess I was naïve, but I thought he was gone for good."

Milloy raised an eyebrow.

"Apparently," Fina said, "all is forgiven. It makes me want to throw up."

They were moving away from the photo when Michael Reardon appeared before them.

"Hi, Fina. I didn't know you were coming."

"I'm always happy to support a good cause."

Milloy coughed into his cocktail napkin.

"Michael, this is Milloy Danielson. Milloy, Michael Reardon." The men shook hands. Michael stood up straighter in an unconscious attempt to compare more favorably with Milloy.

"Well, enjoy yourselves," Michael said. "I'd like a progress report tomorrow."

"And I'd like to give you one. Just give me a call."

Michael walked off. Across the room, Fina caught sight of Danielle, who was in rapt conversation with a Red Sox player. He was a recent trade, and Danielle was probably trying to dive into his deep pockets before Juliana did.

"I'll be right back," Fina said to Milloy.

She wended her way through the crowd until she found a waiter to direct her to the ladies' room. He pointed toward the back of the gallery.

The hallway was long and poorly lit, with doors leading off in various directions. Since she'd never met a closed door she didn't want to open, Fina tried each one. The first was locked. The second was a supply closet. The third was a large studio space, and the two beyond that were the restrooms.

Fina looked around before ducking into the studio. She didn't want to turn on the lights, and luckily it was a clear night and the moon shone brightly through the large windows. The space was filled with tables on which sat projects in various stages. It looked as if artists had their own workstations. There were oil paintings and watercolors on one table, a set of pottery on another.

She took out her penlight and examined the shelves and closets that lined the walls. They were filled with paints and brushes, pencils and clay. In one corner, there was a pile of smocks that were ripped and stained. It brought back memories of art class in school. Fina had never liked art class—not because she didn't like art, but because her own talent was slim to nonexistent. Maybe you weren't judged on your ability, but nothing could ease the shame you felt when your sculpture looked like the Michelin Man.

Fina moved her light in a steady arc, but then stopped. She negotiated her way around some easels and stood in front of a table with chunks of stone. Off to the side, a wooden box held what looked like hammers with small square heads. Resisting the urge to pick one up, she sunk down onto a nearby stool. The light pointed away, but in its beam she caught sight of something else that gave her pause. It looked like an igloo, but it was actually the opposite.

It was a kiln.

Fina urged Milloy to go home once his interest in the art had been satisfied, as well as his limited appetite for cheap wine.

"You don't want me to stay? I think you're up to something," he said.

"Moi?"

"That was an awfully long bathroom break."

"Don't you worry about my lady parts."

"Be careful."

"Always."

Fina took another lap of the room and made sure that Danielle saw her in the thinning crowd. When there were only a dozen guests left, Fina pulled out her phone and texted Cristian before heading back down the hallway to the studio. She returned to the stool between the sculpting hammers and the kiln and waited in the dark.

Five minutes later, the lights flickered on and Danielle glared at her from the door.

"I didn't invite you," she said.

"I thought the more the merrier. It's a fund-raiser, after all."

"We don't need your money." Danielle shut the door behind her and started walking across the room.

"Did you really think threatening my niece would get me to stop?"

Danielle stopped walking. "What are you talking about?"

"The pictures you took of my niece—at her school, playing field hockey—not really a good showcase for your talents."

"You're not making any sense. I don't know your niece."

"Really? Because some of the photos in your studio looked awfully familiar."

"I take pictures all over the area. That's coincidence, nothing else."

"Photos at a school? A school to which you have no connection? That's just creepy." Fina thought for a moment. "Why don't you have any photos of Aubrey?"

"My child is none of your business."

"I understand why you'd keep her out of the public eye, but I haven't seen one in your own home, not even in her nursery."

Danielle glared at her.

"I am sorry about her situation, for what it's worth," Fina said.

Danielle put a hand out and steadied herself on one of the tables. "What?"

"I'm sorry your child has cystic fibrosis. That must be heartbreaking, especially since nowadays it can be detected prenatally."

Danielle's eyes scanned the room.

"Why wasn't she tested when you were pregnant?" Fina asked.

Danielle barked a weak laugh. "Because her father wasn't a carrier, or at least that's what we'd been led to believe."

"But Hank was, right? And so are you. His test results were falsified by Walter Stiles at the cryobank twenty years ago."

Danielle avoided her gaze.

"So Hank had his physical and found out the truth, and either you were too far along to end the pregnancy or he didn't want you to." Fina adjusted her butt on the stool. She was perched there, ready to pounce if necessary. "I watched some videos this afternoon about breathing techniques and the treatments you have to give babies with CF. It was awful. I can't imagine having to do it with my own kid."

"I don't want your pity," Danielle said.

"Trust me, I don't pity you." Fina tried to relax her back muscles. "I don't understand why you're keeping Aubrey a secret. No one will think less of you because your child is sick, and the prognosis for CF isn't nearly as dire as it used to be."

"Really? You think nobody judges me?" Danielle spat out the words. "When it's just *my* child who's sick? Not all the other children my husband fathered? And they keep coming out of the woodwork, like that degenerate Brett Linder!"

"You were jealous of the cryokids?"

"I was pissed." Her voice rose. "I didn't even want a baby, but he insisted. So we finally have one, and it turns out that she's not a regular baby, she's a baby that needs so much. She never stops needing things!"

"Isn't that the definition of a baby?" Fina yelled back.

"You have no idea. She needs care all the time and special medicine and interventions and even then, she'll never get better."

"So that's why you keep her out of sight? So people won't know you have a baby with health issues? That's your solution?"

"Stop being such a judgmental bitch. This is not the life I signed up for."

"Nobody gets the life they signed up for."

"Really? Hank did. Having a sick child didn't change his life one bit."

Fina glanced over at the box of hammers. "How did you get into the garage that night?"

"I didn't kill him."

"Really?" Fina watched as Danielle's gaze drifted over to the kiln. "I'm pretty sure you did. That's why you took the pictures of my niece. Even if I didn't figure out you were the murderer, I was digging around too much for your comfort. You didn't want Aubrey's situation to come to light."

"Believe whatever you want."

"You were enraged that Hank had gotten you pregnant with an imperfect child that you had to care for, only to find out that he'd fathered healthy children for other women. And then those women and their children were going to stake a claim to him and his money."

Danielle snorted. "They were welcome to him."

"That would have been the better choice. Divorcing the guy and not killing him. I'm still working on my theory of the crime. Do you want to hear it?"

"Not particularly."

"Come on. Be a sport. I think you were in the car with Hank when he drove into the garage, but you bent over so you wouldn't show up on camera."

"That's ridiculous."

"Really? You know where the cameras are at your house and at Universum. So you bend over and pretend you're getting your phone or some lipstick. Hank wouldn't think anything of it, but there'd be no record of you sitting next to him in the car."

"And I just happened to have a murder weapon handy?"

"I saw your bag, remember? You had a lot of crap, including art supplies. I don't think it's a stretch to think you had one of those in there." Fina gestured toward the table of mallets.

"You need to leave," Danielle snarled, "and if you make these ridiculous claims public, I'll sue your ass."

"You want me to leave so you can clean out the kiln? I don't think so." Fina folded her arms in front of her. "I'm betting there's some good trace evidence in there."

Danielle took a few steps toward her. "What is it that you want?"

Fina shook her head. "Nothing."

Danielle came closer. "We could figure something out."

"I have money, thank you."

"Not the kind of money I have."

"I don't want the kind of money you have, you stupid bitch, and you can forget about plan B."

"What are you talking about?" Danielle walked another step. Her hand wandered behind her back.

"If you think you're going to knock me out and stuff me in the kiln like some demented Hansel and Gretel fantasy, think again. I will kick your ass."

Danielle shook her head as if pitying Fina's overblown confidence. Her gaze wandered to the side, and Fina stood. Danielle's hand reached out, and she swung at Fina, a sharp rasp cutting Fina on her upper arm.

Fina grabbed Danielle's wrist and bent it backward, smashing it down onto the table until she released her grip on the weapon. Disarmed, Danielle tried to twist out of her grasp, but Fina had other plans. She hauled off and punched Danielle, who cried out in pain and crumpled to the floor in a heap.

Fina pressed a hand against her bleeding arm. "You know, everyone busts my balls about getting beaten up, but I do all right."

Danielle huddled on the floor. Fina pulled out her phone and dialed with her blood-sticky fingers.

"What the hell is taking you so long, Cristian?" Fina asked, just as the cavalry arrived.

35

Fina passed Danielle the next morning on the steps of the police station. Danielle was wearing a large pair of designer sunglasses, flanked by her attorney and a couple of bodyguards. Photographers and reporters tossed out questions, but she swept by them and climbed into a Cadillac Escalade with tinted windows. Fina's hand instinctively went to her upper arm, which was sore and tender with fifteen stitches pulling on her skin.

"Where's she going?" Fina asked Cristian, who met her at the front desk.

"Home."

"She's not going to be charged?"

"The only thing we can charge her with now is assault, assuming you press charges."

"What about the kiln and the hammer? She practically admitted the whole thing to me."

"Don't worry. We're testing the hammers and sifting through the ashes, but that's going to take time. We can't hold her in the meantime."

She followed Cristian to an interview room where another detective took her formal statement about the preceding night's events. Fina was reviewing it when a flash of color breezed by the door.

"Hey! Lieutenant!" Fina hollered.

A mass of curls peeked around the door. "Yes, Fina?"

"What? Not even a hello? I've helped you wrap up two cases!"

"'Wrapped up' is an overstatement," Pitney said, coming into the room. She sat down across from Fina. "How's your arm?"

"It hurts."

Pitney tugged on the front of her polka-dotted shirt, which was riding up her ample bosom. Her fuchsia-painted nails matched the background of her top.

"Well, I made the connection between Walter Stiles and Denny Calder," Fina pointed out, "and I led you guys to Danielle and possibly the murder weapon. Seems like a good day's work to me."

"I don't deny it, but you haven't given me much in the way of hard evidence."

Fina reached across and patted Pitney's hand. "I have faith in you, Lieutenant. You'll find it. Am I free to go?"

Pitney gestured to the door.

Back in her car, Fina took a deep breath and closed her eyes. She wanted nothing more than to go home and curl up in bed with some pain relievers and a pint of ice cream, but that would have to wait. She had some loose ends to tie up.

She met Marnie Frasier at the same hotel in Cambridge, but instead of a drink, they convened at the breakfast buffet. Fina had also invited Renata to join them. She believed they both deserved an explanation, but she was hopeful that Marnie's clear head might temper Renata's impulsivity. Technically, Michael Reardon should have been her first order of business, but the Reardons had annoyed her to the point of abandoning professional conduct, at least temporarily.

"Thanks for meeting me on such short notice," Fina said once the women were seated with food and drinks. They both looked at her expectantly. "I don't know if you saw the news this morning, but Danielle Reardon and I had a run-in last night."

"Are you okay?" Marnie asked, her fork poised over her eggs.

"She stabbed me, but I'm fine."

Marnie gasped, and Renata reared back in surprise.

"I'm fine, but there are a couple of things I want you to know."

Marnie put down her fork.

"Danielle is now a person of interest in Hank's murder, so I think Rosie and Tyler are off the hook."

Renata nodded her head, and Marnie took a deep breath before speaking. "Wait. Are you saying that Danielle Reardon killed her husband?"

Fina looked at her. "I'm not saying anything, although I will say that society wives don't usually stab someone unless the stakes are pretty high."

"Holy shit," Renata said under her breath.

"But that isn't the main thing I wanted to tell you. I have reason to believe that Walter Stiles committed fraud around the time of your children's births."

"What do you mean?" Renata asked, straightening in her chair.

"Get ahold of yourself, Renata," Fina said. "Seriously. I know I'm taking a risk by telling you this. Don't make me regret it." Fina stared at her. "I don't think he performed the medical tests on the donor sperm that he claimed he did. You might want to speak with an attorney about verifying the health records you were given at the time of insemination."

"An attorney like your father?" Renata asked.

"It doesn't matter, although I will say that my father is a damn good attorney, and he enjoys ripping people to shreds. It's a gift."

Fina decided not to tell them the details about Hank's genetic tests and Aubrey's cystic fibrosis. The baby's health wasn't their business, and the revelation would serve no purpose.

"Do you think other SMCs may have had a similar experience?" asked Marnie.

"I think it's possible. It might not make any difference. It seems like it's a healthy group of kids, but you may have made decisions under false pretenses. It won't be long before some of them have kids, and they should probably have accurate medical histories."

Renata was off and running, debating the ins and outs. Fina begged off and walked back to her car.

Michael Reardon was in a lather by the time she got to Ludlow and Associates. He was sitting across from Carl, who had a weary look on his face and was fiddling with his tie.

"I've been calling you all night!" Michael exclaimed.

Fina grabbed a diet soda from the bar and sat in the chair next to him.

"I was busy being stabbed by your stepmother, but here I am! Bright-eyed and bushy-tailed!"

"I don't even know where to start," Michael said.

Fina looked at him.

"Michael is not happy with the direction of your investigation," Carl said.

"Thank you, Father. I hadn't noticed." She turned to Michael. "You've been paying me for my service and skills as an investigator. If you thought that ensured a particular outcome, I'm afraid you're mistaken."

"You think I'm going to pay you for dragging my family through the mud and creating a scandal?"

"Damn skippy you're going to pay her," Carl said, leaning forward. "You pay people the money you owe them. Didn't your father teach you that?"

Michael pulled back. Fina sipped her soda. These were the moments she liked being Carl's kid.

"Whatever, but I'm going to bad-mouth you all over town."

Fina exchanged a look with Carl. They both burst out laughing. "Good luck with that, son," Carl said.

Michael jumped up and stomped out.

"Thanks, Dad," Fina said. She adjusted her arm on the armrest, but couldn't find a comfortable position. "My stab wound is fine, by the way."

Carl waved his hand in the air. "Just another day at the office for you."

Fina filled him in on the Walter Stiles situation. As she talked, she recognized the gleam in his eye. He was practically rubbing his hands together with glee.

A knock on the door brought their conversation to a stop. Rand stood on the threshold, wearing a suit and tie. Fina bristled when her father invited him in.

"Well, well. I heard you got stabbed last night," Rand said, taking the seat Michael had vacated.

Fina looked at him. Sitting so close to him made her skin crawl. "When's your flight?" she asked.

Rand grinned. "I'm not going anywhere."

Fina looked at her father, who was studying his eldest and his youngest.

"Actually, I think you are." Fina reached into her bag and pulled out a folder. She handed it to Rand.

He flipped through the contents, his expression clouding over. "Where the hell did you get this?"

"Those are copies, in case you're wondering."

Carl stuck out his hand, and Rand passed the folder to him. Carl's face got stony as he examined the contents. "Where did you get this, Fina?"

"It just fell into my lap. I'm no expert, Rand, but it looks like you were bilking clients. That's a pretty serious crime."

A flush crept up her brother's neck.

"While you were working for Dad," she added, "which puts him in an awful bind."

Carl dropped the folder onto the desktop.

"Don't threaten me," Rand said.

"It's not a threat."

"Dad?" Rand looked at Carl, whose mouth was set in a rigid line.

Fina looked at her brother. "Go. Away."

Rand turned to his father. "You're going to let this happen?"

"Let me talk to your sister, Rand."

Rand left the room, slamming the door behind him.

Carl stared at Fina. "You wouldn't do it."

She shrugged. "Maybe, maybe not."

"You're not just threatening him, you're threatening me, too."

"I'm sorry about that, Dad. Collateral damage. But are you really so sure he's an asset? Not just a liability?"

Carl drummed his fingers on his desk. Fina stowed the folder in her bag and left.

She was on her way home when Risa called. She banged a uey and wished the day would end.

Risa was sitting on the front porch stairs, watching her boys play a pickup soccer game in the yard with some neighbor kids. Fina took a seat next to her and winced when she put weight on her arm.

"Now what happened?" Risa asked.

"Nothing. Let's not talk about me. Let's talk about you. I didn't expect to hear from you so quickly."

"I didn't sleep at all the last two nights. Everything kept running through my mind, and I don't need any more sleepless nights from this particular topic."

"Understood." They watched one of the teams celebrate a goal while the other huddled in serious discussion.

"I'm willing to meet her," Risa said, "and, if I like her, get tested."

Fina didn't speak for a minute. "That's very generous of you."

"You think I'm nuts."

"I think you're an amazing person. A better person than I am."

"I don't know about that."

"I don't think I'd give up body parts for anyone, even family."

Risa stared at her. "Fina, you injure your body parts on a regular basis for strangers."

Fina shrugged. "It's work."

"It's not just work, and you know it. There are easier ways to make a living. I know you like the excitement, but it's more than that."

The boys were debating another goal. Voices were raised for a moment, but then died down of their own accord.

"Maybe," Fina conceded. "So you want me to be in touch with Greta?"

"Yes, and let's set something up quickly. If I'm not going to help her—and I may not—at least we shouldn't waste her time."

"She doesn't deserve you, Risa." Fina struggled up from the step.

"Who's to say what any of us deserve?"

"I don't know. I think I'm a pretty good judge."

Risa grinned. "Go home and take care of yourself."

Fina gave her a wave and dodged a pass on the way to her car.

It was good there were people like Risa in the world. They made up for the Danielle Reardons.

Fina went home and took care of herself with a long nap, a few hours of bad TV, and a bag of miniature Reese's peanut butter cups. She was feeling better when Scotty called and invited her to dinner. Moving off the couch didn't hold much appeal, but she missed Patty, Haley, and the boys and thought that some quality family time might offset her recent encounters with Rand.

Dinner hit the spot—both the food and the company—and the Lego session after the meal reminded her why she loved her nephews and why she didn't have kids. Patty shepherded the boys off to bed, and Haley plopped in front of the TV in the upstairs family room. Fina helped Scotty finish up the dishes.

"So you haven't said anything about Rand," he said, handing her a dish to dry.

"What's there to say?"

"He went back to Miami. Flew out this afternoon."

Fina suppressed a smile. "Glad to hear it."

Scotty folded the dish towel and placed it on the counter. "What did you do?"

"Who says I did anything?"

"Remind me never to piss you off."

She faced him and grasped his shoulders. "Have I told you recently that, of the two brothers I like, you're one of my favorites?"

He patted her lightly on the cheek. "I've got work to do."

Scotty retreated to his office, and Fina started to climb the stairs to the family room. She felt a deep sense of satisfaction. She'd done it, and it hadn't even been that hard.

Fina's steps slowed as she reached the top of the staircase.

Why hadn't it been that hard? She leaned back against the railing for a moment. Had getting rid of Rand been her idea, or someone else's? Had she risen to the bait yet again?

She felt a tingle in her hands and closed her eyes. Goddammit.

"Aunt Fina!"

"I'm right here, Hale."

"Hurry up. *Romance Renovation* is about to start."

Fina took a deep breath. "I'm right here," she repeated, and started down the hall.

ACKNOWLEDGMENTS

"Thank you" seems woefully inadequate, but it's a good place to start.

Thank you to all the readers, booksellers, and librarians who supported *Loyalty*. I hope this is the beginning of a beautiful friendship!

Once again, Davenie Susi Pereira provided terrific feedback and encouragement throughout this process, and Catalina Arboleda can always be counted on for guidance and support. Allison Walker Chader is the best cheerleader a friend could ask for, and Lauri Bortscheller Nakamoto contributed to the cause with insightful observations and restorative lunch dates.

I have been embraced by the Putnam and Penguin Random House family and couldn't be more pleased to be a member. Katie Grinch, Christopher Nelson, Lydia Hirt, Kate Stark, Alexis Welby, Mary Stone, and Meaghan Wagner have helped me navigate this new world with tremendous support and good cheer. Alan Walker, Howard Wall, and Dominique Jenkins helped smooth my way at key events, which I won't soon forget. I'm tremendously grateful for Ivan Held's support and continued vote of confidence.

Mary Alice Kier and Anna Cottle have been Fina's advocates in Los Angeles. Thank you for being such fierce protectors of my creative vision.

I'm immensely lucky to have two amazing women as my stewards for this journey. Helen Brann is savvy and fearless, and I love having her in my corner. Christine Pepe makes me a better writer and does so with grace and humor. I have no doubt I hit the publishing jackpot with these two on my team.

My family has made this an even more joyful experience. Thank you to Kirsten Thoft, Ted Nadeau, Zoë Nadeau, Ella Nadeau, Escher Nadeau, Lisa Thoft, Cole Nagel-Thoft, Arden Nagel-Thoft, Erika Thoft-Brown, Chris Thoft-Brown, Owen Thoft-Brown, Sophie Thoft-Brown, Riley Thoft-Brown, and Sharon Padia Stone. You guys are fantastic!

Last, but never least, my mother, Judith Stone Thoft, and my husband, Doug Berrett, make all of this possible. Truly, since my mother gave birth to me, but that is the least of her contributions. Her love, humor, and endless enthusiasm sustain me each day. Doug Berrett is my go-to guy for everything. He is the best, and my heart still skips a beat when he walks in the room.